BEEKEEPER

BEEKEEPER

J. ROBERT JANES

ORION

First published in Great Britain in 2001 by Orion
an imprint of The Orion Publishing Group
Orion House, 5 Upper St Martin's Lane, London WC2H 9EA

A CIP catalogue record for this book is available
from the British Library

Typeset at The Spartan Press Ltd,
Lymington, Hants
Printed in Great Britain by
Clays Ltd, St Ives plc

This is for Anne Prewitt who stood on her hands in a canoe at the age of sixty and is a heroine to many, myself included.

Acknowledgements

All the novels in the St-Cyr–Kohler series incorporate a few words and brief passages in French or German. Dr Dennis Essar of Brock University very kindly helped with the French, as did the artist Pierrette Laroche, while Professor Schutz, of Germanic and Slavic Studies at Brock, helped with the German.

A very special thanks must also be extended to Dr Cynthia Scott-Dupree, of the Department of Environmental Biology at the University of Guelph, for her very kind assistance with the technical aspects of beekeeping. Should there be errors in any of the above, they are my own, and for these I apologize but hope there are none.

To the worker there is but slavery; to the drone but constant leisure and the good life until its single task is done.

Author's Note

Beekeeper is a work of fiction. Though I have used actual places and times, I have treated these as I saw fit, changing some as appropriate. Occasionally the name of a real person is also used for historical authenticity, but all are deceased and I have made of them what the story demands. I do not condone what happened during these times. Indeed, I abhor it. But during the Occupation of France the everyday crimes of murder and arson continued to be committed, and I merely ask, by whom and how were they solved?

1

The Restaurant of the Gare de Lyon was huge, a prince, a god among all others. But now under the blackout's hauntingly blue and ethereal light from Paris's infrequent lamps, its gilded cherubs and buxom nymphs were cloaked in grime. They shed their gilding, clutched their bouquets of daisies and looked offended as if wanting to cry out, Monsieur the Chief Inspector of the Sûreté Nationale, how could you – yes, you! – of all people have let this happen to us?

Gone were the diners in their splendid dinner jackets and tails, the beautiful girls in their magically tantalizing gowns, the *femmes du monde*, the society women, too, and those of little virtue. The gaiety . . . the laughter . . . the sounds of silver cutlery and crystal, the pewter plates upon which the porcelains had been set.

Gone, too, were the bankers, politicians, industrialists, the men of solid cash and much power. These days most of them had found other pastures upon which to graze.

But now . . . now after more than two and a half years of the Occupation, the restaurant's crumbling horns of plenty let fall a constant rain of golden fragments and plaster dust which littered the mountains of crates, barrels, sacks and steamer trunks – suitcases, too, of all sizes – that climbed high into the vault of the ceiling to where once Gervex's magnificent painting, the Battle of the Flowers, had portrayed the city of Nice.

'It's like an Aladdin's Cave that's all but been forgotten,' breathed Kohler, aghast at what lay before them.

Distracted, St-Cyr ignored his partner. The restaurant, that triumph of the Mauve Decade and the *Belle Époque – le Train Bleu*, some had begun to call it – stank of sweat, mould, sour produce and rotten meat that the inevitable delays in transit had left to languish. Soot, too, of course, and urine, for what better 'terrorist' action when forced to store things destined for the Reich, than to piss on them in secret – or do worse – in the name of freedom and of *Résistance*?

'"*Produce . . . a gift from the people of France to their friends in the Reich*,"' snorted Kohler at a label. 'Walnuts, Louis. Sacks and sacks of them from Périgord.'

'A warehouse, Hermann. This was its *Salle Dorée*!' Its Golden Room.

'Easy, *mon vieux*. Hey, take it easy, eh?'

'Now just a minute. Look what you Boches have done! My grandmother brought me here on 9 April 1901, just two days after the grand opening. We sat right over there. Yes, over there! Right next to that great big window with all the soot on it.'

A kid of ten. Jean-Louis St-Cyr was now fifty-two years of age, himself fifty-five, and where had the time gone? wondered Kohler. To the Great War – they had both been in it, but on opposite sides – and then to more murders, arsons, rapes and other 'common' crimes than he'd care to count. Munich first for himself, then Berlin and finally, after the Defeat of France, Paris and partner to Louis, since all such Frenchmen needed someone to watch over them. This one especially!

'Oysters baked golden in champagne sauce, Hermann, and laid piping hot in the half-shell on a bed of coarse salt.'

'Von Schaumburg, Louis. Old Shatter Hand said we were to take a look at this.'

'*Le côte de boeuf à la moëlle . . .*'

Rib of beef . . . 'Louis . . .'

'*Gaufres de Grand-mère Bocuse*, Hermann.'

Waffles! *Merde*, were they to have the whole of the meal? 'Louis—'

'Yes, yes, the Kommandant von Gross-Paris. How could I have forgotten one of my many, many masters?'

It was Friday, 29 January 1943 at 23:55 hours. Just five minutes to curfew and colder than a bugger outside. In here, too, thought Kohler. At least five degrees of frost, the inky darkness of the blackout, no sleep, no food, no homecoming to Giselle and Oona, his lady loves. No pleasure at all; damp, too, and this after a bastard of an investigation in Avignon whose result, totally unappreciated, had seen them all but shot to pieces and kicked to death.

Von Schaumburg had sent him and Louis a telegram which had found them on the train somewhere between Lyon and Paris and hours late. Hours.

'We couldn't have known the *Résistance* would blow the tracks, Hermann,' offered St-Cyr apologetically, having intuitively gauged the trend of his partner's thoughts. 'We were lucky, that's all.'

Lucky that the *plastic* – the cyclonite – hadn't gone off right under them.

The telegram from von Schaumburg had exhibited the usual Prussian gift for brevity: RESTAURANT GARE DE LYON. TELL NO ONE. It hadn't even ended with the customary Heil Hitler. A Wehrmacht orderly, one of the Kommandant's staff, had met them on arrival and had given them a key. No guards had been on the doors, though there should have been.

'*Merde*, Hermann, just what the hell had he in mind?'

Paris's 'trunk' murderers were always sending their victims to Lyon in steamer trunks with no return address. Thinking they had yet another corpse on their hands, and not liking the thought, Kohler disconsolately ran the beam of his blue-blinkered torch over the trunks and turned again to hunting through the labels.

St-Cyr let him be. Always these days there was conflict among the Germans, one faction against another. And always Hermann and himself – who were practically the only two honest cops left to fight common crime in an age of officially sanctioned, monstrous crime – had to come between them.

Von Schaumburg was a soldier and the armed forces – the Wehrmacht – still hated the SS and the Gestapo, distrusting entirely the Führer's faith in those two organizations and jealous of it, too.

Boemelburg, on the other hand, was Hermann's boss and Head of SIPO Section IV, the Gestapo in France. His telegram had preceded that of the Kommandant von Gross-Paris by nearly twenty-four hours, having arrived just as they had reached the station in Orange to begin their homeward journey:

3

BODY OF BEEKEEPER FOUND IN APIARY NEAR PÈRE-LACHAISE CEMETERY REQUIRES IMMEDIATE AND URGENT ATTENTION. HEIL HITLER.

'Urgent' meant, of course, trouble, and trouble was something they did not need, but this was, of course, not the Père Lachaise. Not yet!

'Bees, Louis. Something to do with them, I guess.' Hermann's voice was muffled by the crates.

Threading his way through to that same window at which he had sat so long ago, St-Cyr looked down over the inner concourse of the Gare de Lyon. Surreal under its wash of dim blue light, people sat or stood as if caught frozen in time. Locked in now because of the curfew and forced to spend the next five hours waiting to leave. Most were shabby, the suitcases they guarded, old or of cardboard and no longer made of leather. Hungry always, they confined themselves to patience, accustomed now to the lengthy delays, the endless queues for food, food tickets, travel papers . . . papers, papers of all kinds.

A Wehrmacht mobile soup kitchen was dishing out thick slices of black bread and mess tins of cabbage soup with potatoes and sometimes meat, but only to others of their kind in the ever-present grey-green uniforms. A crowd of children stood silently watching as *les haricots verts*, the green beans, the '*Schlocks*' spread margarine on their bread and wolfed down their soup.

Gone were the days of those first few months of the Occupation in 1940 when many of the troops tried to behave themselves and play the benefactor. Now, with the imminent defeat of von Paulus at Stalingrad and the loss of what remained of the Führer's Sixth Army, they and others were afraid lest the conquered and oppressed begin to turn against them en masse.

Hermann's two boys had been among the Wehrmacht's one hundred and fifty thousand dead at Stalingrad, but being Hermann, he didn't hold this loss against his partner and friend, nor the French or anyone else but the Führer. Instead, he had become a citizen of the world. France had been good for Hermann.

4

'Louis . . . Louis, there's beeswax in lard pails but half the shipment is missing.'

'Half?'

'The dust on the floor. I can count, can't I? The rings where the pails once sat. Taken two, maybe three days ago at most.'

Kohler crouched to indicate the lack of dust in circular patches. Prising off a lid revealed the contents and for a moment neither of them could say a thing. Frost caused their breath to billow. Louis was transfixed. The dark, golden honey had been squished out to fill the crevasses and grow stiff with the cold. The wax was of a paler, softer amber under the blue of the light. Hexagonal platelets – the cappings that had once covered the cells – were smeared over one another.

'Squashed honeycomb that hasn't even been drained let alone spun, Louis. Smashed and mangled bees. Whoever did this didn't give a damn about keeping the colonies alive and robbed the hives blind.'

A big man with the broad shoulders, big hands, thick wrists, bulldog jowls and puffy eyelids of an ageing storm-trooper, which he'd never been, the Bavarian gazed up at him. They both knew exactly what the robbery meant: the hunt for *Banditen*, for bandits – *résistants* – in the hills and some poor farmer's hives that had just happened to be there.

'A lot of them, so a lot of farmers, Hermann.'

'I'm sorry. Do you want me to apologize for all the atrocities of this lousy war or only for being here at this moment?'

Hermann's tired and faded blue eyes were filled with remorse and worry. He hadn't liked what they'd found, but more than this, had sensed trouble in their now having to again work for two masters. Von Schaumburg *and* Gestapo Boemelburg!

'Forgive me,' said St-Cyr. 'It's just this . . . The restaurant, *mon vieux*. It meant so much to me as a boy. I'd never seen such things. Lace and plunging necklines, scented breasts and lovely soft earlobes with amethysts in silver dangling from them, diamonds too.'

'I'll bet your grandmother slapped your ogle-eyed wrists!'

'She said I needed to be educated and that if I would but do as she had wished for herself, I'd go far. That honey, by the way, is from lavender.'

'*Merde*, did you think I needed to be told? The labels, such as they are, say the "wax" is from Peyrane in the Vaucluse, but we both know lard doesn't come from there in such quantity, so the pails were gathered elsewhere and whoever stole from the hives went in prepared.'

'So, why would a Parisian beekeeper's death have anything to do with this?'

'And why would von Schaumburg want us to have a look and not tell anyone? The gatherer of this little harvest, eh?' snorted Kohler. 'Find the bastard's name and whisper it into the shell of Old Shatter Hand's ear, but *don't* let Boemelburg in on it. Christ!'

'We shall have to see,' breathed St-Cyr. Always there were questions and always there were difficulties.

They tasted the honey whose accent was harsh and of the hills, and marvellous. 'Long after it is swallowed, Hermann, the ambrosia remains.'

'Ambrosia's beebread, *Dummkopf*. Pollen and nectar the worker bees store so that the nurse bees can feed it to the brood larvae. Hey, if you're still intent on buying that little retirement farm in Provence after what happened to us in Avignon, I'd suggest you damn well pay attention to your partner.'

Hermann had been raised on a farm near Wasserburg, whereas this Sûreté had but spent wondrous summer holidays at those of relatives. The great escape, now dragged into the dust of years by memory.

'Come on, Louis. We're wasting time we haven't got. You take two and I'll take two as evidence. No one will miss another eighty kilos.'

'What about our suitcases?'

'We'll throw them in the *vélo-taxi* too.'

A bicycle taxi! 'It's too icy. They'll have stopped running in any case.'

The curfew was upon them and, as von Schaumburg had ordered, they could tell no one of what they were up to.

'We'll walk. You take the suitcases,' said Kohler. 'I'll take the pails, then we'll switch halfway.'

'To Charonne and Belleville?'

'Relax, eh? I'll soon find us a lift.'

6

'That is *exactly* what I'm afraid of, given the scarcity of traffic!'

The *gazogène* lorry that Hermann stopped perfumed the air with its burning wood-gas and was on its way to La Tour d'Argent, le Grand Véfour, Maxim's and other high-class restaurants, all of which were doing a roaring business. Half-loaded with ducks, geese, chickens, eggs, cheeses, milk and potatoes – items no longer seen by most since the autumn of 1940 – its driver was speechless.

Louis had simply shrilled, 'No arguments, monsieur,' and had flattened the bastard.

'That'll teach him to deal on the black market and to hand over half his load to some double-dealing son of a bitch of a Feldwebel at a control,' snorted Kohler.

Everyone knew that the charge was 50 per cent. Half for the boys in grey-green; half for the dealers, the big boys who organized things. There were never any complaints. Even then fortunes were being made and yet another class of *nouveaux riches* had been born.

'We'll just drive by the flat and let Giselle and Oona look after these, Louis. Then we'll go and pick up the Citroën before we dump the lorry at one of those restaurants and pay our beekeeper a little visit.'

Never one to take things for himself and his little 'family', had Hermann suddenly shifted gears?

'It's the war, Louis, and what's been happening out there. Hey, don't let it worry you, eh? We're still friends.'

That, too, is what I'm afraid of, muttered St-Cyr to himself, for the *Résistance* didn't take such friendships kindly and this humble Sûreté was most certainly still on some of their hit lists. For working with a Nazi, with Hermann, who was not and could never have been one of those.

No lights showed in the flat that was above St-Cyr on the rue Suger. How could they, with the black-out regulations? Alone, freezing and tired – *mon Dieu* he was tired, for they'd been away for days without sleep – he sat in the lorry's cab and waited.

Sometimes waiting for Hermann could take hours. There were only two beds in the flat, one for Giselle, the other for Oona.

Hermann would try not to awaken either of them. They'd both be bundled in several heavy sweaters, pyjamas, slacks and socks upon socks. Woollen hats, too, and scarves. Mittens probably, and all that under heaps of blankets, but their ears were ever keen, as were most these days. And he knew Oona would be certain to get out of bed to greet his partner silently.

She was forty years of age, all but twice that of his little Giselle. Was Dutch, an illegal alien from Rotterdam who had lost her two children to the Messerschmitts on the trek into France during the blitzkrieg, and had subsequently lost her husband to the French Gestapo of the rue Lauriston. A Jew she had been hiding. Another case, a carousel murder.

Hermann and she got on well. She never complained and he knew Hermann depended on her to watch over Giselle. And, yes, the Bavarian was in love with both of them, and, yes, they were each, in their own ways, in love with Hermann. 'War does things like that,' he muttered to himself. 'It forms instant friendships only to plunder them as instantly.'

Giselle was half-Greek, half-Midi French and with straight jet-black hair, lovely violet eyes and a mind of her own. A former prostitute Hermann had 'rescued' from the house of Madame Chabot on the rue Danton and just around the corner.

Oona's eyes were sky blue, her hair blonde. Tall and willowy, she had a quiet calm, a dignity that was best for Hermann. But like the war, such things would have to sort themselves out and who was this humble Sûreté to judge?

The lorry's gas-producer hissed as he got out of the cab to stoke its firebox. Firewood and charcoal briquets were being used – charcoal in a land where so few had any heat. Hermann's concierge was always bitching about their never having any when he could so easily, and rightly, she maintained, insist that coal and wood were well supplied.

But Hermann wouldn't do that. A bad Gestapo – lousy to his confrères, many of whom hated him – he lived as one of the Occupied. Maybe that, too, was why Oona had grown to love him, and Giselle also. But now things were changing, tightening. Now people were beginning to say, '*Ma foi c'est long.*' My faith, it's taking a long time.

For the invasion to come.

'He's closing the firebox door,' whispered Oona, looking down into the street through parted black-out curtains. 'For just an instant there, I saw a glimpse of its light, Hermann. Ah *mon Dieu*, to sit and watch a fire in the stove and know those bastards can never again come banging at the door to drag us away.'

The Gestapo, the SS, the Paris *flics* and Vichy goons, et cetera. Oona had been stopped in the street. The contents of her purse had been dumped out, her papers scrutinized. Kohler held her. He felt her tears on his cheek, cursed the war, cursed the Occupier, and reluctantly said, 'I have to go. Louis will be freezing.'

And they had another murder to attend to. Never time to live a normal life but then . . . why, then, she told herself, things were just not normal anyway.

'Take care,' she whispered and quickly squeezed his hand.

People didn't hear Hermann when he didn't want them to. He left the house as silently as he had come and she knew then that he hadn't wanted to awaken Giselle, but had wanted to be alone with her.

'He's worried,' she said softly. 'Intuitively he knows there can only be trouble with this murder.'

Taking a spoon, she dug it into the pail of wax to taste the honey, to hold it in her mouth and cry.

'Louis, the *Milice* were after Oona.'

'When?' Oona's papers weren't good. 'Well, when?' demanded St-Cyr. 'Please don't spare me.'

'While we were on the train between Lyon and here.'

That explosion? wondered St-Cyr, alarmed. These days such things could well be the work of others but attributed to the *Résistance* so as to hide the fact. That way the SS, the Gestapo and their associates could settle nuisances such as honest, hard-working detectives, without being blamed.

These days, too, things were very complicated. The *Milice* were Vichy's newest police force – paramilitary but yet to receive their weapons, since Vichy had none to give and no such authority.

Primarily their duties were to give the appearance of the government's actively suppressing the black market. They were also to search out and arrest evaders of the forced labour draft, the hated *Service du Travail Obligatoire* and two or even three years of indenture in the Reich. But they had still other unspecified duties and powers of arrest and interrogation that suggested a branch of the SS.

'They couldn't have heard of what happened in Avignon, not yet,' muttered Kohler, trying to light a cigarette but suddenly finding his fingers too cold.

As in Avignon, so, too, in Fontainebleau Forest and with other crimes, the finger of truth had been pointed by them and not appreciated. And, yes, Hermann wore the scars of such honesty. But in Avignon there had been the *Cagoule*, the action squad of a fanatical far-right political organization of the 1930s, the *Comité Secret d'Action Révolutionnaire*.

That organization had been dedicated to the overthrow of the Third Republic by any means. Murder, arson . . . the dynamiting, on the night of 2 October 1941, of six synagogues in Paris in a show of mutual support for the Nazis, but were they now free to do as they pleased with a certain two detectives?

'In revenge for what happened in Avignon,' sighed St-Cyr. 'Word could so easily have rushed on ahead of us.'

'Then was Oona stopped in the street as a threat to us to leave things alone or else taste what's to come?'

Hermann was thinking of von Schaumburg's warning. He was letting his thoughts run through the many twisted threads of the tapestry Paris and the country had become under the Occupation. Each thread was so often knotted to another it could and did, when yanked, yank on still other threads and on their guts.

'All things are possible, Louis. That's what worries me.'

The *Milice* were not the *Cagoule*, but those same political leanings, those same sympathies were shared. And Boemelburg, as Head of the Gestapo in France, was one of the major thread-pullers and could well have given the *Milice* a little tug just to warn Hermann and himself to behave.

And yes, of course, one of the first things the SS and the Gestapo had done after the Defeat was to empty the jails of their most hardened criminals and put those types to work for them.

'Fighting common crime brings no pleasure these days,' sighed St-Cyr. 'Let's go and have a talk with our beekeeper. Maybe he can shed a little light on things.'

Louis always 'talked' to the victims, no matter how grisly the murder.

Under the blue light from Hermann's torch, the tiny bodies were seen to be scattered everywhere in the snow. All were frozen and curled up. No longer did the cluster of each hive, that winter ball of ten thousand or so bees, shake their wings and jerk their bodies to keep the queen and themselves warm. No longer did each cluster move slowly about the frames feeding on the honey they had stored for the winter and the beekeeper, being wise and kind, had left for their wellbeing. Someone had broken into each of the hives – all thirty of them – and had stolen a good deal of what remained of the winter stores.

'About twenty kilos to the hive at the start of each winter, in eight or ten frames,' said Kohler. '*Jésus, merde alors*, Louis, whoever did it had no thought for tomorrow.'

'Just as in Peyrane, eh?'

'Not quite. Here they left the cluster. In Peyrane they took it and squashed it along with everything else.'

The apiary was in one of those surprising little oases of nature that were often found in Paris: a field of a few hectares that was surrounded, St-Cyr knew, by a high stone wall. Cut off, isolated and quiet, it was right on top of one of the city's smaller reservoirs and not a stone's throw from the Père Lachaise.

'At five degrees of frost the poor little buggers didn't have a chance, Louis. Ten thousand times thirty equals three hundred thousand little murders.'

Using the wooden-handled pocket-knife the Kaiser had given him and countless others in the spring of 1914, Kohler scraped away the worker bees, stabbed at a large fat one in the centre of the cluster and said, 'That little darling was their queen. Not a virgin, not this one. Two years old, I'll bet, since that's the most productive age to successfully overwinter a hive. They're Italians, by the way. Banded yellow over the abdomen and with hairs that are fawn-coloured. Gentle, too, and prolific breeders just like their namesakes.'

'I never knew you were so well versed about bees.'

'There's plenty you don't know! This cluster had lots of honey and pollen to feed on.'

He pointed cells out, pricking some and scraping the wax cappings away. A maze of cells, a warren of them.

Indicating a poorly defined thumbprint, he said, 'Whoever robbed the hives wore gloves and was afraid of bees. They could so easily have scraped the cluster away and taken everything.'

Instead, they had left perhaps a good three kilos of honey in each hive.

Kohler switched off his torch and for a moment the star-filled sky came down to them, the air cold and clear. No hint of smoke or car exhaust in a city of nearly two and a half million. Paris had the most fantastically clear sunrises and sunsets these days, the most beautiful views over its pewter and copper-green roofs.

In '39 there had been 350,000 private automobiles and traffic jams like no others; in July of 1940 there had been, and now were, no more than 4,500 cars and most of those were driven by the Occupier. Sixty thousand cubic metres of gasoline had been required per month before the Defeat; now all that was allowed was 650 cubic metres. Thirteen hundred of the city's buses had disappeared from the streets and virtually all of the lorries.

Now the city ran on bicycles or on two feet, and when it shut down like this at midnight, it didn't open up again until 5 a.m. Berlin Time, 4 a.m. the old time in winter and hell for those who had to get up and go to work.

'So when were the hives robbed and by whom, Chief?'

Hermann was below him in rank. Sometimes he would use this accolade to prod his partner; sometimes, when others were present, to let them know he was subordinate to a Frenchman.

'Footprints,' sighed St-Cyr.

'I was wondering if you'd noticed them. The préfet's boys and those of the *commissariat* on the rue des Orteaux, which isn't far, is it, but did they have to trample everything and visit every hive?'

'A woman, I think.'

'Madame de Bonnevies?'

'Or another, but the matter can be left for now. Why not go and have a talk with the grieving widow? Let me take care of the rest.'

The corpse. 'Are you sure?'

Having seen too much of it, Hermann hated the sight of death. 'Positive. Fortunately the study is separated from the rest of the house and this kept the fumes from it, but it's interesting, is it not, that the woman didn't spend much time in there after she discovered what had happened? We could so easily have had two corpses on our hands. Use the front entrance; leave me to go in by the back. I want time alone and undisturbed with him, Hermann. I need to think and want Madame out of the way and distracted.'

'And the daughter?'

'It would be best if she were to come upon us by surprise, but then these days anything is possible, and a daughter who is absent without a *laissez-passer* and a *sauf-conduit* will have to be questioned about what she missed.'

About the missing permit and safe-conduct pass or the murder? wondered Kohler but let him have the last word, for Louis was in his element.

'Madame . . .' hazarded Kohler on entering the salon.

The woman didn't look up or turn from the stone-cold hearth. '*Oui*. What is it, Inspector?'

'A few small questions. Nothing difficult.'

His voice was gentle but this grated on her nerves, though she told herself he was only trying to be kind. She heard him sit in one of the other armchairs, knew he would have noticed there wasn't a speck of dust in the room and that she must have an obsession about cleanliness. Would he smell the *eau de Javel*, she wondered, or just the lavender water she used when wiping down afterwards?

The Javel, she said to herself. He has the sound and manner of it.

'Your husband, madame. I gather he spent all his time with his bees.'

And didn't go out to work like normal husbands with responsibilities? 'Ours was old money, Inspector. My money.'

Under Napoleonic Law a husband had control of his wife's money and property and could do as he pleased, even to gambling the lot away.

Kohler found his cigarettes and offered one, only to see her vehemently shake her head and hear her saying, 'I haven't since the Defeat. Women aren't allowed a tobacco ration, isn't that so? He . . . my husband refused to share even his cigarette butts and delighted in my anguish as he lit up.'

'I take it, then, that you weren't getting on?'

'Not getting on? We hardly spoke.'

'Then is there anything you can tell me that might help us?'

She pulled the bulky white dressing gown more tightly about herself and thrust her hands deeply into its pockets, still hadn't looked at him. A woman with very dark brown, almost black hair, cut short, kept straight, and worn with a bit of a fringe whose carelessness suggested an irritable, hasty brush with a hand.

'He wouldn't have taken that stuff by mistake, Inspector, not of his own accord.'

In tears, she faced him now, was angry and afraid and didn't really know what to make of things, thought Kohler. Was still in shock, was very much the *Parisienne*, but not of the quartier Charonne. Definitely of the Sorbonne and probably of the quartier Palais-Royal or some other up-market district. Of medium height and slender – weren't so many women slender these days? – she had a sharply defined face with high and prominent cheekbones, skin that was very fair, a jutting defiant chin, dark brown eyes, good brows, lips, a nice nose, nice ears, throat and all the rest probably.

The hair was thick, and as he looked her over and she fought to return his scrutiny, her right hand nervously tried to brush the fringe from her brow.

'Your daughter, madame . . .'

'Danielle, yes. Something . . . something must have happened to her. The Gestapo, the *Service d'Ordre* . . .'

The Vichy goons, the *Milice*.

'A control . . . Was she stopped and taken into custody, Inspector, or did they just "requisition" her bicycle again and force her to walk home?'

Hastily she wiped her eyes with the back of her left hand and snapped, '*Well*?'

The daughter, like so many these days, had gone out into the countryside to search for food, but that had been on Thursday, well before dawn, well before the murder. 'Look, we don't know yet what, if anything, has happened to her. We'll find out. Don't worry, please. She's probably okay.'

The Inspector had been writing notes in his little black book. A big man, broad shouldered and comfortable with himself even though there was a savage scar down his left cheek; others, too . . .

When he didn't look up at her but let her continue to look at him, she told herself he could know nothing and she was not to worry.

It was small comfort. And what about Danielle? she demanded of herself while waiting for his questions. Danielle who had never been the first-born, always the second and had therefore become so defiantly independent and competent. But . . . but these days, even those qualities could go against a person if arrested.

'The timing, madame?' he said, and she realized he was using the notebook to avoid looking at her so as to gain her confidence.

'Last night . . . Well, Thursday night, at . . . at about ten o'clock the new time. Berlin Time. My husband . . . he hadn't left that study of his, that "laboratory" as he loved to call it. When I went to knock on the door, he . . . he didn't answer.'

'And the door?'

'Was locked as usual. *Mon Dieu,* he could have been up to anything in there and I'd not have known, but always with him it was his bees.'

'You went in by the garden?'

'I went outside, yes, and around to that field.'

'You took the footpath that leads down from the cul-de-sac, the *impasse,* here to the gate that's off the rue des Pyrénées?'

'Yes. From there a lane leads to it.'

'The apiary your husband leases from the city?'

'*Yes*! And . . . and then I came in through the garden.'

'The gate to that field's kept locked but you've got a key?'

'No I don't have. It . . . it wasn't locked, nor was the one to the garden.'

'Could anyone else have come in that way?'

'The thief, the destroyer of the hives?'

'You noticed in passing that they'd been robbed?'

15

'Not then, no, but . . .' She shrugged. 'I don't really know when that happened. Yesterday – on Friday, probably, and after . . . after one of the neighbours had discovered he'd been murdered and would no longer have need of the hives.'

Kohler scribbled: *Hives not robbed night of murder but next day (?) Neighbours a problem.* 'Anyone else?' he asked, not looking up.

'Whoever delivered that little gift he drank from, the seller of it perhaps? *Yes!*'

'Do you mean your husband left those two gates unlocked because he was expecting someone?'

'I . . . I don't know. *How could I have?*'

'Okay, okay, calm down. So you found a brick in the garden and broke a pane of glass in one of the doors.'

'I had to. He . . . he did not answer me.'

'And you found him lying on the floor, dead?'

'*Merde alors*, must I shout the obvious to you? The fumes alone were enough!' she shrilled and gripped her head in anguish, shut her eyes and wept – let him see her like this. Ashamed, terrified, completely exposed and totally unable to control herself.

Kohler lit a cigarette and forced it between her trembling lips. '*Merci*,' she gasped and inhaled deeply. Calmed a little, she tossed her head back, but gave him a hard look to warn him off, thinking he was getting too close. Still fighting for control, she turned her back on him.

'I choked. I ran back outside and tried to think. He . . . he hadn't been dead for long, Inspector, because we'd spoken through that damned door of his at about seven thirty, or was it eight thirty? I . . . I can't remember. I'm so confused. Eight thirty . . . yes, it was eight thirty. He hadn't wanted to eat what little I had prepared. Soup . . . endless days of soup. A few cooked carrots. A little endive . . . No wine. We'd run out and you can't buy any, can you? Not here. Not in Charonne anyway, and one must shop at those places where one is known, isn't that so?'

Everyone was bitching about the shopkeepers, many of whom abused their positions and lorded it over their customers, selling a little to their favourites and nothing to the rest.

Kohler told her to sit down.

'And freeze?' she snapped. 'Forgive me. I'm . . . I'm just not myself,' but thought he would only wonder if this really *was* herself. Shattered and unable to think, and so afraid.

Instinctively the woman's fingers sought the gilt-bronze sculpture of a naked young man which stood, perhaps some thirty centimetres high, on a glass and bronze table in front of the fireplace. There was a vase of long-stemmed red silk roses beside it and, as he watched, she fingered the sculpture's shoulders, arms and thighs, couldn't seem to stop herself and trembled at the touch.

Complete in every detail, handsome and virile, the sculpture was one of a pair but its mate, a girl of fifteen or sixteen, stood not on the table but up above it and dead centre on the white mantelpiece of fluted wood, and before its mirror. The girl's right foot was down a step from the other foot on her pedestal, her torso turned towards the viewer, her head away and to the right.

Tiny acanthus leaves made a delicate tracery of chained ovals on the flat frame of the mirror that was as wide as the mantel. Two life-sized white marble faces, those of a boy and a girl, flanked the statue, looking out into the room.

'My son . . . our son, did these,' she said as if afraid of sounding foolish. 'Étienne . . . Étienne is in one of your prisoner-of-war camps.'

Along with one and a half million other Frenchmen, but they aren't *my* camps, thought Kohler and said, 'Look, I'm sorry to hear that. You obviously need him with you.'

'I've always "needed" him, Inspector. Always.'

But not the daughter? Then why put her sculpture up there front and centre and with her gorgeous backside reflected in the mirror? The father? he asked himself. Had de Bonnevies insisted on her placing it there?

The chairs, the sofa and chaise all matched the mantelpiece with white and fluted wooden frames and the clean, sharp lines of the late 1920s. Moderne, then, or post-moderne, and all covered in a cocoa-brown fabric that was almost silvery in the lamplight. Italian silk velvet, he told himself, and very expensive even then. Had the furniture been a wedding gift from her father, he wondered and thought it probable.

The carpet was not an Aubusson or a Savonnerie or any of those to which, as a child and then a university student, she might have been accustomed. But the soft, warm and very light beige of its wool went well with the armchairs and the rest of the furniture. In the mirror he could see the oil paintings she had hung, and knew they were good and must have been in her family for years.

'Inspector, my husband had his enemies – the petty jealousies of other beekeepers. He was president of the *Société Centrale d'Apiculture*, and for the third year in a row, and so had trampled on a good many toes. But . . . but who the hell would do that to him? *Who*?'

And had that person come in through the apiary? wondered Kohler.

For a moment they looked at each other and finally, realizing what she was fingering, the woman let her hand fall away from the sculpture of her son. 'That is Danielle,' she said acidly of the other bronze. 'My son is very talented but his sister did not pose like that for him. Not without her bathing suit. I'm certain of it.'

But not quite, was that it, thought Kohler, and wrote it all down for Louis and himself to digest. 'Your daughter, madame. How old is she?'

'Eighteen. Étienne is twenty-two. Why can't you people let him come home? He was badly wounded, and is still in need of a long convalescence. He can do you no harm, not now, not even then, in '39 and '40. A stretcher-bearer, an artist . . . He who had never wanted to hurt anyone, especially not his dear *maman*, his *bien-aimée*.' His beloved. 'They shot at him, even though he wore a Red Cross armband.'

'Madame, your husband.'

She waited, letting him know she wanted to shriek, That bastard, yes?

'Thirty hives. Were there more?'

Out-apiaries – that was what the Inspector was thinking. 'Several. One here, one there. Maybe two or three. It depended on the locations. A flat with a roof-top that was sheltered and not much frequented; the garden of a private house or villa. The city has plenty of such places.'

Have fun chasing them, she seemed to imply. 'And the honey,

madame. Did he sell it and the pollen and the propolis – the bee glue? The *gelée royale* also, his extra queens and the wax?'

The detective had forced her to look at him in a new light, that of one who was well versed on the little slaves Alexandre had adored. 'He had his "clients", yes. There's a book, a list with all the addresses and details. Your partner will have found it unless . . . unless, of course, whoever poisoned my husband took it away with him, or the sous-préfet and préfet, since both came here briefly to view the body yesterday at noon, and to discuss the matter.

'Now if you will excuse me, Inspector, it's very late and I'm very tired. My bedroom is at the back, overlooking the garden and that field, but while I'm in my bed, avail yourself of the rest of the house. Search all you like. I've nothing to hide and I don't think he had either. We didn't sleep together, not any more, and not in a long, long time. Ours was always a marriage of convenience. I'll not deny it, and you would soon have discovered this in any case, so please don't bother to ask the neighbours. Life is hard enough.'

Alone in the study, St-Cyr drew on his pipe as he sought out each detail, but this killing had not – he was now certain – been as it had first appeared.

The smell of bitter almonds, of nitrobenzene, though minor, was still present, for the corpse exuded it. Some, too, had been spilled on the worktable and tiled floor, and some had been absorbed by a fistful of rags. These things had had to be cleaned up and removed by Hermann and himself, both wearing rubber gloves and before they had gone out into the apiary to find that the hives had been robbed. Hermann had put a match to the stains and had burned the rags in the stove – no other course of action had been possible. The damned stuff was just too dangerous.

He, himself, had capped the bottle of ersatz Amaretto and never mind the fingerprint artists fooling around with it while open. He had picked up and had capped the tin container of nitrobenzene that the beekeeper, in his panic, had taken down from a shelf and had hastily opened.

Flung wide, the doors to the garden still let in the cold night air as an added precaution, while the heavy black-out curtains kept in the light. Fortunately, the Occupier hadn't chosen to switch off the electricity to this quartier or the whole city in reprisal for some act of 'terrorism' or because the Citroën and Renault works, et cetera, were in desperate need of the power to make things for the German war machine.

'Nitrobenzene is nothing to fool with, is it, monsieur?' he said to the dark blue-suited, scarved and cashmere-sweatered victim who lay on the floor near the desk, curled into the fetal position by a final spasm, and in rigor. 'The poison is rapidly absorbed through the skin and lungs, and that is, I fear, what really killed you. Death by misadventure, albeit with intent.'

The right side of the head, and a portion of the white woollen scarf, were awash in now frozen vomit. Everything, at first glance, had pointed to the bottle of Amaretto that sat on the desk among his papers. Oil of mirbane was soluble in alcohol, not in water, so there was, perhaps, no problem there. But drinking it was to experience its fiercely burning taste and to die long after ingestion.

De Bonnevies had probably first smelled the liqueur, and finding its bouquet acceptable, for Amaretto's flavour came normally from apricots and their stones which have the odour and taste of bitter almonds, had apparently taken a sip or a mouthful and then had instantly spat it out and set the bottle down.

'In panic, you thought the worst, monsieur – your wife, perhaps?' he said, gesturing companionably with his pipe. 'You rushed over to the shelves and took down the tin which you had kept in here for safety's sake, and not in the honey-house in the garden. You had to see if it had been the source of the poison. You had to, *mon ami*. Let us make no mistake about this.'

Giving the matter a moment's thought, St-Cyr then said, 'The container had been put back in haste, *n'est-ce pas*? The cap was loose, wasn't it? Accidentally you spilled some. You grabbed the rags to wipe it up. You were extremely agitated. Angry, I should think. Your fingers shook. Did the realization of what you felt had happened cause your shaking hands to accidentally knock that tin over? Had you argued with your wife, monsieur? Had she threatened you?'

The fingerless gloves which de Bonnevies had used while working in the cold at his desk, had absorbed some of the spilled nitrobenzene. He had dragged them off and, yes, they, too, had been burnt in the stove by Hermann.

'You tried to wipe the residue from your hands with the rags, monsieur. There was also some on the workbench. In your haste, your panic, did you then knock the tin over again and is this what caused it to fall to the floor?'

Suddenly feeling very dizzy, had he cried out to madame? Had he seen in the container lying on its side on the floor, the truth of what he felt she had done to him?

'Did you then look at the door which you had kept locked so as to shut her out? A door that opens into a narrow corridor and a set of stairs down which that woman would have had to walk each time she wanted to talk to you?'

The rest was clear enough. Breathing in more and more of the fumes and unable to get the pale, lemon-coloured oil from his hands, de Bonnevies had started for the garden. 'Suddenly you felt very drunk, monsieur. You had a splitting headache. You began to throw up – first over there by the table you used when selecting queens for your colonies, then by the one on which is the apparatus you use for artificially inseminating them. You had left the tin lying on its side on the floor. You had to get out. Out!

'You tripped and fell. You hit your head and threw up violently. Your vision was blurred, your skin began to itch. Drunk . . . you felt very drunk and as you got up, you stumbled, only to realize then that you had just put your hand down into the spill and that container had rolled across the floor towards you.'

A bloodied froth of vomit and mucous had erupted from the mouth and nostrils. The rictus was far from pleasant and exposed tobacco-stained and gold-filled teeth. The lips and mucous membranes, the fingernails also, were the deep shade overripe blackberries give to their juice when crushed. The skin was but a paler shade of the same.

At fifty-eight years of age, de Bonnevies had once been

21

distinguished-looking – tall, but otherwise of medium build, and with a face that was broad and strong. The hair was iron-grey, coarse and rapidly receding, the eyes grey and with heavy, horn-rimmed glasses that had been knocked askew.

The nose was long and broad, fierce and determined, a full Roman even in death; the eyebrows those of an academic, a professor perhaps: thick, bushy, well arched and demanding. The cheeks were cleanly shaven . . . Had he been about to go out? These days shaving was not a priority due to the scarcity of soap, razor blades and hot water but de Bonnevies *had* shaved early on Thursday evening.

The lips were thin, their expression probably often tight with impatience. The white shirt had been freshly laundered in cold water without soap, of course, and with fine sand for the collar stains – there were still sufficient grains to indicate the shirt hadn't been well rinsed but had been washed in a hurry. The tie was a dark royal blue and had many golden-threaded bees woven into it. A meeting of the Society? he wondered.

The gold signet ring bore the image of a honey hive with a tiny cloud of departing workers – a swarm perhaps.

Madame de Bonnevies was deeply asleep. Exhausted, no doubt, thought Kohler has he stood in darkness at the foot of the woman's bed. She had closed and had locked the door, but had left the key in the lock. And as any housebreaker worth his salt knows, he snorted inwardly, that's as good as giving him the key.

Her breath came easily – a clear conscience, he wondered, or relief at last that it had finally been done?

As with the rest of the house, the room smelled strongly of Javel and he had to wonder about this too. Lavender water had been liberally sprinkled and used when wiping down the furniture, but it couldn't begin to suppress the other. He had found bottles of Javel in the armoire by the bathtub, more of it in the toilet down the hall and still more in the kitchen. All from late 1940 or even up to mid-1941 probably, but as with so many things people had taken for granted, now it was no longer easy to come by unless she had a ready source.

There were lace and silk in the mirrored armoire, the soft wool of a dress, another of crêpe de Chine, a suit, a pair of slacks, a chemise, full and half-slips . . . Silk stockings were in a bureau drawer. Five, maybe six pairs and virtually unobtainable except in certain places. And oh *bien sûr* women kept those with runs in them – nothing was thrown out these days and one of the pairs had laddered runs in it. He could imagine her despair.

The brassiere he fingered was light and airy. There were two garter belts, and these had the same lace. But so, too, were there serviceable, everyday undergarments of cotton, linen and satin. All prewar. Nothing ersatz for her in that department, and damned hard to get in any case.

She sighed and murmured in her sleep, and turned on to her other side. He wanted to switch on the torch to see the faces in the photographs on the bureau and those that hung on the walls and were on her writing table.

Had she, unlike the husband, only those of the son; he only those of the daughter? The girl, Danielle, had had plenty of both herself and her brother in her room, and of happier times. A country house, a weekend retreat before the war. The boy lithe and handsome and laughing, with an arm draped fondly across his mother's shoulders, both in their swimsuits.

When he ran his fingers over what he knew to be a foundation sheet of wax for the combs in the hives – the bees built on these – Kohler felt each hexagonal indentation, the design covering the whole of the sheet. She'd been making a candle, but had left this off.

Gently he eased open the drawer of her writing table and began to explore its contents. He looked towards the bed; he put his back to her and, wrapping a hand over the end of the torch, let only a sliver of light escape.

There was a photograph of her son in uniform and taken before the Defeat. Clipped to it was a menu from Maxim's, no less, and at the bottom of this someone had scribbled *100,000 francs.* The going rate. Half down, half on arrival.

Searching for a cheque stub, a bank passbook – something to indicate monies had been paid out – he found none, simply a small oval badge in silver with the letters F.M. – *Förderndes Mitglied* – the runic double 'S' and the swastika.

Sickened by its implications, Kohler silently closed the drawer and returned to the foot of her bed. Again he listened to her breathing until satisfied she hadn't awakened.

Quietly he left the room, locking the door behind him while leaving the key in the lock on her side.

'Louis . . .'

Hermann had returned to the study. 'A moment, *mon vieux*.'

Louis was bent over the beekeeper's microscope. He had taken off the battered brown fedora that had seen such rough handling in Avignon. The shabby overcoat with its threadbare collar had been flung open – had he been tucking things into his jacket and waistcoat pockets, wondered Kohler and answered, Probably.

A fisherman at heart, though that pastime was forbidden and subject to forced labour or imprisonment, Louis was not tall or short, but something in between and still a trifle portly in spite of the extreme shortages. A muse, a reader of books in winter when he could get the time, which was seldom, he had the brown ox-eyes of the French, the wide forehead of the police academy's boxing champ and *flic* he'd once been. The hair was thick and dark brown, and carelessly brushed to the right. The eyebrows were bushy, the nose that, too, of a boxer. The lips were broad and determined, the moustache thicker and wider than the little corporal's and grown long before that ranting maniac had ever come to power.

'Talbotte was here, yesterday at noon,' said Kohler.

The préfet of Paris, on Friday. 'I could have told you as much. I recognized his footprints in the snow. Flat and expensive leather shoes, not those of a real cop nor the soles of wood most of us have to wear these days. Now, please, I've the corpse of a bee before me and it's not one of our beekeeper's.'

A half-open matchbox held several said corpses. The broad and somewhat rounded shoulders of the Sûreté hunched closer to the instrument. A meaty, no-nonsense thumb was jerked up and behind to indicate a framed collection under glass on the wall nearest the desk. 'The varieties and their clans, Hermann. The offspring of their unfettered inbreeding.'

Each bee in the collection of nearly two hundred had been

stabbed with a tiny silver pin. '*Apis mellifera carnica* . . .' began Kohler, trying not to think of the corpse on the floor. '*Apis mellifera caucasia* . . .'

'The Carniolan and Caucasian bees,' said St-Cyr, not looking up from the microscope, 'and beside them, the dark German bee, *Apis mellifera mellifera*, and the golden-banded *Apis mellifera ligustica*, the Italian bee.'

'You're learning,' quipped his partner. De Bonnevies, like many French beekeepers, had kept Italians primarily because they were gentle and productive, while the Germans, as with their human counterparts, thought Kohler wryly, had strong tendencies towards aggression.

'So, what's the verdict, Chief?'

'Acarine mites in Caucasian bees. Our beekeeper had collected some of the diseased corpses and was proving his diagnosis.'

'Only to be poisoned by a remedy for them. Fumigation with . . .'

'Yes, yes. Here our beekeeper has cut off the head and forelegs, then has used a needle to expose the tracheae which bear the characteristically brownish stains caused by the mite.'

'You've been reading his reference books.'

'It's not a simple murder, Hermann,' sighed St-Cyr, as if warming to the thought of a long and complicated investigation.

'That of the bee or of the human?'

'*Both*! Now listen, forget about the colour of the fingernails and the rigor – forget all such things. Take a look around you, eh? The well-ordered, well-loved shelves of a dedicated scientist. Two microscopes, Hermann, and good ones. The watercolours of flowers, the oils – the catalogue he kept of pollen in bottles, of honey, too, and its many varieties.'

The sketches, painstakingly executed, of dissected workers, drones and queens. All sacrificed, thought Kohler, to the greater good of others. 'So, why hasn't Talbotte got his boys working on the case?' he asked.

Charonne, like all of Paris and the Île de France, was the préfet's beat; theirs the rest of the country. 'And préfets tend to stick together,' said St-Cyr, leaving the microscope to pick up the trend of thought.

Both knew that word of what had happened in Avignon must have been passed on ahead of them. Those in power so seldom liked being challenged and did tend to stick together.

'Perhaps Talbotte doesn't want to dirty his hands with this, Hermann, for fear ours won't be dirtied enough.'

'And von Schaumburg has asked for us,' said Kohler, not liking it.

Caught between the Occupier's opposing factions, they had simply had to tough it out. But these days events were piling up and everyone was uneasy.

And suspicious too.

'Death occurred sometime between eight thirty and ten p.m. on Thursday,' said Kohler. He'd save the worst until the last. 'The couple weren't getting on, Louis, and didn't sleep together, but . . .' He shrugged. 'I can't see her as having tried to poison him. I really can't.'

Hermann always had a soft spot for the pretty ones. 'But she may well have laced that bottle,' chided St-Cyr gently and led him patiently through how the killing had come about. 'She'd have felt he wouldn't have taken more than a sip, Hermann. His every reaction would have been known to her. The instant suspicion, the anger, the race to check the tin – a woman can't have lived with a man for more than twenty-two years and not have known about such things.'

'The son . . .'

'What about the son? Well, come on, damn it, tell me.'

'F.M.'

Out in the garden, not a sound came up from the city at nearly 5 a.m. Far beyond the Bois de Boulogne, far over England and freedom, a shooting star streaked long and hard and cleanly until snuffed out.

Up from the ground came the terrible dampness and the cold.

'F.M., Hermann. What, please, have the Honorary Members of the SS to do with this little murder which was not murder at all, simply the attempted variety, if what we have seen of it so far is true.'

'It could so easily have been a black-market mistake, idiot.

How else these days is one to find the smell or taste of bitter almonds?'

Everyone knew there were hazards with black-market products. No questions were ever asked. To complain was to get nothing further and to have one's name passed on to other traffickers. 'Well, what about the F.M., Hermann? Please don't spare me.'

In 1932 there had only been about 13,000 Honorary Members, recalled St-Cyr. Collectively they had contributed a modest 17,000 marks to the SS's 'cultural, charitable and social pursuits'. But in 1934 membership had grown to over 342,000, with an increase in funds of nearly 600,000 marks. Since then he had lost track, but the sky must be the limit.

'*Jeder an seiner Stelle*, Louis,' said Kohler. '*Es ist eine Ehre, förderndes Mitglied zu zein.*'

Each in his appointed place, translated St-Cyr. It is an honour to be an honorary member. By caving in and joining the F.M., not the SS or the Party, one made a little contribution every year, thereby avoiding the strong-arm boys and the constant squeeze. Guaranteed a little peace, the Honorary Members and another, similar group, the Friends of the Reichsführer-SS, got on with their business interests – shoes, beer, tanks, cigars or whatever. All were involved.

'Siemens-Schuckert, Hermann. I.G. Farben. The Krupps, the Norddentsche Lloyd and Hamburg-America Shipping Lines, the Dresdner and Deutsche banks – all of the really big companies sent board members to join the Friends, and often the F.M., and in doing so, dragged in the little fish.'

'Himmler still has a good thing going with them, Louis. That little badge I saw only proves it. Silver no less, not zinc.' As were many of the medals these days.

'And the name?' asked the Sûreté, looking up to that God of his with tears no doubt, thought Kohler.

'We haven't got a name yet, but we've got a menu.'

Everyone who was anyone listened to rumours these days and knew that among the waiters at Maxim's there were some who would offer to help those wealthy enough to want to free their loved ones from POW camps in the Reich.

'Fifty thousand down, as the menu says, Louis. The rest when the "meal" is delivered.'

Madame de Bonnevies had been trying to buy her son's freedom. 'But why does she have the badge, Hermann? Why keep it with a photo of her son and with the menu?'

'Why, indeed, when her husband had control of all of her money, eh, and let her have only enough for the house?'

'You found expensive underwear. If she's having an affair with a Nazi . . .'

'We'll have to go carefully.'

These days things were always so complicated. 'Our beekeeper had planned his rounds for Friday and had made a list of those he intended to visit,' said St-Cyr.

'You've found his little book,' sighed Kohler.

'His is an eclectic list.'

'And?'

Hermann could nearly always sense when there was more. 'Old Shatter Hand is a valued customer. Three jars of honey.'

Shit! 'And?'

'The honey, the royal jelly and pollen were to have been delivered first thing yesterday morning to his villa.'

'Then I'd best deliver them, hadn't I?'

It was a plea, a cry to God for help. 'Yes, I think you'd better.'

2

Alone once more, St-Cyr again surveyed the study. He was grateful for the silence, for the opportunity, but were there things he had missed?

De Bonnevies had had a real love of bees. Pollen, sealed in 100cc jars, formed a collection as eclectic as the directory of his clients. Several of the samples were from prewar Poland; others from Russia. Italy was represented, Belgium, Holland – England, Wales and Scotland. Shades of yellow mostly; those of green, too, and orange and purple but muted, the tiny, microscopic grains being packed together by each forager to form granules from about two to three millimetres in diameter and irregularly rounded. All would possess the scent of the blossom most prevalent. Lavender, clover, linden, pear or apple. When mixed with nectar or honey, and stored in the cells, the pollen would form the beebread Hermann had mentioned.

Elsewhere in the study, filing cabinets held correspondence that, before the war, had gone on at a pace. America, Brazil, South Africa, Kenya, India . . . Wherever bees were kept, de Bonnevies had sought answers or given advice. An address to which he had been making last-minute revisions was entitled: '*WILL NO ONE SPEAK FOR THE BEES OF RUSSIA? Reliable estimates tell us that over one half of all Russian honey bees have already perished. When will this madness stop?*'

And never mind the human casualties at Stalingrad. A brave man to have thought to speak out like this. Foolish, too.

Folding the address – planning to read it later – St-Cyr tucked it away in a pocket. The desk was functional, not big or wide, but with a rampart of pigeon-holes that would take much time to go through. Could they be left for the moment? he wondered.

Something . . . was there still something in plain sight that he was missing?

Pens lay on the desk with a spare pair of glasses. Snapshots covered a tackboard on the wall behind. The daughter was attractive in her own right: not too pretty but secure enough in that department. There were lots of photos of her, but none of the son. 'And why not?' he asked. 'Surely a few of the boy in uniform to remind the father of him?'

There weren't any in the drawers or even in the pigeon-holes, many of which contained letters of one sort and another.

The Amaretto bottle had probably once held gin, not olive oil or wine. The new label had been stained by the contents when the bottle had been quickly set down. Of brown sticking-paper, its bold black letters had been crudely executed. An associate, perhaps, or a client – one of the less fortunate. Or had the bottle really been purchased from a black-market supplier and was that all there was to it? Death by mistake.

Then there would surely have been other poisonings. But would the préfet and his men make Hermann and himself aware of them? Not likely.

Though their visit could only have been brief due to the fumes, Talbotte hadn't taken the beekeeper's directory of clients, and neither had the sous-préfet of the local *commissariat*. A puzzle unless it had been left as a warning.

When Juliette de Bonnevies came downstairs, she found the Chief Inspector sitting in Alexandre's chair quietly perusing the directory, and she couldn't help but ask herself, How could he be so calm with that lying so near?

Alexandre hadn't been covered. Retreating, she went softly upstairs to find a bed sheet in the walnut armoire, the one from Aix that her mother had treasured, as had she and Étienne who had often, as a boy, hidden in it.

In play, never in fear of me, only of Alexandre, she told herself and touched the compartment where he had curled himself in with his bony knees pressing against his chin.

'*Mon cher*,' she whispered. '*Mon petit*, I mustn't cry, must I? He's gone now, Étienne. Gone.'

Everything would pass to Danielle – she knew this, knew that

Alexandre would have left her son nothing in his will. Nothing of hers. But it would take time to settle things, and there would have to be a funeral.

Knowing she couldn't face one, she took a moment to steady herself, then blurted softly, 'Maybe they will let you come home for it. *Home*, Étienne.'

Compassion? Had the Occupier any? she demanded bitterly, and using a corner of the sheet, dried her eyes.

In the study, she said nothing, only covered the corpse and then stood waiting patiently.

He'd let her wait, thought St-Cyr.

Every detail was there, she told herself, in that little book Alexandre insisted on keeping. The names, the clients, the people who kept bees for him too. The out-apiaries . . . The Inspector seemed glued to the precisely crisp, neat handwriting. He'd see that keeping the directory had begun long before the war. In October of 1921, Inspector? she silently demanded. The 31st to be precise. The day he brought me here to this house of his mother and its awful furniture that my father soon rectified.

He'd see that there were actors, doctors, lawyers, but among those less fortunate, Madame Roulleau, the concierge who kept bees for him on the roof of her apartment house and had done so for all those years and even some that had not been recorded. Mme de Longueville, too, and Monsieur Durand.

He'd see that there were socialites, politicians and businessmen, and now German generals and others of the Occupier, and that Alexandre had had access to the grand salons of the elite. He'd see that they had all trusted him with their little secrets.

'Madame, you will forgive me, but I'm puzzled.'

'Puzzled?' she heard herself yelp.

'Yes. Did you, perhaps, remove this little book from the desk and then replace it?'

How could he have guessed? 'I . . .'

The woman swallowed. Flustered and defenceless, she fought to answer but couldn't. 'You see, madame, in spite of the need for haste to avoid the fumes, Préfet Talbotte should, by rights, have taken it. A first police procedure is to seize all such records in case they should yield the identity of the killer.'

'I . . . I did remove it, yes, for safety's sake, you understand. But—'

'But felt it best to replace it after the préfet and sous-préfet had departed?'

She knew he was going to force her to answer yes, and wondered why it was so necessary for him to humiliate her like this. Her cheeks felt hot.

Abruptly pulling the white woollen robe more tightly about herself, Juliette folded her arms defiantly across her chest and answered, 'One does things in the instant of such a discovery, Inspector, that one later feels differently about and rectifies.'

Instinct had driven her to protect something in the directory, but he'd not mention this, not yet, nor that she must have known of the danger and had ducked into and out of the study to get it. 'Then can you tell me anything about these people?'

Anything at all, or nothing. 'It's been a long time . . .' she hazarded. 'He kept things to himself.'

'You didn't help him in his work? A wife . . .'

Had the crisis passed? she wondered and felt herself beginning to relax. Unfolding her arms, she said, 'At first, yes, but then . . . why then Étienne came into this world and, with the house to look after and Madame de Bonnevies, I had little time to spare. She was ill and confined to her bed. I—'

'You did not have *une bonne à tout faire*?' A maid of all work.

'My husband and his mother thought it too expensive, too "ostentatious" of me.'

The Inspector would leave that titbit for now, she knew, but would come back to it like a vulture.

'Did he like Amaretto?'

Was it safer ground? 'Not that I knew, but what you mean to ask, Inspector, is did he go out of his way to buy that bottle or did someone give it to him?'

'You've been thinking it over.'

Ah *merde*, he didn't miss a thing! 'The café on the rue Saint-Blaise is a possibility and just down from the church. He always went there for a marc or a glass or the *vin ordinaire*, but not on the no-alcohol days, of course. Sometimes an *eau de vie de poir ou de pêche* from one of the little orchards in Montreuil – he rented out hives to them and still does. Well, not any more, I guess. Perhaps that's why there are so many in the apiary. He must have been overwintering some of them here and would have set them out again in the spring.'

And you really have thought things over, madame, he said to himself. You've planned your strategy and want, I think, to lead me away from too close a perusal of this little book.

'A vineyard, an orchard – pear and peach brandies or the plain and rough,' said the Inspector, and she heard herself saying yes too quickly, and felt her heart sink at being caught out so easily.

'The vineyard is in Saint-Fargeau. It's not far and . . . and is not very big, but before the war, the . . . the wine was exceptional, the brandy passable.'

Did the Inspector know it well? she wondered. Did he, perhaps, live nearby? Again her heart sank, then again and deeper as she heard him say, 'The rue Laurence-Savart. My mother's house also.'

'Was she old and ill, too?' she heard herself asking and knew he could be cruel for he did not answer.

'Your partner . . . ?' she asked.

'Has gone to interview one of the names on this list your husband had written for Friday's deliveries and consultations.'

'List . . . what list? I saw no . . .' Ah *Sainte Mère*, he had got the better of her again!

'It was in your husband's jacket pocket,' he confessed. 'Now, if it's not too much trouble, might we have a look at your son's room?'

'My son's . . . ? Inspector, you've no right. Étienne can't have had anything to do with this. He doesn't even know of it and won't for weeks and weeks, if then!'

She had broken into tears and he hated himself for doing it to her but had had to. 'Do letters take so long to reach him?' he asked.

The hint of kindness in his voice only grated. 'Months, sometimes. My son was being held at Stablack but then they moved him to Elsterhorst and now he's at Oflag 17A. It's . . . it's somewhere in what was formerly Austria, I think.'

Officers' Lager 17A. 'Did your son help his father, madame?'

'With the bees . . . ?'

She had blanched and now realized this. Angrily she brushed the fringe from her brow and glared at him before stammering, 'I . . . I don't know why you should need to ask such a thing? I really don't!'

'Then let us take a look at his room. He can't have had anything to do with this murder, of course, but let us make certain of it.'

Monstre! she wanted to shriek, but found the will to softly say, 'Then, if you will follow me, I will take you to it.'

Twenty-four avenue Raphaël was tucked against the Jardin du Ranelagh and not a stone's throw from the Bois. Once the villa of François Coty, the perfumer, it had been requisitioned like so many others. Drawing that splendid front-wheel drive of Louis's into the kerb and locking the Citroën's doors, Kohler stood in darkness as the faint blue lights of workmen fretted feverishly over the lower stonework of the villa. White paint was being removed with wire brushes and cloths soaked in gasoline. There were large, dripping letters nearest to the windows . . . *MORT AUX BOCHES . . . VICTOIRE! LIBERTÉ!*

Death to the Germans . . . Victory! Liberty! Von Schaumburg would be in a rage. Not only had the *Résistance* done a job in the deepest darkness of the night, they had taught the sentries a damned good lesson: both could so easily have had their throats cut.

'Relax, eh? I'll see what I can do to calm him,' he said to a pink-cheeked Grenadier who couldn't be any more than sixteen and was dreading the Russian Front. 'Kohler, Kripo, Paris-Central.'

Cigarettes were passed to both of the boys for later. '*Danke*,' said the other one softly. 'He's in there frying our balls, I guess.'

It was very quiet in the spacious foyer where tapestries hung and gilded Louis XIV armchairs offered respite. But the doors to the salons were all closed, the adjutant not at his desk, the secretary . . .

Ilse Gross came through to take one look at him and shake her head. 'Von Paulus,' she mouthed the name. 'Der Führer . . .'

Prising off his shoes and dumping coat, fedora and gloves on top of them, Kohler headed for the grand salon. Clearly the rolling drumbeat and trumpet call of *Die Wache am Rhein* came to him and then words over a wireless that crackled.

Radio-Berlin were broadcasting von Paulus's faint-voiced gratitude to the Führer who had just made him a Field Marshal and expected him to carry on to the death.

Looking ill, a grey, bristle-headed giant struck down, von Schaumburg was huddled under blankets before a roaring fire. Field-grey, regulation-issue woollen long johns were pulled up to the knees; the big bare feet plunked into a tin basin of steaming water that smelled strongly of Friar's balsam. Both his adjutant, Rittmeister Graf Waldersee, and his aides, Major Prince Ratibor and Oberleutnant von Dühring, were with him.

But only von Schaumburg had the flu. And why must that God of Louis's do this to them?

The radio message came to an end as the Führer's Headquarters signed off.

'Kohler, *ach du lieber Gott, Dummkopf*, what has happened? Why aren't you working?' Phlegm was hawked up, choked on, and spat into a handkerchief.

'Nothing's happened, General. It's just a small delivery my partner and I thought you would . . .'

'*Das Bienen . . .*' he coughed. 'Have you brought them. *Idiot?*'

The bees . . . ah shit!

Startled, Kohler threw the others a puzzled glance only to see the three of them quickly retreat and softly close the doors.

'Well?' demanded von Schaumburg. 'My knuckles, they're swollen. *Swollen*, Kohler.'

Arthritis, and Louis hadn't told him everything that had been in that little book of de Bonnevies'. 'The bees were all dead, General. As soon as we can find replacements, we'll send their owner to you.'

'Ten stings a week, one on each knuckle. He was to have come to me yesterday.'

'Yes, General, we know that.'

'*Verfluchte Franzosen.*'

Damned French . . .

'*Banditen*, Kohler. *Terroristen*. Did you see what you and that . . . that partner of yours let those people do?'

Gott im Himmel, were they now to be blamed for everything? 'General, I've brought your honey and pollen, the royal . . .'

'ANSWERS. I WANT ANSWERS, DAMN YOU!'

A coughing fit intruded, the nose erupted. Mulled wine was taken deeply. The Nordic eyes, with their sagging pouches, were filled with rheum.

The throat was cleared. 'You see what the filthy French have done to me, Kohler? Now tell me how he died.'

Here was the man to whom Vichy was now forced to pay not 400 million but 500 million francs per day to the Reich in reparations and costs: £2,500,000 at the official exchange rate of 200 francs to the pound sterling, or at 43.5 francs to the American dollar, all but $11,500,000.

Pine needles littered the surface of the foot-bath. Rheumatism, too, thought Kohler ruefully. Nearly seventy, and long past retirement, the general waited. The unshaven jowls were grey, the blunt, high forehead and prominent nose damp with perspiration.

Briefly he gave him an update on the murder but for a moment Old Shatter Hand's thoughts were transfixed by the flames of other matters. 'Von Paulus will surrender tomorrow, Kohler, and for this, the Führer will call him a traitor. Cut off, surrounded, outnumbered and out-gunned, should he lay down the lives of those of his men who remain?'

'General, I leave all such matters to those who know best.'

'And the Führer is always right, is that it, eh?'

'General . . .'

'Yes, yes, you don't believe it for a moment and have just recently lost both of your sons. War isn't pleasant. Condolences, Kohler. Condolences.'

Another deep draught of the mulled wine was taken. A Gevrey-Chambertin, the 1919, and *mein Gott,* was he draining Coty's cellars in preparation for the Wehrmacht's packing up and heading home?

'In 1935, de Bonnevies visited my family's estates in Mecklenburg on the Plauer See. He remembered our beekeeper fondly – they'd spent an afternoon discussing a mutual interest in bee-breeding and making mead.'

'Acarine mites in Caucasian bees, General . . .'

'From Russia, Kohler. *Russia!*'

It had to be asked. 'Brought in with squashed honeycomb, some of which might then be used for supplementing the winter stores of Parisian bees?'

Kohler had been to the Restaurant of the Gare de Lyon, so *gut, ja gut!* but that honeycomb hadn't been from Russia. 'To the Gare de l'Est, you idiot. Rerouted through the Reich to find its way to Paris thereby denying the needs of the Fatherland. I want the practice stopped.'

Oh-oh. 'A name, General?'

'That I can't give you and you know this. All I can tell you is de Bonnevies was aware of it and deeply concerned for the health of not just his own bees, but those of his colleagues and all others.'

'And was that why he was poisoned, General?'

'Questions . . . must you ask me questions when you find me like this? He had a sister in the Salpêtrière, the women's asylum. He may have gone to see her on Thursday. He always did.'

Frau Gross came in with one of the Wehrmacht's doctors. Two nurses followed. There was talk of putting the general in hospital, of at least getting him back to bed.

'Candles, Kohler. I think it had something to do with candles.'

'The wax.'

'Yes, yes, that's it. The shortages.'

And the *marché noir*, the black market? wondered Kohler, but let the matter sit. Louis might have something by now. Louis . . .

The candle was no more than ten centimetres in length and one in diameter. Made from tightly rolled foundation sheet, the wick, a simple piece of string, would work well enough, thought St-Cyr. First soaked in salt water and then dried, it brought back boyhood memories of homemade fireworks and other forbidden explosive devices. The pewter candleholder would have entranced a boy of ten and filled his head with dreams of brigands and seaside inns.

Madame de Bonnevies was tensely watching him. 'Do you light one of these every day?' he asked and saw a faint, sad smile briefly touch her lips.

'When I can, yes. It perfumes the air. Étienne loved the smell of it. He . . .'

'Madame, your son can't have occupied this room in several years. Not, I think, since beyond the age of . . .'

How could he do this to her? 'Sixteen,' she gasped.

'And did your husband know you were using his foundation sheets for such a purpose?'

'No! There, are you satisfied?'

'And this practice?' He indicated the candle. 'Has been going on for how long?'

The police were always brutal, the Sûreté only more despicable. 'Since the Defeat, since my son was taken. A mother has to do something, hasn't she? Well?'

She wouldn't cry, she told herself. She would face his scrutiny bravely. But he turned away and, setting the candleholder down on Étienne's desk next to the windows, found Sûreté matches and lit it.

'One name,' he said, and she, like him, watched the flame splutter to life. 'There are well over forty in this book of your husband's, madame. My partner and I have little time. I think you know the one we need.'

'I don't. I haven't seen that book in . . .'

'Then why, please, did you take it?'

'Did I look through it – is that what you're implying?'

'You know it is.'

'Then I must tell you I saw nothing untoward.' There, she had him now. Defeated, he picked up one of the tiny Plasticine sculptures of ducks, pigs, geese and horses, too, in the farmyard Étienne had made at the age of four and which she had saved all these years.

'Beautifully done,' he said.

'Please don't touch them. You've no right.'

'Is it that you want me to obtain a magistrate's order? It will take much time, but if you have nothing to hide, why imply that you have?'

Salaud! she cried inwardly and swiftly turned away.

'Sixteen, madame. Why did your son feel he had to leave this house at such a tender age?'

Tender . . . 'It has nothing to do with my husband's murder! Nothing, do you understand? He . . . he simply couldn't stand seeing what was happening to me.'

There were photographs of the boy with his mother in happier times, some of the sister, too. In one snapshot, the two youngsters, at the ages of perhaps twelve and eight, were shyly holding hands at the water's edge; in another the boy was moulding river clay into a pregnant female form. In yet another, he and his mother were fondly embracing.

'One always looks for answers, madame. You must forgive the detective in me.'

Had he seen something? she wondered and looking up, knew at once that he was now watching her closely in the mirrored door of the armoire and had positioned himself so as to do so.

'Is there anything else you want?' she asked harshly.

'The watercolours, madame. Your son is also an accomplished painter. Very sensitive, very accurate. Lupins, achillea, dogwood in flower, roses, but . . .'

'But, *what*?' she spat.

He shrugged and parted the black-out drapes to peer down into the garden and then to pull them aside. 'But in your husband's study, madame, there are those of Pierre-Joseph Redouté and others. *Un bouquet de pensées, Rosa x odorata, lilium superbum . . .*'

'And?' she shrilled defiantly.

'But none of your son's work. It's a puzzle, isn't it?'

Pinching out the flame, St-Cyr heard her suck in a wounded breath and stammer, 'I . . . I never do that. Not . . . not until the candle's burned out.'

'Then let us hope your prayers will be answered.'

Wax and candles and a sister in the Salpêtrière. Acarine mites from Russia . . . Old Shatter Hand hadn't given them a hell of a lot to go on, thought Kohler, finishing a cigarette while standing next to a newspaper kiosk inside the Gare de l'Est.

People were everywhere; uniforms, too, the smell of boot grease, sweat and urine mingling with those of cheap cologne, unwashed bodies, stale tobacco smoke, farts and all the rest. *Jésus, merde alors*, why did the French have to make their railway stations so huge?

High above him, the glass-and-iron dome of the roof was lathered with regulation laundry blueing, each pane criss-crossed with brown sticking-paper, but now daylight fought to get in to discolour everything in this perpetual gloom. More than thirty platforms fed lines to and from Eastern France, the Reich and Switzerland. It was from here that trainload upon trainload of goods left the country. Fully 80 per cent of the country's wheat, nearly all of its potatoes, eggs, cheese, wine, copper, lead, zinc and steel. There were goods-sheds upon sheds in the yards to the north of the station, warehouses upon warehouses. So how the hell did honeycomb from Russia bypass the Reich to find its way into this, and where was it being kept?

Tucking the cigarette butt away in his *mégot* tin for another day – a real butt collector like everyone else – Kohler took a moment longer to look around.

People came and went or milled about in their thousands, or joined seemingly endless queues at the controls which solidly blocked the traffic up. Some had burlap sacks of onions – firewood even – on tired, worried shoulders. Others lugged suitcases – the better dressed, their briefcases. A crate of carrots, one of cabbages – artichokes in a hamper that was stuffed to the limit. Sacks empty, on occasion, and oh, *bien sûr*, it was a city and a nation on the scrounge and most here had been out foraging the countryside or were on their way to it. And those returning with the spoils had to face the lottery of the controls.

Paris had become a city of police and nowhere did one see this better than in places like this. The *flics* in their dark blue capes and képis patrolled endlessly looking for trouble or just being damned officious to show that they still had some power. The Feldgendarmen, the military police, in field-grey great-coats and with badges of office that looked like miniature breastplates dangling from the neck, were here in force. The *Kettenhunde*, they were called behind their backs: the chained dogs. They, too, carried black leatherclad, lead-weighted truncheons.

Gestapo . . . there were lots of those and invariably they carried thin briefcases and looked like down-at-the-heel undertakers who'd had a bad year. But the Wehrmacht had its plain-clothed secret police, too: the GFPs, the Geheime Feldpolizei, on the hunt primarily for deserters.

And wasn't this matter of the mites a question for the railway police? he asked himself and said, Go carefully. Remember that these days there has to be a system for every commodity.

The Reichsbahn supervised the railways, so he'd have to go to them. But in France they didn't wear the becoming light blue-grey they did at home. Here they wore coal black with silver piping on their tunics. Swastikas and eagles also, of course.

Where . . . where the hell to start? Soldier-boys were every-where, arriving and departing, laughing, shouting, crying, too, as they kissed their girls goodbye. There were boys from the Kreigsmarine and also from the Luftwaffe, for Paris was Mecca to all and probably the closest one could get to how things had been before the war – no bombing; well, hardly any. Rest and recupe' and this really was the Führer's little showcase of how the Occupied should behave.

Good luck then, *mein* Führer, he snorted inwardly at the thought of what wasn't so easily seen, that vast undercurrent of dissent and deceit that would one day erupt into outright hatred.

When he found the appropriate office, a burly Bahnschutz-polizei corporal from *Schwaben* was standing guard over a bench filled with kids. Some were young, others older, but all had dutifully crossed their knees. Books were open on each of their laps – one, two, three, four, five in all. Scruffy shoes needed mending, mismatched kneesocks drooped, and all were obviously from the same family, for a mismatched sock found its mate well down the line . . .

Would a sweet voice help? '*Guten Morgen*, Herr Offizier. A moment, *bitte*. I seem to be lost.'

Suspicious blue eyes raked him savagely. 'Lost? Don't give me that crap! *Gott im Himmel, mein Schweinebulle*, since when was a cop ever lost?'

Was he really that easy to spot? wondered Kohler, somewhat taken aback. 'Okay, I'm looking for something.' Affably he grinned and offered a cigarette as a token of peace.

41

The packet was taken in expectation of more to come. The kids didn't look up. A page was turned and then another and on down the line.

It would be best to get it out and over with. 'A railway truck in from Russia recently. Honey or beeswax.' He gave a futile shrug. 'My boss wants to know.'

'Your boss,' sighed the corporal.

'Sturmbannführer Boemelburg.'

'That's better.'

Reluctantly Kohler dragged out a wad of bills. Cursing the constant need to pay for information that should rightly be shared, he peeled off five hundred *Reichskassenscheine*, the Occupation marks and equivalent to ten thousand francs at the official rate.

'It's important,' grunted the corporal. 'Your boss must really want to know.'

Another five hundred were found. A page was turned, another and another and on down the line.

'Try Shed fourteen, line twenty. Enjoy yourself.'

'*Danke*.' Kohler started to leave but curiosity got the better of him. 'So, why are the kids being held?'

'Why do you think, *mein lieber Detektiv?*'

Knees were uncrossed and recrossed and this continued on down the line. A thin skirt was primly tugged into place beneath its book. Trousers were tugged . . . Another skirt . . .

'Your sergeant has arrested their mother,' sighed Kohler.

'Detained her.'

'For how long now?'

A lifelessness entered the corporal's gaze. 'Long enough.'

'Kohler, Kripo, Paris-Central, *mein* Herr. I'm sorry but I'd better check into it.'

'He won't like it.'

'Nor will I.'

The door was locked. The kids had all stopped reading. People came and went constantly. None looked up. None were curious.

When a woman who couldn't possibly be old enough to be the mother of those kids came out to urgent banging and cries of 'Gestapo! *Raus*! *Raus*!' she was carrying two big and obviously freshly emptied old suitcases. There were tears in her wounded brown eyes, those of rage and those of humiliation and despair. Her overcoat was unbuttoned, the little pillbox hat with its bit of veiling askew. Blouse and sweater were also unbuttoned.

'Get out of my way,' she said fiercely to Kohler.

So few of the Occupier spoke French, he knew his use of it would startle her. 'A moment, madame. Hey, let me settle this properly, eh? Just wait here. I won't be long.'

Louis wasn't going to like it. They had enough trouble as it was but what the hell. Chance was everything these days. One could go through a control and nothing would happen or there'd be an absolute disaster, but this one's misfortune could have its silver lining.

Stepping into the office, he closed the door and locked it behind him. Out in the station they'd be waiting, the kids not turning a page, the woman trying to button her things and finding her fingers were shaking too much.

The beret and earmuffs were dark brown, the belted brown suede, three-quarter-length jacket and grey woollen gloves old. As St-Cyr watched her from inside the honey-house, Danielle de Bonnevies hesitated. The girl had entered the garden from the Impasse de champ de parc de Charonne, and now stood just inside the tall wooden carriage doors through which she had come.

The once dark blue Terrot bicycle was caked with dirt and badly scratched, its mudguards dented, the glass of its blue-blinkered lamp cracked. A torn bit of towelling padded the seat. Wires secured the tyres to their rims – a bike no one would want to steal or requisition, but it was the load she had brought that begged closer scrutiny. The front carrier basket held a large, worn brown leather suitcase, tied round with old rope; on the rear carrier rack there was a wooden cage that held two worried rabbits beneath an oft-mended burlap sack that bulged.

Above the hiking boots, coarse grey woollen socks hid the turn-ups of the heavy khaki trousers she had made over for herself. Originally from quartermasters' stores, the trousers had been left on the beaches at Dunkirk in early June of 1940 like thousands of other pairs, boots, shirts, et cetera, as the Allies had fled to Britain. Such garments had been rarely worn at first, but now in the third winter of the Occupation, were increasingly being seen, and with the defeat at Stalingrad, would be even more in demand.

The girl's breath came hesitantly, as she sensed that things were not right but couldn't put her finger on the cause. The police photographer had been and gone, the corpse would be in the morgue, yet not one of the neighbours had thought to stop her in the street to tell her. Not one.

Cautiously she wheeled the bike towards the honey-house. Noting the footprints of others trampled in the snow, she held her breath, looked questioningly over a shoulder towards the house – searched its windows on the first floor, one in particular. That of the brother, he thought. Then she looked towards the gate in the wall at the back of the garden.

A girl of eighteen, with pale, silky auburn hair that didn't quite reach her shoulders. The large, wary eyes were gaunt and darkly shadowed by fatigue under finely curving brows. The forehead was furrowed with anxiety and chalky, the nose that of the father, although in her it made the face appear narrower than it was, giving height to the brow but a fine, soft curve to the chin. The lips, unreddened by anything but the cold, and slightly parted in apprehension, were not thin like the father's, but more those of the mother. Good kissing lips, Hermann would have said. The cheeks, though rosy, were frost-bitten under that same chalky whiteness as the brow. Was she ill?

When she opened the door to the honey-house and saw him waiting for her, Danielle sucked in a breath and blanched.

Quivering, she waited for him to . . . to arrest her? wondered St-Cyr and sighed inwardly as he told her who he was.

Alarm filled her grey eyes. Faintly she found her voice. 'What . . . what has happened? The Sûreté . . . ?' she managed.

Not the *flics*, not the Gestapo either, or the *Milice*. Although it would be best to put the jump on her and find out what he could, he told himself he would have to be kind. 'An accident, I think.'

'An accident,' she repeated.

'Your father, mademoiselle. I regret the news I must impart, but . . .'

'Dead?' she asked emptily. '*Dead*?'

'Please go into the house, mademoiselle. Take as long as you need. A few questions, nothing difficult . . .'

'An *accident*, you said.'

'Well, perhaps it was attempted murder.'

'*She did it. He always said she would. Maman!*' she cried in anguish and began to run towards the house only to be caught by an arm and pulled back.

Vehemently shaking her head, she stammered, 'I . . . I shouldn't have said that. I . . . I told him she would never do it. *Never*, do you understand? *Maman* only threatened to because she . . . she was so unhappy. Murder was never in either of their hearts, Inspector. How could it have been?'

The urge to say, That is what we must determine, was suppressed. St-Cyr released his hold on her, the girl instantly dropping her eyes and pressing a fist hard against her lips to stop herself from crying.

Turning away, she began to pluck at the ropes that bound the cage and sack to her carrier. Breaking a fingernail, she tore off the offending shred with her teeth. 'Bacon . . .' she wept. 'Some sausage . . . The last of the late pears, wrapped in newspaper . . . Butter. I managed a kilo this time. Cheese, too, and eggs – enough for an omelette.'

Taking her by the shoulders, St-Cyr stood behind her saying, 'Cry, mademoiselle. Go on, please. You're exhausted and now in shock and deeply distressed. Things will sort themselves out in time. Leave the unloading and the rabbits to me. They're to go under the kitchen stove, isn't that so?' he asked and saw her nod.

'The cage there is bigger. I . . . I made it for them. He . . . he really would have been pleased. I know he would.'

It was a cry of despair.

Turning from her, he began to untie the ropes that bound the suitcase to her front carrier. Danielle knew he would open it – that he'd see both what she'd brought back and what she hadn't been able to barter or had hung on to by never giving in and always sticking to her price.

She knew he'd see her for what she had become – a travelling stall-keeper, a peddlar – and that the crucible of her very being was in those things, and that the bike was not nearly so beat-up as it appeared. The sack bulged where those of others did not; the rabbits were not two males as others often discovered, but a buck and a doe whose mating had been performed before her as proof positive and at her insistence.

But would he find in that stained and slag-encrusted crucible, the button of gold at the bottom of its white-hot melt?

'Excuse me, then, Inspector. I . . . I'm not myself, I'm afraid. *Papa . . . papa* and I, we were the best of friends. I understood him, you see. I alone appreciated what he did and what he had worked so hard to become.'

St-Cyr watched and, as he had felt she would, the girl turned to look back at the honey-house before entering the study to pick her way through it and wonder what really had happened there.

A little thread, some buttons on cards, a few safety pins and hairpins met his eyes as he opened the suitcase. Carpenter's nails were like gold and she had them in several sizes and neat little bundles, and had hung on to them in the hope of a better deal. Shoelaces, string, glue – what else had she carried in trade?

Unlike most, she hadn't taken small valuables from the house but had built up a stock of necessities and simple luxuries. Toothbrushes were extremely rare and she had them, elastic bands, too. Hairbrushes, hair-combs, pencils, playing cards, dice, lipsticks, cigarette lighters, small tins of black-market lighter fuel but watch out, it's gasoline!

Matches, too, but from the Reich, not French. Cigarettes – Russian, these. Pipe tobacco – Dutch. How had she come by it?

Chocolate – real chocolate!

Balls of wool – blue-grey, black and white – recovered from unravelled sweaters. Some reasonably good perfume, face powder and compacts. Tins of tuna fish. A christening dress for a baby, a bonnet, too. Three brassieres and several pairs of underwear, both male and female, not new, of course, but well laundered and with, yes, that same clean, white sand . . .

Jammed into the suitcase were the spoils of bartering: a small sack of chicken manure to be mixed with wood ash if possible, and used to fertilize the soil under the forty or so inverted glass bell jars, the *cloches* beneath which the girl would soon start growing Belgian endive, green onions, radishes, lettuces, et cetera, in the garden.

The smoked pork sausage with garlic, smelled also of savory and mushrooms. Six chicken eggs were cradled in a cigar box that was lined with straw and secured by elastic bands. The bacon, a slab of about two kilograms, was wrapped in newspaper and tied with string. There was a small crock of pâté. Two jars of redcurrant jelly were nestled beside others of plum jam. Dried cherries and dried apples filled a small tin box. There was also a rope of garlic.

The sack held beets, but among them were potatoes, carrots and a stalk of Brussels sprouts.

Among the tins of face powder she had to offer was one whose shade would easily have matched the pallor he'd seen and he realized then that here was a very resourceful young woman. At each control she would have coughed, looked like death, and gasped, 'A fever. The flu, I think, Herr Offizier. Forgive me.'

'Pass. Let this one pass.'

Not only would it have discouraged a close inspection but also flirtation. And yes, the road controls were normally run by the Wehrmacht, not the Gestapo, not the *flics*, the *Milice* and other Vichy goons as at the railway stations. But how had she come by so many things to trade, and where the hell was Hermann? Surely he should have been here with the car by now?

There wasn't just one man in the *Bahnschutzpolizei* office at the Gare de l'Est, a hole in the wall with stove, table and chairs. There were three of them, and the contents of the woman's purse was still strewn across the table, so they weren't yet finished with her, thought Kohler. Ah damn . . .

Putting his back to the door, he took in the competition. The Bzp Obergruppenführer who had watched the other two at play, didn't smile. A climber who would have liked to have worn a different uniform, the man was about forty years of age, clean-shaven and serious.

'So, *mein* Herr, you have a problem?' asked the Bzp in *deutsch* – in German. 'The woman is suspected of being a courier for the terrorists.'

Black tunics and flies were undone on the other two, not on this one. He even wore his cap.

'Several times we have noticed her,' eagerly sang out an eighteen-year-old boy in French, the younger of the two *miliciens*. 'When I was with the *Service d'Ordre*, she would come and go twice a week. I watched her.'

'Always she has those kids with her as a distraction,' grunted the older *milicien*, grim-faced and smug about doing his 'duty'. Both wore the regulation-issue brown shirts, black ties and trousers. Her suitcases had been emptied into a corner, but they'd not had time yet to pick through the loot – winter beans, dried and still in their pods, potatoes . . .

'You raped her,' sighed Kohler in French. 'Under OKW ordinance eighty-four, section thirty-six, article seven – that's Oberkommando der Wehrmacht to you two – what you've just done is a criminal offence and subject to the death penalty. Look, I'm sorry but I'm going to have to report it.'

'To whom?' asked the Obergruppenführer softly.

'To the Kommandant von Gross-Paris. How's that for an answer?'

Herr Kohler's German was still perfect, of course, but his French had really been very good and far better than most. 'I wouldn't if I were you.'

Deutsch again. 'And why not?'

'Word gets around. Besides . . .' The Obergruppenführer thumbed her identity card. 'This, I believe, is a forgery.'

What else was the bastard to have said? scoffed Kohler silently as the other two quickly buttoned themselves. The boy found his *chasseur alpin* beret and truncheon, the older one, his cigarettes and those of the woman, her lipstick, too.

Was there nothing for it, then? asked Kohler silently. Louis wasn't here to back him up. Louis wasn't anywhere near. Had she been arrested by the Gestapo or the SS, things would have been far harsher and still would be. Yet if a courier, then wasn't the item these bastards wanted not on her person at all, but being passed from child to child out there on that bench!

'Look, I can't have trouble. Not at the moment. My partner and I are on to something really big and need a little help.'

'So, are we to let the whore go in return? Is this what you're saying?' asked the sergeant, finding the thought mildly amusing.

Neither of the other two could comprehend a word, so *gut, ja gut*, thought Kohler. 'That's it. Old Shatter Hand wants me to have a look at . . .' He found his little black notebook and flipped it open to any page. 'Shed fourteen, line twenty. Help me out and I'll put in a good word for you and forget all about what happened here.'

Kohler . . . Kripo, Paris-Central . . . where had he heard that name before? wondered Obergruppenführer Karl Otto Denke. The rue des Saussaies, he told himself, and something about the SS. A rawhide whip and their not liking this one. The scar on the left cheek – yes, yes that was it, so he could go to them if Kohler should reveal anything useful. 'Okay, you've got a deal. Let her go, you two. *Vite, vite*. Orders from above. *Orders*, idiots!' He swept an arm across the table and, dumping the contents of the purse back into it, handed the bag to the boy.

Kohler took it from him. 'The cigarettes and the lipstick,' he asked the older *milicien* in French and snapped his fingers. 'Just to calm her nerves, eh? Then maybe if she really is working for the terrorists, those *salauds* won't come looking for you.'

Unable to comprehend all that had been said, suspicion registered in the Bzp's countenance; doubt and fear were in those of the other two.

'So, okay, we've got ourselves a deal,' quipped Kohler, 'and the three of us will visit the shed.'

Out on the concourse, he told the corporal to make certain the suitcases were refilled. 'We wouldn't want her going home empty-handed, especially since her papers are in perfect order.'

She would change them within the hour. She had that look about her. One after another the storybooks were closed and the staircase of kids got to their feet to dutifully wait.

'Take care of her,' he said to the littlest one. Nothing else. Just that.

Madame de Bonnevies was in the kitchen, sipping the leftover of the daughter's tisane of linden blossom, perhaps sweetened with honey. She didn't look up when St-Cyr put the last of the things the girl had brought on the counter, but when he shook the matchbox the husband had used to hold its little corpses, the woman set the bowl down.

'Acarine mites in Caucasian bees,' he said. 'An address entitled, "Will no one speak for the bees of Russia?"'

'Danielle can perhaps help you, Inspector, but you will have to wait.'

'Murder seldom does.'

'*Merde alors*, I've already told you I know nothing of these. The child is exhausted. Have you no compassion? No thought for the worry she has caused her mother?'

The Inspector wasn't buying it. He set the matchbox down on the table in front of her and found his pipe and tobacco pouch.

'Your husband was freshly shaven, madame, and had dressed as if for an evening out.'

'I . . . I don't know what he was up to. Believe me, I wouldn't have. Danielle . . . Danielle is the only one who might be able to tell you.'

'The girl stayed at the family's country house?'

She met his gaze, asked herself, What the hell has Danielle already told him? and said with a shrug, 'It's near Soisy-sur-Seine. She . . . she goes there sometimes – it's on one of her "routes", but she tries not to visit it too much. That way it's . . . it's safer.'

'And unoccupied otherwise?' he asked and heard her acidly answer, 'Of course. Fortunately the Occupier has found no need of it.' But then she calmed herself.

'My father loved it, Inspector. Danielle never really knew him but feels the same and I know she . . . she would like to live there, too.'

'As your father did, madame, or as your son, before the war?'

Ah damn him. 'My son, yes. My father left the property to him.' There, he could make of that what he wanted!

The table, one of those exquisite pieces from the provinces, had the warmth of old pine boards that always seem to ask, How many have sat here in days gone by? Bare but for a decorative bowl which would, before the Defeat, have held fruit, it would have easily seated eight or ten.

And this one has realized I love the table, she warned herself as he sat down to examine the beets in the bowl.

'The names in this directory, madame. If we could just run through them.'

'It's . . . it's been a long time, as I've already told you.'

'Of course, but . . .'

He paused to light that pipe of his and to look steadily at her until he had forced her to bleat, 'But what, Inspector?'

'One name, that's all my partner and I need. Enough to make a good start and save much time.'

Again he forced her to wait. Taking out his little black notebook, the Inspector struggled to find a pencil stub and at last rescued one from his jacket pocket.

Alexandre's signet ring was among the debris that had come out of that pocket – he would have had to remove it from the corpse. Why had he done so? Why had he left it on the table like that?

Elastic bands were also there, burnt-out matchsticks, a cigarette butt that had dribbled its tobacco on the table, the *mégot* tin it was to have gone into, a tin that was years old and had once held sweets: *Anis de l'Abbaye de Flavigny* . . .

'Does the name Frau Uma Schlacht ring any bells, madame?'

'Schlacht?' she heard herself saying.

'Age: forty-four. Address: 28 quai d'Orléans. She's not one of the *Blitzmädels*, not with a schedule that allows for visits during the day.'

The Île Saint-Louis, and not one of the grey mice, the girls who had come in their droves from the Reich as telegraphists, typists, clerks, cooks, canteen help and other jobs like prison warders and interrogators.

' "Treatments: Mondays," madame, "at four p.m." What sort of treatments?'

'How the hell am I supposed to know?'

'Would your daughter have carried out those treatments?'

'Instead of my husband?'

The woman was shaking, and as he watched her, more tears fell. 'You know that's what I mean, madame.'

'Then, no! Alexandre would have insisted on attending to this . . . this foreigner himself.'

'Then did your daughter help him with other patients, other clients?'

She would toss an uncaring hand and shrug, thought Juliette, would say acidly, 'Ask her, don't ask me. *Mon Dieu,* those two had shut me right out of their lives. We . . . we hardly spoke.'

There, he'd make what he wanted of that, too, she told herself. A son who had left the house at the age of sixteen and now a daughter who had loved her father, not her mother because she hadn't wanted her to be born.

' "Two litres of mead a month, madame. Six hundred grams of pollen – apple or rose if possible. Honey in two 400cc jars." Again Frau Schlacht prefers the apple or rose. "For facial masks and for the throat." Is she a singer?'

'*Pouf!* You think you can pry answers from a head that is empty? *Quelle folie,* Inspector. *Quelle absurdité.* For the sake of justice, I hope you find his killer, but for myself, I sorely feel you are not up to it! A Sûreté? A Chief Inspector? *Pah!* I ought to have known not to hope.'

'I'll keep your objections in mind. But it says here "the honey, mead and pollen to be left, if necessary, at the Palais d'Eiffel"?'

A beautiful townhouse on the avenue Matignon, the *palais,* so named by those who worked there, had once been the residence of Alexandre Gustav Eiffel, the builder of the Tower.

'The Offices of the German Procurement Staff, madame. *Das Deutsche Beschaffungsamt in Frankreich.*'

Of all the names in that little book, why had he chosen the one she most wanted him to avoid?

Intuitively anticipating her question, the Inspector slid the book across the table, forcing her to look at it. Inadvertently, when she had discovered Alexandre's body and had taken the book to search through it, she had slightly crumpled the top-right corner of the page. Alexandre had always been so meticulous, so fussy. Perfect pages elsewhere. In just such things as this would the detective find his answers.

'My husband was a strong advocate of the healthful benefits of taking pollen, Inspector. A spoonful a day. The Père Michel has taken it for years . . . Ah! here is his name. The Église de Saint-Germain de Charonne. It's but a short walk. Père Michel could, perhaps, help you greatly and then . . . why then, you could come back to see Danielle.'

She was desperate and would have to be given a breather, but one must do so curtly and leave her with doubt in mind.

He wagged a forefinger at her. 'That is exactly the help I want from you. *Merci.*' Hermann . . . where the hell was he? 'If my partner should turn up with my car, please tell him not to hot-foot it about the city but to wait patiently. In the honey-house perhaps. He used to keep bees on his father's farm and will find much in there to touch on memories I sadly fear he has long been too busy to recall.'

Shed fourteen, line twenty was well to the north of the Gare de l'Est through a wind-blasted Siberia of rails and a taiga of switches. Trains came and went, huffing, belching steam and coal-smoke; electric ones, too, and noise like you wouldn't believe, thought Kohler. Donkey engines roared as track was lifted on to flatbed wagons destined for the Reich. Crates of produce were over there . . . People . . . a long double line of them. Kids held by the hand, mothers and older daughters . . .

Though the roundups of Jews and other so-called undesirables had largely gone on last year and Louis had documented as much as he could, there were still some who had hidden and then been caught. Gypsies, too, and Communists, Allied agents and *résistants*, et cetera.

Wehrmacht boys with carbines slung over their shoulders and dogs on the leash, patrolled the shuffling line, while those with the Schmeissers covered the flanks, and those who had come to supervise the deportations stood nearby.

Suitcase after suitcase was being left to one side of the tracks, but the 'carriages' the passengers were to take were still some distance ahead.

'We're there,' said the Bzp Obergruppenführer, indicating a corrugated, rusty-roofed shed of grey concrete block that looked exactly like all the others.

'Your name . . .' began Kohler. 'I seem to have heard of it years ago. Where'd you say you were from?'

'I didn't.'

'Then tell me.'

'Münsterberg.'

'Near Breslau?'

Kohler was just ragging him. Of course everyone in 1924 had heard of Karl Denke, the mass murderer and butcher who had smoked and then sold the meat of his victims. 'We weren't related.'

'I just wondered. Police work – you know how it is. I was in Munich; the wife at home on her father's farm. We hadn't yet had our two boys, Jurgen and Hans. *Mein Gott*, the inflation, eh? I wheeled a barrow full of marks to buy a dinner of boiled cabbage and a toothbrush!'

There'd been famine. Real hardship. From an official exchange rate of 4.2 marks to the U.S. dollar in 1918, the mark had fallen to 1,000,000 to the dollar in 1923. Those who had had work, had instantly spent their wages on anything they could get.

The smoked 'pork' Herr Denke had marketed had sold very well. Buttons from the bones, too, and soap from the fat and ashes.

I can't let what's happening to the deportees set me off, said Kohler to himself. I mustn't.

They were climbing into cattle trucks and would freeze in them. *Jésus, merde alors*, how could anyone do this? He was glad Louis wasn't here to witness it; Oona neither, nor Giselle.

'Look, tell your *miliciens* to wait outside, eh? This is between the two of us. The less who know of it, the better.'

Charonne was still very much the village it had once been. As he left the house and began to walk uphill along the cul-de-sac towards the rue Stendhal, St-Cyr knew he was being watched from more than one window. 'A *mariage de convenance*,' Madame de Bonnevies had said to Hermann and told him not to ask the neighbours. 'Life is hard enough.'

Whispers . . . rumours . . . there would have been lots of those, for when all was said and done, the beekeeper had been an *original*, an odd character, an eccentric, and in any village or small town such idiosyncrasies always singled one out. Her money, too – they'd not have missed such a juicy thing.

But had she been carrying on an affair? If so, she would have done it discreetly but even then, the women of this street would have noticed and commented on a made-over skirt, a newly polished pair of prewar high heels – those silk stockings Hermann had mentioned; a *chapeau cloche* or beret set at a more determined angle, the hair perhaps curled.

Since the Defeat there had been a flood of anonymous letters to the authorities. Vichy and the Gestapo encouraged them, to the shame of the nation. Old scores were being settled, lies told upon lies. Even children – especially children – could be useful to those who would encourage such trash, but had there been letters of complaint about de Bonnevies?

Which of you smashed those hives and robbed them? he demanded silently. Is this why you watch me so closely?

The matter of the hives would have to be settled but for now it was the least of his difficulties. Something had caused madame to hide the fact she had known very well who Frau Schlacht was and that could only spell trouble for Hermann and himself if things turned sour.

At the intersection of the *impasse*, the rue Stendhal ran downhill past the graveyard and church to end in a set of stone steps. Although the day was almost half-over, the sun had failed to show itself. But here was history, he reminded himself. Architecturally there were those, he knew, who thought the Église de Saint-Germain de Charonne frightful. Only its bell tower remained of the original structure. Fires, wars, dedicated, well-meaning parishioners and determined priests had seen what had been in place since the twelfth century all but completely rebuilt in the fifteenth, gutted of its transepts in the nineteenth and left with a clock in its bell tower to give the time of funerals, confessionals, weddings and christenings, in verdigris-stained Roman numerals.

An *original* in itself.

Père Michel wasn't at home in the presbytery or in the church. He was downhill from them a short distance along the rue Saint-Blaise, sitting at a corner table in the Café au Rendezvous, waiting for the Sûreté to question him.

One saw it at a glance on entering. Word had somehow been

telegraphed on ahead. *Mon Dieu*, there were so few telephones in such quartiers, one seldom considered their use.

No, this had been done whisper by whisper and as if through the walls, but how had they known madame would be certain to send him to the priest? Oh *bien sûr*, it was logical. A death in the parish, the murder of one of their own, but the Sûreté could have come at any time.

They'd seen it, right from the moment he had stepped from the front entrance. They'd known it in his walk. *Merde*, these villages, he said, letting a rush of affection pass through him, for he was of Belleville, had been born there, and knew it and Ménilmontant and Charonne like the palm of his hand, as would this priest.

In the faltering light of a single electric bulb, shadows seemed to fill Shed fourteen. The smell was overpoweringly of buckwheat, of ripening fields, of straw and wax and beebread, cordite, blood and burning barns. The image of peasant women and children on their knees was clear. Pistol muzzles pressed to the backs of their heads. Bang, bang and into the mud and shit. The men were being hanged.

Kohler sucked in a breath and heaved a defeated sigh at the stupidity of it all, only to notice that Obergruppenführer Denke was watching him closely. The smug little bastard would report his reactions . . .

'*Mein Gott*,' he said and tried to flash a grin as he indicated the contents of the shed. 'The Wehrmacht's boys sure did a job, didn't they?'

Denke probably wouldn't know a damned thing about bees. 'They didn't just take the heaviest and lightest of the hives – those of the old, well-established colonies that might harbour disease, or the youngest that were too light to overwinter,' said Kohler. 'They took everything.'

Inverted straw skeps, grey and golden, the thimble- to basket-shaped hives not used in ages in the Reich, nor in France for that matter – except for catching a swarm – had been piled one on top of another right to the roof. Russia . . . the Ukraine? he asked himself, and going in among the stacks, touched one and then another.

'My grandmother used to make these,' he said, the sound of

56

his voice flat in the freezing, pungent air. 'Toothless and so old, the arthritis in her hands caused her constant pain she ignored. And forget that crap you hear about bee stings helping. They didn't.'

The iron skep needle had been like a skewer, twenty centimetres long and sharply pointed, but with a circular loop at its opposite end. 'Peeled, split willow and blackberry shoots are used to bind the tightly coiled ropes of straw. My brother and I used to gather them for her.'

So why the trip down memory lane? wondered Denke uneasily. Some of the hives had been removed, and because of this there was a gap in the stacks. Kohler had wandered out of sight.

'Okay, so who's bringing these in?' called out the *Detektiv*.

'We can go through the manifests, if you like. The Frenchies keep them in the main office.'

A shot rang out, puncturing the metal roof and killing a rat with a sweet tooth.

'Herr Kohler, what is the meaning of this? What's going on?'

Nervous was he, at the sound of gunfire and yet wanting a different uniform? 'Just tell me who it is. Whoever set this up had help – lots of it – and long lines of communication.'

Where . . . where the hell was Kohler now? 'I . . . I simply don't know, *mein* Herr. How could I?'

'And you an Obergruppenführer in the Bahnschutzpolizei who'd look better in a Leutnant's grey-green? Hey, *mein Kamerad* from Münsterberg, I know you're sharper than that. Cough up and I'll put in a good word for you like I said.'

Another rat fell from the roof timbers, and then another. The *miliciens* didn't try to enter. In his mind's eye, Denke could see them running back along the tracks towards the stationhouse. Had Kohler planned it this way? Of course he had!

'He's . . . he's important,' faltered Denke only to hear Kohler quip, 'He'd have to be.'

'He's one of the *Bonzen*.'

The bigshots. That was better, but teasing the name from the sergeant would be like coaxing the rats to show themselves.

Verdammt, the lousy *Schweinebulle*, thought Denke. The shed had dropped to silence.

'Oskar Schlacht. He has an office in the Palais d'Eiffel but is seldom there, or so I've been told.'

A busy man, then. 'So who does Herr Schlacht ring up in a Wehrmacht supply depot in Kodyma or Krivoy Rog, or maybe Lugansk?'

Kohler had worked his way right round the stacks and was not two metres from him! 'I . . . I really couldn't tell you, *mein* Herr.'

'It's *Detektiv Aufsichstbeamter* or Herr Hauptmann.'

'Sorry.'

'Look, relax, will you? Don't worry about it. A cousin – is that who Herr Schlacht rings up?'

'He has relatives stationed in several places. In Russia, Czechoslovakia, Poland, too, and the South of France.'

A man with a big family. '*Gut*! So come and have a look, eh? You never know. Maybe what I'm about to show you could be the key to your future.'

They went among the hives. There was little else he could have done, thought Denke warily. Kohler still had the Walther P38 in hand, but held loosely.

With each stack, the lowest hives had all but been crushed. Others above them were distorted – squished this way and that – but all gave ribbed shadows where light struck the bound coils of straw.

Except in the uppermost hives, where near-dormant bees stirred and fanned their wings, everything was frozen. Dead bees littered the floor. Wax and honey were underfoot. 'These are Caucasians,' confided Kohler, handing the pistol to him to hold. 'You can tell that by their big size and grey hairs. Here, let me gather a few for you to take to the Kommandant von Schaumburg. You can tell him I'm still looking for others. He'll be at home today. I'll write the address down for you, no problem. Just hand him this matchbox and he'll understand.'

Von Schaumburg . . .

Kohler's expression was companionable. He found a pencil and a little black notebook, and tearing out a page, wrote the address and then: Herr Kommandant, this is a man the OKW could use. It's not right to let the past of a relative stigmatize what could be a promising and very successful career. Heil Hitler.

He had even signed the note.

'Why, *danke*, Herr Hauptmann *Detektiv Aufsichtsbeamter*. For a moment there, I thought . . . Well, that young woman and those two. I found them in the office on their hands and knees, the younger one rutting at her like a wild beast while the older one pinned her wrists and head to the floor. I . . . I didn't quite know what to do, and then there you were to settle the matter.'

'Your lucky day, just like I said. Oh, have you ever tried chewing this? It's propolis – bee glue, the bees get from trees. The sap. My boys used to love chewing it, like gum, only this is way better.'

Louis would be pleased. A call to Ilse Gross would suffice. One Obergruppenführer who should have known better, two *miliciens* the world could well do without, and a charge of rape. Flu or no flu, Old Shatter Hand would hit the roof, and as for Herr Oskar Schlacht, why, the fun had just begun.

3

The Café au Rendezvous was like so many St-Cyr had experienced
as a boy. The stand-up bar, with its rows of cloudy, overturned
glasses on their metal tray was just the same; the copper coffee
machine still exactly like a boiler-works out of Jules Verne.

Several of the linoleum-topped tables were occupied, and the
hands of the patrons still identified their owners: a clerk in a
menswear shop, a glazier, piano teacher, plasterer, carpenter and
stonemason . . .

Burn marks the size of bullet-holes marred the linoleum floor
where countless cigarettes had fallen in the heat of argument.

'Inspector . . .'

Father Michel Audet had chosen his position well. From the
back of the café, and flanked by posters that cried out, *Vous Avez
la Clef des Camps* – You Have the Key to the Camps – and, *The
Good Times are Here Again, Daddy's Working in Germany*, the
priest waited.

Overly large, black horn-rimmed glasses magnified the inten-
sity of sharp, dark eyes. The brows were thick and had been
defiantly dyed black, and they matched the beret which was clean
but so obviously had the dust of age and obstinacy clinging to it.

'Father, I am—'

'Yes, yes, I know who you are. I've followed your career for
years with much patience.'

Ah *merde* . . .

'Sit down. Marcel,' he signalled to the *patron*. 'A pastis for the
Chief Inspector. He looks like he could use it, and put that idiot
signboard out of sight at least until our guest has refreshed
himself.'

The chalked *pas d'alcools* board was quickly tucked behind the zinc, a Ricard bottle produced as if by magic and set on the table with two glasses and a small carafe of water.

'You read my mind, Father,' said St-Cyr gratefully.

'It's my job to do so, as it is your own.'

A cigarette was offered – it was extremely rare for one to do so these days, so the priest was not only telling him they had things of importance to go over, he was warning him to tread carefully. And, yes, he was also telling the assembled that here was a Sûreté they would have to recognize but that it would be wise to first funnel everything through himself.

'This murder . . .' began Father Michel, adding a touch of water to the pastis in both of their glasses.

'My partner and I are not absolutely certain yet that it really was murder, Father. Amaretto isn't common, even on the *marché noir*, but it could have come from there. Did our beekeeper buy such things?'

'Not from around here. Alexandre didn't even care for the stuff, but what you really mean to ask is, could Madame de Bonnevies have added the poison to it.'

'I'm waiting, Father.'

'Then wait. God is still hearing dispositions on the matter. Madame de Bonnevies tried repeatedly to get me to intercede on her son's behalf. She begged me to find her three skilled workers who would willingly leave their jobs, their families and loved ones, to work in Germany, in return for which, her son would have been released.'

This was the *Relève*, the exchange programme whose poster, of a male Germanic fist holding an upraised key, was to the right of the priest. But now that scheme, having been introduced in mid-1942 and having failed utterly, had been replaced by the *Service du Travail Obligatoire*, the forced labour draft, so even posters like that of the radiant young mother telling her four children money was now on the table, were passé. Now all non-essential males born between 1 January 1912 and 31 December 1921 immediately faced being called up.

The priest cleared his throat, then wetted it.

'I refused, of course, and advised patience. It was wrong of me.'

'Why so?' asked the Sûreté.

'Alexandre might still be alive. It's a question that haunts me. Madame de Bonnevies has suffered greatly and is a very distraught, very desperate woman who has had two and a half years of agonizing over that son of hers and has, I should surmise, tried everything possible to free him.'

The hands that fingered the glass so delicately were not big, but finely boned. Beneath the jacket, the priest wore a grey cardigan that had lost none of its original buttons yet had probably been purchased back in 1930.

'The past is food for the present, Inspector, but at its table the future is nourished. If ever there was a woman wronged it was Juliette de Bonnevies. Oh for sure, Alexandre was not only one of my parishioners but also a very dear friend, and I am much saddened by his unfortunate and untimely death. And certainly I tried to intercede in that marriage. Love for his wife – a wife who had borne him the son of another man. Pah! He refused her this just as she refused it him. They tried, of course, at first, but very soon it became apparent both were prisoners of the other; she to dote on her son and ignore the daughter she and Alexandre shared; he to do exactly the reverse.'

'He lived on her money.'

'He married her because of it. He *knew* she was pregnant with the child of another. It had all been arranged. Her family, his family, the matter settled. You see, I married the couple, and when I leave here to walk back up the street, I will see my church's beautiful and ancient bell tower stained by the mistake I made.'

'They hated each other.'

'Of course they did.'

'And Danielle?'

'Has always felt she meant nothing to her mother, and everything to her father.'

It would be best to give St-Cyr a moment, and to replenish his pastis. 'Inspector, that child has no other choice than to peddle merchandise. Alexandre had no head for filling the family larder, even in the good times, except for the produce of his bees. Since the Defeat, the mother has had little head for it either. Those two existed solely because the child they had produced chose to hold them together and feed them.'

It had to be asked. 'Could Danielle have inadvertently picked up that bottle during one of her trading circuits?'

'Then why did he choose to drink from it days or perhaps weeks afterwards?'

A good point, but was Father Michel still trying to suggest the mother was guilty?

They finished their second cigarettes in silence. None of the other patrons watched them now. All were huddled in close conversation. But two women had entered the café so quietly, thought St-Cyr, he was troubled by the fact he hadn't noticed them and the priest hadn't let on.

Both women were in their mid- to late forties, and one Sûreté glance at them sufficed. Both turned away to look out at the rue Saint-Blaise through curtains that held that same gossamer of tired lace he'd seen as a boy. Lace that cried out in despair for a wash or an airing in the rain but, even so, wore the patina of stains – those largely of tobacco smoke and fly spray – with a frayed dignity.

'I've asked them to come, Inspector. As a man who was denied his conjugal rights, Alexandre made his visits to the house of Madame Thibodeau. A sin, God, I am certain, readily forgave but never would his wife. Never. And the question is, Why did he continue to visit a house so close to home? Was it to humiliate her?'

Both women were hard, time-worn *filles de joie* well on their way to that charlady-Valhalla of all such types.

'Though a scientist and *Président de la Société Centrale d'Apiculture*, Alexandre prided himself on his roots. His father was head clerk in the shop of Juliette de Goncourt's father on the rue du Faubourg Saint-Honoré. One *de* was simply exchanged, admittedly, for the dubious respectability of another, and with it eventually went her father's money.'

'And the son's real father?' asked St-Cyr.

'She never told anyone, not even that father of hers, though de Goncourt loved his little grandson and did come to the boy's baptism. I insisted, for her sake, Inspector, as much as for the child's. In Charonne, as in any village or on any street, for that matter, the women always seem to be able to count better than

63

their menfolk. Six months was all it took, and everyone knew it and that she had come from being far better off than them.'

'De Goncourt must have been a very stubborn man.'

'But he loved his Juliette and thought he was doing what was best. Now let me call those two over to our table. They'll talk more freely if I'm present. Together we'll find what answers they can give, for I see that you will need help with this murder and that it was not so straightforward and simple as I had at first felt.'

'Juliette?'

'And an end to the agony of his refusal to help her free the son for whom he had no love and little use.'

Leather, lead and copper, beeswax and candles, thought Kohler as he sat behind the wheel of the Citroën in the avenue Matignon. Flowers . . . *mein Gott*, hothouse roses and a birthday cake. Picnic hampers stuffed with pâté, Brie, caviar and champagne. Beautiful society women and *très chic Parisiennes* were being accompanied by well-turned-out Wehrmacht NCOs, many of whom were old enough to have fathered them.

There was constant traffic into and out of the former *hôtel particulier* of Gustav Eiffel. The boys of *Das Deutsche Beschaffungsamt* sure knew how to do things. Not a stone's throw from the Rond Point of the Champs-Élysées and the rue du Faubourg Saint-Honoré, the Wehrmacht's Procurement Office had been here right from the start in June 1940. Specialists in banking and industry, most of the staff had been drafted, of course, or had volunteered their expertise but why not make life enjoyable while you're away from home?

Vélo-taxis drew up to the entrance of that tidy little mansion whose soft grey stone, Louis Philippe ironwork, tall French windows, and slate-covered, mansard roof, fitted in eloquently with the rest of the street. A Peugeot negotiated one of two arched carriageways. People on the street said hello, the men politely touching the peak of a cap or brim of a freshly blocked fedora.

Cement for the Todt Organization which was building the fortifications of the Atlantic Wall. Iron and steel. Gold and silver, too. Butter, eggs and cheese, the French big shots of the black market, the BOFs as the people called them – the *beurre, oeufs et fromage* boys – were everywhere and the cars they drove made the avenue like a dream of what the city must have been like before the Defeat.

There was even an open carriage parked in the snow of the courtyard, the poor nag too old and decrepit for the Russian Front. Ignoring its driver, he stroked the mare's muzzle and, finding a lump of sugar deep in a pocket, whispered, 'You're beautiful, *chérie*. This is for you.'

Leather, priced officially by Vichy at nine francs the kilo, became fifteen and then thirty by the time the middlemen had got through with it. From there it went through still more dealers until here, bought on the black market, for that was the express, if unofficially acknowledged purpose of the Palais d' Eiffel, it would skyrocket to seventy or eighty.

Lead went from six to thirty; copper from fifteen to eighty-five. But nearly everything was paid for in Occupation marks and since the Occupier printed these, and they couldn't be spent anywhere but in France, why everything worked out just fine and didn't cost a pfennig.

A gangster's dream, a gambler's paradise. 'A *palais de l'illusions*,' he said to the mare who wanted more sugar.

Purchases were also made in neutral countries – Sweden, Portugal, Spain and Switzerland – but paid for in pounds Sterling or Swiss francs. Unlimited bankrolls, then, and temptation like you wouldn't believe, since no records were ever kept, especially of the pay-offs to those who found the goods for them. Again, everything worked out fine. One happy family, with secretaries, interpreters and clerks all anxious to assist, since they, too, shared in the dream. No wonder von Schaumburg was edgy. The Führer might not like it if he knew what actually went on here.

'Wait, let me help you with that hamper,' he called out to a delivery girl. 'It must be heavy.'

Uncertainty registered in her brown eyes. He was too tall, too big, and there was a cruel scar down his face . . .

'Relax. Look, I'm going in and right upstairs. Who's it for?'

He *did* have a nice smile. 'The General Thönisen.'

The boss himself. 'He's just the man I have to see.'

'It's almost noon, m'sieur. They close for three hours over lunch during the week but on Saturdays, stop completely.'

And this in an Army office? *Mein Gott!*

Five hundred francs was five hundred more than she would have got as a tip from the orderly on the desk. '*Merci*, monsieur,' she hazarded, then finally grinned hugely and was gone before he could change his mind.

Silk- and brocade-covered armchairs and sofas made waiting in the hall pleasant. Cigarettes and cigars had been laid on. Helping himself to the freshly opened tin of pipe tobacco for Louis, he went over to the desk, waited his turn, and said, 'Herr Schlacht. A little something for him but I'd like to take it up.'

'Third floor, turn right. He's not in. He seldom is, but Käthe – Frau Hillebrand – should be able to help you. She usually stays for a bit, in case someone has to contact him or one of the others.'

'*Danke.*'

A plaque on the door read: *Scrap Metals*, but that could encompass a lot of things. The foyer was unoccupied, the office small, but with windows overlooking the gardens of the Champs-Élysées, the view nice even in winter.

'*Mein* Herr . . .' came a pleasant, if hesitant voice from the outer corridor.

'Magdeburg,' he said and grinned. 'You're from Magdeburg.'

'Not quite. Schönebeck.'

She had a welcome, if nervous grin, and why, really, was she nervous? he wondered and sighed, 'On the Elbe,' as if it was home. And lifting the hamper up, said, 'These are for Herr Schlacht. I'll just keep the card.'

Had he really noticed her accent? she wondered. 'And from yourself?'

'Two tonnes of scrap lead. We came across it in an abandoned quarry in Charonne, near a graveyard. The leftover coffins they used hundreds of years ago, I guess. All flattened, of course. I thought Herr Schlacht might be interested.'

Coffins! 'Very, I should think,' she managed and, turning her back on him, led the way out of the office and along the corridor to her desk, where she sat down and reached for a pencil, had to hold on to something – anything, she told herself.

Although one of the *Blitzmädels*, the similarity ended here, thought Kohler. Blonde, blue-eyed, about thirty-five and wearing a soft blue woollen dress that accentuated every curve, she was a *Hausfrau* who had heard the call of duty and had left child and home to take it up. But somewhere along the line she'd forgotten to wear her wedding ring. A snapshot of her little boy, and one of his father in a Luftwaffe uniform faced her anyway.

'Your name, *mein* Herr?' she asked again.

He had to hand it to the boys of the Procurement Office. She was really very pretty. 'Look, you wouldn't know where I could find him, would you?'

'I might.'

And still tense about it? wondered Kohler. He'd open the hamper and take out a box of chocolates from Fouquet's, one of the city's foremost restaurants and over on the Champs-Élysées at number 99.

She shook her head. The offer of champagne was no better.

'You're not a businessman, *mein* Herr, so I must ask myself how would such as yourself really have found a load of old coffins?'

Her fingers were no longer fidgeting; the nails perfectly manicured and as red as her lips. 'We were looking for something else,' he confessed and, grinning, offered her a cigarette and lit it for her.

Warily her eyes fled down over him and up again. 'And what, exactly, were you looking for?'

'A little badge, about the size of my thumbprint. He didn't lose one, did he? The letters F.M.?'

Moisture rushed into her eyes. Hurriedly she stubbed out the cigarette and, trying to still the quaver in her voice, blurted, '*Bitte*, how did you know?'

'I didn't. I just guessed.'

And you're from the Gestapo, she told herself, sickened by the thought. He didn't quite have the manner but sometimes a person couldn't tell with those types. 'Herr Himmler presented it to Herr Schlacht on 31 August 1937. Oskar, he . . . he has worn it ever since.'

'He didn't accuse you of losing it, did he?'

'*Me*? Why would he?' she yelped.

The urge to say, 'when partly undressed and in the heat of the moment' was there, but it would be best to shrug and tell her something else to ease her mind. 'Rudi told me about it.'

Everyone who was anyone knew of Chez Rudi's on the Champs-Élysées, across from the Lido. Both restaurant and centre of all gossip.

'Oskar may still be at the smelter on the rue Montmartre. It's near a café called À La Chope du Croissant and is run by some Russians. A narrow courtyard . . . Lots of little ateliers. If he isn't there, he might have gone over to the Hôtel Drouot to . . . to look things over.'

The Paris auction house. 'And afterwards?'

'Lunch at Maxim's, I think.'

And a bull's-eye.

As he turned to leave, she called out desperately, 'Your name, *mein* Herr?'

'Oh, sorry. Denke. Tell him Karl Otto was in. He'll understand.'

'And the badge?' she asked. 'He . . . he really did blame me for losing it.'

You poor thing. 'Then tell him not to worry, eh? Rudi says it's in good hands for now. No problem.'

The two prostitutes were sisters, and it hadn't taken a moment to see this, thought St-Cyr, surprised that Father Michel had still not mentioned it. Both had implored this Sûreté to guarantee the sous-préfet and préfet wouldn't have them hauled in for questioning or worse, a licence suspension. They were really very worried and had kept coming back to the matter so much so, it was abundantly clear the priest had used the threat to get them to the table.

But why that of a licence suspension? he asked himself and sighed inwardly at the intricacies of life under the Occupation. 'Danielle de Bonnevies trades in many items,' he said, looking from one to the other of them. 'Toothbrushes, compacts, razor blades and carpenter's nails . . . Two bars of beautiful hand soap. With all of these she must have had help in acquiring them.'

'Not us, Inspector,' swore Josiane, the elder of the two, reaching for a sip of the red.

'Inspector, what has this to do with the murder?' demanded Father Michel, as if, in having set it all up, he could now claim innocence.

'Only that the J-threes are very busy these days, Father.'

Everyone knew the teenagers were working the black market for all it was worth. Designated J-threes by their ration category, many were roaming around after classes flashing thick wads of fifty- and one-hundred-franc notes. Five-hundreds also.

'Danielle deals with some of the local kids,' admitted Josiane, her auburn hair permed and piled beneath its *petite chapeau*. 'They buy and sell, and then she sells for them and splits the profit, I guess.'

'Lipstick,' murmured Georgette, not daring to look up from her playing cards, for Père Michel was sternly watching her. 'Cigarette lighters. I . . . I have bought one from her. Was it a crime, Father?' Was the Chief Inspector on to her and Josiane? she wondered.

'You know that the Church has now advised everyone that it is perfectly within the will of God to deal on the black market,' chided Father Michel. 'It's no longer to be considered a sin, Georgette.'

Like some? she wondered, sickened by the thought.

St-Cyr had been assigned to the pussy patrol in his early days as a policeman, recalled Father Michel, satisfied that the Chief Inspector had finally gauged the drift of things. 'Neither Georgette nor Josiane would ever have anything to do with underage clients, Inspector. Now would you both?' he asked, and saw another moment of panic rush through them.

'No, Father,' came Georgette's hushed answer, she still concentrating on her game of solitaire.

'Just one,' confessed Josiane. 'I swear I didn't realize it, Father. Madame put him out of *Le Chat* before . . . before anyone else had noticed him.'

'Then the matter is settled,' said the priest, calling for another carafe of the red to soothe the sore throats of his two guests who had obviously, thought St-Cyr, been up to things with more than one of the local teenagers.

They settled down, each of the sisters no doubt silently cursing their parish priest for having exacted a promise from them by using a confrontation with a Sûreté over the unfortunate death of a former client!

Warming to the interview, for it was so much of Belleville and Charonne, St-Cyr took out his pipe and prepared to stay for as long as it took to get what he could from these two. Both were heavily made-up. Still in their fur-trimmed overcoats, thin scarves and hats, only their gloves had been removed. Both had the same broad faces, wide lips, double chins and carefully tweezed eyebrows. But whereas Josiane had dark brown, cataract-clouded eyes, Georgette's were sea-green and clear, but with a pronounced cast in the left one. Hence the cards and the endless games of solitaire, though even here one of those nuances of character had caused her to taunt the good father and tempt him into distraction, just for the fun of it and to have something to recount to the other girls!

'Now tell the Inspector a little about Alexandre and your dealings with him,' grunted Father Michel. 'Go on. You can speak freely. God knows everything and will understand.'

Trust a priest to say such a thing! thought Josiane. 'God would have shut His eyes, Father. Besides, it's a private matter. The rules of the house, isn't that so?'

'Private,' echoed her sister.

One by one the greasy, well-thumbed playing cards, each with a full-length portrait of a naked girl in an awkward pose, were placed face up.

'He liked to take you both, didn't he?' prompted Father Michel, helping himself to more pastis and another Gauloise Bleue from the packet of cigarettes they had brought.

'Sometimes,' said Josiane a little stiffly, 'Alexandre would . . .'

'Father, details of his sex life with these two really are of little interest. I want to question . . .'

'Then they should be, my son. Please don't be so impatient.'

'Oh *là, là*, Josiane, will you look at that!'

The younger one had lost her game.

'He . . . he liked to call us names,' she confessed and began to gather the cards.

'What sort of names?' prodded the priest, exhaling cigarette smoke and fastidiously picking a shred of tobacco from his sleeve.

'Father, you know very well what sort of names.'

'Angèle-Marie,' whispered Georgette darkly, again concentrating on the game before her.

Merde alors, why had he had to ask? cursed Josiane. 'And Suzette, and Élène or Michèle. *Pouf!* Father, it meant nothing. Just a whim of the moment.'

Retreating behind his little cloud of cigarette smoke, the priest waited.

Finally the dark eyes of the older sister ducked away.

'Angèle-Marie . . . ?' hazarded St-Cyr. The cards had stopped.

'Alexandre's sister, Inspector,' sighed Father Michel. 'I rather thought you might be interested, especially since he went to see her last Thursday. Teased as a child by an older brother who loved bees and knew all about virgin queens; raped repeatedly on a summer's evening in 1912, and so violently at the age of fifteen, by some animal or animals in the Père Lachaise – we never did get the story of it in full; the custodians had forgotten about the poor child and had locked her in for the night – she has long since become a permanent resident of the Salpêtrière.'

Almost the size of a small town, the Paris asylum for women held more than six thousand inmates and had a staff of over a thousand.

'Alexandre was very worried about her safety, Inspector,' said Father Michel. 'Given the willingness of our German friends to destroy all such signs of mental or physical weakness, he had, I should think, cause for alarm.'

'It was only play,' hazarded Josiane, picking at her handbag. 'Georgette would take her name, I would watch and when . . . why, when his little moment was over, we would sit and talk for old times' sake.'

Jésus, merde alors, these village quartiers and their priests! 'And how old, please, was Georgette when Monsieur de Bonnevies first visited *Le Chat*?'

71

'Fifteen,' grunted Father Michel. 'Alexandre would have been . . . Now, let me see . . .'

'Twenty-seven, Father,' said the older sister.

'And two years later he went off to war and we saw him only twice in all those years,' confessed Georgette, moisture coming readily to her eyes. 'These . . .' She indicated the playing cards. 'Are the deck I gave him. You can still smell the mustard gas – I swear you can.'

Gathering the cards, she held them out, the cut-glass rings on her pudgy fingers, with their red-lacquered nails, flashing in the thin light.

'He loved them,' she said. 'He used to say they reminded him constantly of me.'

'Of me, too, Georgette.'

'Yes, of you, too, *chérie*.'

At a nod from the priest, another carafe of the red was brought – the third, or was it the fourth? wondered St-Cyr. People had come and gone. Left alone in their little cocoon, the four of them had lost all sense of time.

'The hives,' prompted Father Michel.

'Ah, *oui*,' said Josiane. '"A field lying fallow is a portion of France dying."'

It was one of the Maréchal Pétain's many sayings, just as was *Travail, Famille et Patrie*, but not the *Liberté, Egalité et Fraternité* of prewar days.

'I take it the field was leased from the city for the apiary,' sighed St-Cyr, 'but the neighbours felt it would be best to grow vegetables there.'

'And Alexandre would have no part of such a thing, Inspector. You see, to remain content and productive, bees need peace and quiet,' acknowledged the priest.

'There was lots of room,' countered Josiane. 'He could have freed up half the land. We . . . we told him this.'

'We did,' insisted Georgette. 'And now the hives are in ruins and what the neighbours wished will soon be possible.'

'Who stole the honey?' asked St-Cyr.

Both of the sisters shrugged. Josiane glanced at the priest and then dropped her gaze to her wine.

72

'The neighbours,' sighed Father Michel. 'Which of them, and how many, will, I'm afraid, be all but impossible to ascertain and take much time.'

'A *fait accompli*, is that it, Father?'

' "Life is not neutral," Inspector,' grunted Father Michel, giving him another of the Maréchal's sayings. ' "It consists of taking sides boldly." Alexandre was very much a *Pétainiste*, but not when it came to giving up his precious apiary.'

'He could be so very stubborn,' offered Georgette. '*Mon Dieu*, if I didn't submit *exactly* the way he wanted, he would get angry. I was to stretch out my arms above my head so as to grasp the little black iron bars of the fence around the tombstone while . . . while knocking the flowers over as I smothered my cries in them. They . . . they tickled my nose. That stone . . . it was so shaky sometimes, so heavy I was afraid it would fall and . . . and crush my head!'

'I had always to urge him on, Inspector,' confessed Josiane.

'Until he would cry out his sister's name as he released his little burden?' bleated the Sûreté.

'Ah *oui*. Then he would stroke Georgette and tell her to be calm, that she hadn't really lost her virtue, that this was of the heart, not the hymen, and I would stroke him until . . . until all three of us were calm.'

'Tears . . . were there tears?' he heard himself asking.

'Always,' confided Josiane with a touch. 'Always and without fail.'

'Father, you could have warned me. Did he rape his sister?'

They had left the café and were heading up the rue Saint-Blaise towards the church.

'No, he did not. He was at the Jardin du Luxembourg assisting one of the Society's beekeepers. Alexandre simply blamed himself. You see, that morning he had asked his sister to pick some flowers in the cemetery but to be careful not to let the custodians see her doing so. He wanted a sampling of their pollen to compare, under the microscope, with that found in his hives.'

'Then why play a game of rape with those two?'

'Why not? It was harmless, a punishment – self-humiliation. And there was Georgette's sister to witness it.'

'But she had always to urge him on?'

'That's of little consequence. Oh *bien sûr*, he confessed this strange desire to me many times – God won't punish me for telling you; but I felt it best you should hear it from those two.'

'You told me he went there, you thought, perhaps to humiliate Madame de Bonnevies.'

'He *did*! But by the time of their marriage he had discovered he couldn't stop himself. Those two understood him far better than Juliette could ever have done.'

'They said nothing of his wife.'

'Because they had nothing to say about her.'

'And did he tease his daughter the way he teased his sister?'

They were shouting at each other. 'Absolutely not. Danielle was everything to him – everything that is, except his bees, but he included her among them, so it really didn't matter.'

'Included her among them . . . ? As a virgin queen? Well?'

'Don't be an ass, Inspector. He knew very well she wasn't a bee.'

'Even so, Father, I'm going to have to talk to those two again.'

'Of course. It's understood. Now that the introductions are over, feel free to contact them whenever necessary. They'll answer you truthfully, or they'll answer to me.'

Parting at the church, Father Michel watched as the Sûreté, somewhat disgruntled, it had to be admitted, plodded up the steps into the driving snow. Had he been right, he wondered, to short-circuit things and open that door into a very private and tragic matter now seldom mentioned?

'I had to do it,' swore Father Michel. 'Otherwise that one and his partner would have looked elsewhere and this they must not do.'

More snow began to fall, and with the wind, it made life miserable, thought Kohler, wishing he'd driven over instead of leaving the Citroën in the place de la Bourse. But he'd wanted to come upon Herr Schlacht on the quiet.

Most people didn't look up as they hurried along. Bundled up in anything they could lay hand to these days, all pretence of fashion had long since vanished from the minds of everyday citizens. Even the boys in grey-green had given up on their

74

seemingly endless window-shopping. And as for the *filles de joie* who had migrated from the vast emptiness Les Halles, the central market, had become, the girls were listless and frozen stiff.

Bicycle-taxis vied with one another and with the bicycles. Pedestrians took their lives into their hands at the white-studded crosswalks. At the corner of the rue Réaumur and the rue Montmartre, sandbags were being unloaded from two Wehrmacht lorries. Here, too, as elsewhere in the city, the air-raid shelters were being converted into bunkers and machine-gun nests.

Instinctively, Kohler flicked a glance down the rue Montmartre towards the central market to gauge the field of fire, was right back at the front in 1914 and '15. Bang on. These boys knew what they were doing and that could only mean the OKW – Old Shatter Hand and von Stülpnagel, the Military Governor – still feared an uprising once the defeat at Stalingrad was officially announced, as it would have to be.

Louis and he had seen such pillboxes before heading south to Avignon. Unsettled by the thought, he went on up the rue Montmartre searching for the smelter.

A big Renault was parked outside the café À La Chope du Croissant. No sign of its owner, nor would Herr Schlacht have wasted time in that café.

A nearby signboard, in flaking off-white paint, read: *Imprimerie.* Printers.

Pushing open the tall, wooden doors, he found himself in a rubbish-littered, ice-encased courtyard. Soot all over the place. Soot in these days of so little coal. Soot and iron bars on the windows. Were all the doors locked? he wondered. In one broken window the wind teased a peeling paper notice in German and in French: *Jüdisches Geschäft.* Jewish business. All were gone now. Gone since July of last year. But the smelter would have coexisted with the printers for as long as the years immediately after the Russian Revolution, when so many had fled to Paris.

The courtyard was narrow and at its far end it must take a bend to the right. Tattered handbills rattled around inside the printing shop, the presses as silent as a frozen tap that had burst its lead pipe.

Merde, where was the place? The smell of burning charcoal was in the air, soda, too, and bone ash.

As he neared the bend, the soft roar of pot-furnaces came to him. A little farther on, he came to a window and, reaching between the bars, cleaned off a bit of the glass to peer inside.

Flames danced, coals glowed. Crucibles were held by two-metre-long iron tongs. Everyone wore goggles, most asbestos suits, gauntlets and toe-capped boots . . .

The smell of nitric acid reached him and of hydrochloric, too. *Aqua regia*, Louis would have said. A mixture of the two, Hermann. One part nitric acid, three to four of hydrochloric; the name from the Latin for Royal Water. Gold can be dissolved by it and then later extracted.

End of lecture. Louis was always coming up with things like that, but Louis wasn't here. And why *did* he feel he needed backup? Why the constant tingling in his spine?

Among the half-dozen or so grey-clad zombies with their hoods and goggles that made them look like naval gunners in the heat of battle, Herr Schlacht watched a pour. White-hot, the gold was being cast into wafers the size of calling cards. An assistant, to one side, was polishing those that had already cooled.

Schlacht, though hidden behind goggles and under a wide-brimmed felt trilby and tweed overcoat, had the stance, the look of a Berliner. Solid – maybe weighing as much as 110 kilos. A real *Bürgermeister* type. The face was round, fleshy and double-chinned, the forehead wide and blunt, the nose not unlike Louis's but no boxer, no such refinements – simply a pugilist come up from the streets. The lips were a little thin, but maybe that was because the stub of a cigar was clamped fiercely between his teeth.

Two Alsatians, guardians of the smelter, slept on the cooling firebricks of a nearby hearth.

The pour came to an end, the goggles were pushed up until they covered the forehead. *Ja, das ist gut* – Kohler could almost hear Schlacht saying it. Gold and candles . . . What the hell else was this little entrepreneur into?

Again the tingling in his spine came to him, again he thought to step back from the window and did so this time.

Frozen in its little cage beside the door opposite to the smelter, a dead canary watched him through hollow-eyed sockets. The hanging wire cage had been dented several times and often straightened to no effect. *Mein Gott,* why had someone left the poor creature out here to sing its heart away until no more?

There was a notice on the door. *Avertissement: Peine de mort contre les saboteurs.* Sentence of death against saboteurs.

For the acts of terrorism on 15 November, 3 and 16 December 1942 . . .

Father, brother, mother, sister, cousins, too – all had been taken, since that was the rule these days. But whereas the *résistant* would have been shot right away, the other men would be held as hostages, as *Sühnepersonen* – atoners – until needed in retribution for some other act by some other poor idiot whom they wouldn't even know. And goodbye to the rest of the family. They'd all have been deported.

Oberg had added these little twists to the ordinance. The Brigadeführer und Generalmajor Karl Albrecht Oberg, Höherer SS und Polizeiführer.

Judging by the custom-made wafers, Herr Schlacht could well have friends in high places and that could well be von Schaumburg's greatest worry.

Stepping into the canary's abandoned building, Kohler prepared to wait and find out what he could. Louis would preach caution. Oberg was simply not a nice fellow and they'd already had too many run-ins with him.

Behind closed doors, through slightly parted curtains, the neighbours watched and held their collective breath, thought St-Cyr. Once on the Impasse de champ de parc de Charonne, the feeling was only more intense. Father Michel had orchestrated the whole interview, but why, really, had he seen fit to take him back to 1912 and the sister?

A parted curtain fell into place, another and another. Were the women of these houses afraid of what Hermann and he might discover and what their parish priest could well have initiated? Certainly a field for vegetables was one thing, the smashing of the hives and theft of the honey directly related to it, but did their guilt run deeper? And why, really, had Josiane always, it seemed, to play the part of a witness?

All of these former villages, once suburbs, had had their gangs of toughs. As a boy, he had had to defy that natural fear of all such boys when venturing into the territory of others. And in the summer of 1912, as today, de Bonnevies, no matter his penchant for taking a drink in the neighbourhood café or visiting the local house, would still have been classed as an *original*. Had the sister been picked on because of it? Had she not been alone in the Père Lachaise at all but with a friend – a witness who had hidden in terror, only to later confess to her mother the names of those who had raped the girl?

Father Michel might always have suspected this and now could not fail to see a connection between the murder and the rape, or had he deliberately begun by almost accusing Juliette de Bonnevies and then used the past to distract the investigation so as to hide something else?

'I don't quite trust him,' said St-Cyr to himself. 'I can't afford to, not yet.'

Knowing that he had best talk to Josiane and her sister before the priest got to them again, he retraced his steps. Father Michel had made no mention of the Caucasian bees de Bonnevies had been examining, none whatsoever of the address to which the beekeeper had been making last-minute revisions. Either he hadn't known of these, or had simply chosen not to discuss them.

At the rue de Bagnolet, St-Cyr crossed over and, once beyond the parish church and heading down the rue Saint-Blaise past the café to a side street, was right back in his days on the patrol.

Like all such houses, *Le Chat qui crie* had no need to announce its presence to the rue Florian or to this Sûreté. But like them all, there was intermittent traffic, the steps either hesitant or dogged, and then, of course, the absolute ease of entry. Swift and secure, and no one the wiser, perhaps.

The Charonne métro station was just behind the house and perfect for those who liked to travel from another quartier for their little moments, but had it been closed to save on the electricity? Rapidly he counted off every second station, concluding that it must still be open.

Between the glass and the lace curtain of the door to the house, a small card stated simply: *Entrer*.

'Monsieur, what can the house do for you?'

Sûreté had registered in the sixty-year-old madam's eyes. Instant suspicion, total defiance. Outrage, even. So *bon*! *Oui, oui*! He'd heard it all before, and many times. 'Josiane and Georgette, madame, and hurry.' He snapped his fingers. 'A few small questions, nothing difficult unless, of course, you feel I had best call in a little help.'

Bâtard! she silently cursed, tossing her head in a huff and saying tartly, 'You may sit with the girls or wait here.'

'Here will suit perfectly.'

He was already thumbing through her accounts ledger. There were no names of the clients there for him to peruse, only those of the girls, but once her back was turned, he would put the lock on the door and then what? she demanded.

St-Cyr . . . wasn't it St-Cyr those two had said?

She let a breath escape and murmured to herself. 'The ave' Ménilmontant. The house at number six.' And now? she wondered. Why now it must be more than thirty years since that house had been raided. Would he have remembered her from among those who'd been swept into the *panier à salade* – the salad basket – the Black Maria?

Deciding that their brief encounter of today was more than sufficient to last her for the rest of her life, Madame Thibodeau hurried into the waiting room to hush the whispers.

'Josiane and Georgette, that parasite from the Sûreté wishes to prolong his moment at the expense of the house. Take him up to the graveyard. Strip if you wish, but watch out with him. He's a bloodsucker.'

'It's freezing up there. It's always so cold,' lamented Georgette.

'Cold or not, *ma petite*, it is exactly what you will do. Now go. Hurry. *Hurry*! Then get him out of here!'

No cat would venture down the courtyard to the smelter, no rat either, thought Kohler, for here they'd all been trapped and eaten. He was certain of it, was damned cold and tired of waiting in the building across the way. But at last Herr Schlacht left the smelter.

Seen briefly through the grime of a broken, iron-barred window, the Berliner appeared even more of a pugilist, very sure of himself and satisfied with the latest of the day's efforts. Business was booming, and all that really mattered to one such as this was business.

The chubby chin wore its midday shadow, not brown, not blue-black but something in between; the collar of the beige tweed, herringbone overcoat was tightly buttoned up under it. Pausing to relight the cigar stub, Schlacht then collected the shiny black attaché case he had set on the paving stones at his feet. A man in his mid-fifties with beautifully polished, alligator-leather shoes – Italian? wondered Kohler. The case was hefted, the grey eyes passing swiftly over the window to come to rest on the canary in its cage.

Crossing the courtyard, Schlacht looked up at it through narrowed eyes and said, '*Meine Liebling*, are you cold? As cold as those who put you in your cage? Forgive me but I had to send them away. They were taking too much notice of things and I couldn't have that.'

Berliners, like Parisians, loved their birds, and this one, by his accent, was solidly of the Luisenstädter Kanal. Scrap metals, Kohler reminded himself. And, no doubt, crowded tenements near the Schlesischer Bahnhof in the Fiftieth Precinct.

'The charge was over nothing, *meine Liebling*. A mere mistake on my part, but . . .' Schlacht savoured his cigar as if searching for the right words. 'But these days, little one, such mistakes once made cannot be retracted and unfortunately seem always to lead to far-reaching consequences. You should have warned them to move, or at least to take no notice of my comings and goings.'

He was gone then. Too soon he had reached the bend in the courtyard and had passed from view.

As Kohler stepped from the building, he realized Schlacht had seen his footprints in the snow. Louis, he said silently. Louis, I think we've got a problem.

The room with the gravestone was in the attic of the brothel. Like all such *maisons de tolérance*, the house catered to the special needs of as many of its regulars as possible. But here . . .

'*Sacré nom de nom*,' breathed St-Cyr softly as Josiane and her sister stepped aside. Floor-to-ceiling murals covered the walls, giving ersatz views of the Père Lachaise's tree-lined boulevards. The tomb of Honoré de Balzac was in the near distance – was it really Balzac's tomb?

The entrance to the Ossuary was a parody of Bartholomé's magnificent high-relief sculpture. Instead of a naked couple standing hand in hand ready to step through the doorway into the pitch darkness of eternal peace, here each had a hand on the buttocks of the other.

'My partner should see this,' he said drolly. 'Hermann is a student of all things French, especially its *lupanars*.'

Its 'rabbit hutches'.

'This is the stone,' said Georgette, picking her way down a narrow aisle between bits of sculpture and other stones. 'Her name, as you can see, is beautifully inscribed.'

'The stone is real, as are all the others,' said Josiane quickly. The Inspector would immediately see that others must also have used the room to fulfil their fantasies or to view it in fun, but would he accept that Alexandre had never once complained of this, that to him the room had still been just as sacred a trust as when it had begun, secure and totally private?

A low, Louis XIV iron fence surrounded the plot where masses of silk flowers were forever in bloom. Verbena, fuchsia and hibiscus, thought St-Cyr. Chinese Bell Flower, too, and Mignonette, but not the dreary bunches of red and white carnations so typical of such places.

'When Alexandre asked his sister to gather flowers for him,' confessed Georgette, 'he told her to take only the not-so-common.'

Carved into the grey granite was the name *Angèle-Marie de Bonnevies*, and then: *Born 17 June 1897; taken in the flower of her youth, 20 August 1912.*

'But . . . but she isn't dead?' he heard himself saying.

It was Josiane who, ever wary of his reactions, answered, 'Ah no, Inspector, but she might just as well have been.'

'Did de Bonnevies pay for this room?' he asked and saw her start, heard her sister saying, 'Everything, and for its continued maintenance. Inspector, none ever knew at whose stone the girl had been violated, so no other name was possible, isn't that right? I would pretend to be gathering samples of these flowers, Josiane would be over there out of sight. The custodian had forgotten all about us and had locked the gates, so we were both a little nervous and would . . . would call to each other.'

'Angèle-Marie, have you found any other flowers? Hurry. We must hurry,' sang out Josiane softly and no longer seen.

Georgette was now on her knees, awkwardly reaching well over the fence to almost touch the foot of the stone . . .

'I would say, "I've found some," but so soft was my voice, the name of my friend could never be heard.'

'They would come upon her,' grated Josiane. 'Two, maybe three of them – four sometimes. Young, not old. Boys, he thought but never really knew. I swear it. He . . . he always changed his mind about the number and . . . and the ages of them.'

'First one and then another would take me, Inspector. My clothes would be torn from me, my legs forced apart, my head pushed down . . . down . . .'

'Yes, yes. Enough! And this friend of Angèle-Marie?' he asked grimly. 'What of her, please?'

They didn't say a thing, these two. Josiane made her way among the stones to help her sister tidy the flowers.

'The friend cried out encouragement,' sighed St-Cyr. 'Instead of watching in horror at what was happening, she egged them on and had probably agreed beforehand to set the whole thing up. Did he find out who this "friend" was? Please, you had best tell me now.'

Both shrugged and shook their heads. 'Afterwards, as we would soothe him and ourselves,' said Josiane, taking her sister by the hand to comfort her, 'he would always speak of a settlement of accounts, Inspector. Things were to be done on the quiet, though.'

'But at any price; at all costs,' managed Georgette.

'How many were there?' he asked. 'Come, come, you must have some idea.'

'Four,' confessed Georgette. 'He had finally settled on four of the local boys.'

'When?'

'Last Thursday. After he had been to see his sister,' said Josiane, 'and . . . and before he was poisoned.'

With a flash, the last of the lead was oxidized and carried away by the strong jet of air from the blowpipe, leaving a white-hot bead of gold and silver in the bottom of the cupel. Kohler was entranced. '*Mein Gott*,' he exclaimed, 'bubbles are erupting from the surface. It's like a tiny volcano.'

'That is oxygen the silver has absorbed. It sprays the metal up.'

The Hauptmann Kohler nodded. As he continued to peer into the cupel, sweat made rivulets down the savage scar on his left cheek. 'And the temperature now?' he asked.

Andrei Dmitreyevich Godunov looked into the cupel through his goggles and said, 'Below one thousand and dropping fast. A skin is forming.'

'It gets shinier as it cools.'

The silvery bead was soon dumped into an iron saucer where it rolled about. 'Now we will weigh it, *mein* Herr, and that will give us the combined assay and tell us how best to refine this latest batch.'

Louis would be intrigued but horrified and in despair at what Schlacht was up to most probably for Oberg and the SS of the avenue Foch, among others. Scrap jewellery that had been stripped of its gemstones, unwanted or no longer needed wedding rings and dental fillings, smashed wrist- and pocket-watches, even bits of gilded picture frames and worn or clipped louis d'or – some of the earliest of these – had been run through the chopper and blended. Pale yellowish soda, the peroxide of sodium, would soon be added, along with bone ash, lead oxide, charcoal and sand, after which the whole mass would be melted in large crucibles. As the precious metals sank to the bottom with the lead, the lighter, glassy-brown to greenish-brown siliceous slag would rise to carry upwards the unwanted copper and other metals found mostly in the cheaper grades of jewellery.

When cooled sufficiently, this slag would then be broken away and the lead, containing all the gold and silver, would be subjected to cupellation, a process as old as 2,000 years.

'We can handle most things with little or no problem,' said Godunov. 'All we need is a few days. Once we have the gold and silver together, we then dissolve the silver with nitric acid but recover it later by electrolysis.'

A tidy operation. 'And you get to keep the silver?' asked Kohler. 'As our fee, yes.'

Pot-shaped, rectangular and square furnaces constantly roared, their firebrick linings glowing degrees of yellow. One man broomed slag into a heap. Another began to weigh the bead they had just made. Sterling silver flatware was being thrown into a pot furnace. Charcoal dust and acrid smoke were everywhere, the ventilation terrible. While the Alsatian guard dogs took no interest in him, they did look hungrily away. Along one entire wall, and nearly to the ceiling, wire cages held several dozen pairs of guinea pigs, the latest of the Occupation's food fads and another source of income for the smelter boys. Stews . . . had they a recipe he could get? wondered Kohler.

To a man, the Russians and their families ate, lived, slept and worked here. 'Your papers can't be very good,' he said.

Wearily Godunov pushed up his goggles. 'Herr Hauptmann, is it that you are asking for a little silver or gold perhaps?'

A pay-off, so it would be best to grin and offer a cigarette. 'Not at all. Just a little information. Has someone been bothering you?'

Was this one really from the Procurement Office as he'd claimed? Only a fool would have believed it. 'The local *Milice*. Herr Schlacht is aware of the matter, but says it is entirely up to us to take care of it. What can one do?'

'But keep silent and roll it around your little finger, eh?'

Thinking it over and remembering it. A Russian saying, so at least the Hauptmann was trying to be polite!

'How much do you pay them for the privilege of being left alone?' asked Kohler.

'Four of the wafers each week. One hundred grams.'

'Out of how much?'

'It varies. Sometimes we are busy refining silver only, on consignment for others, you understand. Sometimes Herr Schlacht has sufficient gold for twenty or thirty wafers. Perhaps two hundred at the end of each week. Perhaps and often much less than this.'

Or more. 'So you set aside a little something to pay off the *Milice*?'

'We have to. After all our employer . . .'

'Told you to take care of it. So, where does the gold end up?'

It would be best to sigh and say, 'That we do not ask.'

'Switzerland?'

'Perhaps. Perhaps Argentina, too, or Spain or Portugal.'

'And what's Schlacht's take from here?'

'That, also, we do not ask, but I should tell you he came here once with two SS, a Generalmajor with thick glasses, and an Obersturmbannführer. They were pleased, I think, but one can never really tell with people like that, and they did not stay long.'

Oberg, then, and his right-hand man, the Herr Doktor Helmut Knochen. Christ! 'Forget I was in.'

'Certainly.'

'But let me have the bead, will you? A small souvenir.'

'Of course. It shall be exactly as you wish. Polished, and like a ball bearing to facilitate its rolling around your little finger.'

Out in the courtyard, Herr Kohler took the birdcage down from across the way and carried it off. Now why, please, would he have done such a thing? wondered Godunov, not that they would miss it.

There were cellars below the smelter, and from one of these there was access to the sewers. An alternate escape route had been fashioned through the attics from house to house and then across the roofs, but would either of them be of any use if they had to escape?

Sadly he shook his head. The Germans would block all exits and bottle them in. No one would be left alive here, not even the children. There were far too many secrets in the furnaces.

'Life is like that,' he said to one of the guinea pigs he had taken from its cage. 'You just think things are sailing along like the moon when some son of a bitch of a tovarisch decides to tip the old man right upside down!'

He kissed the guinea pig and stroked his bristly, sweat-streaked cheek and damp, grey-white moustache against it. 'Don't worry, little one. We won't eat you today.'

Closeted in the kitchen with the brothel's cook and two of the girls, Louisette Thibodeau looked up from her soup and choked.

'Madame,' said St-Cyr and saw her wince, 'when, please, was the *Salon du cimetière* constructed?'

Had he not recognized her? Had she changed so much from the girl he had dragged naked from the arms of her client? wondered Madame Thibodeau. 'Constructed?' she bleated. 'In . . . in 1919, after Monsieur de Bonnevies came back from the war. He . . . he said he had felt the need when on the battlefield and had had plenty of time to . . . to think it over.'

'And for twenty-four years now he has used that room?'

'Yes. Yes, that is so. Always the tombstones, always those two.'

It had to be said. 'Yet he never takes Josiane.'

'Never.'

The whole neighbourhood would have heard of it ages ago, no matter how private the house claimed things were. 'Your ledger tells me the room was used mostly on Tuesdays and Thursdays, presumably by the victim, but there are also visits on Saturdays, in the afternoon, and on Sundays.'

'By him, but not at the times of the Masses,' she said swiftly. 'This is a God-fearing house.'

'Of course, but on Sunday evenings, once a month and late, the room is used. Charlotte attends.'

With Father Michel – was this what he thought? Well let him! she told herself and, shrugging, set her soup spoon aside. 'Charlotte is always in demand.'

'She's pretty,' said one of the girls coyly, 'and pretty young, too.'

'Eighteen,' said the other one.

'*Milou, please leave us this instant*! Élène, go with her. Some coffee, Inspector?' asked Madame Thibodeau, her words brittle. She'd deal with those two later, and as for this one from the Sûreté, well, now that he had whetted his appetite, one had best feed the leech a few bits of flesh so as to send him away happy.

His kind are never happy, she silently said and steeled herself to meet all onslaughts.

He took out his pipe and tobacco pouch, preparing to stay for as long as necessary. Ah *mon Dieu*, she thought, it's just as it was when we last met and my licence had expired.

The cook thought it best to be busy. Setting the steaming pot with its roasted acorn-and-barley water on the table, she took refuge next to the sink where carrots were to be peeled and onions sliced.

'Louisette Thibodeau née Grégoire,' he said and sighed at the memory.

Her heart sank. 'Inspector, what can I do for you?'

'That depends,' he breathed and let the threat of silence hang in the air while he stuffed that pipe of his until he had forced her to finally yelp, 'On what, please?'

'On your reading of history, I think.'

Nom de Jésus-Christ, he hadn't changed a bit!

She'd been an ample woman in her late twenties and not beaten by her pimp as so many he had encountered. But down on her luck and with a five-month-old baby boy to nurse. 'We both know the beekeeper's use of that room must have attracted the attention he wanted, madame. Save my partner and me a lot of time. Help us out.'

For old times' sake – was this what he thought? *Maudit salaud*, the nerve!

'Whoever tried to poison him may poison others, with even more success,' confided St-Cyr. 'It's just a thought – please don't trouble yourself. But my presence here . . . Our having talked things out.'

The bastard! 'All right, it is as you have ascertained. Some of our clients – the female ones, too – ridiculed his strange desire. Others tried out the room once or twice, but found it not to their taste. A few have come to use it on a regular basis, yes.'

He'd want the names of those few; he'd want every little titbit he could get!

Feigning boredom came easily to him. He examined a fingernail, said only two words. 'Four names.'

'I . . . I can't tell you. I mustn't.'

'I think you'd better. While there's still time, that is.'

'One was killed at Sedan in 1940. A corporal.'

He waited for her to crucify herself. Had he no heart? Did he not think of the slashed face she would earn, the wrists also, her body stripped naked at her age and dumped into the Seine with ropes and stones? 'One no longer lives in this quartier but comes by métro when he feels the need.'

'And takes Charlotte once a month, late on Sunday evenings in that little graveyard of yours?'

May God forgive her for telling him. 'Yes.'

'That's perfect! Now let me have the whereabouts of the other two.'

'Both are married. Both have families . . .'

'Of course.'

She had him now and rejoiced in it! 'Both are in prisoner-of-war camps in the Reich!'

'Which camps?'

'I . . . I don't know.'

'Oflag 17A, madame?' An officers' camp, but . . . The same as Étienne de Bonnevies . . .

'I . . . I couldn't say, Inspector. Really I couldn't.'

He'd sigh, thought St-Cyr. He'd put his tobacco pouch and matches away. 'Then all we need is the address and name of the one who comes by métro.'

'Or those of the wives, the mothers, fathers, sisters and brothers of the other three?' shrilled Madame Thibodeau. 'Each of them will want to keep silent the identities of those who violated that sister of his!'

'I'm listening, madame.'

Why had he had to come here like this today? Had her number come up? wondered Madame Thibodeau. 'Angèle-Marie de Bonnevies was *très belle, très intelligente,* but flirted with the boys and wanted to be like the other girls. Her father had to beat her but not about the face, you understand. He wouldn't let her ask her friend into the house. The friend was "dirty", he said. "The poor always have lice."'

'And the name of this friend, madame?'

The Inspector had taken out his little black notebook. 'I will have to sell the house and move to the country. *Les Allemands* don't like issuing such permits. I'm getting on – you can see it for yourself. Would you throw me out on the street?'

The urge to say, You've been hiding the identity of one who aided and may even have incited a crime, to say nothing of those who committed it, but one must be kind. What she had said was absolutely true. 'My partner and I will go carefully.'

'It won't be enough.'

'Then I will still need the name.'

Even as a *flic* he'd been a lousy shit! 'Madame Héloïse Debré, 7 rue Stendhal, top floor, but . . . but there's no husband and no one knows where he got to. He used to knock her about terribly but then . . . why, then, one day he vanished. Just like that, and she swore she did not know where to.'

'Please don't try to distract me, madame, with suggestions of another domestic killing. Just give me the names of the three families.'

Hermann would be pleased with the progress. The hive of this little murder, if it really was murder, had been truly opened, its cells disgorging honey and uncovering the larvae.

But was there a rival queen?

The Paris auction house wasn't far from the smelter. Just up the rue Montmartre and over past the *mairie* of the ninth arrondissement. It was in a large building on the corner of the rue Chauchat and the rue Rossini. All alone, and by itself, the Renault was parked out front – big, blue and shiny in the wind-driven snow. 110 kilometres per hour, no problem; 120 and still none. A b. . .e. . .a. . .utiful set of wheels for a hot little scrap-metal dealer.

Kohler plunked the birdcage down on the bonnet, right up by the windscreen where it wouldn't be missed, then drove back up the rue Rossini to leave the Citroën next to the town hall and walk back.

No one would steal the birdcage. No one.

It being noon-hour and at its tail end, no auctions were in progress. Instead, the public were allowed to peruse the up-and-coming items. Room upon room of bailiff's gleanings were on the first floor; those, too, of lesser items being sold off to settle a grandmother's or dead husband's estate. Beds, bureaus, cutlery, pots and pans, stacks of dishes – linens. Housewives mingled with shy newlyweds, the bridegrooms all a lot older than their brides. Hell, most of the younger men were dead or in POW camps in the Reich, or on the run from the forced labour and hiding out with the *maquis*.

The second-floor rooms were reserved for the better quality merchandise. Here there was silence, although the undercurrent of muffled conversation from below formed a constant background. Tiffany, Lalique and Gallé glass filled a room with lamps, vases and figurines. No sign of Herr Schlacht, though.

Limoges and Sèvres porcelains were in another room, the *belles mondaines* and the dealers noting the lot numbers and jotting down, after much deliberation, the sums they would be prepared to bid. One glance was enough. The ebb tide that Paris had become, had left its wide strand littered with the debris of all such items. Things that had been in the family for years had had to be parted with. If one wanted to eat, let alone to eat as one had before the Defeat, then one had to pay black-market prices.

But one had to be so very careful. All items over one hundred thousand francs in value had had to be reported to the authorities in the early fall of 1940 and couldn't be moved or sold without permission.

A Regency mirror gave him a glimpse of Schlacht. The overcoat collar was still tightly buttoned up under the double chin; the wide-brimmed trilby was still pulled down a little over the brow. He was feasting his eyes on a pure white sculpture, something that would once have been set on a table in a place of honour.

'Hermann . . . Hermann, is it really you?'

Merde, it was Gabrielle, Louis's girlfriend, a chanteuse, a White Russian who had fled the Revolution in 1917 and had arrived in Paris at the age of fourteen and all alone.

Kohler took her by the elbow and hustled her into the adjacent salon, to stand among beautiful pieces of marquetry. 'Beat it, please,' he begged. 'We got back late last night and . . .' He shrugged and grinned. 'And haven't had a moment since.'

She was a good head taller than Louis, was almost as tall as himself, and when her lips brushed his scarred left cheek, he felt the warmth, the lightness and gracefulness of her. Breathing in the scent of her perfume, of Mirage, he recalled, as he always did when coming upon her like this, their first meeting.

It had been during the investigation of a small murder in Fontainebleau Forest, the murder that had earned him the scar she had just kissed and the one from his right shoulder to his left hip. She'd been a suspect then, had lost a small pouch of diamonds . . .

'How are René Yvon-Paul and the countess?' he asked. The boy lived with his grandmother at Château Thériault, near Vouvray, overlooking the Loire.

'Fine. Both are fine.' René was ten years old and had been missing the two of them, Jean-Louis especially, thought Gabrielle. René had also saved Hermann Kohler's life, and Hermann, to his credit, had never forgotten it. But, then, he liked children almost, if not more than Jean-Louis. 'You look beat, *mon vieux*. Are you hungry?' she hazarded and ran a slender hand over a table whose marquetry glowed in shades of amber, some so soft they matched her hair.

She had the loveliest eyes. Violet, just like Giselle's. Tall, willowy, a gorgeous figure – Louis was an idiot not to have gone to bed with her yet and now . . . why now, might never get the chance! 'Look, this isn't easy, but it's best we not be seen together.'

'Not by the one you are following,' she said and sadly nodded. 'Is he so important you would deny me the pleasure of your company? Ah! He must be. Don't look so pained.'

'Let's just say he's connected to the avenue Foch, Gabrielle. I wouldn't want . . .'

'Them to take an interest in me? They already have, as you well know. Bugging my dressing room at the club, keeping track of when and where I go, so . . .' She shrugged. 'What's the problem?'

She was a member of the *Résistance*, had been detained during a previous case, but had managed to get away with it. 'Gabi, please.'

'Do you like this table? It's Russian. Eighteenth century. I'm going to buy it.'

She would, too, and then would slap heavy coats of paint on it!

'For to hide best is to expose those things you value most to view,' she said, having read his mind. 'Now take me by the arm like the gentleman – the wishful lover, perhaps – that I know you to be. Escort me into that room, Hermann, so that you may better study this man you want to follow.'

Grâce à Dieu, Schlacht had departed. There were others in the room – four Wehrmacht officers and their *Parisiennes*.

'Your Führer has a passion for Leda and the Swan,' confided Gabrielle, conspiratorially clucking her tongue as she ran her eyes over the voluptuous, classical nude in alabaster. 'Nineteenth century and by Albert Carrier-Belleuse. It's exquisite, is it not? *Mon Dieu*, your man has very good but expensive taste.'

Asleep, the swan was nestled over upraised, cloth-draped knees and thighs, with its head next to a plump, soft breast and Leda's hand resting on a feathered wing.

'Both of them are asleep,' he said. But it was true, the Führer *did* have a passion for Leda and her Swan, and she did figure heavily in Nazi art. And every time she'd been just as voluptuous, just as slender, just as asleep and waiting to be ravished. 'She was the Queen of Sparta,' he said. 'Zeus came to her in the form of a swan.'

Hermann's tone of voice indicated how distracted and worried he was. 'And now?' asked Gabrielle, turning to search his pale blue eyes. 'Now will the one you wish to know more about, come back to bid on this?'

'To send it to his Führer as a little gift?' he bleated.

She touched his hand in sympathy. 'I'll bid against him, if you like.'

'No you won't. You'll find out what he pays for it and if he asks to have it crated and shipped to you know where.'

Outside, on the street, the Renault was gone but in its place were the flattened remains of the birdcage and its canary.

4

It was freezing in the study, and when the one from the Sûreté indicated the tin, Danielle told herself she must listen to his voice as if from beneath the ground and she already in her coffin.

'One part safrole by volume, mademoiselle. Two of nitroben-zene, and the same again of gasoline. A small amount of the solution is dabbed on to a rag which is then stuffed through the entrance to the hive, so as to place it in the centre of the floor.'

'Normally the fumigation is repeated every second day, Inspector, until all four decimal-five cubic centimetres of the mixture have been used.'

On waking, the girl had changed into a dark grey, woollen skirt, white blouse with Peter-Pan collar, and a knitted, powder-blue pullover. No pearls, no rings, no jewellery of any kind, not even a wristwatch. She was not nearly so tall as the father, but taller than the mother and thin, now that he could see her without the coat. Thin and small-breasted, underweight and no doubt this was all due to the severe lack of calories, and the energy expended in the hunt for food.

Becoming aware that she had remained just inside the doorway to the study, the girl thought to come forward, hesitated and then thought better of closing the gap between them.

Would the Sûreté understand that most of the honey they had produced had been taken from them? wondered Danielle. Would he realize that the rest had been severely rationed except for that given to clients among the Occupier and their sickening friends?

'A lot of the bees are killed and must be removed from the hives, Inspector, but they are usually the ones with the acarine mites. *Papa* . . . My father felt the best time for such a fumigation was in the late winter, and after the bees had had a good flight to clean themselves. Bees are very clean, you understand. They will not defecate in the hive unless very ill, and fly away from the hive before doing so. But some people don't realize this at first and hang their laundry near the hives in the garden, only to . . . to find it yellowed by the droppings.'

Modestly she had lowered her eyes, and when he gently said, 'And the fumigation, mademoiselle?' she looked up suddenly and swallowed with difficulty.

'He would seal the entrance after placing all of the solution in there at once. "Quick and easy and thorough," he said. "Danielle, never mind doing it bit by bit. Get it in there and over with! Hurry, *petite*. Hurry!"'

'The . . . the carnage was terrible but . . . but if you ask me, Inspector, he was invariably correct.'

Inadvertently the girl had recounted the first time the father had made her do it. And for how many years had she carried the guilt of those first little murders? he wondered. 'How old were you then? Five or six?'

'Seven. We . . . we had had a scare and *papa* wanted me to know best how to deal with it. I cried myself to sleep for nights afterward.' There, he could think what he liked of that!

'And was the recent infestation the reason so many of the hives had been brought into the apiary?'

Say only what is necessary; look steadily at him, she warned herself and answered flatly, 'Yes.'

'And the number of hives?' she heard him ask and dug her fingernails into her palms to more firmly awaken herself to the threat of him before answering, 'Usually about twenty here. Sometimes a few less or more. It depended.'

'On the need to service an orchard or vineyard.'

'The out-apiaries also. He . . . *papa* has – well, he had . . . Well, we have; I have, fifty-seven to . . . to look after.'

'Then twenty-seven of them are still out on rooftops and in gardens?'

'*Papa* . . . *Papa* and I were still bringing them into the apiary. He . . . he felt it necessary due to . . . to the threat he perceived. The disaster he said would happen.'

'Acarine mites.'

'Yes! But . . .' She clamped her eyes shut and turned away, burst into tears and tried to stop herself. 'Forgive me,' she blurted. 'He . . . he would not tell me *why* he felt so certain there would be such a terrible infestation, only that . . . that we must guard against it for the good of France.'

And has he believed me, this Chief Inspector of the Sûreté? she silently asked herself and heard that one gently saying, 'Would you like to sit down?'

'In his chair, at his desk? No. No, I . . . I will stand over here. Yes, here.'

And next to the microscope under which a Russian bee had been opened.

Her back remained ramrod stiff, her hands gripping the edge of the workbench, but when she realized that he would notice this, the girl relaxed her hold and turned to face him. She hadn't yet dried her eyes or wiped her nose – did she want him to see her like this so as to engender sympathy? he wondered. *Merde*, what was she attempting to hide?

Everyone hides things these days, he cautioned himself. And please don't forget grief takes many forms and she is in great distress.

As in the honey-house, he'd have to be kind, but was she hoping to block him from further viewing what was under that microscope? She'd admitted to the presence of acarine, but not to its source in Russian bees. 'Mademoiselle, it's good of you to have come downstairs. You must still be exhausted and are understandably in shock.'

'I want to help, Inspector. There is only myself who can. She . . . *Maman* won't be of any use. *Papa* didn't . . . didn't tell her anything about his work or . . .'

'Or even about his private life?'

That brothel? That filthy place and those two bitches – was this what he was implying? 'Yes. Yes, that is how it was with my parents. Mother didn't do it, Inspector. I made her tell me. I said we had to talk, that the time for insulating herself from me must end.'

'And her response?'

Instinctively the girl touched her left cheek, disturbing a

camouflage of last-minute powder whose pale chalkiness had hidden the welt.

'Mother slapped me hard. I . . . I forgave her immediately, of course.'

'Would you prefer we didn't talk here?'

'No. No, here is fine. I . . . I will just have to get used to it, won't I?'

The girl waited for him to say yes, but he would simply take out his pipe and tobacco, thought St-Cyr.

'Inspector, I don't know who could have poisoned him. That bottle of liqueur was not in the study when I left here early on Thursday morning. My father was already at work at five when I came in to kiss him goodbye. He was happy – earnest, that is, about his work. *Our* work.'

'And did you know the contents of the address he was revising?'

'I knew only that he was working on an important paper, but . . . but not the subject of it. *Papa* refused to tell me. "It's too controversial," he said. It . . . it had to be about his bees, of course. They are our dedicated and loyal little friends, isn't that so? Tireless and always bringing beauty and the gold of their honey, the light from their wax, while at the same time pollinating the very plants without which we could not survive.'

Quickly Danielle wiped her nose and eyes with a hand and tried to smile, and when she heard him ask, 'Was he to have given the address that evening?' vehemently shook her head.

'Tomorrow at two p.m. The Jardin du Luxembourg. A . . . a room in the Palais is still not possible so, again, as since the Defeat, the Society must meet in one of the greenhouses, but it . . . it is really quite pleasant and perhaps far more in keeping with the subject. I, myself, though forced always to sit at the back, have never objected to our holding the meetings there. The bees love it, and one can watch them going about their tiny lives as if in total peace.'

Her voice had strengthened but was she now on firm ground? he wondered. She was also, in a way, striking a blow for equality and the injustice many women and young girls felt at the hands of men who often knew far less than they.

'Aren't you going to light your pipe?' she asked.

'Ah! I've forgotten. I often do. Would you like a cigarette?'

Would it help? 'No. I don't. I haven't ever. I've had no desire to use them.'

And now need no such crutches? *Merde*, what was there about her? The need to constantly be on her guard, the need to hide the fact she must know the mites were from Russia? 'While away, you stayed, I believe, at the family's country house.'

'Only at night. My route took me too many kilometres from it otherwise. I arrived after dark on Thursday, crept into bed and was up and away before dawn on Friday. Today also. It's . . . it's just an old place. Not much to look at and sadly in need of repair.'

And nothing for you to worry about – was this the impression she wanted to impart? 'You use it only once in a while.'

'Yes.' And damn *maman* for telling him of it. 'I must vary my route and so must stay overnight in other places. Sometimes where we have out-apiaries. That way I can check on the hives also.'

And let me give you those locations? Let us talk no more of the country house – was that it, then? 'Could someone have come here on Thursday evening to see your father?'

'And bring him such a gift?'

The frown she gave was deep. 'Well?' he heard himself ask.

'Perhaps one of the Society might have arranged to visit him, but he didn't tell me this, and I . . . why I did not ask. I was in too much of a hurry to be on my way. I did not think. I just assumed everything would be the same when I returned – *fine*, do you understand?'

Flinging herself around again, she stood with head bowed and her back to him. Tears spattered the workbench, hitting the hands she pressed flat against it. Splashing between her fingers. Hands that, washed in ice-cold water and without soap, still held dirt and looked chapped and worn.

The Inspector took hold of her by the shoulders. 'There . . . there were those in the Society who did not *want* him to give that address,' she said bitterly. 'They . . . they were afraid *les Allemands* would close down the Society and arrest everyone. *Cowards, papa* called them. *Cowards!*'

97

Her hair was very fine and light and when he released her left shoulder, his right hand remained in comfort, deliberately touching it and she knew – yes, knew now – that he would stop at nothing to get his answers, that he had, indeed, the eyes and insidious curiosity of a priest! Of Father Michel, yes!

'But he was determined to give the address?' she heard him ask and felt herself instinctively nod then blurt, 'It was his duty to do so. His *duty*, he said!'

The girl *was* thin, and she shook hard when he wrapped comforting arms about her. 'Please go upstairs, mademoiselle. Go back to bed. There will be time enough for questions.'

But will there? she silently asked, still clinging to him but opening her eyes now to see, through the mist of her tears, the desk, the wall with its collection of bees under glass, the paintings, the whole of it, of life itself and what it had become. The French windows to the garden also.

'*Inspector* . . .'

It was Madame de Bonnevies and the look she gave condemned both himself and her daughter for sharing grief's moment in such an intimate way.

The girl released her hold but remained defiantly standing beside him so that her right arm touched his and now . . . now that hand found its timid way into his own and he felt her close her fingers about his and tightly. She was still trembling.

'Mother, what is it? What's happened?'

Had the girl been expecting an absolute disaster? wondered St-Cyr and thought it probable.

The mother's voice grated.

'That one's partner has arrived and is waiting in the car for him. A matter of some urgency. *This*,' she said acidly, and held out the flattened remains of what must once have been a birdcage!

'All right, Hermann, enlighten me.'

'Not here, idiot. Somewhere quiet.'

Was it as bad as that? wondered St-Cyr as the Citroën roared up the *impasse*, crossed over the rue Stendhal, made a hard right on to the rue de Prairies, a right again and then shot down the rue de Bagnolet. Of course there was so little traffic these days, it really didn't matter if one stopped where one was *supposed* to stop. *Mon Dieu*, it took only ten minutes to cross the city from suburb to suburb at peak times, even with the clutter of bicycles, bicycle-taxis and pedestrians, far less to reach Chez Rudi's on the Champs-Élysées, especially with Hermann behind the wheel!

'This is *not* somewhere quiet!' seethed the Sûreté acidly.

'But it *is* the centre of all gossip and gossip is what we need, *mein lieber Französischer Oberdetektiv*. Let me do the talking – that's an order, eh, so *don't* object!'

Hermann was really in a state but one mustn't take crap like that! '*Inspektor*, my lips are sealed. After all, you, too, are one of my German masters.'

'Piss off. This is serious. Act natural.'

'I am.'

'Then don't look as if the ground had just fallen out from under you! Try smiling.'

'You know how much I resent having to come here when most of the city is starving!'

'But you do get fed, so please don't forget or deny it. And *don't* seal your lips to a damned good feed. I'm going to order for you.'

Nom de Jésus-Christ, must Hermann be the same as all the others of the Occupier only more authoritarian, more forceful, more blind and insensitive to even the simplest wishes of his partner?

Of course. After all, like Rudi Sturmbacher, he was a Bavarian.

Beerhall big and at the tea-and-coffee stage at 3:47 p.m., the restaurant was in one of its more genteel modes. Couples here, couples there. Uniforms and pretty girls who should have known better than to consort with the enemy in a place so visible.

But none of this caused Hermann to stop on the threshold, to gape in surprise and dart his eyes over the walls and ceiling, then hesitantly grin only to caution himself and finally croak, '*Mein Gott*, Louis. Was it done overnight?'

From wainscoting to ceiling, and over that too, huge murals revealed the heart, the mind, the sympathies and loyalties of the restaurant's owner.

'It's Rudi's little contribution to morale,' whispered St-Cyr. 'Be sure to praise it. You'll have to and so will I.'

Across the far wall, Arminius, conqueror of *three* Roman legions in AD9, rode a white stallion through the brooding forests of the Teutoburger Wald. Chained centurions and legionaries were among the captives, their former slaves, too, and in front of the pommel of his saddle was bent all but double, a naked maiden, she forced to moon her gorgeous backside to the heavens and to all and sundry, her long, blonde tresses trailing.

There were crowded shields and swords and drinking horns of mead among the barbarians who wore wolfskins and whose women were dressed in blowsy, off-the-shoulder gowns that were belted at the waist. Smiles and grins were on most of the conquerors, outraised arms of welcome from the humble citizens of their forest abode. Babes in arms, babes on shoulders to better see the victorious, and babes voraciously suckling from under bearskin comforters. Kids everywhere.

'I like the helmet, Louis.'

It was big and it was winged. 'What about his brassiere?'

'Did they wear such things – the men, that is? I don't think the women did.' It was of iron – two mounds shaped like tumuli that had been forged by Vulcan himself. A battle-axe in hand, the expression on that thick-bearded, big-boned Teutonic countenance was ever-grim even in conquest. 'Muscles . . . *mein Gott*, look at his arms and thighs!'

'Look at the prize he's brought home. There is something vaguely familiar about her but I can't quite put my finger on it. The hair perhaps.'

'Her ass, *Dummkopf*! and the women who are looking on.'

Most of the female faces were similar. 'Rudi's little Yvette and his Julie were models.'

'Helga, too, idiot!'

Rudi's youngest sister waited on tables and was still hoping for a husband. 'But they all wear boar-tooth necklaces?' hazarded St-Cyr.

'That's because they like the feel of teeth!'

There were always a few plain-clothed Gestapo about, a few of the SS too, in uniform, and burly Feldgendarmen, et cetera.

Saying hello to some, ignoring others, Hermann found a table right in the middle and, throwing himself into a chair, sat staring up at the ceiling in wonder to where Stukas dived through thunderclouds, Henkel-111s dropped their bombs and Messerschmitts chased Spitfires which exploded into flames.

'Well, my Hermann. You say nothing?'

It was Helga. The round, milkmaid's eyes were bluer than blue, the blonde braids cut shoulder length, the chunky hips firm under a pale-blue workdress that hugged them.

'Helga, *meine Schatze*.' My treasure. 'I can't believe it,' swore Hermann, still taken aback and trying, perhaps, to find a deeper meaning where there was absolutely none.

She indicated the other wall on which a naked Brünnhilde rode a comparable white stallion but at one of the Munich torch-lit fêtes. Surrounded by lusty, young torch-bearing Brown Shirts with swastika armbands, the girl had risen up in her stirrups for a better look at the bonfire.

'That's you,' he murmured, half in surprise perhaps, half in interest – it was hard to tell.

'I modelled for it,' gushed the girl. 'Rudi let me.'

The blaze was huge, a pillar of fire whose light glistened in her eyes and on her pale white thighs and ample breasts, but lost itself among the tangled mat of pubic hair which glowed more softly.

'Good for Rudi, Helga. You deserve it. *Alle Halbeit ist taub*, eh, Louis?' Half-measures are no-measures.

'Such poise, *mein Kamerad der Kriminalpolizei*. Were you one of the BDMs?' asked Louis of her.

The *Bund deutscher Mädchen*, the League of German Maidens. 'Of course. It's *gesunde Erotica*, is it not, my Hermann?'

Healthy eroticism designed to increase the birthrate and produce cannon fodder. 'This . . .' Kohler indicated the murals. 'Is fantastic, Helga.'

'If only the Führer knew,' exclaimed Louis.

'He does. Rudi sent him photographs,' she said and proudly blushed.

'The murals are bound to be the talk of Paris and Berlin then,' enthused St-Cyr. 'Ah! not Braque, you understand, or Picasso who is also out of favour but also thinks he's so good. Still . . . what can I say, Hermann? I, a lover of art?'

And bullshit! Braque and Picasso were the fathers of cubism! 'Art for the people and of the people.'

'Yes, yes, that's it *exactly*!' said Louis, still full of enthusiasm.

'Pea soup with pig's snout and trotters, Helga,' said Hermann positively.

She screwed up her face in distress and frowned deeply. 'Rudi won't like it. You know how he is. Meals at mealtimes. Coffee and cakes at other times.'

Kohler put a hand firmly on her hip. 'Tell him it's necessary and that I've managed something sweet for him. Now after the soup, we'll have the grilled Franconian sausages with pork rind, sauerkraut and boiled potatoes. And two big steins of that Münchener Löwen he saves for friends like us. The sight of you up there on that wall has made me hungry.'

But had it made him see her as she really was? wondered Helga, and wetting the end of her pencil, took longer at this than necessary.

'Encouraging her will only get you in trouble!' hissed St-Cyr when the girl had disappeared into the kitchens.

'Trouble,' muttered Kohler. 'Our days are clouded with it just like those of the Romans on that wall.'

From a pocket he took a small ball bearing of silver perhaps, and after rolling it around in a palm, let it trickle slowly across the table towards his partner and friend. 'Don't bite on it, Louis. I already have.'

The days of the Munich Putsch, the uprising of 8 November 1923, lived on in the triumph of murals. A Brown Shirt from them, a survivor with fists, the mountain of flesh that Rudi Sturmbacher had become weighed 166 kilos. The hair was flaxen and cut short in Wehrmacht and SS style; the eyes were small, red-rimmed, pale-blue and wary.

A moment ago there had been greed and larceny in those eyes – the expectation of profit which had accompanied the huge platter of sausage, potatoes, sauerkraut, et cetera, to the table.

Uneasily the mountain's gaze flickered over the little silver ball bearing Hermann had placed in an ashtray. That gaze passed beyond this humble Sûreté, thought St-Cyr, and took in at once the whole front half of the restaurant, the reward for years of service and loyalty, the murals, the entrance – everything. Even the newspapers and magazines that had come straight from the Reich that very morning.

Rudi hadn't touched the ball bearing and wouldn't. 'Something sweet,' he breathed and pursed the big lips that had only just lost their grin.

'Honey,' confided Hermann, conspiratorially leaning over the table, and why must he do this? demanded St-Cyr silently. Didn't he care about the SS and Gestapo who were now taking note of them, even the GFPs, the Secret Police of the Army? Didn't he know that gossip was instantly passed to, and generated here at the centre of it?

'Honey from Russia,' confessed the Sûreté – one had to say something, especially after having had to listen, over their soup, to Hermann's long-winded discourse on the subject.

Steam rose from the platter, and with it came an aroma which made the juices flood to remind one that meals, even though from the Occupier as this one was, were seldom seen and often taken on the run.

'We could get you some,' offered Hermann – *merde*, even when bluffing he could be blithe about it!

'*How?*' asked Rudi. He wouldn't let on to these two what he knew. Not yet. But in the past Hermann had often been a useful source, a student of the black market, so one had best make a pretence of being attentive.

'Two lorries. Drivers who won't say anything. Yourself and myself, I think,' said Hermann. 'Tonight would be best. Let's set it for 22:00 hours, me to meet you and the lorries, you to choose the meeting place.'

'Honey . . . Whose honey, *mein Lieber*?' puzzled Rudi softly.

Hermann gave the shrug he always did when meaning, It could be anyone's, so why bother worrying?

Was Hermann slipping? wondered Rudi. Had the Kripo's most disloyal *Detektiv* left little messages along his route today only to forget all about them? 'Oskar,' he indicated the little ball bearing of silver and gold, 'is very well placed, my Hermann. But it's good you've come to me – yes, yes it is. Oskar could do a lot for you and this one.' He indicated the Sûreté, the traitor, the patriot who was, at the moment, being treated with felt gloves simply because Gestapo Boemelburg needed him to fight common crime and keep the people quiet. 'I'm certain of it, Hermann. Herr Schlacht is a man of many talents and a valued client. Enjoy your dinners. Drink your beer. They're on the house.'

Rudi abruptly got up, deliberately knocking the table a little and sloshing their beer. 'Now wait!' bleated Hermann. 'Sit down, eh? Come on. We're friends.'

'And friends are what you and this one need.'

Sacré nom de nom, were things that bad? cursed St-Cyr and managed – yes, managed somehow to dig the serving spoon into the platter and load his plate without spilling a drop.

'You've such splendid linen, Herr Sturmbacher. Everything complements the meal.' *Beer* instead of wine!

Louis stabbed a chunk of sausage and brought it up to let those nostrils of his flare as he drew in the aroma – no cat meat, no rat meat, no sawdust either, thought Kohler.

Repeatedly dumbfounded by Louis's coolness in the face of a crisis, he watched as his partner and friend blew on the morsel, chewed it slowly as a connoisseur would, and pronounced it magnificent.

'Don't try to flatter me,' breathed Rudi. 'I know it's perfect. So, eat, yes, and let's talk a little. This is serious, Hermann, and you'd better listen.'

Word had got to Rudi from Frau Hillebrand of the Procurement Office. Whispers of a birdcage had come from Schlacht himself.

'The Hôtel Drouot, Hermann. As you were consorting with a certain chanteuse who shall remain nameless, a call was being placed from the ground floor. I could even hear crockery in the background.'

'He's lost his little badge,' swallowed Kohler. 'I should have told him where it was.'

'Certainly not here and not with the Bzp Obergruppenführer Denke who is, I believe, already heading for the Russian Front, courtesy of the Kommandant von Gross-Paris. Your *miliciens*, by the way, were taken directly to the Santé and shot. I . . . why I just thought you ought to know, Hermann, that when a flea tickles an ear these days, the elephant is likely to sneeze.'

Or fart! 'It's the trunk you mean. The flea tickles the elephant's trunk, Rudi,' muttered Hermann. He hadn't meant for those two to be shot, thought St-Cyr, but had merely felt a few years of forced labour would have been good for them.

'Eat,' urged the mountain. 'Don't let that little taste of home you wanted go to waste. It'll be in every mouthful.'

The two of them dug in. *Mein Gott,* but they discovered they were hungry! Beer was taken. Bread – good Bavarian *Roggenbrot* – was broken and savoured with tears, so *gut. Ja gut*! 'Now listen. you get that little badge for me, you two, and I will forget we even spoke of it. Oskar separates the honey when he recovers the wax, and a little of that "sweetness" already comes to me.'

Ah *Scheisse*! 'He also makes little wafers for you, doesn't he?' gulped Kohler.

Rudi brushed ham-fat fingers over the linen before sampling the sausage. He toyed with a curled wedge of pork rind, judged it crisp enough and fully flavoured. 'I did not hear that, Hermann. The restaurant pays for itself. What little is left, is sent home to my parents who are getting on and finding things somewhat more difficult than anticipated.'

But to send money home from an occupied territory was illegal, therefore Rudi had to have another route. Switzerland . . . ? The wafers are going there, thought Kohler. *Merde* but hadn't he stepped in the shit this time! 'I'll get you the badge, Rudi. That's a promise. No problem.'

'If this beekeeper of yours was murdered, who cares, eh, Jean-Louis? What? Is the sauerkraut not to your liking?'

'No. No, it's perfect, Herr Sturmbacher.'

'And you're not even sure it was murder, are you?'

Had the news travelled so fast and in such detail? 'Not yet, but I believe we will soon be satisfied. One thing does puzzle me, but I . . .'

Louis left the thought dangling while he helped himself to more from the platter and then peered deeply into his stein.

'Helga . . . Helga, *meine Schwester*, another beer for each of my friends,' sang out Rudi.

The whole restaurantheard it, a good sign. '*Danke*,' said St-Cyr. 'You see, Rudi – may I call you that when in . . .' He indicated the cosy friendship of their table and said, 'In such *Gemütlichkeit*?'

'Herr Sturmbacher, I think.'

'*Gut*! It's always best for me to be reminded of where I sit in this Occupation of yours. You see, Herr Sturmbacher, the victim was what we French call an *original* and this, I feel, must have contributed much to his demise.'

'He doted on his daughter,' confided Kohler, quickly picking up the thread Louis wanted him to pick up.

'But hated and despised his son,' said the Sûreté.

'Whom the mother loved with a mother's love, thereby all but totally rejecting the daughter, Rudi,' insisted Kohler.

'Who held the couple together and fed them as well as she could.'

'And helped her father with his bees.'

'While revering her brother.'

'Who hadn't shared the same father with her,' tut-tutted Hermann.

'And remains lost in a prisoner-of-war camp in the Reich.'

'Oflag 17A, Rudi,' swore Hermann, sadly shaking his head. 'A *Kriegsgefangener*.'

'A *Kriege*,' echoed the mountain, giving the slang for such and immediately taking note of what these two were really after. 'I'll see what I can do, Hermann. The badge in return for a little help.'

'Maxim's,' breathed Hermann conspiratorially. 'Did our *Bonze* of the gold wafers and the candle wax pay the fifty thousand francs down for her to get her son released? Save us time, Rudi, and the expense of going to that restaurant. You know the beer there always gives me gas, the soup also.'

'Candles . . . ?' asked the mountain, ignoring the question of Maxim's, but had he forgotten he'd mentioned Schlacht separated the honey when recovering the wax, wondered St-Cyr, or was he but testing the air for the perfume of how much they really knew?

'Old Shatter Hand coughed up that crap about the candles,' confessed Hermann, shrugging broadly.

These two were known for the speed and ruthlessly thorough determination with which they sought their answers and steadfastly upheld the truth. One law for all and only one, the fools. 'Oskar does make candles, yes.'

'Where?' shot Hermann, forgetting about Maxim's for the moment.

'That I do not know nor ask. Really, *meine Lieben*, have you not listened? Can you not realize who your friends should be? *Der* Führer has . . .'

Rudi leaned over the table, looked to one side and to the other for listening ears not wanted, then thinking better of confiding it to both of them, got up and crooked a finger at this fellow countryman of his who was so delinquent, and whispered, '*Der* Führer has a secret weapon, Hermann. Yes, I have heard this. Everything of such interest passes through here, but one must be careful to whom one imparts such confidences? The *Vergeltungswaffe-Eins*, Hermann. Even as we speak, the ground is being prepared for the launching ramps from which they will be sent. Normandy and Picardy have been mentioned.'

'V-1s?' Revenge weapons.

'*Fliegende Bomben*, Hermann.'

Flying bombs.

'Some kind of rocket. So you see, Stalingrad is but a minor reversal and we are still going to England.'

That little saying hadn't been heard since the Führer had abandoned such plans in the fall of 1940.

'Behave,' said Rudi. 'Become a good Nazi. Join the Party. Now you must excuse me. My kitchen calls.'

'And Maxim's? Did Schlacht . . .'

'Pay to get the woman's son released? Really, my Hermann, how could I possibly know of such an intimate matter?'

The city was now pitch dark and, at 17:22 hours, bitterly cold. Infrequently, pale dots of blue penetrated the darkness from struggling *vélo-taxis* and *vélos*. Pedestrians were caught but momentarily in the slim blue slit-eyes of the Citroën's headlamps. A mother and two little children . . .

Hermann jammed on the brakes – skidded, and then stopped. The three of them had remained standing right in front of the car . . .

'*Hermann, we haven't time.*'

'Her kids are hungry, Louis. She's prepared to commit suicide.'

'*Merde*, how soft can you get?' But it was happening all over the city. Desperate measures for desperate times, and every car would have to hold the privileged, since no one else was allowed to drive.

'There'll be a Wehrmacht soup kitchen at the Gare d' Austerlitz. I can fix things for her there, then drop you off, and come back to take them home.'

Hermann was rolling down his side window. The woman and her children were approaching . . . '*Jésus, merde alors*, idiot! We've a murder investigation on our hands!'

'We could simply say the beekeeper's death was an accident.'

'Was that what Rudi advised? Well, was it, eh?'

'Monsieur,' began the woman. 'Could you . . .'

'Well, was it?' demanded St-Cyr.

'Something like that. The heat's on, Louis. We can't afford to get burned, not with the *Milice* after Oona and her papers not so good.'

'And Giselle? Were they also after her?'

'Monsieur . . .'

'Get in the back. *Vite, vite*, before this one changes his mind. I'm going to have to see about Giselle, Louis, but that explosion on the tracks between here and Lyon could really have been a warning to us. Please don't forget it!'

'And this one, Hermann? Has she a grenade or a revolver hidden beneath that shawl she has wrapped about the children?'

'A grenade . . . ?' managed the woman.

'You worry too much. *Mein Gott*, your ears are even bigger than Rudi's!'

'And you are far too trusting and forget entirely, *mon ami*, that the *Résistance* still have my name on some of their hit lists!'

A problem, a little misunderstanding. 'There's a rumour of

something big,' said Kohler stiffly. 'I'll tell you about it later. I promise.'

'A rumour?' managed the woman. 'Bread here, milk there. Cheese . . . has one of those *salauds* really got cheese, or are we simply to eat rumours, messieurs?'

Many of Paris's forty thousand concierges were grassroots black-market traffickers. Flour from one, cheese from another, but always a city of rumour.

Her tears were very real, and when Hermann stopped the car outside the railway station, they both looked into the back seat at her through the darkness.

'Forgive me,' she said. 'Some bastard stole my purse and all of our ration tickets.'

To say nothing of her papers, but such 'petty' crimes were happening all too frequently. 'Look, I'll fix it. Don't cry. Chewing gum, Louis. In the compartment. It's banana flavoured. I was going to give it to you-know-who, but . . .'

To Oberg, the Head of the SS!

'Banana . . . ?' hazarded the woman only to see the big one toss a carefree hand and hear him say, 'Well, something like that. Here . . here, take it. Look, I know it won't do much but . . .'

'But that is all you can do. I might have known.'

'No! Now just calm down, madame. You'll see.'

'*Merde*, you're too easy, Hermann. One of these days I'm going to be picking up pieces of you.'

Like those of Marianne and Philippe – Louis's second wife and little boy? wondered Kohler. Louis was right, of course. The mood of compliance was bound to change. The *Résistance* would warm up. Though still disorganized, widely scattered and few in number, they *had* tried to kill Louis last November, and Gestapo Paris's Watchers, not liking the finger of truth these two humble servants of justice had pointed, had known all about that bomb on his doorstep but had deliberately left it in place. His wife had been coming home to him after a torrid affair with the Hauptmann Steiner and Louis hadn't been able to warn her there might be trouble – they'd been out of the city at the time. And, yes, Steiner had been the nephew of the Kommandant von Gross-Paris who had packed him off to Russia to protect the family's honour. And, yes, Steiner had died there just as would likely happen to the Bzp Obergruppenführer Otto Denke. Ah Christ!

'A bomb?' asked the woman with difficulty.

'Madame, please don't let it trouble you. Just go with this one. He'll look after you like he does everyone else.'

The Gare d'Austerlitz was indicated somewhere out there in the cold.

'Relax, Louis. I won't be a minute.'

There was a can of pipe tobacco without a lid next to where the chewing gum had lain. The Procurement Office? wondered St-Cyr.

Somewhat mollified, he began to pack his pipe, and when he had it alight, sat waiting and waiting. Thinking, too, and asking, Murder . . . had the beekeeper's demise really been intended, and was Hermann honestly suggesting they avoid the issue entirely so as to make life easy for once?

Madame de Bonnevies had gone through her husband's book of clients and had tried to keep them from finding the name of Frau Uma Schlacht.

Danielle de Bonnevies hadn't wanted him to look through the microscope at the mite-infested innards of a Russian bee. Her father had been terribly worried about an infestation, but also about the decimation of French bees, though she had claimed not to know the contents of the address he had planned to give.

She had also not wanted him to take any notice of the family's country house near Soisy-sur-Seine. And ever since the Defeat, the mother had been trying desperately to free her son, the child of another man. Had the son been freed, then? Had the girl known this and feared her stepbrother had come in through the apiary and garden to poison that bottle? It hadn't been in the study at 5 a.m. on Thursday. Early in the evening de Bonnevies had shaved, had spruced himself up – a woman? he wondered again. Perhaps the childhood friend of his sister, a Madame Héloïse Debré of 7 rue Stendhal? A woman whose husband had repeatedly beaten her until one day he had vanished and she had sworn not to know where to.

Had Father Michel been hiding something? Why else, but to

distract this Sûreté, would he have mentioned such a parish disgrace as the gang rape of Angèle-Marie de Bonnevies? And ever since 1919 there had been a cemetery room at *Le Chat qui crie* and word of a settlement of accounts at any price. A very stubborn beekeeper, then, and one with not only a very troubled conscience, but a long memory.

When Kohler got behind the wheel all Louis said was 'Four names, *mon vieux*. One of whom was killed at Sedan during the invasion of 1940. Another who no longer lives in the quartier but visits a certain *lupanar* late on Sunday evenings and takes Charlotte whose age is eighteen in that very room.'

'What room?' blurted Kohler, baffled by the thought trend but intrigued.

'Please don't interrupt me. Two others, Hermann, who are married and with families but are locked up in POW camps in the Reich just as, supposedly, is Madame de Bonnevies' precious son.'

'Oflag 17A.'

'It's just a thought.'

'Louis, Rudi says Schlacht's fucking Madame de Bonnevies.'

'Did he really say that?'

'Not really, but enough.'

'In return for which?'

'Schlacht must have put the fifty thousand francs down at Maxim's for her to get her son back. Why else was that little badge of his in her drawer? Why else the expensive lingerie and the menu?'

'The son, then, and that's what the daughter tried to hide from me, but really, Hermann, Herr Schlacht could have any . . .'

'He has.'

'Who?'

'His secretary.'

'Then you will have to prove to me that he really is consorting with madame.'

'Why me? Why not you?'

'Are you ordering me to keep a watch on her when I have already too much to do?'

'Louis, this is serious. Boemelburg has warned us to lay off.'

'Even though the Kommandant von Gross-Paris is insisting we do no such thing?'

They'd be shouting at each other in a moment. 'Oberg won't stand for our interfering again. Let it lie, Louis. Say it was an accident.'

'An accident.'

'Misadventure. Rudi says there are flying bombs and that they're to be pointed at England from launching ramps that are already being built in the north. He wouldn't have told me that had he thought it wouldn't convince me to be a good Nazi for once.'

'And has it convinced you? Is the one-thousand-year Reich really here to stay, Hermann?'

'I don't know. *Verdammt*! I wish I did.'

'Then in the interim, *mon ami de guerre*, let me visit the sister while you . . .'

Hermann knew he'd have to say it. 'Visit Frau Schlacht.'

'Who may have paid our beekeeper a little visit on the night of his death – is this what worries you, Hermann?'

'Not really, but now that you've brought the possibility to my attention, I'll be sure to ask her.'

'*Bon*! For all we know at present, she could just as easily have given him that bottle as anyone else!'

'Idiot, it's the wife she'd have wanted to get rid of, not de Bonnevies, particularly if Schlacht is running around with madame!'

'And that, *mon enfant*, is precisely what I meant.'

Ah *merde*, the Amaretto, thought Kohler. Had it not been meant for the beekeeper at all, but for madame?

Out of the darkness and the falling snow, the silhouette of the Salpêtrière grew, and the line of its many roofs stretched from the rue Jenner almost to the Gare d'Austerlitz, along the south side of the boulevard d'Hôpital.

Pausing to search for a visible light – some sign of life within – St-Cyr found only one tiny pinprick of blue above the main entrance. Every window and door would be secured behind heavy black-out curtains. Oh *bien sûr*, the staff would open those curtains during the day – they were really very conscientious, so much so, the hospital ranked among the finest. But still there would be that mesh of stiff steel wire, still the bolts, the necessary locks, guards, warders, nurses, doctors, cooks, et cetera.

'Angèle-Marie de Bonnevies,' he softly said and wondered what he'd find. She'd be forty-six years old now.

The patients would be at their evening meal. Soup . . . would it be soup? And how many of them did they really have – six thousand . . . eight thousand? Was the cost what troubled the Occupier as much as an unwillingness to recognize that mental illness was not something society should wipe out with injections of potassium cyanide or air?

There was wing after wing to the hospital – those for the criminally insane, others for the suffering of amnesia, depression, hypochondria and senile dementia. On visiting days, the triangular foyer would be crowded with relatives and loved ones – two thousand, perhaps three thousand of these, with vendors, too. Ersatz chewing gum – yes, yes, banana-flavoured, cherry also, and apple; flower sellers as well; paper collages and cut-outs, picture books done in cloth or otherwise. From the administrative centre, avenues opened up and these were named after the permanent shops they led to. And which one would he follow? Which would she walk every day of her life? The rue de tabac, where now no tobacco would be available? The rue de la pâtisserie where painted plaster and papier-mâché mock-ups would give the lie of plenty as they did all over the city? Éclairs, petits fours and babas au rhum? Would they allow such lies or simply have empty shelves?

The street of the market was one of the most popular, since the hospital was to be as much like a small town as possible.

Of the two bronzes at the entrance, only one remained: that of Dr Philippe Pinel who, in the 1790s, was one of the great pioneers in the humane treatment of the mentally ill. The other, that of the world-famous neurologist Dr Jean Martin Charcot, had been removed by the Occupier last year. Cast out for having influenced Freud, among others of his students. A man who had pioneered the use of hypnotism in the treatment of hysteria, Charcot had lived from 1825 until 1893; Freud had, of course, been Jewish.

Shaking his head in despair at the long memories of the

Occupier and what had happened to France, he went in to the administrative desk, pulled out his badge and ID and said, as always in such places, a stern, grim, 'St-Cyr. Sûreté. It's urgent, so please don't argue. Just get me whoever is in charge of the wing in which Mademoiselle Angèle-Marie de Bonnevies resides. Her dossier also.'

'That's impossible.'

'As are most things these days until a little persuasion is applied.'

Namely the Gestapo. 'Wait here. I'll ring for him.'

'*Bon.*'

The smell of *eau de Javel* was pungent. Water dripped constantly from leaking faucets. The white, enamelled cast-iron washtubs were chipped, the light so dim it was as if a fog had seeped into the corridor.

All that remained of Louis XIII's gunpowder factory were this wet, grey marble floor and these two limestone walls with their black iron bolts and the heavy ceiling timbers. Later, sconces of wrought iron had been added to give torch- and candlelight, but that had been in 1656 when the Salpêtrière, then so named, had been an asylum for vagrants.

'Inspector, please be careful. She is . . . How should I put it? Almost normal. Deceptively so,' said the doctor.

The woman wore grey – an undershift – and the dress she frantically scrubbed was grey, too, as were the galvanized iron ripples on the washboard she used. Her hair was blonde, but pale and cut short so that it stood well out from her and above the shoulders. Thick and teased by constant, rhythmic brushing.

Apparently she paid no attention to them, to the dripping of adjacent faucets, the damp cold, dim light, fog and constant smell of Javel. And her voice – she was talking to herself – was not shrill but earnest. 'You *will* be poisoned, Angèle. I drank water, idiot. You know the poison wasn't in it! Ah, you think I'm crazy? I know where you are. You were in the chapel. I'm in the garden. There were clowns. You were on the trapeze, Angèle. Madame la sous-maîtresse Durand was riding an elephant. You were . . .'

114

'Angèle-Marie,' said Dr Henri-Martin Lemoine gently. 'It's me. You have a visitor.'

'I played the drums. *He's a Communist! He's been sent to poison me*! Why am I here?'

'One of the others spilled their soup on your dress. Remember?' he said.

'Will he tune my piano?'

'Perhaps. Now come along.'

'A lake. I went swimming. You *did*!' she said to herself. '*Marie-couche-toi-là*, you were *naked*! You sported yourself!'

Harlot . . . 'Inspector, please. Let me get her to her room.'

'They're going to poison you. You know they are,' she said to herself and then, 'Try biscuits, not water. Be reasonable. Take air. I can't. It burns. There are spies. They're watching you, Angèle. They've seen you peeing!'

'Please,' said Lemoine, nodding slightly towards the wash-house entrance. 'Let me talk to her. We'll only be a moment.'

The woman lifted her head and listened intently. As if struck by something, she stood rigidly, still clinging to the dress on the washboard. Hesitantly her chest rose and fell in fear, but then the frown she now gave changed swiftly to a smile.

Merde, thought St-Cyr. That bit about the poison not being in water. Does she know why I've come?

The wrinkles were there again across the deeply furrowed brow. The large brown eyes were dark with worry, the lips tight as she watched for his every move and he heard Lemoine saying, 'Go, for God's sake.'

'Go?' she asked, and watched – one could feel her doing so, thought St-Cyr, as he walked to the end of the corridor.

Poison . . . was her concern over being poisoned normal to her condition, or had she been told and had it registered that her brother was dead?

The Schlacht residence at 28 quai d'Orléans might well be pleasant, for the house it was in faced the river. But at 6:17 p.m. it was shrouded in darkness, fog and softly falling snow.

Kohler stood beside the Citroën. He had no love of the Île Saint-Louis, this ancient kernel from which Paris had grown.

115

Oona had nearly been killed at its upstream end, a matter of his having used her as bait, and ever since that affair, he'd been shy of the place.

Regrettably so, Louis would have said but Louis wasn't here. And anyway, that had been back in mid-December and, yes, there'd been gold involved then and now there was more of it. Gold and candles, squashed beehives from Russia and acarine mites. Shit!

Though he listened intently, the city was all but silent. Only the gentle lapping of the river came to him, just as it had when Oona had had that knife at her throat. She had trusted him implicitly then and he had put her at risk.

'I've got to find her a really decent set of papers; Giselle, too,' he said and swore he'd do so. 'I've got to get them both out of France before it's too late.'

Spain . . . he'd always felt that would be best. Louis and he had often discussed it. A small café, a little *bar-tabac* with Giselle behind the zinc and Oona? he asked himself. Oona at home, tending Giselle's babies, eh? Oona waiting. Oona lying in bed night after night never knowing if he loved her, too, or what the hell would really happen to her.

Fed up with himself and the life, he yanked down on the brim of his fedora and took a little walk. Paused to light a cigarette and tried to think.

He'd have to go carefully. Louis and he couldn't have Oberg breathing down their necks again. And yet . . . and yet, had Frau Schlacht really intended to poison Madame de Bonnevies? Had the woman gone to that study only to find that the beekeeper, thinking the Amaretto quite safe, since he hadn't yet poisoned it, was in the throes of death? Had the intended victim added that poison? Had Juliette de Bonnevies beaten them to it?

A soft whipping sound cut the air to interrupt his thoughts and, curious, he leaned over the stone parapet to gaze down through the inkiness at the lower *quai*. There was a set of iron stairs here, he remembered. There had been chestnut trees, or had they been lindens?

Someone was fishing. Before the Defeat, before this lousy war and Occupation, this *quai* and all the others would have been lined with fishermen, especially on a Sunday afternoon. Now one could only do it under cover of darkness and still that was a terrible risk to take for a few roach or chub.

He let the fisherman be. He went along until he found the door to Number 28's courtyard. Rebuilt in the mid-1800s, the house, of five or six storeys, would have superb views of the Notre Dame, the Left Bank, too.

As if totally ignoring him and the war and what had happened, the bell of the Église de Saint-Louis tolled the half-hour as it had for centuries. Christ! was it cracking the ice of the bloody Volga?

'*Fliegende Bomben*,' he muttered disconsolately and asked himself, was the rumour even partly true and if so, must the war go on and on with no end in sight?

Louis would be certain to tell Gabrielle, who would pass the information to her contacts in the *Résistance*. 'And God help us all if she's dragged in again for questioning. I should never have put that responsibility on his shoulders. Never.'

Not one for using the elevators – he'd been caught hanging by a thread once too often – he started up the stairs only to be softly reminded. 'Monsieur, you have not stopped with me.'

There were concierges and concierges, but to most there was that same look of utter bafflement as to why a visitor – any visitor – should call at such an hour. At any hour!

Brusquely Madame Jeanette-Noëlle Jouvand turned the ledger towards him, having retreated into her *loge*.

She was not old, not young any more, and of medium height and build, was a war-widow as so many of them were. A quite pleasant-looking woman in a neat, prewar woollen suit of dove blue, with silver Widow's League button, a constant reminder.

'Please,' she indicated the ledger and held her breath while he wrote: Kohler, Kripo, Paris-Central, and glancing at the military wristwatch, the time: 18:35 hours, the Schlacht residence.

'That one has gone out, monsieur.'

He grinned, and it was a nice grin, thought Madame Jouvand, even though he was a Boche and there was the scar of a terrible slash down the left side of his face from the eye to chin. Other scars, too, but from shrapnel and from a bullet graze across the brow.

'The war,' he said. 'Not this one, but the last one.'

'Barbed wire,' she said and nodded sadly even though he had lied about the slash and the graze – both were far too fresh. '*Mon mari* was found clinging steadfastly to it with his face absent. Come back in three hours, monsieur. Madame dines. The Monsieur seldom goes with her since he is not often home and is, perhaps, too busy elsewhere.'

'I'll just go up and leave my card with her maid.'

'It is as the monsieur pleases, but I will note this in my ledger, should madame wish to question me.'

Verdammt, she was a cool one! A look down at her from the stairs revealed that same puzzled concern. 'You do not take the lift?' she asked and heard him say, 'They're like some of the people I have to deal with. I never trust them.'

A shrug was given and, delighted by her, he knew she was exclaiming to herself that the Germans were crazy, but instead she said, 'Well, of course, m'sieur, it's the exercise. Always *les Allemands* are at it. Rowing on the river, in the most tragic of weathers. Swimming when full of champagne and where none are allowed to swim even if fully clothed and there is ice. But it's as God has said. He is with them.'

'*Gott mit Uns*, eh?' he chuckled gently. It was written on every Wehrmacht belt buckle.

'She will have gone to the *salon de beauté* first, monsieur, and then to the brasserie.'

'It's near the *passerelle*, isn't it?'

The iron footbridge that crossed over to the Île de la Cité. The Germans had ordered it thrown up in 1941 to replace the bridge that had been knocked down by a disgruntled barge in 1939.

'*Oui*. The *salon* and brasserie are very close to each other and to it. First the one and then the other, the place of the Alsatian.'

'And no ration tickets, eh?'

'None. It is also as God wishes, is it not?'

There was even the innocence of wonder in her deep brown eyes, but concierges seldom offered information and this one had.

Kohler hated to spoil the fun but returned to face her as a Gestapo would. '*Ihre Papiere, bitte*, Frau . . .'

'Jouvand. Jeanette-Noëlle, age forty-five.'

Tonelessly she gave her address and position, et cetera, but it didn't take him a minute to find what he wanted, and when he drew out the slim, bright red- and green-covered little book from under *Paris-Soir*, where she had hidden it, she shuddered.

'Relax,' he said in French. 'Forget I ever saw it. Look, you've a nice coal fire in that furnace of yours. Why not go down to it and do us both a favour?'

Dear God forgive her, thought Madame Jouvand, for being so stupid as to have accepted that little book in the street when it was passed to her.

'*Poésie et vérité*,' said Kohler. Poem and truth.

Paul Éluard's poems were *Verboten* but were being published and distributed by the *Résistance*.

'I will do so immediately, monsieur.'

'*Bon.* And now that we're friends, I can ask you anything I want about Herr Schlacht and that wife of his, and you'll be sure to answer without telling anyone else you did. Right?'

Ah *merde!* 'Yes. Yes, of course. It shall be as you wish.'

The grainy photo in the dossier was of Angèle-Marie de Bonnevies in 1912. Staring blankly at the camera, the fifteen-year-old clutched the bundle of her clothes tightly to her chest, had just been showered and admitted, was still wet. The hair, worn no longer then than now, was parted in the middle and had been combed flat to cling behind her ears and drip. There wasn't a frown, a tear – not one hint of anything.

'Empty . . . her expression is exactly as it is as she looks at us now,' said St-Cyr sadly. 'It's as if she can never forget.'

Lemoine turned up a companion photo. 'The father blamed her,' he said. 'A walking stick.'

She'd been severely beaten. There were welts, bruises and inflamed cuts across her back, buttocks and thighs; rain after rain of blows. Her arms and shoulders had suffered. The calves, the ankles, the heels . . . 'Is there no hope for her?'

'There is always hope. Why else would we struggle?'

From the wash-house, she had led them to the rue de la

pâtisserie and then up staircase after staircase and through common wards which seemed to stretch on for ever.

There were two tall French windows behind the heavy blackout curtains that hung in the centre of each of the outer walls, the corner room having lots of light during the day. The floor was of bare planks, except for a colourful carpet of woven rags. A rescued Louis XIV settee had lost all upholstery but that on the seat and needed repainting and regilding. A worm-eaten narrow table, with a mottled grey marble top, held the grey-stone bust of an unhappy saint; an armoire with mirrored doors, her clothing. A chipped, yellow-and-white-enamelled sink on feet, served both as private bath and basin.

An unpainted, tin, hospital table-cum-bedside-cabinet held Bible, rosary, lamp, tin carafe of water and one tin cup. There were books with leather bindings but could she even read them for any length of time and make sense of them? There were several Jumeau, Bru and Kaestner dolls with feathered chapeaux and long, flowing gowns of dark blue, emerald green, deep red and gold velvet. Silk and satin, too, with rings, necklaces, pins, bracelets and cameos. Dolls with rouged cheeks, painted lips and long dark or blonde lashes. Had she given them names?

'My piano,' she said, at last losing that blankness of expression and indicating the upright. 'It whispers. It tells me it wants to be tuned, that its strings are hurting. Are you here to paint the room? You did once.'

A metronome had been silenced long ago by the removal of its arm. There were thin stacks of frayed sheet music – waltzes, he supposed, and sonatas. There were cobwebs, too, and flaking varnish, split cabinet wood, and lifting or missing ivories to match the broken plaster of the walls where large gaps exposed the stones.

'Her brother makes this possible,' confided Lemoine, discreetly taking the dossier from him. 'Humour her, Inspector. Sit down and tamper with the keys. She'll soon pass on to other thoughts.'

'The brother's dead.'

'Pardon?'

'I meant what I said.'

Lemoine heaved a contemplative sigh. 'I felt you must have a good reason for coming. She'll have heard us, by the way, and is very conscious of everything that goes on around her. How did it happen?'

'Poison,' she said to herself. 'You will also be poisoned, Angèle-Marie. I won't. I drank the roasted barley-and-acorn coffee they have to serve us in this place. I was a squirrel.'

'Later . . . I'll tell you later,' confided St-Cyr.

Clothing lay drying over a small wooden rack, but the room was damp and cold. She hung the dress with the other things and, finding a nightgown in the armoire, modestly turned her back to them and got ready for bed. Fought with the voices she heard; refused to respond to them; said earnestly, 'I *won't*! I *mustn't*! Not now.' And then, 'He's dead. I'm free and can no longer hate him. He hated you. He really did!'

'Angèle-Marie, you know that's simply not true,' said Lemoine. 'Your brother loved you. He'll be sadly missed.'

'His honey is sweet,' she said and smiled and arched her eyebrows questioningly before again speaking to herself. 'You tasted it, you little fool. I had to! I begged you not to, Angèle-Marie. He said I had to. He did. He really did! Poison . . . it was poison. Honey . . .'

'Touch the damned keys, Inspector! Play something. Anything!' whispered Lemoine urgently.

The piano was not the euphonium that he had played in the police band and still practised when time allowed, which was never, thought St-Cyr, but he did know the keys and with effort, picked out *Au Clair de la Lune.*

Entranced, Angèle-Marie sat down on the settee, then got up quickly to pull an all-but-threadbare Louis XIV armchair over to the piano. 'Please,' she said, and nodded at the keyboard. 'Already it sounds better. As if it *wants* to be healed.'

'Find out for me if she had any other visitors last Thursday,' he sang out, the deep baritone of his voice delighting her.

'She'll not be fooled, Inspector. I warned you.'

'Agreed. But please call downstairs to the desk. There is an intercom in each of the wards. Choose the closest.'

'There is no need. She had a violent attack early on that afternoon. It took us ages to calm her down.'

'An attack?'

'The keys,' pleaded Lemoine.

'The keys,' whispered Angèle-Marie.

'Please double-check for me,' sang out the Sûreté.

Il Pleut Bergère – It's Raining Shepherdess – followed and then, though the piano was desperately in need of tuning, St-Cyr thought he'd try *Sur le Pont d'Avignon* only to be reminded of Hermann and the agony of their last investigation and to strike up *Les Beaux Messieurs*.

'He *did* bring me honey,' she said earnestly and then, sharply, 'He wasn't supposed to, Angèle-Marie. I told you not to taste it. I did!'

'Honey . . . ?' asked St-Cyr. Lemoine had left the room.

She indicated he was to search for something and watched intently while he did. Five minutes passed, perhaps a few more. Baffled, he stood before her and the smile she gave was one of absolute delight.

'The curtains,' she whispered and nodded excitedly towards them. 'Flowers. Stones. Undervest and drawers. *Hands*, Angèle-Marie. I warned you. *Cheese!*'

Lying on the floor, and well hidden behind the black-out curtains, was a wooden honey-dipper. 'Bees,' she said. 'You heard the bees, Angèle-Marie. They were in the walls. No they weren't! *Yes they were.* Those were mice, idiot! *Mice don't live in solid stones.* BEES, ANGÈLE-MARIE! BEES . . .'

Ah *Nom de Jésus-Christ*, what was happening to her?

Lemoine tore back into the room. 'Inspector, what the hell did you say to her?'

The woman was on her knees by the bed holding her hands tightly over her ears and crying. The sound of bees was clearly all around her. From every wall, the floor and ceiling, too. Tearing her hair, she began to moan, to rock back and forth and then to shriek, 'DON'T DO IT TO ME! PLEASE DON'T! I'M A GOOD GIRL. I'M NOT A QUEEN . . . A queen,' she sobbed.

Holding her tightly, Lemoine indicated the dipper and demanded to know how she had come by it.

'The brother, apparently.'

'Inspector, that's impossible. He wouldn't have, and in any case, I was certain we had taken that wretched thing from her in the concourse last Thursday. Angèle-Marie, I'm sorry but your visitor must leave immediately. Get out, Inspector. *Out,* damn you!'

'*No! No!* But you want him to go, Angèle? He was going to poison you. Drink . . . I must not drink the liquid. You did! You *did!*'

'What liquid?' snapped the Sûreté. The woman sucked in a breath and glared at him through her tears.

'A bottle of Amaretto. After we'd got her calmed down and thought she was well enough to see her brother, some fool must have momentarily set it near her during visiting hours.'

'And did she drink from this bottle as she claims? Well, did she?'

'The brother caught her doing so and, in a rage, took it away with him.'

Nothing could have been wrong with it then, said St-Cyr to his other self when alone and out in the corridor. Only later could the poison have been added, but de Bonnevies, believing the liqueur was perfectly safe, had thought no more about it and must have tossed off a stiff shot – Dutch courage perhaps – only to then, in panic, blame his wife for having tampered with it. But for this to be so, he reasoned with his other self, the bottle must have been left alone in the study and Madame de Bonnevies must have had a chance to get at it. Honey . . . someone among the crowd of visitors on that afternoon had earlier given Angèle-Marie a taste of honey.

De Bonnevies had gone to the brothel. That evening he had left the outer gate to the apiary unlocked and that to the garden also. He had an address he was to give to the Society, had settled on the names of the four who had violated his sister.

'A woman . . . ,' he said, he and his other self churning things over. 'The visit that evening would be difficult, hence the stiff shot from the bottle.'

The French windows to the study and garden had been locked – madame had had to break the glass to get in, or had she simply lied? To hide what, then? he asked his other self and, after holding

123

a breath, finally answered, 'The identity of the visitor she knew only too well would come calling.

'Frau Uma Schlacht.'

5

The flat at 28 quai d'Orléans had once been the property of a retired antiques dealer, felt Kohler. In the grand salon the floral trim of the panelling exuded that warm, soft glow of gilding that had been applied a good one hundred years ago. Portraits were of counts and countesses who had lived well before the Revolution. But in amongst this feast of ormolu, oil paint and Baccarat, of gilded, silk-covered Louis XIV and XV armchairs, were the bits and pieces of their new owners.

'Madame collects,' quavered the *bonne à tout faire* timidly.

The girl, a brunette of medium height in a neatly pressed uniform, was all of sixteen and still terrified of him. Mariette Durand, he reminded himself, so caught up in things he couldn't yet quite comprehend them. 'Porcelains from the 1920s,' he went on. '*Mein Gott*, cheap figurines of bathing beauties.'

Some naked, most not, they were everywhere, even on the mantelpiece against a gorgeous ormolu clock whose figurine depicted Minerva, the Roman goddess of wisdom. They were between mounted Imari vases. Green, red, or navy-blue bathing suits on some of them, and all poised as if for a plunge, or simply lounging about on bits of coral, on red lobsters, or sunning themselves flat on the sand. Figurines from ten to fifteen centimetres in length. No chips, no cracks that he could see.

'Madame swims,' offered the girl, as if an explanation for such a strange passion was needed. 'Every day she goes to the Lutétia pool.'

One of the sweat-relieving havens of the Occupier. 'Even when it's open to others and not *nur für Deutsche*?'

And only for Germans. '*Oui*. She . . . she says it is good for the figure.'

'And she's conscious of that?'

'Very.'

One had best prise off the shoes – it was that kind of carpet. An exquisite white porcelain, Sèvres damsel with harp *sans* clothes but with open cloak in a stiff breeze, caused him to pause. One arm was uplifted, that breast higher than the other; one foot placed back, the girl proudly dancing into the wind, while at the feet of this little goddess of perfection lay a Russian table whose marquetry would have made Louis's Gabrielle green with envy. Yet here, too, there was a clutter of the flea-market gleanings of Frau Schlacht.

'They . . . they help her to think of home,' offered the girl.

'And Herr Schlacht – are they here to help him think of her?'

The girl sucked in a breath and fought for the correct words. 'She . . . she hopes so. During the early twenties she was a bathing beauty. Her father ran a concession at Wannsee, one of the pleasure lakes and suburbs to the north of Berlin. *Bier, Wurst und Schnitzel,* with ices and soda drinks. That is where Herr Schlacht first met her.'

'A romance made of all the good things, eh?'

The detective moved on through the flat. He wished, perhaps, that others he knew could also see it. Quite obviously the owner had left Paris during the exodus of June 1940 and hadn't returned, thereby forfeiting all right to the flat and its contents. Those, too, of his safety deposit boxes and bank accounts.

There were music boxes – girlhood things Frau Schlacht must have once admired and now found possible to buy in quantity, thought Kohler. There was even a mechanical bank – man and his best friend, which when fed a sou, danced around to a scratchy tune. 'Nothing but the best,' he snorted.

'Every Saturday she visits Saint-Ouen to spend the morning among the stalls. They remind her of home, I think. I . . . I have to accompany her because of the language, you understand. Madame can't speak a word of French.'

Or won't, like so many of the Occupier. 'And Switzerland – does she take you there when she visits it for her husband?' It was just a shot in the dark. Well, not really, but what the hell, one never knew . . .

'Four times a year. At . . . at every quarter. Herr Schlacht has relatives who are old and . . . and in need of comfort.'

Once again, a man with a big family. 'And are her suitcases heavier when you leave or when you arrive?'

She would duck her eyes and say it modestly, thought Mariette. 'Heavier when we arrive. Always it is this way.'

'And how many banks does she visit for that husband of hers?'

Madame would kill her if she knew about her telling him, but he was of the Gestapo and had shown her his badge. 'Three. One in Zurich, another in Bern, and the last in Lausanne. It . . . it is best that way, is it not?'

This kid wasn't dumb and had figured it all out, had damned well known it was illegal for any citizen of the Reich to send or hold money in a foreign bank, yet they all did it, those who could.

In the master bedroom a flowery dust of icing sugar fell from the Turkish delight the detective sampled. Herr Kohler noticed this dust as he noticed everything, and even as he nodded and said, '*Pas mal, pas mal* – not bad – she knew he was thinking she was counting the *bonbons* because Madame would most certainly do so later.

'I'll leave her a little note,' he said, eating another.

'Please don't. You . . . you mustn't. Just let her blame me as she often does when she loses count. I . . . I will eventually be forgiven.'

'What does she pay you?'

'Fifty a week.'

Two hundred francs a month! And yet . . . and yet such maids, even those who had taken the trouble to learn a little *deutsch* – and this one knew far more than that – were dirt cheap and easy to come by. The French bourgeoisie had seen to that. And one did get fed, clothed and have a room, even though it was usually nothing but a filthy garret and as cold as Siberia in winter. But this one must have been treated far better and, under Frau Schlacht's firm hand, no doubt, had learned to bathe and groom herself every day or else.

'Saturday afternoons, after the flea market, I am allowed to visit my family and to . . . to take them a few little things that are no longer needed here.'

A stale loaf of bread, a half-litre of wine – the dregs of a dead soldier? wondered Kohler. A suspect egg, a few withered carrots, even the icing sugar that would soon be left in the bottom of this box.

The detective set the *bonbons* on the bedside table among the clutter of figurines. He touched the Art Deco alarm clock Madame had found last Saturday. He sat down on the edge of her bed and ran a hand over the antique lace of its spread, but did not say *pas mal* this time, for he was now concentrating on the photograph of Madame's son whose frame was draped in black.

'A sergeant and so young,' said Mariette, surprised by the steadiness of her voice, for the room had grown quiet and the clock, it must have stopped. Ah no!

'A midshipman on a U-boat, a *Fähnrich zur See in Unterseebooten*,' muttered the detective, and there was to this giant with the terrible scar the sadness of a father who had, perhaps, lost a son himself. The postcard he picked up had the photograph of men firing the bow cannon of a submarine, and beneath this, the words of a song. '*Kameraden auf See*,' he snorted sadly. 'That's an eighty-eight millimetre gun, probably the most versatile thing to have come out of this lousy war so far. Is this the medal she kisses before bed? It's the boy's *Kriegsabzeichen*. Every man aboard a U-boat gets one after two sorties. Two is good and damned lucky. Three are possible. Four is . . . Well, you must know all about that.'

He ran a forefinger over the eagle and swastika above the badge's U-boat, then indicated the oval wreath of oak leaves around it. 'When did his boat go down?' he asked.

'In December. The fifteenth. A Tuesday.'

And still fresh in Frau Schlacht's mind.

'Madame lost her brother in the Great War. She . . .'

'Hates you French.'

'But myself not so much, I think.'

This kid had really learned her lessons.

There were photos on the wall next to a landscape of Renoir's: black, cheaply-framed snapshots of the three Schlacht daughters. The youngest was a fresh-faced Luftwaffe Signals Auxiliary; the middle one, a Red Cross nurse, but taken in the summer of 1941 during the blitzkrieg in the east and not among the shattered, snow-covered ruins of Stalingrad. The eldest, a big, round-faced replica of Herr Schlacht, wore the grin, the uptilted goggles and dungarees of a scrap-metal cutter with torch in the yards along the Luisenstädter Kanal.

The detective eased the bedside table drawer open and ran his pale blue eyes over the contents. He touched the neckerchief Madame's son had worn on parade as a *Hitlerjugend* and noted that it was tightly crumpled and damp.

'She still cries,' said Mariette softly. 'A mother must, is that not so, monsieur?'

The boy's pocketknife – black-handled and with an oval portrait of the German Führer and stainless steel eagle and swastika – was there, too, and as the detective fingered it, she heard herself saying, 'Klaus forgot to take it with him when he last visited Paris in November. Madame . . . Madame feels his leaving it behind was an ill omen for which she blames herself for not having sent it on to him by special courier. But you see, she did not know where to send it.'

'Lorient, probably. It's on the Breton Coast. My partner and I were there not so long ago. A dollmaker. The Kapitän zur See Kaestner.'

'But . . . but could it have been the same boat and now you've come here, too?' she blurted, revealing at once that she, herself, might quite possibly be superstitious.

The detective looked up at her and shrugged, but there was not the emptiness that had just been in his gaze. Now there was a warmth, the loss of loved ones, the feeling, yes, that all were a part of this war and that he had had enough of it.

Unlike Madame, he spoke French and well, and this was a curious thing, but had it made her tongue loose? wondered Mariette and hazarded, for it was not her place to demand, 'Have you seen enough, monsieur?'

'I'll leave in a minute. Don't worry. Just don't tell her I was here, eh? and remember your concierge, Madame Jouvand, is also on board and won't say a thing.'

He examined the Louis Vuitton *trousse de toilette* Madame had bought – an extravagance she had lamented but had not denied herself. He examined her jewellery, such as it was.

'Marcasite,' he said, fingering a bracelet. 'Onyx and carnelian – most of these are from what was once Isaac Kahn's factory in Pforzheim. *Mein Gott,* does she not realize he was Jewish? I may have to report it. You remember I said so, eh?' And *grâce à Dieu* for that little bit of ammunition!

There were plastic bracelets and bangles, chrome neckchains – the gaudy, cheap and plain, when Madame could have had the very best.

There were sturdy black leather shoes fit for walking all day, lisle stockings, no silk ones, not her, thought Kohler – silk was for parachutes. There were stiff, prewar woollen skirts and jackets, a small pin on the lapel of one. 'The Honour Cross of the German Mother,' he said. 'A bronze . . .'

A Tyrolean hat *à la* Fräulein Braun caught his eye and he asked, 'Like Eva, does your mistress spend her time waiting for the light of her life to come home?'

'He's never here. Well, not never. Only sometimes.'

'In and out, eh?'

'She hopes he will stay and invariably begs him to, but he's . . . he's very busy.'

'So, okay, tell me where you went last Thursday?'

The detective had not said why he had come to the flat. 'She . . . she went out at about two in the afternoon. That . . . that is all I know.'

A cautious answer. 'Did she take anything with her?'

'I . . . I do not think so, monsieur. Just her handbag. The big one.'

'You can do better than that.'

The emptiness had come back into his eyes. He patted the bedspread and indicated she had better sit down beside him. 'It helps,' he said tonelessly. Would he now beat her, force her to answer – torture her? wondered Mariette and felt tears rushing into her eyes.

'Look, I won't hurt you,' he said. 'My partner and I don't do that sort of thing. I just have to know.'

'She . . . she went out, that's all. She did not say where to, nor when I had got myself ready, did she want me to accompany her. Always she does, but . . . but not that time.'

'And when she came back?'

A hesitation had entered the detective's voice. 'She said, "There, it's done."'

'What was done?'

Hurriedly the girl dried her eyes. 'I . . . I really don't know. Something she had to do. Something important, I think.'

In defeat, the girl's shoulders drooped, and she folded her hands in her lap.

'Now tell me about the beekeeper. Give me all you can about his visits. My partner will be sure to ask and gets bitchy if I forget something. You've no idea, Mariette. A Sûreté. A Chief Inspector, no less, but *impossible! Merde*, you should hear him sometimes!'

'And where is this "partner" of yours at the moment?' she asked with wisdom well beyond her tender years.

'The Salpêtrière.'

'Ah!' She tossed her head and nodded. 'The sister. A tragedy Madame is only too aware of, since Monsieur de Bonnevies always speaks of Angèle-Marie at length when questioned by her.'

Startled, Kohler hazarded, 'And she never fails to ask him?'

'Never. Not for some time now.'

'Is it because of something Madame de Bonnevies did? Well, is it?'

Merde, why had he had to ask, how had he known?

Hastily the girl crossed herself.

'May God forgive me, yes. *Yes*, it is because she suspects her husband is having *une affaire de coeur* with the woman. It's crazy. I tell her this. I plead with her but . . . but Madame is of her own mind, monsieur. Of her own mind!'

The detective let a sigh escape. 'And Herr Schlacht does mess about with the ladies, doesn't he?'

'A lot, but not with me. I swear it. She . . . she put a stop to that before it ever got started. I screamed and she . . . she heard me.'

There was more to this, there just had to be.

'She badgered Monsieur de Bonnevies until finally he agreed that, yes, his wife was probably seeing Herr Schlacht,' said the girl.

'And not just for an isolated lunch at Maxim's?'

'Other places. He . . . he did not know where.'

'A candle factory?'

The girl bit a knuckle and tried to stop herself from crying. 'The Hôtel Titania, on the boulevard Ornano.'

A *maison de passe*, a seedy hotel where prostitutes, licensed or otherwise, took their 'lovers'.

'I know this because I . . . I have followed Madame de Bonnevies there for Madame.'

The life had gone right out of the kid but he'd have to ask it. 'Did you see Schlacht go into that hotel?'

'He . . . he came in his car.'

She'd have to be told. 'Then watch yourself. If you feel you have to bolt and run, go at once to 12 rue Suger, in Saint-Germain-des-Près, and ask for Oona or Giselle. They'll know what to do and will probably hide you in the house of Madame Chabot, around the corner. Failing that, go to the Club Mirage on the rue Delambre in Montparnasse, but use the courtyard entrance and be careful, since the Gestapo's Watchers may still be taking an interest in the place. Ask for Gabrielle, and tell those Corsican brothers behind the bar that Hermann says it's urgent and they're to keep you out of sight or else.'

Shiny brass cowbells hung from dark ceiling timbers and made little sounds when vibrated by the din as Kohler squeezed himself into the Brasserie Buerehiesel. Loud laughter, boisterous, good-natured banter and argument competed with orders for meals, for beer and wine. Crockery clacked, copper pots were banged – there were no signs on the rows of bottles behind the bar saying *Nur Attrapen*, only for decoration. No coloured water. Not in this establishment.

Schiefala, smoked pork shoulder, served with hot potato salad; *Baeckaeoffe*, a long-simmered stew of lamb, pork and veal with onions and potatoes; and *choucroute*, sauerkraut with several types of ham and sausage – the fabulous golden-crusted *tarte à l'oignon* also – were constantly on the move. One hustling waiter had seven heaped dinners perched in a row on an arm and three in his right hand. How the hell did he do it?

'Monsieur, your coat, please, and weapon. You do have a weapon?'

The coat-check girl was cute but firm. There were off-duty Felgendarmen on the door and hired especially to bring ease, so everything was okay in that department, but what the girl really meant was the SS ceremonial daggers so many of them would wear. They simply got in the way when sitting cheek to cheek in such long rows. 'No weapon. Not tonight.'

'Then please find yourself a seat if you can.'

'*Danke.*'

Neighbourhood pub and feedbag, the waiters, cook's helpers and cook-owner had all been Alsatian fifth columnists prior to the blitzkrieg of 1940 and were now in their element. Meteor Pils, straight from Hochfelden, was on tap; Ackerland too – both the light and the brown. 'Mortimer . . . have you Mortimer?' he shouted at the balding barkeep who had little time and simply said in *deutsch*, 'Ah, *ein Kenner*,' a connoisseur, and filled a large, clear-glass stein with the dark, strong mother of beers.

'I needed this,' said Kohler, squeezing sideways to better look the place over.

A slab of Münster cheese, ripe and seasoned with caraway, passed by – well, actually, there were six slabs of it. There were signs for Schutzenberger beer on the walls, signs for sabots made by a François Schneider, portrait pipes carved by an Adolf Lefèbvre, signs for the red Vorlauf from Marlenheim that surpassed most French burgundies.

There were life-sized tin sculptures of storks wading in ponds or nesting on the roofs of half-timbered bits of home. There was even a gaudy poster of the Baron von Münchhausen in his hot-air balloon; others, too, of ruined castles – Hohenburg, Löwenstein and, yes, Fleckenstein which even Louis XIV couldn't quite destroy in 1680.

There were alpine scenes and alphorns, one of which some idiot had taken to blowing until silenced.

There were the business suits of the collaborators, of the butter-eggs-and-cheese boys with their *petites amies* and those of the Occupier. All down the long tunnel of two sets of tables, and under lamps whose light fought with the haze of tobacco smoke and the heady aroma, there were the uniforms, most with tunic buttons undone.

And there, sitting jammed into a far corner beneath the guild sign of a wrought-iron hunting hawk, and staring out over glass and bottle of *eau de vie*, was Frau Schlacht. The new permanent wave was perfect for the short, thick blonde hair which was parted on the left, the expression empty though, the lips tightly pursed as if deep in thought.

A cigarette, untouched for some time, wasted its life in a saucer before her. In a place of conviviality she sought solitude.

A chalkboard gave the menu. Five hundred francs for the *prix fixe* of *choucroute*; a thousand for the roast quail stuffed with goat's cheese and served with a creamy sauce of preserved white grapes. Other items were in between, and for a bottle of the Pinot Blanc: four hundred francs; for that of the Reisling, six hundred francs; the spicy Gewürztraminer requiring three hundred more.

When what looked to be a seat became free a few places from her, he squeezed himself down the long tunnel between the tables and gave a nod the woman completely ignored.

The *eau de vie de framboise* she downed required four kilos of raspberries per bottle of the brandy and was priced accordingly at four thousand francs, yet she sipped it constantly until her *pâté de foie gras* came *aux truffes sous la cendre*, wrapped in chopped truffles and baked under the ashes, and served with a dicing of beef jelly whose colour was that of old amber.

Her eyes were very blue, the forehead clear and smooth and broad, the lips good, the chin and nose and all the rest really something.

Kohler ordered another beer and the *Baeckaeoffe*. Louis would just have to wait it out at the Salpêtrière. This spider in her little corner was simply too important to leave.

When the seat directly opposite her became vacant, he moved in, but there was no surprise from her, no smile of anticipation or welcome. She simply stared at and through him, then went stolidly on with her pâté until every last bit of it was gone and the bottle half-empty.

Then she ordered two servings of the grated potato pancakes with toasted goat's cheese, and the chicken in mushroom sauce.

'It is good,' she said. 'I had the same last night and will do so again.'

A Berliner through and through, but *Jésus, merde alors* what a conversationalist! 'Do you live nearby?' he asked. The racket around them intruded.

'Not far,' she said, and for a time that was all.

He'd take to studying her now, she felt, this giant of a Bavarian with the terrible duelling scar, the bullet graze across the brow, and the shrapnel nicks from that other war. He would want to get fresh with her, but would wait a little – he had that look about him. Great ease with loose and stupid girls, the younger the better, she told herself and said silently, Men! They are all the same.

'I have three daughters,' she announced straight out of the blue, but offered nothing further until he said, 'I had two boys. Both were killed at Stalingrad.'

Moisture filled her eyes making them clearer, brighter, but causing him to despise himself for using the boys to crack her armour.

'I have lost a son, too,' she said and took a deep draught and then another of the *eau de vie.* 'He left his pocketknife with me and I did not send it on to him.'

Verdammt! she'd be bawling her eyes out if he didn't do something. 'Waiter . . . Another beer, please!' he shouted. 'And for you, Frau . . . ?'

'Schlacht. Uma. A bottle of the Riesling, I think. Yes, that will suit.'

They would settle down now, this *Scheisse,* this *Schweinebulle* and herself, and maybe that crap about his sons was true, and maybe it wasn't. We will eat and I will let him strip me naked with those cop's eyes of his, she told herself. He will get nowhere but I will let him try just for the fun of it.

Oskar . . . had Oskar finally done something the Gestapo did not like? she wondered. Oskar was always up to things. But this one couldn't have come because of him. He was just hungry for a woman, like all the others.

'*Guten Appetit,* Herr . . . ?'

'Kohler. Hermann. From Wasserburg, the one that's on the Ihn.'

Ja, mein Herr, and you are lonely, aren't you? she said silently to herself and nodded inwardly. A veteran from the Great War, he had big, capable hands whose thumbs, first and second fingers were deeply stained by nicotine.

A smoker, a drinker, and a fucker. She would show him and his kind. She would ask for a steak knife when her dinner came. Yes . . . yes that would be best, and she would give him a lesson he would not forget.

Louis . . . Louis wasn't here to back him up, thought Kohler desperately. Louis must still be with the beekeeper's sister. But what the hell is it with this one, *mon vieux*? he bleated silently. She *can't* know why I'm here, yet is as uptight as a queen bee with her hot little stinger in my balls.

Line 5, the place d'Italie-porte Pantin métro was a bitch, the evening rush horrendous and lengthy as usual.

Jostled, shoved – crushed – St-Cyr cursed aloud to none and all in particular, 'Hermann, you *salaud*! Where the hell have you gone with my car?'

No one bothered to pay any attention to his frustration. No one cared. '*JÉSUS, MERDE ALORS,* MONSIEUR, THERE IS ROOM FOR NO MORE!' he shouted.

'*FOUTEZ-MOI LA PAIX, BÂTARD.* I'LL SHOW YOU!'

'*SÛRETÉ! SÛRETÉ!*'

The whistle fell from his hand. The whistle was lost. He was jabbed in the small of the back, was jammed against two *Blitzmädels* who managed to squeeze sideways to fit him in and reeked of the cheap, foul colognes that were now so common.

Sweat, farts, colds, coughs, sneezes, the sour stench of thawing, wet overcoats and clothing that hadn't been washed since the Defeat, roared in at him!

'A patriot,' he muttered under his breath. 'I am still of such a mind.' *Mon Dieu*, the heat of so many bodies . . .

The train rattled on. There were so few seats, all thought of getting one simply did not exist. A Wehrmacht gas-mask canister dug into his groin, a jackboot trod harder on his left foot as the soldier turned at his objection of, 'Monsieur . . .'

The burly Feldwebel grinned hugely and began to chat up the girls from home. St-Cyr hung on but the acid could not be stopped. 'The Wehrmacht ride free, *mon Général*,' he said in French, 'while the rest of us have to pay!'

'*Salut, mon brave!*' sang out a listener somewhere. Was it the one who had told him to bugger off? he wondered.

Another began to whistle Beethoven's Fifth.

Monsieur Churchill's stubborn V was soon on several lips until the protest died through the gaze, perhaps, of a Gestapo. French or of the Occupier, the difference would not matter.

Packed in like sardines – unable to even look down at the floor to search for a whistle that Stores would accuse him of carelessly losing, he tried to hold on, tried to avoid eye contact – it was impossible! Smelt the garlic breaths of a thousand, that of boiled onions, too, for few had grease or oil to fry them in, *tried* to think. I *must*! he said.

Angèle-Marie de Bonnevies had seldom received any visitors other than her brother. The father hadn't even come to see his little girl, had renounced her, and the mother had had to obey him.

Locked up, confined to a common ward, she had regressed constantly, but after the Great War, and the death of the father, the beekeeper had returned and had done what he could. A room – it had taken him years to convince the doctors such would help. And even though still deeply troubled, she had improved – Lemoine had been convinced of this. 'Monsieur de Bonnevies had asked for weekend passes for her, Inspector. First to take her out simply for an afternoon, then . . . then, by degrees, to get her used to living at home once more. He was determined she could do it. Never have I seen a man so convinced.'

'And afraid of what the Occupier might well do to your patients?'

'Yes.'

But had Madame de Bonnevies decided to put a stop to things? After all, it was her money they were living on and she had been forced to look after the mother. Had the beekeeper's death then really little or nothing to do with Frau Schlacht? If so, then why the fear of our discovering that one name among all others in the husband's little book, particularly if the poison had really been meant for herself?

De Bonnevies had never allowed Danielle to visit her aunt. 'Madame, of course, has never visited,' Lemoine had said. 'Nor has her son – I understand it was not his child and therefore of no relation.'

'And Father Michel, their parish priest?' he had asked.

'Years ago, but not since Monsieur de Bonnevies returned from the war. The two of them must have come to some agreement.'

'Why?' he had demanded.

Lemoine had shrugged and said, 'The priest was interfering in the girl's recovery. Hearing the confessions of the deranged, troubling her unnecessarily. That sort of thing. Always after one of the good father's visits, Angèle-Marie would be silent for hours and would insist on standing in a corner, facing the wall.'

'No tears?'

'None. Just voices, but those of the inner mind and never spoken or cried out. We came to dread these visits and I think, in some ways, so did she.'

The train shot into the Saint-Marcel Station. At once there was extreme pressure from those who wanted to get off or on. Dislodged, St-Cyr was shoved brutally out on to the platform, was caught, dragged, heard the doors shutting . . . shutting, and finally managed to get back in.

'I've received a letter from home, Freda,' said one of the *Blitzmädels* to the other in *deutsch*. 'All nonessential businesses have been ordered to close. Every male from the age of sixteen to sixty-five has to report for duty. All are being mobilized.'

The Reich had finally done it. The situation in the east must be far more serious even than the defeat at Stalingrad indicated.

'*Scham Dich, Schwatzer!*' said the shorter, plumper *Blitzmädchen* sharply. Shame on you, bigmouth. 'The enemy is listening – silence is your duty!'

The quote had come from a popular poster which showed a duck in coveralls quacking loudly. The temptation was more than he could resist, but perhaps caution had best prevail. '*Mein Partner* says it's even rumoured they are watering the beer at the

Adlon,' he said pleasantly enough in German. One of Berlin's finest hotels.

'What can't kill me, strengthens me,' retorted the Feldwebel with a broad grin. Another popular saying, but enough said by all concerned for now!

The train began to cross the first bridge – one could feel the change. Elevated – out in the open air; in darkness, too, it had once been possible to see almost the whole of the Salpêtrière even at night, but now the city was plunged into darkness, now even the dim lightbulbs of the carriage didn't glow through the ether of their times.

From two million passengers a day in 1940, the métro's ticket sales had leapt to four million. And we live as a nation of moles when not on our bicycles or walking, said St-Cyr to himself, but had Rudi Sturmbacher been right? Had the enemy some monstrous new weapon that would rain flying bombs on England?

On our hope, our strength, as is America.

Rudi could do with one of those posters. He'd have to suggest it to Hermann who would immediately insist on it.

We are two *originals* ourselves, he said, but in this, though there has been the greatest of good fortune, there can only be danger. War, like small-town and village neighbourhoods the world over, frowned heavily on all but the ordinary.

Once through the Gare d'Austerlitz, the train headed out over the Seine and he could feel this, too, and knew there had formerly been splendid views of the river, the Île de la Cité and the Notre Dame.

When the train began to dive underground, he decided he'd had enough of it. 'The morgue,' he said in *deutsch*. 'I've a murder investigation to see to and must get off.'

The Feldwebel shoved several out of the way and stooped – yes, actually stooped – to retrieve the whistle. 'This is yours, I believe,' he said and grinned hugely again. 'It was under my jackboot. So sorry.'

And had been flattened just like a certain birdcage!

The warmth, the sounds of the restaurant were all around them but the former bathing beauty still had a gaze that was even emptier than his own and he was getting nowhere, felt Kohler uncomfortably. *Mein Gott*, what was running through that mind of hers?

'You do not eat,' she said, jabbing with her fork to indicate his stew. 'It is not good to let it get cold.'

Steadily marshalling food and drink, she had downed potato pancakes and chicken with cream sauce and mushrooms as if there was no tomorrow and to hell with keeping one's figure. The bottle of Riesling had all but been sunk. The steak knife she had requested had yet to be touched but was unfortunately far too close to hand.

From time to time one of her shoes would brush against his trouser leg under the table, as if daring him to make a pass at her. He'd have to use the son again. 'Lorient,' he lied. 'I was just thinking . . . Well, one of the boys we had to question at the submarine base there looked a lot like you, but . . . *Ach*! It can't be possible.'

Caught off guard, she winced and set her fork down. 'What boy?'

'A *Fähnrich zur See*. There was some trouble – not with its crew or the boy, so don't let it worry you. My partner and I had to visit the base to ask a few questions. A local thing. Nothing else. You know how the French are. They kill each other in the most diabolical ways and then try to blame it on their friends from the Reich, when we've only come to put a little order into their lives.'

Louis would have shuddered at that. 'The sergeant would have been about nineteen, Frau Schlacht. A quite handsome young man. Promoted often. Eager to do his duty for Führer and fatherland and proud of it, too.'

'Klaus . . . was it my Klaus?' she stammered. 'I . . . I have a photo. Yes . . . yes, it is here in my purse. A moment, *Herr Inspektor*.' Could he really have spoken to Klaus? wondered Frau Schlacht. Was it possible?

Lorient . . . so Klaus's submarine had been based there.

Herr Inspektor, thought Kohler. So she'd figured that one out. Then it would be best to be firm. 'An *Atlantikboot* Type 1XB. U-297, but that's confidential.'

'Yes . . . yes, of course.'

'*Gut.* There are spies everywhere these days.'

The Inspector took the snapshot from her fingers, hesitating long enough to look at her with compassion and no longer such emptiness. 'He . . . he was the best of boys,' she said earnestly. 'A *Kapitän* . . . I could see him with his own command one day.'

Not in the Freikorps Doenitz, the U-boat Service. Not likely! 'That's him, Frau Schlacht. I never forget a face. Men like myself are trained to remember and I've had years at it.'

Years . . . 'U-297 . . . And this boat was sunk?' she asked and heard him say, 'Last December, the fifteenth. A Tuesday.'

Then it was true. *True!*

Pale and badly shaken, the woman swallowed hard, touching the face in the photograph, forcing herself not to kiss it and cry, but to simply put the thing away for later.

And I'm a cruel bastard, said Kohler to himself, but as the Maréchal Pétain is so fond of saying these days, *La cause en vaut les moyens.* The cause justifies the means.

'Frau Schlacht, you'll forgive me, but we've not met by accident. I need to ask you a few questions. Nothing difficult. They're just routine.'

'Questions . . . ?'

The emptiness of her gaze returned, the mask perhaps that of the rejected forty-four-year-old housewife whose husband was fucking someone else and who had come to hate all men as a result.

'*Bitte, mein guter Inspektor*, ask.'

The shrug she gave was that of one who had known all along he was a cop. 'Let's begin, then, with last Thursday.'

'Not until I know the reason why.'

'You'll not have heard yet, but the beekeeper who used to visit you was murdered.'

'On Thursday?' she asked without a hint of surprise or other emotion.

'That evening.'

'And is it that you wish to know where I was?'

This thing was going to go round and round unless he was careful. 'The afternoon, I think. Let's begin then.'

'The Lutétia Pool. I go there regularly.'

She was lying, but must he dig a deeper hole for himself and Louis? 'Can anyone corroborate this?'

He still hadn't begun to eat. 'Any number of people. The Standartenführer Scheller; his sister, Hildegard also. Both instruct me.'

The SS and a colonel, no less!

She'd let him have it now, thought Frau Schlacht. 'The one who collects the tickets, the one who tends the lock-up. My little maid, too. She will swear to it, since she was with me. I've taught her to swim and now am teaching her to do it much better.'

'Then that's settled. No problem,' he lied. 'Now tell me what you can about de Bonnevies and his visits.'

'His treatments. But . . . but how is it that you knew he came to see me?'

This one had been tough since birth! 'Your name, and others, were in a register he kept. Treatments Mondays at four p.m. Six hundred grams of pollen. Apple or rose, if possible. Two litres of mead a month. Honey in two . . .'

'*Ja, ja.* For the facial masks and to soothe the throat when taken with glycerine and warm lemon juice. So how, please, did you know enough to find me here?'

It would have to be convincing. He couldn't let her go after Madame Jouvand and Mariette. 'Kripo, Section Five, Frau Schlacht. We've files on everyone. The Reichsführer Himmler insists on it.'

'Files on my Oskar?' she hazarded and for a moment found she could no longer look at him, but sought solace in the chequered, rough linen beneath the steak knife.

'My partner and I believe he's been making candles and selling them on the black market. That's contrary to Article sixty-seven, subsection eighty-two. Look, he could well have told you nothing – we understand this. Some men are like that with their wives, but . . .'

'But he is under suspicion for making *candles?*'

'Yes.'

Switzerland. They must want more about the trips she took! 'I

142

know nothing of these candles. My Oskar is a very private man who has always believed emphatically that his business dealings were not for the tender ears of his wife. And as for this black market of which you speak, does such a thing really exist?'

Jésus, merde alors, Louis should have heard her! 'I'm really more concerned with getting some background on the victim, Frau Schlacht. What sort of "treatments"?'

'Are we now to forget the matter of the candles?'

Verdammt! 'Yes.'

'Then I must tell you that the knuckles of my left hand have been troubling me for some time. A little arthritis. A girl does not like to admit to such things, but . . .'

Herr Kohler tried to grin. 'My grandmother had the same,' he said earnestly. 'Two stings a week and do you know, it worked like a charm. After three months, just three, she could go back to weaving skeps like she once had. The best in our region.'

'Skeps?'

'Beehives.'

'Hot waxing is good, too, and pollen. I take a spoonful a day, with milk.'

And never mind the scarcity of the latter or that the kids in Paris hardly ever saw a drop! 'Royal jelly . . . have you tried that?'

He was all business now, this *Detektiv* from the Kripo. A little black notebook was flipped open; he'd a pencil in hand.

'It's said to improve the body's resistance to colds and other infections,' she acknowledged. 'I, myself, take it once a month.'

'It's collected by killing queen larvae and robbing the contents of their cells with a little spoon.'

If she thought anything of this she didn't let on.

'Some say it prevents ageing, but Herr de Bonnevies had no patience with such thoughts. I shall miss him. He was good, for a Frenchman. Very professional.'

'And discreet but . . .' It would be best to shrug and lie again. 'But do you know, in spite of this, he wrote down a lot in that little book of his.'

'Such as?' she asked, and finding her purse, decided to skip the dessert and coffee.

'Such as, that you've told me almost nothing when I need to

know everything if I'm to make life easy for you and that husband of yours.'

There, he'd said it, thought Kohler, and God help Louis and him now.

'Then you had best give me a lift home and we can discuss things in private. You do have a car, don't you?'

Like an idiot, he'd left it in front of her building and now she'd know for sure he had talked to her concierge and maid. Now the steak knife was missing from the table!

'The car's just around the corner,' Uma heard him say, and there was a coldness to his voice she well understood.

'Then I will wait here until you bring it round, yes? That way I will not get snow on my shoes.'

And not see where the car's parked, thought Kohler grimly, since she'd already figured that out. She'd grill the two, was as swift as a fox and would make damned sure of it!

With the falling snow there was a little more light, a little less darkness, and this light was suffused and it magnified the hush of the city.

St-Cyr stood a moment in the centre of the place Mazas. Above the entrance to the morgue, a faint, blue-painted electric bulb glowed forlornly, but clear against the eastern sky, the dome of the Gare de Lyon raised its dark silhouette, reminding him of the restaurant and of the years gone by. The years . . . but there was no time to dwell on them.

Had de Bonnevies gone to the restaurant-cum-warehouse at the Gare de Lyon and discovered the squashed honeycomb and mangled bees from Peyrane? Had he then informed the Kommandant von Gross-Paris of what was happening?

Then why, having found a sympathetic ear, had he taken the suicidal step of planning to give an address that could only have raised the hackles of Old Shatter Hand and the rest of the Oberkommando der Wehrmacht, to say nothing of der Führer and all others of the Occupier? Their friends as well.

And who had told von Schaumburg of the Russian beehives in Shed fourteen at the Gare de l'Est.

Irritated by the constant need for haste, he stubbornly turned

144

his back on the morgue and began to walk downriver towards the quai Henry IV. Suddenly he had to hear the river gurgling softly, had to know that it was still there and that the city . . . this city he loved so much, would survive the war, this terrible war.

Hermann must have been delayed – why else would he not have returned to the Salpêtrière? They'd not eaten yet since Chez Rudi's, hadn't even had an evening's decent apéritif or one of the frightful coloured waters that were so common and made with ersatz flavouring and saccharin.

Frau Schlacht – had the woman proved difficult? he wondered and, suddenly needing the comfort of the river, hurried his steps.

In 1697 the quai Henry IV had been the south bank of the Île Louviers, a small island. In 1790, the Ville de Paris had acquired ownership. In 1806 there had been a market for firewood on the island, but long before this duels had been fought here at dawn. In 1843 the channel between the island and the Right Bank had been filled in to make the quai. The Canal St Martin began here, too. And, yes, the city had its history, every place its past, its intrigue, its matters of state.

'Monsieur, I will love you for ever tonight.'

'I will spend a moment with you, the half or the hour,' said another.

'Or all of us could go somewhere warm with you, *n'est-ce pas?*' said yet another. 'And you . . . you could have the pleasure of the three of us, but for the price of one.'

Kids . . . they were just school kids! Fourteen, if that! 'Go home. You don't, and I'll have you arrested!'

They said nothing. They simply strolled away, arm in arm, and he could see them clearly enough in their thin coats, no kerchiefs or hats tonight. No stockings either, probably, for stockings could not be had by most and beige paint was used instead.

'I was desperate,' cried out one from the safety of distance. 'I begged.'

'I needed to be warm,' shrilled another.

'*Grigou!*' Cheapskate! '*Trou de cul!*' Asshole! 'I hope when we next meet you are stretched out in that place on a slab!'

'Gripped by your lover, eh? Another bum-fucker like yourself!'

'*Pédé! Salut*, my fine monsieur. We're going to find a *flic* and tell him you're one of those. He'll fix you. He'll run you in and beat the shit out of you!'

Merde, the young these days. No parental guidance, no soap either, with which to wash out their mouths! Prostitution was now such a problem, bilingual licences had even been issued to more than six thousand of those who regularly plied the streets but did not work in any of the one hundred and forty legalized brothels. At least this way they were forced into regular medical checkups. But syphilis was still rampant, gonorrhoea a plague, illegitimate births too many, though seldom spoken of until that day of retribution came as surely it would, although sadly for them.

They'd have their heads shaved, these 'submissive girls', so, too, the 'honest' women who had found another, or others, among the Occupier while their husbands languished behind barbed wire or lay beneath the clay.

The morgue was dimly lit. 'St-Cyr, Sûreté, to view the corpse of Alexandre de Bonnevies of the Impasse de champ de parc de Charonne.'

'They said you'd come.'

It would be best to simply raise the eyebrows.

'Monsieur le préfet, and the sous-préfet of the quartier Charonne,' acknowledged the attendant.

'Did they ask for Dr Tremblay, or tell you to wait and let me do the asking?'

'Dr Arnaud has already performed the autopsy. The heart, the lungs, the liver, spleen and all the rest, including the stomach and its contents.'

'Arnaud is a fool and careless, and is aware that I am fully cognizant of his failings. I want Tremblay. They know it and you will now get him here immediately!'

'Tremblay. It shall be as you wish. I can only try.'

'But first, *mon ami*, you will roll out the corpse and put it in a quiet place. I want no noise, no ears but those of the dead and my own, so please don't get any smart-assed ideas, and forget all about what the préfet told you to do.'

This one 'talked' to the dead. 'Préfet Talbotte will be disappointed.'

'Let him be. If he's happy, there will only be trouble for others. Myself, yourself, who knows? So it is always best not to hear. Then . . . why then you can claim you know nothing and I will be certain you do and not come after you.'

The sheet drawn fully back, St-Cyr let his gaze move slowly over the victim. If anything, the skin's pale blackberry hue had increased. There was still rigor, still the smell of bitter almonds.

De Bonnevies had been wounded three times in the Great War – shrapnel or machine-gun fire had torn a deep gouge across the left thigh. The bullet from a Mauser rifle, a sniper, perhaps, had hit him just below the right shoulder. It would have lifted him off his feet and thrown him back.

Barbed wire and metal splinters had ripped their way across and into his chest, the wire probably whipping about as a result of exploding shells and de Bonnevies lucky not to have lost half his face and sight. Otherwise the corpse was what one would have expected of a fifty-eight-year-old who was tall, of medium build.

Drawing the sheet back up to the chest, he said apologetically, 'It can't be pleasant for you to lie here like this, but there are things we have to discuss and it is best I get to know you as well as I can.'

According to the wife, death had occurred between 8:30 and 10 p.m. Thursday, 28 January. It was now nearly 8 p.m. Saturday.

'You were a man who loved his little sister, monsieur. You had made a tragic request of her in the summer of 1912, for which you have suffered ever since and now . . . why now, for all we yet know, this same request, and your desire to settle accounts at any price, may well have led to your death.

'Madame de Bonnevies would certainly not have appreciated the news of Angèle-Marie's anticipated visits and your plans to have her again living in the house. But did you tell her of them?'

He would pause to walk back and forth a little, gesturing now and then, thought St-Cyr. 'Knowing what we do so far of your relationship with your wife, monsieur, I have to doubt you confided in her. But if aware of the planned visits, and in despair, could she really have tried to poison you in the way that you so obviously thought? Would she have known enough about your beekeeping?

'*Bien sûr*, it's possible, but I have to say no. And if not to her, then to whom? You see, you had shaved. You had unlocked the outer gate and that of the garden. You must have been expecting a visitor, a woman. Frau Uma Schlacht, I believe.'

Bending over the corpse, he examined the cheeks closely, the throat also, ignoring its crudely stitched incision and the stench.

There were two small nicks on the left side of the neck, just under the jaw. 'A straight razor was used, and you were a man who would not have used a dull one. Were you nervous?' he asked.

Water was dripping somewhere and he turned suddenly at its intrusion. The attendant, in a bloodstained smock, was standing in a far corner, beyond the rows of pallets. 'Beat it,' said the Sûreté. There was no need to shout. 'Sounds echo here,' he said apologetically to the corpse, and then again, 'Were you nervous?'

There was a scrape on the right side of the chin. 'A lack of lather?' he asked. 'No hot water?'

De Bonnevies had got dressed as if to go out to a meeting of the Society. 'You *were* nervous, weren't you,' said St-Cyr, 'and now I am quite sure of it.'

Frau Schlacht, coming to the house, would most certainly have caused this, but had she really done so and why?

It was an uncomfortable thought, but had he missed anything here?

Pausing, he threaded his way among the Occupation's fresh take of corpses and demanded the beekeeper's clothing from the disgruntled attendant. A vacant pallet was sought, the Chief Inspector taking time out from his conversations with the dead to examine each item thoroughly.

'I told you to leave me alone with him. I meant it,' he said, not raising his voice.

Sand had been used on the shirt collar during its laundering. Vichy advised its Occupation-weary citizens to do such a thing instead of lamenting the lack of laundry soap. The finer the better, and *voilà*, the sweat stains could be erased with a little patient scrubbing. A market had even developed for the stuff. 'Clean, washed sand, Monsieur de Bonnevies but, I'm afraid, a shirt that was quickly laundered and not rinsed sufficiently.'

Gently tapping the shirt collar over a slip of notepaper, he collected the sand. Had the daughter picked it up on one of her foraging trips? he wondered. 'It's not from around here,' he said. 'The local sand has tiny filings of iron which are rusty, if they've been in the river long enough and there was oxygen available. Grey or black otherwise, and with organic matter even after washing.'

This sand was clean, very fine, and of white quartz with only a few grains of naturally occurring black magnetite and ruby-red garnet.

And the girl had had freshly laundered undergarments in her suitcase of trade goods and these had been washed with the aid of the same sand.

'Danielle has the perfect alibi,' he muttered, still not looking up. 'Not only was she not in the city, she simply couldn't have poisoned you, and I'm convinced of this, so please don't trouble yourself unduly.'

And the son of that bitch my wife? the victim seemed to demand. What of Étienne, eh? Oflag 17A, *mais certainement,* but she was trying her utmost to secure his release.

The son of another man, a former lover of Madame de Bonnevies who was still alive? wondered St-Cyr. They'd have to find out and get the man's name.

'Did you tell anyone about what the taste of honey would do to that sister of yours?' he asked. 'Someone knew only too well what would happen and made certain it did. They wanted the doctors to see her true state and to stop all this nonsense of your having her home.'

Then that person must have been my wife, Inspector, the corpse seemed to answer, and continued: There was a crowd of at least two thousand visitors, people coming and going all the time. Juliette would have known the approximate time of my visit and could have been there earlier.

A small jar of honey, a wooden dipper, a gift and gone. Damage done and message certain.

'But . . . but your sister said it was a man who had given her the honey, monsieur,' said St-Cyr, 'and I have to ask could the same person have left the Amaretto?'

He seemed to smile, this victim of theirs, to take academic delight in the dilemma, and say, Inspector, *pardonnez-moi*, but have you forgotten the list you took from my pocket?

'Ah *bon*! *Merci*. But at the time I found it, I asked myself why should anyone you were to visit on the following day have felt a need to poison you, and I ask it again?'

There was no answer.

Searching his pockets, the Chief Inspector at last found what he was looking for. Unfolding a scrap of paper, he stood a moment in silence as he studied it beside the corpse. Then he said quietly, and without turning or looking up, 'We've a visitor again. *Merde*, the nerve! I knew his father well. M. Victor Deschamps, but so often a son fails to please or live up to the aspirations of a parent. Piss off, *mon ami*, before I personally wipe the floor with you!'

Had he eyes in the back of his head? wondered Deschamps.

'I have!' shouted the Sûreté.

There were four names on the list de Bonnevies had planned to visit on Friday. No further details were given but, laying the list on the shroud, he found the victim's little ledger and soon had paired addresses with all of them.

After the General von Schaumburg, the beekeeper had intended to visit the long-standing keeper of one of his out-apiaries. Madame Roulleau was the concierge of the building at 14 rue d'Argenteuil, in the first arrondissement and not far from place Vendôme and the rue du Faubourg Saint-Honoré where Madame de Bonnevies's father had once had a shop, and where the beekeeper's father had been head clerk. A person, then, who quite possibly might have known the victim from years and years ago.

The third name on the list was that of a Captain Henri-Alphonse Vallée, the visit to deliver a small bottle of pollen and a little honey, 'for the energy of an old and much-valued comrade in arms, and for wise counsel on all difficult matters.'

The address was 2 place des Vosges and not too far from the morgue, if time allowed. A *vélo-taxi* . . . would one be possible? he wondered.

The fourth name was that of a Jean-Claude Leroux. No reason was given for the visit, simply the address: 53 rue Froidevaux. It was in the Fourteenth and overlooking the Cimetière du Montparnasse.

'From one cemetery to another,' he muttered. 'Is this the one who visits *Le chat qui crie* on Sunday nights once a month and takes only Charlotte who is eighteen?'

The corpse did not reply but seemed to silently return his gaze.

Not waiting for Herr Kohler to open the gate for her in the convenient absence of the concierge, Uma did so herself and stepped into the lift at 28 quai d'Orléans. She'd fix this one from the Kripo; she'd deal with the girl and, afterwards, with that bitch who managed the building. She'd show the two of them that they couldn't talk about an employer behind her back and think to get away with it. The girl would be on the train first thing tomorrow – straight to Dachau; the woman to one of the camps in the east.

Reluctantly Kohler followed her into the elevator. One had always to make these little sacrifices. But *Gott im Himmel*, what the hell was he to do? She'd accuse her maid of being one of the terrorists and it would be game over. Oona's and Giselle's names and the address of the flat he rented would come up – the kid would have to spit them out; that of the Club Mirage also, and Gabrielle. Water . . . would the boys down in the cellars of the rue des Saussaies use the torture of the bathtub on the kid? Of course they would. They'd strip her naked just for the fun of it.

He's afraid, this *Schweinebulle*, snorted Uma inwardly. In a moment he will be on his knees begging me to forget all about his disturbing a quiet meal after first having questioned my maid and that other one.

'Oskar is clean, mein Herr. I really can tell you nothing.'

The woman had reached the door to her flat. Unlocking it, she entered and shouted angrily, 'Mariette . . .'

'*Oui*, Madame,' sang out the kid, from somewhere.

'*Komm' hier!*'

'*Oui*, Madame.'

The kid still hadn't appeared, but the woman went on in a rage, 'Tell the *Detektiv* Kohler you were with me at the pool on

Thursday afternoon. Stop him thinking otherwise, then repeat for me exactly what you said to him when he was here earlier.'

'*Oui*, Madame, *mais qu'est-ce qui s'est passé?*' But what's happened? 'I know of no detective, Madame,' she said in German.

Sacré nom de nom! swore Kohler silently. The kid had icing sugar smeared on her chin and lips. Frau Schlacht had seen it . . .

'*Hure*, how many this time?' shrilled the woman. '*Bitte*, you little *Schlampe!*'

Brutally pushing the girl aside, she headed for the bedroom and when she had the box of Turkish delights in hand, raced her eyes over it. 'Three!' she shouted, stung by their absence.

'Madame . . .'

Violently the box was thrown at Mariette, the kid slapped hard and hard again.

Bleeding from the lips, she fell backwards on to the rug, winced, cringed as a hard-toed shoe drove itself into her stomach.

'Enough! *Verdammt!* They're only candies, Frau Schlacht!'

'And she has stolen *three* of them! Arrest her. Do it, or I will call in others who will!'

The woman was livid. One had best not grin. 'Now look,' he said, 'I've accepted your word that she was with you all afternoon on Thursday and probably throughout the evening. Isn't that right, mademoiselle?' he asked in French.

Badly shaken, the girl hurriedly nodded then bowed her head and shut her eyes. Tears were squeezed.

'There, you see, *meine gute Frau*,' said Kohler. 'The perfect alibi. Why not give her another chance?' And *grâce à Dieu* for a kid who had the brains and guts to think ahead and take the rap herself to protect the concierge and hide the fact he'd been here earlier.

'A week's wages. No, two, and no half-days off for a month!' snapped the woman.

'*Gut!* That's perfect. Now everyone's happy.'

The girl was told to leave them and dutifully curtsied before doing so. Frau Schlacht led the way into the grand salon but didn't suggest they sit.

'Your questions, *mein* Herr?'

'May I?' he asked, pointing to one of the Louis XIV sofas.

'As you wish. For myself, I will remain on my feet.'

Tough . . . by Christ, she was tough. 'A drink would help – for the two of us, Frau Schlacht. You see, my partner and I have this theory, and evidence to back it up, that your beekeeper was murdered for one reason.' This wasn't exactly true, but what the hell . . .

'Coffee will be ready in a few moments, Madame, should you wish it,' sang out the kid in *deutsch* from the kitchen.

No answer was given. The woman's arms were folded tightly across her chest, her feet spread firmly for battle.

'What reason?' she demanded, her gaze fixed hatefully on him.

'He got in the way. That husband of yours has been using relatives in the occupied territories to send him beeswax. The problem is, his collectors know nothing of honey-gathering or bees, and have been sending him squashed hives, buckets of mangled comb, and one hell of a lot of sick bees.'

'Explain yourself.'

'Acarine mites in Caucasian bees, some of whose honey may well have been used to augment the winter stores of Parisian bees.'

'The sickness spreads . . . ,' she said and, losing herself to the thought, abstractedly added, 'Candles. You mentioned a factory, but I do not know where it is.'

'But did de Bonnevies ever mention it?'

'Only to say that bundles of altar candles were being left regularly on the doorstep of a church. The one to which he belonged.'

And Father Michel, the parish priest, hadn't told Louis a thing about them!

'Your husband controls a precious-metals foundry. What else does he do?'

This one was not going to go away until he had something to chew on. 'I've already told you Oskar is a businessman and that I know nothing of his affairs.'

Nothing about the trips to Switzerland you make for him? wondered Kohler, but this couldn't be asked – he had the girl's safety to think of.

'Is he into real estate, do you think?'

153

'I wouldn't know.'

Maisons de passe? wondered Kohler, but he really couldn't ask that one either. 'The beekeeper had a son. Did he ever say anything of him?'

'Lazy. Not like my Klaus. A coward who hid behind a Red Cross armband but was badly wounded by mistake, of course, during the blitzkrieg in the west. The boy was no good. An artist, a sculptor who made nude statues and drawings of his half-sister. Herr de Bonnevies said it wasn't proper and that the girl should not have posed like that for the boy. Her one mistake, he said, was to trust her half-brother blindly and to encourage his every endeavour.'

That was two mistakes, but no matter. 'Trust?'

'Be the best of *Kameraden.*'

'And the son, where is he now? Two metres under?'

'Really, *mein lieber Detektiv,* you must already know where he is. Why, then, ask it of me?'

The woman hadn't moved and still stood in exactly the same way. '*Bitte,* Frau Schlacht, just let me hear it from you.'

'Oflag 17A, in what was formerly Austria,' she said, gazing emptily at him.

'And the boy's mother? How does she feel about it?'

'I wouldn't know. He seldom spoke of the woman.'

Except to tell you he thought she was having an affair with your husband, thought Kohler, but he couldn't ask it. 'There was a sister,' he hazarded. 'Now where did I write that down?'

The *Schweinebulle* took time out to flip through the little black notebook he had been holding all this time. '*Ja.* Here it is,' he said and showed her the entry. 'The Salpêtrière, the house for the insane. Was he worried about this Angèle-Marie?'

'I wouldn't know, Inspector. Such family disgraces are best kept hidden, are they not?'

That bit about her not knowing of the sister was another lie but he'd best say something. 'You're absolutely right, of course. A disgrace. It was dumb of me to have even asked.'

'Then if there is nothing more, it is time for you to leave.'

'There is just one other thing, Frau Schlacht. Minor, you understand – you must forgive the plodding mind of a *Detektiv.*

154

Always there are these little details, but one never knows when something might turn out to be important.'

'Why not just ask?'

It would be best to give her a nod and to consult the notebook again. Any page would do. 'Your husband is one of the *Förderndes Mitglied*, is he not?'

'*Verdammt*! Just what the hell has the fucker done?'

Schlacht's infidelities had wounded her, all right. 'Nothing but what we've discussed, unless there is something else you'd like to tell me.'

You bastard, swore Uma silently.

One had best leave her with a little something to worry over. 'Apparently he lost what the Reichsführer and Reichsminister Himmler took great pains to present. It might well have fallen into one of those pot-furnaces of his – maybe he was checking the melt – but I still have to think that badge is a problem.'

'What problem?' she asked and swallowed, blanching.

'You see my partner and I tend to believe he must have left it somewhere and we'd like to know where and with whom.'

'Idiot! I know nothing of his affairs. Ass here, ass there,' she said and flung an arm out to emphasize the sweep of territory Paris presented. 'Certainly he has had many, but . . .'

She actually managed to smile ingratiatingly.

'But what is a forgotten wife to do, Herr Kohler? You're married, aren't you? You've left your wife at home, haven't you? Well?'

'My Gerda married an indentured French farm labourer after the divorce came through by special order, since a relative of hers had pull. But war's like that in any case, Frau Schlacht. It splits couples apart and puts others together. German with French; French with German. Love – even carnal love – knows enough to find its greenest pastures in times of strife. I'll be in touch if I need anything further.'

At the door Mariette Durand showed him to, the girl smiled wanly and whispered, '*Merci*, monsieur.'

'Did she go to that brasserie as usual last Thursday evening, or did she come home hungry?'

'Hungry, but . . . but why do you ask?'

Kohler put a finger to her lips and, giving her a fatherly kiss on the forehead, said softly, 'Don't worry, eh?' and then sternly, and in *deutsch* Frau Schlacht would hear, 'Remember what I said, eh, Fräulein? Behave yourself and do exactly as you've been told or I really will have to arrest you.'

And then he was gone from her and Mariette could feel every muscle in her body weaken. I must escape, she said to herself, and he has let me know I have no other choice but to pick my time and go.

The Brasserie Buerehiesel was full. There was hardly space to reach the bar. 'A beer,' shouted Kohler above the din. 'Münchener Löwen, if you have it.'

'We haven't.'

'Then give me another of what I had before.'

'And here I thought you were a connoisseur.'

'And you a barkeep with a memory? *Merde*! A Mortimer, *Dummkopf*!'

'She tell you to keep your hands to yourself?'

'Something like that, yes.'

'She saves it for the husband she never sees. So, did she stick that steak knife into you?'

Taking it out, Kohler set it on the zinc. 'We were too busy, but I found it in her overcoat. The thing had cut a hole in her pocket. You're lucky not to have lost it, and should be grateful.'

'Then what can we do for you, Herr Hauptmann *der Geheime Stattspolizist*?'

'A bottle of Amaretto for my partner.'

'No one drinks that stuff in here.'

'I didn't think they did. I only ask because I want to keep him happy. Pastis and that almond crap, he loves them both!'

'Then try the one who's selling the condensed milk. Maybe he can help you.'

It was now forbidden to even have condensed milk without a doctor's certificate. Such as the supplies were, all of it had been confiscated during the past week. Laying five thousand francs on the bar, Kohler turned to fight his way through the crowd.

On the passerelle Saint-Louis, and in pitch darkness, he caught up with the man simply by calling out, '*Halt! Was wollen sie?*' as a sentry would. Halt! Who goes there?

'Franzie Jünger, *mein Kamerad.*'

'Unit?'

Ach Schiesse, ein Offizier! 'Attached to Wehrmacht Supply Depot Seven. I drive a lorry.'

'Then you're just the man I want.'

'The lorry's not with me.'

'That's no problem. I've got a car. The lorry will come later, eh? For now, we line things up.'

'Such as?'

'A customer for that milk.'

'Can't she breastfeed her brat?'

'She hasn't one. She uses it with honey, for facial masks. It cleans and moistens the skin, I guess.'

'And?'

'I need to find a bottle of Amaretto.'

'What the hell is it?'

'Drink.'

'But for that, *mein Kamerad*, you don't need a lorry.'

'It's for the frozen beehives and the buckets of honey and wax I've found. They've got to be moved or we'll lose out on them.'

'How many men will we need?'

'Four, and yourself. Oh, and we'll need a place to store the stuff.'

'The honey.'

'Yes, and the wax.'

'Okay. Lead the way. Thirty for you, fifty for me, and twenty for the boys.'

'Thirty-five for each of us, and thirty for the boys.'

'Agreed.'

6

The rue Froideveaux ran alongside the southern wall of the Cimetière du Montparnasse, and here the quartier was perhaps at its quietest, thought St-Cyr. Distant were the hustle and bustle of the Carrefour Vavin, boulevard Raspail and avenues du Maine and du Montparnasse where flocks of servicemen and their girls crowded the cafés, cinemas, bars and legendary brasseries. The Club Mirage also. Its rue Delambre was just off the northern wall of the cemetery, Gabrielle really quite near, yet he mustn't visit her. Things were far too close to the Occupier, though Hermann could well go there, thinking to meet up with him, and he might well need to do likewise.

Number 53's roof rose among the jumble across the street. Mansard windows haunted the steeply sloping slates. Wind stirred the barren branches of the chestnut trees. It was 11 p.m. and the métro's lines would all have begun their final runs. Soon the streets would be cleared, the city dead quiet except for the sudden squeal of Gestapo tyres or the approaching tramp of a patrol.

'And number 3 rue Laurence-Savart, in Belleville, is one hell of a walk,' he sighed.

The entrance was steep. Threadbare carpet exposed raised nails. The stairs, given off a small courtyard, rose to a cramped landing and a small window behind a grill.

His fist hit the bell, though there was no need since he could see the concierge through the slot. 'St-Cyr, Sûreté.' How many times had he heard himself saying it like that? *Mon Dieu*, must he be so hard? 'To see M. Jean-Claude Leroux, monsieur. Hurry, I haven't time to waste.'

The day's *Paris-Soir* was carefully set aside. Thin pages, controlled reading . . .

'Leroux . . . Leroux . . .' came a voice thick with the gravel of disinterest and too much black-market tobacco. 'Ah! Here we are, Inspector. That one has gone out again. Always when the moon is on the wane he gets anxious.'

'Don't give me an ulcer, monsieur. They bleed.'

'*Merde*, all that is required is a little patience!'

'That takes time, and as I have already indicated to your tender ears, I haven't any. Now hurry, or I will call in reinforcements.'

'The catacombs.'

'They're closed at this hour.'

'Of course. But he's one of the custodians and always, towards the end of the month, the complaining increases.'

'What complaining?'

'The Germans. He says they are always buggering off on him and he's afraid one of them will get lost down there in those tunnels and go mad, and he'll be held responsible.'

'And madness, is that a fear he harbours?' hazarded the Sûreté.

Harbours . . . were they talking about ships? wondered Hervé Martin. 'He gets his kicks out of recounting how, in 1848, some fool tore up the graves of our cemetery to uncover the bodies of recently buried females, the younger the better, I'm sure.'

The Inspector said nothing, only waited for more of the meal. 'They were laid out in less travelled places among the stones and undressed, or so it is maintained by those in authority, and then were mutilated savagely. The breasts, the womb, the private parts. One was shaved. A girl of . . .'

'Yes, yes, I've heard it all and every time my ears are exposed to that canard, monsieur, it has been embellished by the fool who tells it! How long will M. Leroux be underground?'

'Hours, perhaps. It really depends on how agitated he is and if he can calm himself.'

'Let me have the rest of it. I'm listening.'

They still hadn't looked at each other, this Sûreté and himself. The wall was between them, the door closed but for its little window.

'He's like a woman, Inspector, only his time may differ from some, you understand. Every month, as I've said, when the moon is on the wane and down, he gets agitated. The constant pacing in

159

his room at night – *merde*, the racket! The sounds of him . . . Well, you know, eh? A little relief, oh *bien sûr*, but with silence, if you please! It's then that he has to check the catacombs more often than usual; it's then that he finally leaves the quartier of a Sunday evening and returns much calmed.'

A visit to the *Chat qui crie*, then, and Charlotte, and de Bonnevies must have known of it, but still something would have to be said. 'A woman?'

'The younger the better, Inspector, but not from around here, not with that one. Others would talk, isn't that so?'

'Returning when?'

'Before curfew, of course. Inspector, this one spends much time with the dead and not just with their bones. On his day off, he often visits our cemetery or one of the others.'

'The Père Lachaise?'

'Perhaps.'

'Any friends? Any visitors?'

The Sûreté was anxious. 'None that I know of. Not to see him here, in any case.'

'And letters? Well, come on, eh?'

'Seldom. But he did receive one this Tuesday after he returned from work. Yes, yes, from a woman, a Madame Héloïse Debré, number 7 rue Stendhal. Urgent, I think, since he immediately went outside to read it and stayed away for hours.'

Héloïse Debré had been the 'friend' of Angèle-Marie de Bonnevies in the summer of 1912; the girl who had accompanied her to the Père Lachaise . . .

'Then another today, Inspector, and from exactly the same source and urgent!'

The grille shot aside, the grizzled moon face and large brown eyes of the concierge filling its slot with determined concern. 'Inspector, it's a good thing you people are finally taking an interest in him. My daughters are afraid and whisper bad things to each other when in their bed at night. They're only fourteen and fifteen, and one can understand such innocence, but when left alone here on duty they shudder when he approaches and later tell my wife he looks at them in such a way they each feel violated.'

Two letters . . . One before the poisoning and one afterwards.

From the house at number 53, and eastward along the rue Froidevaux, it wasn't far to place Denfert-Rochereau and the entrance to the catacombs. But everything was in darkness or its shades of grey, and memory struggled. Always there was this problem during the blackout, only the more so if in the car with Hermann at the wheel.

Something . . . something had to be seen with which to fix location and find direction. The silhouette of a building, statue, bridge or *quai* . . .

'The twin pavilions,' muttered St-Cyr. Neoclassical villas. Marvellous with their friezes and perfect lines, they'd been used as tollhouses in the early days and had been built in 1784.

The entrance was in the west pavilion. The custodian would, of course, have locked the door after himself. One would have to beat a fist on solid oak; the sound would be certain to bring a *flic* or worse. The bell . . . you can ring the bell, he reminded himself and, feeling for it first, hesitated still as he gripped a wrought-iron ring that must have dated from when construction of the ossuary had begun in 1785.

The bell's jangling would reverberate within, the sound finding its way throughout the building and straight down the twenty-metre-deep spiralling stone staircase to where the accumulated bones of 500 years and more had been placed. Those of the Cimetière des Innocents, the main Paris cemetery, had filled only a portion of the designated abandoned and reinforced quarries. The contents of other cemeteries had joined them. The ground beneath him was honeycombed with quarries and the maze of tunnels that led to them. Even after individual houses and whole streets had vanished due to underground caving, the quarrying had gone on. *Le vieux* Paris had been built of the limestone, gypsum, clay and sand that had been removed. A city of moles even from years and years ago.

In 1823 further excavations had been forbidden. Fully 325 hectares of openings riddled the bedrock upon which the city had been built. And in one small region of these openings, the bones of the centuries had been piled, arranged, festooned with rows of empty-eyed skulls and gaping jaws, crossed tibia and femurs, too, such artistic licence being variously attributed to Louis, Vicomte Héricart de Thury, Inspector General of Quarries in 1810, and to Frochot, the Préfet of the Seine, who had thought it best to cheer the place up!

The entrance door was unlocked. Pushing it open, throwing a hesitant glance over a shoulder at the darkened *place* where the snow still fell softly and one single blue-washed streetlamp glowed, he stepped inside, said silently, I'm a fool to do this without backup. But Hermann had seen too much of death. The bones would only have driven him mad – who knows? They'd have brought back terrible memories of that other war, the trenches, the shelling and bayonet charges, the bloodied chunks of flesh, those of rotting corpses, too. The murders, yes, of millions of young men.

One would need a light and there were candles in plenty. Boxes and boxes of them.

Striking a match instantly gave their price. 'One hundred francs,' he sighed. 'In parties of forty at a time, at least twenty candles – two thousand francs an hour. Plus the admission charge of ten francs. Two thousand four hundred, then.'

The candles looked as if all had been dutifully returned many times to be offered for sale again and again until too short.

'Eight . . . ten . . . a dozen parties a day – twenty-four thousand francs gross at least, and seven days a week.

'Candles,' he muttered, not liking the implications. And taking two spares in case of need, soon found the staircase and started down.

There was no sound but that of his own breathing. The air was heavy with mould – was someone raising mushrooms? he wondered. The air was also damp and cold. Hoarfrost clung to the stone walls and to places above him. Tiny crystals and little icicles, warmed by candlelight, glimmered.

At the foot of the staircase, a narrow tunnel accepted his light, but drew it in only so far. This passage, he knew, would end in a door upon whose lintel had been inscribed '*Arrête! C'est ici l'Empire de la mort!*' Stop! Here starts the Empire of Death!

A thick line, patiently drawn and redrawn over the years in

charcoal on one of the walls of the passage, and then on the ceilings of the galleries, gave guidance. A sort of Ariadne's thread.

'Ariadne . . .' he muttered, at the thought, for she'd been a necessary part of what had happened in Avignon. A coin, then, with a maze in relief on its reverse and the suggestion from the victim that they find the thread. 'And now here she is again,' he whispered. Hermann wouldn't have liked it. Hermann could, at times, be very superstitious.

Everybody had to have their piece of paper these days, thought Kohler. They'd bitch and fart about in abject misery, but if you slapped a freshly franked wad of nonsense into their hands, they might or might not read any of it in the freezing cold and blue-blinkered light of their torches, and like as not they'd say, '*Jawohl*, Herr Oberst, this way.'

Herr Oberst . . . it sounded good. But getting receipts and requisition orders had meant stealing them from the appropriate desk at Gestapo HQ, 11 rue des Saussaies; HQ, too, of the Sûreté Nationale. Even at 23:42 hours that little hive had been busy. Trouble in the halls; trouble on the main staircase with two teenagers. That bastard Heinemann had been on the duty desk but had rushed to help out, a stroke of luck but bad for the kids. Boots and fists, et cetera.

God only knew what the papers were really for. Works of art or gold coins, cognac or someone's prized stamp collection. And using Herr Oberst could well yield difficulties of its own, but what the hell, they were on their way at last!

'You sign here,' he said, leaning in on one of the lorry's opened side windows. 'And you, here,' he indicated where the fresh stamp had been applied. Swastikas, eagles and all.

They'd brought two lorries and lots of help, and that was good.

'And you?' asked Franzie Jünger, lorry driver for the Wehrmacht's Supply Depot number seven.

'What does it matter, since you both will have lied and neither of you had to pay Occupation marks to get these. Five thousand *Reichskassenscheine, miene lieben Honig-Bienen* – that's one hundred thousand francs, eh? so please don't forget it.'

Stuffing the papers into a pocket of his greatcoat, Kohler thumped the bonnet of the lorry and strode off to the Citroën, giving them a nonchalant toss of a hand. Easy . . . this was going to be easy.

The honey bees would follow. They'd hit the restaurant of the Gare de Lyon first, would plunder its lard pails from Peyrane and then would empty Shed fourteen at the Gare de l'Est.

'Confidence is everything,' he sang out and grinned as he got behind the wheel. Louis should be with them but wouldn't agree, of course – he'd be terrified. 'Trouble . . . we're already in enough trouble, Hermann.' And worry, worry. 'Your horoscope, *mon vieux* . . . Permit me to tell you that it said you *weren't* to venture out after dark!'

'Piss off. You know I don't believe a word of that crap.'

'You do! Don't lie to me. Giselle reads them faithfully.'

Schlacht wasn't going to like it. Relatives would have to be contacted. New supplies brought in. Production halted. But maybe, just maybe, the hive of this whole thing, having been well stirred, would open up with the truth.

In any case, Mariette Durand would have a far better chance of running to Giselle and Oona, and if not to them, then to Gabrielle. Frau Schlacht would miss her little maid and begin to put two and two together – he'd have to trust her concierge would use the girl's absence to cover her own indiscretion.

But word of the missing F.M. badge would reach Schlacht via that wife of his or from Rudi, and one Nazi big shot would come to realize exactly with whom he was dealing!

'And we'll have something he needs,' sighed Kohler. 'His wax, which we'll return with pleasure via the Kommandant von Gross-Paris or not at all.'

The Gefreiter on guard at the restaurant of the Gare de Lyon wasn't helpful. Reluctantly Lance-Corporal Kurt Becker moved out of his little nest to shoulder his rifle and stare bleakly at the papers that had been stuffed into his hand. 'Herr Oberst, this is highly irregular.'

'We're simply shifting it to a more secure location. *Gott* alone knows why Old Shatter Hand wants it done or insists guys like you should numb your balls guarding it, but an order is an order, eh, and I've mine.'

Kohler stabbed at the papers but the Lance-Corporal breathed, 'I'm not alone.'

Oh-oh. 'Who's with you? Well, come on. Out with it.'

The concourse below was indicated. 'The soup kitchen,' said Becker. 'Unterfeldwebel Voegler is warming his toes. Apparently this "Old Shatter Hand" of yours feels the two of us are necessary, especially as the curfew has begun and the doors are all supposed to be locked.'

A wise one; and a sergeant too! 'And how long will he be down there?'

'A half-hour, maybe a little more. You see, Herr Oberst, he was a shoemaker in his other life and likes to keep his boots warm and dry and away from the Russian Front so as not to spoil the leather.'

'Okay, okay, I'll speak to him.'

'I wouldn't, if I were you. He's a very loyal member of the Party and a true believer in the Führer.'

Jésus, merde alors, this guy was really something! 'Got any suggestions?'

Becker folded the papers and stuffed them into a pocket. 'Ten thousand *Reichskassenscheine* for the little dent you will put in the back of my head.'

'Ten . . .'

'And please don't bother to go through my pockets looking for it while I'm asleep, since Herr Voegler will most certainly order me to empty them, and I will have tucked your little reward inside my shirt.'

'Look, you can trust me.'

'It's the others who are with you that worry me.'

A cigarette was offered to cement the bargain and then a long pull at the antifreeze of the bottle of three-star cognac that would be used. 'Another,' said Becker, 'and another. It's always best to take precautions when expecting pain.'

'Idiot, he'll accuse you of drinking while on duty!'

'Please don't trouble yourself. I'll leave enough to be showered. That way he won't think of it, particularly if you take my rifle and cartridge case and I tell him it was the terrorists.'

Mein Gott had things among the troops in Paris really degenerated so far?

'I'd hurry, if I were you,' said Becker. 'Once the mind is made up, it's best to carry through. Take the walnuts, too. Then I can say the terrorists were after potatoes and made a mistake.'

The guard on Shed fourteen, was not so easy. Retaliating against the rape of a young woman and collusion between the railway police and the *Milice*, von Schaumburg had placed Wehrmacht sentries two by two with Schmeissers and dogs.

It wasn't good. Even from a distance this could be seen. Breath billowing from man and beast. Helmets battened down. Greatcoat collars up. Snow softly falling to give the lines of track the uncomfortable look of a lost world just waiting for trouble.

'You've met your match,' confided Franzie Jünger. 'Sorry, Herr "Oberst", but this is too much even for us.'

'Not at all,' breathed Kohler. 'Find the air-raid sirens.'

'You're serious.'

'It's the only way.'

'Just what the hell are you really up to, eh? This place will be crawling with wardens and a person such as yourself must know how those bastards behave. If we get arrested for failing to run to the shelters, it's not only a loss of rank and a few days in the clink. It's Russia.'

'I'll deal with them. This is good. It's everything I could have hoped for. First the terrorists get the blame for the Gare de Lyon job, and now Old Shatter Hand is going to have to think the guy who brought this stuff in, stole it back!'

'Who is he and why are you after him?'

'That's not your concern.'

'It is. You see, *mein* Herr, someone such as yourself, with such easy access to Gestapo Headquarters, must be one of them.'

'He's wanted for questioning in a murder investigation.'

'So you get us to steal his wax and honey?'

'You ask too many questions. That's not healthy and you know it. Now find the sirens and let the world hear them. We won't take everything. We'll just take what we can. That'll make it look even better and will seal the rest so tightly, that little *Bonze* will never get his mitts on it.'

'You're a bastard.'

'The world's full of them, or hadn't you noticed?'

'And this "partner" of yours?'

'Don't even ask. He hates guys like you. I don't. With me, you'll get what you want.'

'Amaretto . . . is that what this is all about? Well, is it?'

'I need its source.'

'Ersatz?'

'Yes.'

'And that bastard behind the bar at the Brasserie Buerehiesel put you on to me?'

'Why ask?'

'To get things straight.'

'Well?' demanded Kohler.

'One of his regulars wanted a bottle. I did it as a favour.'

'When?'

'On Tuesday. The customer had to have it in a hurry. Don't ask me who she was or why. I simply don't know, but you must, since you mentioned she would like a few tins of my condensed milk for her face.'

'And you didn't even bother to tell me,' sighed Kohler.

'There were other matters, if I remember it, Herr "Oberst". The honey and the wax.'

The candle guttered as its flame was quickly teased by the draught that moved constantly through the catacombs. Pinching the flame out, St-Cyr felt molten wax run over his fingers, the smoke smelling strongly of buckwheat honey.

Water dripped. Water hit puddles on the stone floor, and the sound of this was very clear, now near, now far against the muted, constant trickle of a spring.

He was well along the entrance corridor, in pitch darkness, hadn't called out on entering the pavilion above, had decided to go cautiously, but whoever had been whispering must have sensed his presence.

Feeling his way forward, he remained in darkness. A lantern glowed faintly in the chamber ahead. The sound of the spring was now much clearer.

'Héloïse, I tell you I heard something,' came a man's voice, thick with the accent of the quartier Charonne. Madame Debré, could not as yet be seen.

Yellowish, ochre-brown to grey-white femurs and tibiae were packed solidly, their knuckles facing outwards and all along the chamber's walls and to its ceiling high above. Shadows from the custodian passed over them and the empty-eyed skulls that grinned from long rows among the bones. Some skulls had a few teeth, most had none; others were without the lower jaw.

Swastikas had been painted in lipstick on the foreheads of many. Two flagrant violations of the regulations sat on the steps of the spring where Jean-Claude Leroux knelt. Army-issue condoms had been stuffed into the eye sockets and dangled limply from them. Grinning lips had been crudely painted on each skull with lipstick also.

'Bâtards,' hissed Leroux. 'Fornicateurs. If I catch them, I'm going to report those fuckers and their putains to the Kommandant von Gross-Paris himself. I'm not going any lower in rank than that!'

He was so worried he was sweating even though he wore an overcoat, was portly and of less than medium height, but with big hands, a broad, flat nose, and wide lips that were grimly turned down. A short, iron wrecking bar, with a nail-pulling hook, lay on the steps next to his right hand.

Hoarfrost had grown on many of the skulls and knuckles, and this caught the light and made them appear as if varnished.

Suddenly the custodian's shadow flew up over the ceiling. 'Héloïse, I was speaking to you,' he whispered urgently.

Removing the navy-blue cap, with its shiny peak and gold braid, he dipped a hand into the Fountain of the Samaritan Woman and wet his brow and the wide dome of an all but bald and greying head. 'Héloïse, please answer me. Don't wander off!'

Large, wounded brown eyes glistened as he looked up in surprise at some hidden sound and held his breath. Swallowing hard, Leroux cupped a hand and drank a little. 'The water is very cold tonight,' he muttered to himself. 'But, then, it is always cold.'

'The curfew's begun,' cursed the woman from somewhere distant in the darkness of the next corridor. 'Now I'm going to have to stay here until it's over. *Merde*, it was crazy of me to have come.'

'Why did you then? Letters . . . you had to send me letters. Why should I listen to such as you?'

'Because I was fool enough to think you were one of us and that you mattered. I felt I had to warn you.'

'One of whom, please?' he taunted.

'You know very well,' she countered acidly. 'Angèle-Marie, idiot. The Père Lachaise. The four of you.'

And so long ago.

Leroux took another drink of water and wet his forehead again before moving the lantern up on the steps, to the lip of the spring.

'Why did you tell us she'd be there after hours, Héloïse? Why did you promise André and the others the reward of their lives if we took care of her for you?'

'Why? Ah! Why does one do such things when one is told by a dear friend's father that one has lice and is too dirty to enter his house?'

'No one bathes regularly, Héloïse. There is always perfume or cologne. You'd do better to tell me the truth.'

'That brother of hers took me in that shed of his and refused absolutely to marry me.'

'You tempted Alexandre?'

'What if I did?'

'*Merde*, and you got even by making us go at his sister.'

'André first, then Jacques and then Thomas, and after them, you.'

'*Salope!*' Slut!

'*Violeur!*' Rapist!

Very much of Charonne, too, her hands stuffed deeply into the pockets of a charcoal woollen overcoat that had been made over years ago, she hesitantly came out of the darkness, but remained standing in the entrance to the exit corridor.

Leroux got to his feet. 'It was nothing,' he said of the sounds he thought he had heard. 'My nerves, that was all.'

'Your nerves. I'm terrified and you talk of them? Just what the hell are we going to do? You're in this as much as I am. You've *got* to help me.'

Her face was pinched, the frown deep; the eyes and lips heavily made up. A purple woollen scarf had covered her head but was now loose about her shoulders and neck; the raven hair thick, unpinned and of more than shoulder length, and streaked with grey.

'Help you?' he snorted. 'Why? For old times' sake?'

Still she hadn't moved from the entrance to the corridor. Of medium height and thin, she was prepared to run from Leroux if necessary, thought St-Cyr, anxiously gauging the distance between himself and the iron bar.

She shrugged and tried to smile, looked particularly defenceless which, he knew with Sûreté clarity, would not be the case. Not with this one.

'Alexandre was blackmailing you, too, Jean-Claude. Admit it. That's why you went to *Le Chat qui crie* once a month like clockwork. Élène, Nicole, Michèle and others, the latest Charlotte and first when she was sixteen and had just gone to work for that old mare Madame Thibodeau. Girls of such tender ages, I have to wonder if Alexandre didn't see that they were brought in especially for you.'

The custodian said nothing. Her shadow passed over the bones as she took a hesitant step forward and then another.

'Admit it, Jean-Claude. He insisted you do so once a month or else.'

'Why . . . Why would Alexandre have insisted on such a thing?'

'To entice the truth from others. He had to know who else had raped that sister of his. Admit it, you and I are both aware of this.'

'What if I am? He's dead now and that business is ancient history.'

'Not to the Sûreté and the Kripo. Not to me, either, unfortunately. Did he ever let you know he knew you were one of them? Well, did he?'

'Never, and I did not admit it. Always he would go on and on about what I'd done in the war.'

'And what *did* you do?'

'Nothing. I just didn't win any medals. Few of us did, he also.'

'Yes, of course, but . . . but please, Jean-Claude, why would

Alexandre have said of you many times, "A robber of corpses should work among them"?'

Leroux dragged out a crumpled handkerchief and mopped his brow. 'How should I know why he should have said such a thing?'

'But . . . but, *mon Dieu*, Jean-Claude, how ungrateful can you get? He got you this job. Right after the war when so many could not find work, he made certain you were employed.'

' Héloïse, that business of his sister happened a long time ago.'

'And yet . . . and yet he can continue to blackmail you even now. It's curious, *n'est-ce pas*? "The corpses of officers," he said to me. "Their gold pocket-watches, wedding rings and fountain pens – especially their cigarette lighters and money." Apparently you burned the photographs they carried of their loved ones, their last letters from home also.'

'What else did that *salaud* tell you? Well, *what*, damn you?'

She didn't back away.

'That you tried to desert and that he and a comrade caught up with you and forced you to return to the lines. That this other man was then found dead of a bayonet attack in the dark of night when no others were harmed or heard a thing, and that ever since then he felt he had had to watch out for himself.'

'And you . . . What hold did he have over you, Héloïse? A husband who was a drunkard and often beat the shit out of you?'

She stiffened. She glared back at him.

'I lost my babies one after another and now . . . now have no one. When my Raoul went away like that never to return, Alexandre came to tell me he was going to look into the matter. He said that I'd get the . . .'

'Wait! Please wait. Maybe I did hear something. I'll check.'

'Don't leave me in the dark. Please don't! My candle . . . I put it out and set it on the floor. These old bones . . . I hate them.'

'As I have had to, eh?' he shrilled only to calm himself and say, 'Ah! forget that. I will only be a few minutes. Stay where you are. Don't move. You did lock the door behind you, didn't you?'

'Lock . . . ? Ah *merde*, I'm sorry. I . . . I must have forgotten.'

Smoke rose from the kerosene lantern Leroux had set on the floor at the foot of the stone staircase. 'Raoul . . .' he muttered to himself. 'Raoul Debré was murdered by her and now Héloïse is afraid the cops will discover this, so asks for my help. Well let her ask, the bitch!' he said vehemently. 'Now that Alexandre is dead, only she knows what I did in the war.'

He began to climb the stairs, his shadow seeming to reach up the circular well ahead of him. Exhaling, he said, 'But I know the hold Alexandre had over her.'

When he reached the top of the staircase, he held the lantern up and let its light shine about the offices of the Quarries Inspection Service which, with the one small room that served as ticket counter and reception desk to the necropolis below, occupied the pavilion.

'No one,' he grunted. 'I should have checked the door right away. She has slid the bolt home as I told her to. HÉLOÏSE,' he shouted. 'HÉLOÏSE, IT'S OKAY. YOU CAN RELAX.

'Relax? How can I when she knows so much about me and when detectives from the Sûreté are breathing down our necks and the Boches have sent one of their own to add gasoline to the fire?'

Going into the reception office, he found a steel letter opener and, examining it for a moment, decided it would do. Hermann would have said, Stop him, Louis, said St-Cyr to himself, but Hermann wasn't here, and one must wait to hear everything these two had to say to each other.

The custodian's steps grew distant. At one point he paused, perhaps to listen, but no, it was to take a leak.

'No one will notice,' muttered Leroux softly to himself. 'The Boches are always doing it and thinking it funny. Mine will simply add to the stench for when I fetch the Kommandant to witness what those bastards of his have been doing. Fungus . . . There is fungus growing on the bones. It's serious. So many visitors not only warm the caves but increase the humidity and bring it on. The ossuary will have to be closed or else the bones will go quickly to dust. In either case I'll lose my job.'

'Jean-Claude, is that you talking?'

Sounds carried.

'*Oui*. To myself. Don't worry. We're alone.'

'*Bon*. We'll make a night of it, the two of us. You won't leave me again, will you? Not until after the curfew.'

Relief had filled her voice. Sitting on the steps of the spring, she dipped a hand into the water, looked so like that woman from the Biblical past, Leroux told her so.

'Then let me give you a real drink, *mon vieux*.'

The bottle had been in the pocket of her overcoat. 'It's an *eau de vie de poire* from one of the little orchards Alexandre's bees serviced. In a rare moment of concern for what he had just done to me, he left it on my kitchen table. Or perhaps he simply forgot it. But,' she shrugged. 'I never touched it until now.'

'Is it poisoned? Well, is it?' he demanded.

'Would I be drinking it? A pact – you and me both dead in this place – is that what you think I want it to look like?'

He took the bottle from her. '*Merci*,' he said. '*Salut!*'

Momentarily her hand touched his as he returned the bottle. 'To the past, Jean-Claude. To the present, of course – one must drink to it, *n'est-ce pas*? And to the future. You poisoned him, didn't you? You couldn't stand being blackmailed any more than I could. So, what, please, did he confide to you about me and that husband of mine? Was it what the neighbours all thought in any case?'

Leroux set the lantern on the steps at her feet and took the bottle from her, but remained standing.

'First, you tell me what you wanted to warn me of.'

So it was to be like this, was it? thought Héloïse. 'The one from the Sûreté will be watching that house of Madame Thibodeau's for you, Jean-Claude. If I were you I would give Charlotte up and find another somewhere else. Of course, there will not be the cemetery room, but I'm sure you know it well enough to imagine it.'

The slut! thought Leroux. Always that tongue of hers couldn't resist having the razor's edge. 'I didn't poison him, Héloïse. I wanted to – yes, yes, of course and many times considered how best to do it. Down here there are iron grilles that close off countless passages and galleries. Some have locks and I have access to their keys. Any of those would have done and no one . . . Believe me, no one would have been the wiser. The draught . . . I had even calculated that the constant draught we have would carry the stench of his rotting corpse well away from the ossuary.'

The look she gave him hardened. 'Are you threatening me, *mon pauvre*, because if you are, please try to think of whom I might have told where I was going tonight.'

He didn't laugh at her or even smile.

'No one, Héloïse. You would not have told a soul.'

'Then you're forgetting the second of the letters I sent you. Today's . . . well, yesterday's, I guess. It's now Sunday.'

'I burned them both in my room and enjoyed the momentary warmth they gave.'

Was he going to kill her? wondered the woman, or so it seemed, thought St-Cyr, still waiting and watching, still holding back when perhaps he ought to step in and put an end to their little discussion.

'Blackmail,' said Leroux and seemed to relish taunting her. 'I was not the only one to suffer, was I?'

'I didn't poison him.'

'You could so easily have done so. Please don't deny it.'

She tossed a hand. 'All right, all right, I used to help him with his bees, but that doesn't make me a murderess.'

'Which you already were.'

Ah *Sainte Mère*, these two, thought St-Cyr. She took a long pull at the bottle and then offered it.

'Drink with me, then. Two killers, you and I, eh? Yourself during the war; myself some fifteen years after his sister was raped.'

'On the night of 14 July 1927. Bastille Day.'

'He told you?' she asked, and looking up at him, pleaded for compassion with haggard eyes whose tears began to streak their mascara and shadow.

'First you got that husband of yours drunk, Héloïse – a state Raoul welcomed and was used to. Then . . . and this is the fortunate part for you, as a part-time bargee's assistant, he was alone and on duty during the celebrations.'

Emptily she looked down at the lantern. 'And headless corpses, even if weighted down with coal and dredged from the Canal Saint-Martin, are hard to identify. The body was never found – at least I never heard or read about its being found and I searched the newspapers. Believe me, but I did,' she said, suddenly looking up at him and not bothering to wipe her eyes. 'Every day for months and months, Jean-Claude. Years, damn you. Years!'

'Not found,' breathed Leroux and, taking the bottle from her, let a little of its contents piddle on to the top of her head.

'*You cut that out!*' she shrieked and flung herself aside.

OUT . . . OUT . . . the caves echoed.

'A small baptism, just in case,' he said. 'Oh by the way, *ma chère*, Alexandre made certain I knew exactly how he got you to tell him what you'd done and that you had buried Raoul's head on that little farm of your Uncle Marcel's. Near Soissons, isn't it, where old bones are always cropping up in the orchards and fields? An abandoned well the Boches had all but filled in during their final retreat in 1918. What could have been better? A few shovels of fresh earth and a few more stones.'

When she said nothing, the custodian drank deeply from the bottle, then told her to finish it. 'Go on. You're going to need it.'

'Why? Because you will kill me?'

'Now listen, Héloïse. Take it easy. We're in this together.'

'I couldn't move – did Alexandre tell you that, too? I couldn't scream. Always there'd be those damned bees of his, always one of his hives on that roof of mine and no record of it in his little book or with that daughter of his. "The perfect excuse to visit you," he'd say and then . . . then would let them crawl all over me. I was terrified. He'd laugh at me and I can still hear him, and . . . and only after I'd passed water in my bed, would he condescend to patiently scrape them off and return them to their hive. He was a monster, Jean-Claude. Of course I wanted him dead! *Dead*, do you understand?'

'You were naked.'

'Completely! That . . . that's the sort of hold he had over me. Honey . . . he always used honey. The bees then gathered it from my skin.'

'And you poisoned him, didn't you? Confess. There is only me to listen.'

She was in despair and wrung her hands.

'I wish I had. God forgive me, but I do, Jean-Claude. He wanted that sister of his to come home – you knew of this?'

'What if I did?'

Leroux was going to kill her now, thought St-Cyr. Now . . .

'Alexandre confided this to you. Well, he did, didn't he?' she asked of the sister.

'Several times. He was worried the Germans would snuff out her life.'

The woman looked away towards the entrance corridor. St-Cyr stepped back and held his breath. 'Some life, poor thing,' she said tearfully. 'I've begged God to forgive me. Father Michel has heard my confession many times, so please don't think he and that God of his are unaware of what happened in Père Lachaise and who was responsible.'

'Idiot! Did you confess also to murdering Raoul?'

'I had to. I was distraught and couldn't sleep, couldn't stop myself. Father Michel made me tell God everything.'

Father Michel! swore St-Cyr. The bottle was forgotten.

'And yet . . . and yet,' said Héloïse, 'the good father did nothing to stop Alexandre from torturing me like that, and nothing . . . nothing at all to prevent that husband of mine from beating the shit out of me and causing me to lose my babies.'

'And would he have wanted Angèle-Marie to return to the house of her childhood?' hazarded Leroux.

How very cautious of Jean-Claude, thought Héloïse. 'No. No, I'm certain of it. That old priest has much to answer for and no one but his God to confess to.'

The kid on stage at the Club Mirage wore little and was distracting. Momentarily torn between watching her and searching the crowd for Louis, Kohler hesitated, for when she gyrated the silver hoop about her waist, she juggled ersatz oranges to which white feathers had been glued.

Locked in for the night, eight hundred of the Occupier, most in uniform, some with their girlfriends, others entertaining collabos and big shots from the black market, whistled and applauded. Now the torso moved as well and the sky-blue propellers that hid her nipples began to spin in opposite directions as her head was tilted back.

The oranges went higher and higher; the hoop raced the propellers. One knee came up. A falling orange was hit and lifted into the tobacco-fogged air only to be caught with others on its descent as she turned away and . . . *mein Gott*, bounced orange after orange into the crowd with the most beautiful backside on earth.

'*Jésus, merde alors*, her timing's perfect!' he swore.

The piano player flew over the keys, the drummer gave a parade roll and one by one, as they were dutifully returned, the kid caught the oranges.

She was radiant. 'As she should be!' roared Kohler, shoving his way through to the bar. 'Has Louis been in yet?' he called out to Remi Rivard, the one with the open leather jerkin, red plaid workshirt and gut of an iron barrel. The brother of the Corsican with the face and hands of ground meat.

'Not yet. You been rolling around in a beehive or something?' Remi pointed to the greatcoat.

'Oh this. It's just a bit of wax and honey and a few dead bees. I've been robbing hives.'

Two beers were set before him, the froth overflowing.

'Bees or no bees, I'd get that coat cleaned in a hurry.'

Remi, whose face was that of a mountain, all crags and clefts and shadows, with hard dark, empty eyes, gave an almost imperceptible nod in the direction of the balcony. 'Table four over from the clock, front row. You've company.'

An SS major from the avenue Foch sat between two *miliciens*, one older, the other younger but stronger, bigger. None of them had the slightest interest in the kid on stage. They were concentrating hard on the bar.

'Tell Louis I'll meet him at his house.'

A study in perpetual motion, Remi had already surmised as much and had moved away to serve the crush of others. At a run, Kohler headed for the courtyard exit. Crossing the stage, he dragged off his coat and pitched it from him, called out to the kid, 'Hey, *chérie*, look after that for me, eh? You were terrific!'

The three on the balcony were making for the stairs. Leaving the stage, Kohler fought his way past the chorus line where bared breasts wore glued pasties and the girls grinned or smiled. Red lips, bare arms and feathers . . . ostrich feathers . . .

Miliciens jammed the exit. Others were behind them. All wore black *chasseur alpin* berets, dark blue tunics and trousers, brown shirts and black ties . . . Brass knuckles, too, and hatred in their eyes. Hatred for what he'd done to two of their own!

Pivoting, Kohler raced back to the stage, was caught, was dragged down, hit and hit hard. Blood blinded him. Boots felt as if caving in his ribs. *'MAUDIT SALAUD! VACHE!'* COW! they shrieked, the slang for cop. 'Dog-fucker!' The pain was killing him. Curled up, he rolled on to his side and tried to clear his eyes. The kid was stricken. Oranges were bouncing all around her. The crowd was in a rage. Thinking him one of their own, the boys in grey-green were clambering on to the stage. The *miliciens* were dragging him up. 'AN ARREST!' they shrieked at the rescuers but a whistle blew sharply. As one, the men all stopped and stood to attention, or crouched and did not move.

'Take him,' said the SS major, with a dismissive toss of his hand. 'He's wanted for questioning.'

The kid, bless her, was in tears and on her knees, and when she reached out to him, Kohler felt the trembling urgency of her hand on his blood-smeared cheek. 'Gabrielle . . . Gabi asked me to watch out for you,' she blurted. 'But I . . . I had to do my act. Forgive me.'

'Tell Louis I'm in trouble,' he gurgled. 'Trouble, eh? Louis . . .'

With no whistle to blow, what was one to do? wondered St-Cyr, still in the catacombs, in the darkness of the corridor. The lantern was now resting on the lip of the spring between the custodian and the woman, but had Leroux put it there on purpose? The iron bar was uncomfortably close to hand.

If one said, *Sûreté, you're both under arrest*, Leroux would simply tip the lantern into the spring and snatch up the bar. The woman would cry out but not for long.

'That old priest,' said Leroux. 'He'll have to be dealt with.'

'I can't kill a priest, Jean-Claude. I won't.'

'You told him everything.'

Frantic, her eyebrows arched as she spat, 'And what of Alexandre, eh? For years now he's known who the four of you were.'

'You told him, too?'

'I had to. A woman's most private parts are her tenderest. Each time the bees fed . . . Need I say more?'

'Then why the charade of his trying to find out all our names?'

'Another torture of his. Admit it, yours and the other families, mine too, lived in fear of him, as did the four of you and myself. Would he go to the police; would he not do so? When he came back from the war he had that little cemetery of his built and then . . . then started to work on all of us.'

'Never once did he suggest to me that he knew.'

'Of course not! That would have spoiled his fun. He was both examining magistrate and judge, and *wanted* the torture to last. Look how he despised that wife of his? The son of another – he never let her forget it, not for a moment.'

'You'll have to poison Father Michel, too, Héloïse. I'm sorry, but that's the way it has to be. Otherwise . . .'

Leroux took the letter opener from a pocket and fingered it. 'Otherwise, *ma chère compagne dans le meurtre* . . .'

'You wouldn't!' she hissed and began hesitantly to move away.

'Agree,' he said. 'And I'll be generous. Do it within the next two days or . . .'

'Monsieur, please put that down. St-Cyr, Sûreté.'

'*Ah!*'

The lantern went into the drink, the iron bar scraped on the stones as it was dragged up. A skull was smashed. The woman shrieked and began to run – ran into a wall, clawed at the bones, for some fell around her. Cried, wept – begged.

Another skull was smashed. Femurs and tibiae were struck. The bar hit solid stone. The woman shrieked again, and finding the exit corridor at last, ran.

'*Monsieur, give yourself up this instant!*' managed the Sûreté and from the steps of the spring, thought Leroux. '*You're under arrest!*'

Perhaps the custodian shifted the bar to his other hand, perhaps the letter opener. Nothing was said. Water trickled constantly.

In the far distance, the woman stumbled and fell but dragged herself up and went on in terror, screaming for Leroux to spare her. 'HE POISONED ALEXANDRE, INSPECTOR,' she shrilled. 'HE WAS ONE OF THOSE WHO RAPED HIS SISTER.'

His sister . . . His sister . . . came the echoes.

'You killed a comrade, monsieur,' charged the Sûreté, catching a breath. 'You robbed the corpses of your officers.'

'And that . . . that, *mon fin*, was said exactly as one of them would have!'

Leroux began to move forward, feeling always the porous texture of the knuckles in the walls, the skulls also, and recalling every change so as to guide himself.

He'd have to kill this Sûreté. There couldn't be any more than one of them. This one had come alone, and would therefore vanish without trace.

'Monsieur, I'm warning you,' said St-Cyr.

'INSPECTOR, PLEASE HELP ME!' cried the woman.

Help me . . . Help me . . . The chambers resounded with her terror.

Taking out his box of matches, he tried to light three or four of them.

He hasn't moved yet, said Leroux to himself. The spring is to his left . . .

The matchsticks broke, the Sûreté swore and tried to take others from the box. Silently he stepped away from the spring and soon the sound of it was far behind him, for he had reached the corridor Héloïse had taken. Yes, yes, said Leroux to himself, silently following.

Try as he did, St-Cyr knew it would be impossible to hear the exit door being opened. They were just too far from it. Turning back, he felt the draught on his face – searched the impenetrable darkness, smelt the musty damp air, the fetidness of bone meal, the taint of anise, too. Anise and garlic and onions . . . Where . . . where the hell was Leroux? How close now? How close . . . ?

When the iron bar cut the air, it struck the wall, shattering the stone and raising sparks. The woman shrieked as the custodian gave a savage grunt, a stab with the letter opener which flew out of his hand and hit the floor.

'*Bâtard!*' he rasped. 'Let me kill you.'

Each man waited for the other to make a move. The one must

back towards her, the other must advance, thought Héloïse, hastily wiping tears from her smarting eyes. If she could hold the Sûreté, Jean-Claude could kill him and then . . . then maybe he would let her go.

You fool! she said. He will only smash your head in, too.

Franctically her fingers fled over the bones – she was in another of the chambers. If only she could find its exit. If only she could make her way from chamber to chamber and then . . . then climb the stairs back up to the street. This place exits on the rue Dareau*, she told herself. Please, God, help me.

God would only damn her. 'God can't forgive you yet, my child.' Father Michel had said this to her in the afternoon. Today . . . No, yesterday. Saturday . . .

'Candles . . . I lit a candle for our Lady, Father,' she had said.

'God is kind. God is generous. God provides,' he'd answered.

Candles . . . did the Inspector know who left them on the steps of the church? Could she use the information to barter for clemency?

The iron bar was savagely swung. Distant from her, she heard the Sûreté gasp in pain and cry out, 'ARREST, DAMN YOU!'

The bar clattered at his feet. Perhaps he held Jean-Claude in an arm-lock, perhaps he had thrown him up against a wall and was now fastening the bracelets on him.

Perhaps . . . perhaps . . . But *Jésus, merde alors*, what the hell has happened? she wondered. And crawling forward, found the exit, bowed her head into her hands and wept.

At 5 a.m. Berlin Time, the Club Mirage was all but deserted, the air heavy with stale tobacco smoke. Up on stage, in a feather-trimmed pink housecoat that dragged its hem, the wife of one of the brothers pushed a broom but avoided the soiled heap of a Wehrmacht greatcoat. Her slippers didn't match, and the Gauloise Bleue that was glued to her lower lip had a good two centimetres of ash clinging to it.

Silent, the Rivards were giving the zinc a final wipe.

* This portion of the rue Dareau is now rue Rémy-Dumoncel.

'Jean-Louis . . .' said Gabrielle, coming along the corridor from her dressing room to find him staring at the coat. 'Jean-Louis, what has happened to your arm?'

They kissed on each cheek, first the right and then the left, and then the right again, as was her custom. He drew in the lovely scent of her perfume and momentarily shut his eyes, wishing for a calmer time. 'Perhaps you'd best tell me,' he said, indicating the coat on the floor. 'Dead Caucasian bees, bits of willow twigs . . . Buckwheat honey, unless I'm mistaken. That of lavender, too . . .'

'Remi,' she called out softly. 'A pastis for our friend. Please leave the bottle and a pitcher of clean water, then let us have the place to ourselves. This is private.'

'*Oui*, madame.' They often called her that out of respect. She brought in the money and took ten per cent of the take, had the voice of an angel, was regularly heard over wireless broadcasts that reached the front lines of both the Reich and the Allies.

'Arlette, we can do that tonight,' said Léon to his wife who hadn't stopped her sweeping to greet the visitor.

Left alone with Louis, Gabrielle made him remove his own overcoat. 'There is blood,' she said. 'Ah *merde*, you've really been hurt. Is it broken?'

He shook his head, suddenly ached to be at peace. 'I'd like to go fishing with René Yvon-Paul.'

'He'd like that, too.'

She peeled off his suit jacket and the woollen cardigan his mother had knitted for him perhaps ten . . . no, fifteen years ago. There were holes in the elbows, mismatched buttons . . .

'It's a part of me,' he said apologetically. 'Hermann complains.'

'And is that a hint, because if it is, I have to tell you I want to look at this first before letting you know who took him away.'

'Away . . . ?'

She nodded. Tears moistened her eyes, sharpening their violet shade. 'Forgive me,' she said. 'I've missed you terribly and now don't know what's to become of either of you. The *Milice* dump Oona's purse out on the street while you are still on your way home from Avignon. They scrutinize her papers which are not so good, as you know very well, and now . . .'

'Has he been arrested?'

'Later. In a moment.'

'Just what the hell has he been up to, Gabrielle? He was to question a Frau Schlacht, nothing else, and then return to the Salpêtrière to pick me up. A . . . a woman with two small children had stopped us in the street. Hermann . . . Hermann and I gave them a lift to the soup kitchen at the Gare d'Austerlitz. He was going to . . .'

'Calm down, please. For now I need you to keep still.'

The gash in his upper left arm was deep and ragged, and of about ten centimetres in length. 'Who did this?' she asked.

He sighed heavily. 'I tried to arrest two murderers. One was difficult. Both got away and can now await a little visit. There's no hurry even if they should happen to kill each other.'

'There is for this, and you know it.'

'Then please telephone the morgue and ask if Armand Tremblay is going through the autopsy notes on the corpse of Alexandre de Bonnevies and doing his own as I requested. Armand can patch me up. I need, also, the analysis on the bottle of Amaretto.'

'Don't be an idiot. I'll do this myself. Now be quiet.'

Everything that was necessary was kept behind the bar. Deftly she cleaned the wound and refilled his glass. 'I've done this lots of times,' she said.

'You continue to surprise me.'

Her hair, worn loose at this hour, was of shoulder length and not blonde as he'd first thought, but the soft shade of a really fine brandy, and it spilled forward as she set to work. Her hands were slender, the fingers long.

'Hermann was taken by the *Milice* but we still do not know where to. Remi has asked two trusted friends to quietly find out. For now you are to rest and keep out of it.'

'You *like* giving orders. I could sleep for a year.'

'With me, I hope.'

'You know I can't. Gabi, listen to me, please. It's not safe for you to be seen with me. The SS, the *Milice*, will only cause further trouble.'

'Avignon was unpleasant?' she hazarded, not looking up from her needle.

'A handful of madrigal singers. The *Cagoule* caused difficulties.'

'And Gestapo Boemelburg is not happy with the result?'

Still she hadn't looked up. 'We've been warned to behave. An explosion on the tracks, then what happened to Oona. Boemelburg wants us to do one thing; the Kommandant von Gross-Paris another.'

The *Cagoule* had many friends and supporters among the *Milice*, thought Gabrielle. Others were members of it, and their lines of communication throughout the country were tragically getting better. 'Then that must explain why an SS major wanted to talk to Hermann but got those people to haul him in.'

There was a sadness to her voice that said much more. An aching for France and what had happened to a once splendidly humane nation. Refilling his glass, she told him to drink it neat. From a silver cigarette case he knew well, she took two Russian cigarettes, the tobacco black and much stronger than he liked, but . . .

'For me, for you,' she said on lighting them. 'For the first time we met, and for the times since then.'

'For my partner, too, wherever he is.'

Would Jean-Louis and Hermann live to see the end of the Occupation; would she herself, or Oona and Giselle? wondered Gabrielle.

Rolling his shirt sleeve down, she buttoned it. 'You know I want us to have a life together.'

'Don't be difficult. It's impossible. It's far too dangerous for you.'

'For you also?' she asked.

'For all of us,' he said and did not offer to brush her tears away, just looked so steadily at and through her, one instantly saw Sûreté!

'Then you had better come to the house anyway, Monsieur *l'Inspecteur principal*,' she retorted acidly. 'You see, my concierge telephoned here last night and then discreetly came to see me rather than give the news to Gestapo ears, even though those *salauds* are still probably aware of it since they constantly watch the club and I could not tell her this. Apparently I have acquired, through no effort of my own, you understand, a new maid.

Sixteen years of age and very capable, so much so, among her references it is stated that she was trusted implicitly, Inspector – *implicitly* – by her former mistress and made four trips a year to Switzerland with her. Heavy suitcases in; light ones out, in spite of the desperate need for canned goods here. Speaks more than a smattering of German which will be helpful, you understand, since the girl can't possibly stay in Paris and must go underground immediately. Giselle brought her to my place. *Giselle,* Jean-Louis.'

'Not Oona?'

He was desperate. 'No, not Oona.'

'Arrested also?'

'*Oui.*'

The Citroën had remained in darkness in front of the club. No one had touched it or tried to steal it, thought Gabrielle. Things were so bad, word had spread rapidly and it had been avoided like the plague, but left by the arresters so as to give the other half of the partnership wings.

Reaching under the driver's seat, Jean-Louis soon found what he wanted, and dragged them out. 'As keeper of our guns until needed, Hermann is, at times, careless,' he confessed.

She knew his would be the 1873 Lebel *Modèle d'ordonnance,* six shots, the calibre 11mm. Hermann's was a Walther P38, a semi-automatic 9mm Parabellum, with eight cartridges in the clip.

'Jean-Louis, I meant what I said about your sleeping. You can't run on that stuff like your partner does.'

'I will if I have to.'

Digging into the side pocket of the door, he found a spare phial of the little grey pills of Benzedrine the German night-fighter pilots took to stay awake, and downed how many? she wondered.

'Four,' he said. 'After a while the system grows accustomed to them, so one must increase the dosage.'

'*Mon Dieu,* will you not listen to me? Where . . . just where do you think you're going to find him?'

'At a smelter. You know it and so do I, so why try to hide the fact? Just take care of that new maid you've acquired. Let me drive you home and then forget about us.'

'I can't. I won't.'

'You'd best, for the sake of your son.'

The furnace was white hot. The Alsatian guard dogs were restless and had had to be chained.

Awakened in the dead of night and forced from their garrets, the Russian smelter workers and their families huddled in grey nightshirts and nightgowns. Teenagers, kids, thumb-sucking toddlers with runny noses, grandparents and parents mutely watched from the rickety, soot-encrusted staircase that climbed above the wall of cages.

Frantic, one of the guinea pigs was dangled by a hind leg over the gaping mouth of the furnace. Heat roared up, smarting its glistening dark eyes and causing it to madly squirm.

Sweat poured from Kohler. Blinded by it, he tried to clear his eyes. His wrists ached like hell. The bracelets – *his* bracelets – were cutting into them. Strung up, stripped naked, he hung from a chain and hoist pulley near the furnace. Only his toes touched the floor.

There were six *miliciens* and one of them had removed his tunic and beret to don goggles and asbestos. The others, their expressions dark with hatred, waited. There was no sign of the SS major now. No sign . . .

When dropped, the creature didn't even squeal. It simply flashed to steam with little smoke, and this rushed from the furnace, white and sudden and carrying still-glowing bits of its fur.

Frantically Kohler searched for a way out. These bastards weren't just angry about the loss of two of their own. They'd had word from Avignon and were out to put an end to him!

Goggles removed a gauntlet and took from a small, slag-encrusted crucible, a fine gold neckchain and locket.

'*Don't*! Please don't,' managed Kohler. There had, as yet, been no sign of Oona.

The locket was opened. The hoist was released a little, and now his feet could rest flatly on the floor. In relief, he shut his eyes tightly, then opened them.

'Look, be reasonable, eh? It's the only picture she has of her two children. They were lost during the blitzkrieg in the west – killed,

186

she believes, on the trek from Holland, and I . . . I can't make her see that there could still be hope. I can't.'

'Half-Jewish,' grunted Goggles. 'Johan would have been nine years old now; Anna, seven. The father, Martin Van der Lynn, was a Jew the woman you shelter tried to hide in Paris.'

'The French Gestapo of the rue Lauriston killed him in the Vélodrome d'Hiver.' The cycling arena.

'And good riddance,' said Goggles.

The locket was dangled over the furnace. The photograph began to turn brown, to curl and finally to burst into flame.

'Gone,' wept Kohler. 'Ah, Oona . . . Oona, forgive me.'

Blood and sweat trickled from his left eye to run down the scar the rawhide whip of an SS had left a good two months ago at the château of Gabrielle Arcuri's mother-in-law near Vouvray, and overlooking the Loire. Yet another murder investigation whose outcome had definitely not been appreciated.

Blood and sweat found the one that cut diagonally across his chest. '*Maudit salauds!*' he cried. 'What the hell have you done with Oona?'

'That's not for you to know.'

Godonov was summoned and told to charge the furnace. 'We need enough to bathe this one's feet.'

Scrap silverware, sand, charcoal, lead oxide, bone ash and the yellowish peroxide of sodium were added.

'Now we must wait,' cautioned Godonov. 'Please.' He ducked his shaggy head to one side in deference. 'A little vodka, *mes amis*. Pickled cucumber and beetroot will be served on *blini*, the small pancakes we usually eat with caviar. There is *coulibac* also, and made in the old way, you understand. A superb cabbage pie whose origins date from the sixteenth century. *Pel'meni sibériens*, too. These are a kind of ravioli that we have stuffed with a delectable forcemeat of guinea pig.'

He paused to let his gaze sift over the assembled. 'Of course, messieurs, we apologize for there not being any sour cream or caviar, but such things are difficult these days, as is the vodka, although God makes allowances.'

Clothing that was Oona's was dangled over the furnace and allowed to catch fire before being dropped.

Herr Kohler was hoisted up so that his toes no longer touched the floor.

'Forgive me,' said Godonov softly. 'There is, alas, nothing I can do.'

Tendrils of tobacco smoke rose into the beam of the cinema's projector. On the screen, an ancient rerun, approved by those idiots in the Propaganda Staffel, was telling the French how decadent they were.

An abortionist was about to attend to a young girl of misfortune who was afraid and hesitantly undressing. Flames rose from the skirt and sweater she removed. Flames caught at the woollen knee socks, cotton blouse, half-slip and brassiere. Oona . . . was it Oona?

Giselle was sitting all alone beneath the projector beam. Tears streaked her face; she tore her hair. Blood ran from her beautiful lips. Pregnant . . . was Giselle pregnant?

Oona, idiot. She's worried about 'OONA!'

With a shriek, Herr Kohler awoke from his little nightmare as the ice-cold water hit him. Shaking his head to clear it, he realized at once where he was still hanging.

'Were they raping them both,' asked Godonov softly with deep concern, 'or just the one they have taken?'

'What time is it?'

Worried about repercussions, Godonov hesitated. 'Three or four a.m. I have not asked.'

The Russian lowered the bucket and, at a word from behind, deferentially stood aside and returned to the staircase to join the others of his little flock.

Goggles stood beside the furnace, with a gauntleted hand on the pour-lever which would rock the cradle and tip the melt out. Gradually the other *miliciens* came into view. Fists were doubled, arms folded tightly across their chests. Bastards . . . bastards . . .

'So, Herr Kohler, a few small questions,' said the one that was fifty and fast greying but tough, too tough. A butcher, probably, in his previous life. 'Nothing difficult, you understand.'

'DID THEY TELL YOU LOUIS AND I SAID STUFF LIKE THAT IN AVIGNON, EH?'

Sweat ran down Herr Kohler's flanks causing the scars from that other war to glisten, as did those of the whip marks. 'Please, make it easy for yourself,' continued Vincent Soulages, *Chef de Milice du quartier du Mail et de Bonne-Nouvelle*. 'We're not monsters and must go home to our families as loving fathers or sons, so as to sleep peacefully.'

'Piss off.'

Stung, Soulages lashed out with his truncheon, hitting the buttocks. Gritting his teeth, Kohler refused to cry out. The chain creaked as it swung back and forth, finally coming to rest.

'*I will ask you only once!*' shrieked Soulages. '*Where did you take the wax and hives?*'

'*I don't know. Hey, it's not that I won't remember. It's simply that I didn't ask the boys who were with me!*'

'WE'RE WASTING TIME, VINCENT!' yelled Goggles.

'A moment, Félix. He has not quite understood.' Savagely the truncheon was swung back, the blocky shoulders moving with it.

'Okay, okay,' shrilled Kohler. 'Hey, I was only kidding but if you hit me again, my lips will be sealed.'

'Then we await your reply.'

'And then you'll pour the melt – is that it, eh? *Ach Du lieber Gott, meine Idioten*, you've forgotten with whom you're dealing. Old Shatter Hand, *Dummköpfe!* He gave us orders to pluck that crap away from your little *Bonze* and destroy it!'

The furnace, mounted on rollers, was moved a little closer. A trough of firebrick was put in place and sloped to Herr Kohler as he was lowered until his feet once again touched the floor.

'Look, I'm telling you we had orders from the Kommandant von Gross-Paris.'

'And we are telling you ours come from the Général Oberg, Höherer SS und Polizei Führer of France!'

Giving them the location might buy a little time. '*Le Halle aux Vins.*' The central wine store for the city. 'A cave . . . The rue de Languedoc, I think, or was it off the Grand Préau? There are so many caves . . . One hundred and eighty of them – one hundred and sixteen cellars, two huge magazines . . .'

Kohler was just fucking about! 'POUR IT, FÉLIX!' shrieked Soulages.

'NO, WAIT! I . . . I think I've remembered. The rue de Bordeaux, the cellars of J.P. Malouel.'

'We will check it out later. For now, a few other small questions,' said Soulages. 'The dipper, if you please, Félix.'

'The dipper . . . ?' blurted Kohler. *Mein Gott*, they were serious! A scum began to quickly form over the dollop of melt in the dipper. Kohler felt his toes curling up. 'Don't,' he softly begged. 'Please don't. I'll tell you.'

'Make certain of it, Félix.'

A droplet . . . just one was allowed to fall and splash on the floor, but the shriek when it came, as surely it had to, filled the smelter, terrifying the others on the staircase, thought Godonov, and causing the guinea pigs to cease their foraging and to watch.

The dogs urinated at the ends of their tightly stretched chains . . . The pain Herr Kohler experienced was, Godonov knew, excruciating. In and out of the blackness, the detective drifted – he wouldn't know, couldn't tell if he'd ever walk again and what the hell good was a detective who couldn't run?

Weeping, Herr Kohler hung his head, was still too afraid to look down at his feet. *'Maudit salauds,'* he breathed. 'Louis will get you for this. Louis . . .'

'You questioned Frau Schlacht,' said Soulages. 'You were interested in a bottle of Amaretto.'

'She . . . she bought it on the *marché noir*, I think.'

Kohler probably knew more of the source, but that was not important. 'How much poison was in it?' shrieked Soulages.

The detective's eyes leapt as he shrilled, 'I don't know! I haven't had a chance to talk to my partner. Maybe it hasn't even been analysed!'

Analysed . . . Analysed . . .

'How much did the beekeeper take?'

'I don't know! I haven't seen the autopsy!'

Autopsy . . . Autopsy . . .

'But you are certain Frau Schlacht bought this bottle?'

Bottle . . . Bottle . . . Why the hell bother about it? 'Yes, on Tuesday. She . . . Look, I'm almost certain she took it to the visitor's concourse at the Salpêtrière on Thursday afternoon and . . . and must have left it with his sister.'

'The crazy one.'

'Yes.'

'But why would Frau Schlacht not simply have given it to Monsieur de Bonnevies?'

'I . . . I don't know yet. Honest, I don't.'

'Water . . . You must give him a little,' hazarded Godonov from the stairs. 'It's the sulphur in the air, messieurs. It makes one very thirsty.'

'THEN BRING IT, IDIOT!'

'Yes, yes, of course, and right away as you wish.'

The Russian hurried forward with a tumbler in hand, but when he held it to Herr Kohler's lips, the *milicien* held it, too.

'Water . . . It is only water, monsieur. All of our vodka has been drunk by yourself and your men, *n'est-ce pas?* A privilege of ours, of mine, I assure you.'

Soulages backed off. The prisoner tried to take a sip. Some of the water dribbled down his chin. 'Easy,' cautioned Godonov. 'Take just a little at first.'

Fiery, the vodka stung the throat and the prisoner tightened his before gasping, '*Merci.*'

Whetted, the throat eagerly opened to receive the rest. Yanked away, the Russian let the glass fly from his hand to hit the floor and shatter.

'Amaretto,' hissed the *Chef des miliciens.* 'Who did Frau Schlacht wish to poison?'

Poison . . . Poison . . . *Gott im Himmel,* why did they have to know what she was up to? wondered Kohler, sucking in another breath to clear his head. 'Madame de Bonnevies, I think. Frau Schlacht is a very jealous woman and, crazy as it must seem, believes Madame de Bonnevies is having an affair with her husband.'

'So she poisoned the beekeeper instead? Really, Herr Kohler . . .'

'Look, I don't even know yet if there was poison in that bottle when she left it at the Salpêtrière, but it's interesting you should suggest it.'

'I didn't.'

'Then who did, eh? Schlacht . . . Was it Schlacht who asked

you to find out from me if that wife of his was intent on poisoning him? Him! *Merde*, I should have guessed!'

At 6:17 a.m. Berlin Time there were no other cars parked along the rue Montmartre near the café À La Chope du Croissant. Pedestrians, bundled against the ten degrees of frost, hurried silently to their places of work. Cigarettes occasionally glowed in the pitch darkness. *Vélo-taxi* bells sounded warnings, their blue-blinkered lights all but lost in the ice fog that had crept up from the Seine to engulf the city.

Alone and cursing the weather, St-Cyr found the courtyard more by feel than memory. Pushing open the heavy door, he started out. Gabrielle had reminded him that the smelter was down at the far end. Russians . . . she knew some of them. Godonov, he said to himself. The boss man has an admirable handlebar moustache that is grey and bushy like his eyebrows. 'The eyes are very blue, and he plays the balalaika beautifully,' she had said.

As if such titbits of information could be of any use! He didn't know what he'd find, thought only the worst. Now all but convinced the beekeeper's murder was a 'village' affair, if not a 'family' one, he didn't know what Hermann had been up to or why the *Milice* had suddenly decided to jump him.

But it has to have been something to do with Frau Schlacht, he said silently to himself and, pausing by an iron-grilled window, listened hard for nearby sounds.

There was soot in the air. Soot and the acrid smell of sulphur. The taint of nitric acid, too, and above these, as if the top note of a perfume, that of roasting flesh. Sweet and slightly gamey. A puzzle and a worry.

Moving through the darkness, picking his way over and around the rubbish, he cocked the Lebel and looked through the grimy window to where the soft glow from a furnace gave an all but ethereal light to the dingy interior. Figures, dressed in grey nightshirts and nightgowns, ministered to the prisoner who lay with legs sprawled on the stone floor and his back propped against a heap of broken slag.

'*Er ist vom Tode gezeichnet*,' muttered St-Cyr softly to himself. The mark of death is upon him.

Pale and streaked by sweat and soot, Hermann neither stirred nor was aware of the constant ministrations. A woman bathed him with great tenderness. A man . . . the boss . . . fed tea to him, a tiny silver spoonful at a time.

'He'll sleep for hours,' sighed the Sûreté, on silently joining them. 'No, please do not be alarmed, *mes amis.* It's only his partner.'

'We'll take the day off, then,' said the one with the moustache. 'Sit with him, for he cries out and is anxious for you and about the love of his life, his Oona, and needs great comforting. In a little, we will eat and you must join us. Some soup and stew.'

'You're very kind.'

Was it so surprising in this world they shared? wondered Godonov. 'Kindness is like moonlight, is it not? It comes and goes, and one takes strength and joy from it when one can.'

'Hermann won't forget this, and neither will I.'

'Good. That is good.'

A blanket was brought and the patient covered, though Hermann was obviously warm enough. A scarred and broken armchair, was placed nearby and with it, the last two fingers of a clear-glass bottle of vodka. 'We make it ourselves from potato peelings the Occupier has little need of,' confided Godonov, touching the side of his nose with a forefinger to indicate silence in the matter. '*Za vashe zdorov'e,* Inspector. *Salut.*' Good health.

'*À votre santé aussi,* monsieur. *Merci.* Ah! a moment, please. This Oona of whom he speaks?'

One could not avoid it and had best get it over with quickly. 'Is being held by the *Milice* as insurance, but for what, I do not know, of course.'

'Oona . . . ?' muttered Hermann, tossing his head in despair. 'Oona . . . Must get her better papers. Must take her to Spain or Portugal before . . . Too late. *It's too late for that! Ah . . .*'

The faded blue eyes widened then slipped deeply back into slumber beneath their sagging pouches. 'It's the Benzedrine,' sighed St-Cyr. 'His system has finally run out of it.'

Giving a yawn, the Sûreté settled back and, yes, thought Godonov, was, though favouring a left arm, soon fast asleep himself. Two babes in the woods of the Occupier, the moon above.

The burns were small but deep among the toes of the right foot, and surely Occupied France owed much to the refuse that had been left on the beaches of Dunkirk.

Wrapped in British Army tulle gras – a sterilized gauze that had been treated with balsam of Peru and vaseline – and then in khaki that had been cut from trouser cloth, there was, of course, no room for a shoe. Hermann couldn't have worn one in any case.

'Penicillin or sulphanimide powder should be used, if possible,' said Godonov's eldest daughter, her black braids tied out of the way. 'We apologize, but have none to spare, since such wounds are frequent here, you understand. We can, however, let you have a little extra of the tulle gras, as the dressing must be changed frequently. Have you someone who can do this for you?'

'My partner, if he isn't too busy,' retorted the wounded giant, feeling angry with himself for having let it happen and worried . . . so worried, one had to ignore the taunt and a stitched-up left arm to reach out to him in comfort and urge caution. 'We'll get Oona back, Hermann.'

'And what will we find when we do?'

The *Milice* had taken her clothing, had burned it here and in front of Hermann. 'I don't know. *Merde* I wish I did, but . . . but this has to have been a warning.'

'A squeeze! *Jésus, merde alors,* can't you see that they wanted information? Schlacht *had* to find out if that wife of his intended to poison him.'

'Him . . . ?'

'Yes, idiot! Our beekeeper was nervous about his visitor, right? *Gott im Himmel,* why wouldn't he have been? A member of the Occupier. A murder. Schlacht was to have been the victim, Louis. *Schlacht!*'

Must God do this to them? 'We're to meet him in the Jardin du Luxembourg in an hour. He sent a note earlier but . . . but I didn't want to wake you until necessary.'

'I'll kill him, Louis.'

'I'm sure you mean it, and for just this reason and just this once, I'll be the keeper of our guns. Also, since that right foot of yours would only scream if the brake was applied – which it would have to be – I will, once again, drive my beautiful Citroën, if only for a final moment.'

'You're enjoying this.'

'Not after what you've just told me!'

Using a samovar, the girl had made tea and had left a small pot of buckwheat honey to sweeten it. Louis did just that, using a wooden dipper he took from a pocket.

Grimly, the one from the Kripo filled the one from the Sûreté in on things, then listened impatiently for the other side of the affair, observed Godonov, silently watching them from a distance. Both anxious and worried, they shared a cigarette as was their custom perhaps on such occasions, or when short of tobacco.

'They are like comrades in the trenches, *Babushka*,' he confided to the old woman beside him. 'Those two understand each other so well, one will go for a piss when the other needs to.'

'Passing water does not repair the damage life in this place has done to my ears. I would like to hear what they are discussing.'

'A murder, Grandmother. A case of poisoning, but much more.'

'Fornication? Was money involved or simply penetration?'

'Both, I think, but trouble. Much trouble, although I'm no detective, just a worker of small miracles.'

Left to themselves, the detectives soon became calmer, conversing earnestly and quietly, the Sûreté spreading a few handfuls of foundry sand on the floor between them before taking two candles from a pocket.

He set them upright and lit them.

'Made from the wax of hives that were loaded with Russian honey and bees that had suffered from acarine mites, Hermann. Our big shot supplies the catacombs with candles.'

'And that village priest of yours, finds bundle after bundle of them left by an anonymous donor on the steps of his church.'

'Madame de Bonnevies . . .'

'Or Danielle, eh? Danielle, Louis.'

'I didn't find any among the items she brought back from her foraging.'

'Because she'd already left them, *Dummkopf*. Ride by the church on the way home, eh? Walk the bike up the steps beside it and on the way, drop the bundle.'

'Could the donor be helping Schlacht with his factory?'

'We'll have to ask her. One thing's for certain. That factory must be a hell of a lot bigger than the wax we've so far found suggests.'

'Much bigger. Perhaps Herr Schlacht will enlighten us.'

'That wife of his really did mean to kill him, Louis. The poison in that bottle wasn't meant for anyone else – well, maybe Madame de Bonnevies, too, but primarily for our Oskar.'

This was not good. Indeed, it was terrible. 'Please go carefully over things again, Hermann. Leave nothing out.'

'She makes four trips a year to Switzerland and must have the keys and account numbers to the fortune he's had her salt away for him and for others of the avenue Foch, namely Oberg, Louis. He fools around, so much so, she's finally had enough of her Oskar and plans to escape.'

'So she badgers our beekeeper about his weekly visits . . .'

'And gets him to tell her of his sister and the stepson he can't tolerate – here, take two drags. You're going to need them. She finds out everything she can about his little life because she's convinced her Oskar's banging the hell out of Mme de Bonnevies. She even gets her maid to confirm this by staking out that fleabag Hôtel Titania, then demands de Bonnevies admit it's happening.'

The cigarette was handed back.

'Frau Schlacht buys the bottle on Tuesday, Louis. Knowing that de Bonnevies always visits his sister on Thursday afternoons, she takes it to the Salpêtrière and slips it to Angèle-Marie.'

'Whom the brother then caught drinking from it, so the oil of mirabane had yet to be added . . . But why leave the bottle with her, Hermann? Why not simply take it to de Bonnevies that evening?'

'You're too innocent. Have you learned nothing from the years with me? She did so because our beekeeper was proving difficult.'

'He had refused to have anything to do with poisoning her husband,' sighed St-Cyr heavily. 'He was terrified of reprisals and knew he'd be arrested.'

'And that has to be why she visited the house on Thursday evening.'

'To collect the bottle after he'd added the poison.'

'He'd shaved, had got himself spruced up but . . .'

'Was very nervous about his visitor and with good reason!'

'And Madame de Bonnevies knew at least something of what was going on, Louis, and was afraid you'd discover Frau Schlacht's name in that little book of her husband's.'

Another cigarette was found but ignored, so lost in thought had Louis become. 'But when Frau Schlacht arrives, our bee-keeper was either in the throes of death or dead,' he muttered. 'Yet when you confronted her in the brasserie, she showed no fear of being questioned.'

'Because she's as hard as they come and would have done that husband of hers in if she could have, *and* the beekeeper's wife, and then . . . And this is where it's perfect, Louis. She would have pointed the finger at de Bonnevies and put paid to him, too, and Danielle and Madame and the stepson!'

Death to one of the Occupier only brought more of it. 'But . . . Ah *mais alors, alors,* Hermann, there is just one little problem with what you say.'

'Go on, tell me, damn it!'

'There was another visitor to the Salpêtrière that afternoon. A man, since Angèle-Marie, for all the "voices" she hears and the worries she has about being poisoned herself, maintained that it was a "he" who had given her a taste of honey on this little dipper.'

'A man . . .' croaked Kohler.

'Someone who knew exactly how she would react to the taste, as she did, but before she'd received the bottle. Someone who didn't want her coming home and wanted to demonstrate to de Bonnevies and her doctors that she wasn't capable.'

Someone from the quartier Charonne, a member of one of the four families . . . 'The custodian, Louis?'

'His day off doesn't coincide with Thursdays but it could have been switched, yet he made no mention of it in the cata-combs.'

'He was too busy with other matters!' snorted Kohler. 'The son, Louis. Could it have been Étienne?'

'Did Schlacht pay the first half of the one hundred thousand francs at Maxim's – is this what you're now saying? Well, is it?'

'You're right, of course,' sighed Kohler. 'Schlacht wouldn't have paid it. He'd simply have used the offer to nail Juliette's underpants more firmly down around her ankles.'

'Danielle . . . Could Danielle have made a deal with him to buy her half-brother's freedom?'

They were desperate. They were trying to think of every possibility. 'That priest,' said Kohler, finally lighting the cigarette. 'Father Michel . . .'

'Would have known exactly how Angèle-Marie would react to a taste of honey and may well not have wanted her to return to the fold.'

'Yet he opened the past when he could just as easily have left it closed.'

'He's hiding something, Hermann. *Merde*, these village intrigues, these domestic quarrels. Severed heads of wife-beaters, blackmail and rape. A legacy of hatred and a determination for vengeance that reaches back more than thirty years.'

'That bottle, Louis. It must have been left unattended on the beekeeper's desk for a few hours. From when he came home from the Salpêtrière and until he returned from *Le Chat qui crie* and his little cemetery.'

'But were the gates unlocked then?' sighed St-Cyr and said firmly, 'Not likely. Keys would most probably have been needed. Keys, Hermann.'

De Bonnevies had seen his sister drink from the bottle and had thought it okay. Later, he'd had a quick shot, only to discover otherwise.

'Several would have known where he kept the nitrobenzene, Louis. Danielle . . .'

'Yes, yes. How many times must I say I can't see that girl poisoning her father?'

'The wife did it, then.'

'Or Héloïse Debré? Or Father Michel – we can't discount him yet!'

'Someone who knew it was there, Louis, and had had enough of our beekeeper who was far from being the saint that daughter

198

of his thought, and far worse than the lousy son of a bitch his wife considered him to be.'

A torturer, a blackmailer, a hider of serious crimes that had been committed by others. A man so seeking vengeance he would prolong the agony of those responsible for years just for the sweet pleasure of it.

Yet a dedicated scientist who had truly loved his bees and had had the wellbeing of the nation's bees and those of others at heart and suicidally so.

'But he didn't care for Amaretto, Hermann, and there was no guarantee whatsoever that he would drink from that bottle.'

'But would our *Bonze* have done so, Louis? Our *Bonze*?'

7

Beyond the boxwood there were rose arbours, and in among these the puppet theatre that had been rebuilt in 1931 but whose origin dated back to 1881. Beyond it, there was the Palais where the nobility of the Faubourg Saint-Honoré had been imprisoned twelve to a room, during the Reign of Terror in 1792, and a high hoarding had been wrapped completely around the Jardin du Luxembourg to keep them in until called to the guillotine.

And now? asked St-Cyr silently, as Hermann leaned on the makeshift crutches the smelter workers had kindly crafted. Now the Palais is home to the Luftwaffe and a swastika flies from it while we, the people, are the prisoners, but without the wall of boards.

There was snow everywhere, and often with distance-loving spaces between, there were strolling couples, old, young, the Occupier, too, with his *Parisiennes*. Choirboys – perhaps sixty of them – were furiously at war with snowballs among the lindens and under the stern-eyed gazes of their respective choirmaster priests. Each 'soldier' wore his 'colours' in a trailing choir gown. 'The Saint-Sulpice, Hermann, and Saint Germain-des-Prés. It's an annual affair, if God provides.'

The snow! 'They're too silent, Louis. Have they all got sore throats?'

Not a one of them made a sound. All swore or yelled with glee but under their breaths. 'People respect the rights of others here to peace and quiet,' said St-Cyr drolly, trying to calm him down. 'It's a rule that even lovers must conduct their most amorous activities in absolute silence!'

Beyond the war of snowballs, beyond the tennis courts, balustraded terraces, with wide promenades, stepped down to the large, octagonal pond where in summer and days gone by, Louis and his little boy had sailed their toy boats. Statues, most of them of the queens of France, looked silently on, and as the steps on the other side rose from terrace to terrace, they eventually led into a wide promenade that was flanked by stately plane trees.

In the distance, beneath the grey of the skies, sunlight touched the dome of the Panthéon. Breath billowed. Neither of them said a thing. Both simply wanted the moment to last, thought St-Cyr, but all too soon it was gone.

'Herr Schlacht will be waiting for us at the bandstand, Hermann. It's over there, on the way to the *Fontaine des Médicis* and before Valois's Leda and the Swan.'

'Louis, let me talk to him alone. He'll want that.'

'Can I trust you, Hermann?'

'Not to make a secret deal?' Always there was this doubt between them; less now as the years together had sped, but still, it was there. 'I'll do what I can because I have to. Oona's suffered far too much already.'

'Then go. I'll walk about for a bit, and then follow.'

Hermann reached the upper terrace and stood looking off towards the Panthéon. Framed by the lines of plane trees and closer urns where sprays of golden chrysanthemums from the hothouses were coated with ice, he looked old and defeated. A giant with one foot so bundled in rags, he gave the premonition of captured soldiers marching through the snows and into Siberia.

As if on cue, the bell of the Bibliothèque Nationale sounded once, to shimmer on the frigid air. But then all motion stopped; no one moved, for that one bell was taken up by the Notre Dame, and after that by the Sacré-Coeur and others – one by one, and throughout the city.

No wonder the choirboys had fought in silence – they'd known this would happen and now . . . now stood or crouched, as if statues themselves.

'Stalingrad . . .' sighed St-Cyr, a rush of joy and tears of gladness filling him even as he gazed across that frozen expanse towards Hermann, who made a statue, too. 'Von Paulus has surrendered.'

It was Sunday, 31 January 1943.

Behind the bandstand there was a cleared space, a no-man's-land not easily visible from elsewhere in the Jardin. Along one side of this space rows of stacked iron chairs leaned away towards tall trees like a regiment whose legs were spread as if urinating.

Having pulled one of the chairs free, Schlacht sat with forearms crossed and resting on the head of a burled walking stick. The beige, herringbone overcoat was tightly buttoned under the double chin; the grey eyes looked out emptily from beneath the pulled-down brim of a freshly blocked trilby. The gloves were new and of pigskin and all but unheard of these days; Schlacht the well-to-do Berlin *Kleinbürger* wanting yet to rise above the middle class.

The voice, when it came, was thick and still of the scrap-metal yards. 'Well, Kohler, you've me to thank for your being alive.'

'And to blame for this.'

The foot. Kohler still hadn't come down from the bandstand. 'If I understood Godonov's daughter correctly, the burns are small and not serious.'

'The Russians – even the White ones – will say anything these days.'

'And that partner of yours?'

'Louis? He's probably communing with the beehives the *Société Centrale* are overwintering under the fruit trees.'

The Society did keep hives here and regularly held beekeeping demonstrations and gave lectures. 'These papers, Kohler. This Oona Van der Lynn of yours . . .'

'She's not mine. No woman is.'

'No matter. *Diese papiere sind nicht gültig,* Kohler.'

Not valid, not good . . .

'Where is she? What have they done with her?'

'*Bitte. Kommen sie hier.* Sit awhile. Rest yourself. She's fine and will not be harmed.'

'Unless . . .'

'Let's talk first. Then we'll see.'

Tucking Oona's papers away, Schlacht offered a cigarette from a packet with a black cat on a red background. 'Craven A's,' breathed Kohler. 'Taken from downed American aircrew that were stopped while on their way to Berlin.'

'The war's not good, is it?'

'Not good, but then I don't exactly live at the expense of the Occupied like some.'

Schlacht nipped off the end of a small cigar. 'Now listen, be realistic. De Bonnevies got in the road. If that wife of his hadn't poisoned him, someone else would have.'

'And you're sure Madame de Bonnevies did it?'

The cigar was lit. 'What I'm certain of is that my Uma didn't, and that, *mein lieber Detektiv*, is the only reason I'm here talking to you. Leave her out of things.'

'She wanted you dead.'

The cigar was examined fondly like the little friend it was. 'She misunderstood things, Kohler, that's all, and has reconsidered, but wants her maid returned.'

'That girl's free to do as she pleases and has found a better job.'

'With Gabrielle Arcuri.'

'Who has generals and the OKW at her beck and call, the boys in the front lines, too, and all the others.'

Kohler had yet to sit down. 'Then we'll leave Mariette Durand where she is and hope her new boss stays out of trouble, but I must warn you rumours still persist about that woman's loyalties.'

'I'll be certain to let Gabi know.'

'And the war, Kohler? Have you heard how things are at home?'

Schlacht had been sitting on copies of the *Berliner Tageblatt* and the *Zeitung*, and took these from under himself. '*Bombenlose Nacht*, Kohler. Apparently it's what my fellow Berliners now say to each other when parting company.'

Bombless night, instead of *auf Wiedersehen*.

'Even apple cider, our favourite non-alcoholic drink, is no longer available. Rhubarb juice has been substituted! And now . . . now those little *Witze*, those political jokes my fellow Berliners love to circulate, include several about the Bolsheviks. When Obergruppenführer Sepp Dietrich announces on Radio Berlin that Bolshevism is dead, people are heard to whisper, "Long live Bolshevism"!'

As cruel and ruthless as they come, Sepp Dietrich had commanded the Führer's SS bodyguard during the days of the Blood Purge, and since then had blossomed into a Colonel General in the Waffen SS.

Everyone's friend and one to be admired, snorted Kohler silently.

When still no answer had come from him, Schlacht continued. 'We're realists, you and I, Kohler. The American landings in North Africa are only the beginning. We both know time is on the enemy's side and that the Reich has fewer than thirty thousand men here in France to keep order. Not more than two thousand five hundred of them, yourself included, are Gestapo.'*

Paris's police force had damned near half as many *flics* as that 30,000, to say nothing of the *Milice*, the *Cagoule* and all the others but this was heresy coming from someone like Schlacht. 'And *Endsieg* seems a far-off dream, is that it?'

Final victory . . . 'The Führer is not always right, so let us agree it's wisest to take precautions.'

With the help of Swiss banks! 'Are you making me an offer?'

'I'm asking you to keep out of my life. Forget about this business of the wax and honey, forget about my candles. Concentrate instead on Madrid or Lisbon and travel papers for the Van der Lynn woman that won't be questioned.'

Such a tidy offer could only have been suggested by the SS of the avenue Foch. 'And?'

Schlacht didn't let his gaze waver. 'Five million francs; two hundred and fifty thousand marks, Kohler, and not the Occupation ones. Gold wafers if you prefer.'

'Ten million, but let me have it in gold.'

'Don't push. It isn't wise of you. I really will forget about Mariette Durand, and I'll get you the papers quietly.'

'And in return?'

'I'm sure the one you're looking for is a member of the Society Central. A jealous beekeeper, nothing more.'

---

* The number needed to keep order had steadily declined to this figure of 30,000, but later increased to about 200,000 by the end of 1943. There were also operational troops in France – about 400,000 in 1942, but by 1944, nearly 1,000,000 during the invasion.

'And he poisoned de Bonnevies?'

'He would have known exactly how to do it.'

'But . . . but it might still have been an accident. We're not sure yet.'

'Then let it be one. That's even better.'

'And Madame de Bonnevies had nothing to do with it?'

Always the loose cannon, Kohler would know perfectly well the embarrassment he could cause if he went straight to the Kommandant von Schaumburg with what he already knew. 'Juliette was merely an amusement my Uma and I have agreed must end.'

'And the Hôtel Titania?'

'I own and whose front desk Juliette helped to manage, so you see, Kohler, where my wife's misunderstanding lay. Of course . . .' Cigar ash was examined. 'Of course I'll have to find a replacement, and for this . . .' He sighed heavily and looked up again. 'I'm willing to make a trade.'

'Giselle?'

'Think about it. She'd be perfect.'

Kohler was sickened by the thought and at a loss for words. 'A former prostitute, *mein Lieber*. Young, very beautiful – wise in such ways and everything a businessman such as myself could hope for in a prospective employee. The Durand girl will be left alone and your Oona sent to freedom with the gold. Take it or leave it and *don't*, please don't, ever mess with me again.'

Giselle . . . Kohler saw her as she'd been that first time in the waiting room with all the others at Madame Chabot's. Straight, jet-black hair, good shoulders and of a little more than medium height. He saw her turn to smile at him as her name was called, the *négligée* falling open, nothing on under it, the girl asking, 'What, please, is it you desire, monsieur?'

'Fate . . . it was fate,' he muttered sadly. Schlacht had left him cold, had flung that cigar of his aside, and was now gone from the Jardin du Luxembourg, the stab marks of his walking stick all too clear in the snow.

'*Jésus, merde alors*, what the hell am I going to do?' he demanded angrily. He couldn't trust the Berliner and the SS to carry through with the papers. He mustn't even think of it! 'But I want to,' he lamented. '*Mein Gott*, to see Oona safely in Spain would make it all worthwhile.'

But would it?

'She'd only find out what I'd done and would never forgive me; Giselle neither, and certainly not Louis! Yet Oona could buy that little hotel on the Costa del Sol they'd all dreamed of, and not so little now either. She could set herself up really well and be ready and waiting for him and Giselle when . . .

The butt of Schlacht's cigar had gone out. With difficulty, Kohler leaned over – tried to keep his right foot out of the snow – and plucked the thing away.

'You bastard,' he said as he scattered the tobacco in the wind, rather than tuck the butt into his *mégot* tin. 'Two hundred and fifty thousand marks in gold. *Ausweise* and papers no one would fool with . . .' And hadn't Giselle helped him and Louis out before? Hadn't she been plucked from the street and taken to the avenue Foch to Oberg who had made her stand before him as he'd stared up at her through his bottle-thick glasses? Hadn't she been beaten up by the French Gestapo of the rue Lauriston?

'I can't ask her to help us,' he said. 'I mustn't.'

Even so, temptation clawed. All the way back to the pond, he thought about it – tried to figure a way out. Let Schlacht get the papers for Oona. Agree to go along with him, and then . . . then . . .

Louis . . . where the hell was Louis when needed most and not in sight?

'I can't tell him a thing. If I do, Oona will be killed.'

Danielle de Bonnevies stood looking down at one of the Society's hives, some twenty or so of which were wintering among espaliered fruit trees, and when the detective from the Sûreté caught sight of her, she felt herself automatically flinch, but worse than this, knew he had seen her do so.

The flock of sparrows that had been feeding on the crumbled vitaminic biscuits she had scattered in the snow at her feet fled, leaving the yellowish stain of the biscuits and the two of them starkly alone. He'd know all about where she'd got those biscuits

– from the J-threes to whom they'd been distributed at school. He'd know she sold them to others, the very best pigeon bait there was. 'Inspector . . .' she heard herself bleat. 'Why . . . why are you here?'

'Me? I was just enjoying the few moments of peace the investigation seems to have allowed.'

A lie . . . What he'd said was an absolute lie! 'I . . . I've come for the meeting but . . . but am a little early.'

And not at home in mourning. 'The Society. Yes, of course. I'd forgotten.'

Another of his lies. He wouldn't have missed a thing like that. Not when *papa* had been about to tell the world what was happening to Russia's bees. Not when she'd told the Sûreté one of the Society could so easily have been the poisoner.

'Cowards,' she muttered under her breath but loudly enough. '*Papa* called them cowards because they were afraid of being arrested.'

'Some of them didn't want him to speak out, did they?' she heard the Sûreté saying as he came closer, too close, and she could, though not daring to face him yet, see the white breath of his words as they fell on her.

'No, they didn't,' she said defeatedly, but then, as if in anger, she turned and said accusingly, 'I saw Herr Schlacht telling the tall one with the crutches something he did not want to hear.'

The girl must have spotted them as she'd come along the promenade between the plane trees. 'Hermann and he are having a little heart-to-heart of their own, mademoiselle, but it's interesting that you should know of Herr Schlacht.'

'I . . . I don't know him well. *Maman* has . . . has only spoken of him once. Just once.'

'And yet you could identify him so easily?'

'He . . . *Maman* . . . They . . .'

'They secretly met at a hotel in the Eighteenth.'

'Yes.'

Hastily she dragged off a mitten and wiped her eyes – tried to find composure and took to staring bleakly down at the beehive in front of her. Snow capped its flat roof. 'Brood chamber below and honey super above,' she said hollowly of the two-tiered boxes. 'Six to ten frames of comb in the brood chamber should tide the colony over, but here there are extras in the upper chamber so that the worker bees can place the honey and pollen where they feel it best and the wintering cluster can move slowly about the hive as it wishes. *Papa* always put a super like this on top of the brood chamber and then a square of heavy tarpaper to shed the rain and snow melt.'

'He loved his bees, didn't he?'

'As a husband ought to love a wife, only in his heart there wasn't room for one.'

'Did your mother go willingly to the Hôtel Titania on the boulevard Ornano?'

'You're simply trying to get me to tell you she had another reason.'

'And did she?'

Étienne . . . was he wondering about Étienne? 'I wouldn't know, would I, Inspector? We seldom spoke.'

'Yet surely you knew of her repeated attempts to free your brother?'

'My half-brother.'

'Father Michel refused to find three willing workers to be sent to the Reich in exchange for her son. Maxim's, mademoiselle. Isn't Maxim's the reason your mother went to that hotel?'

To prostitute herself. To let Herr Schlacht paw her naked body and rape her, yes rape her in return for his paying the necessary 50,000 francs down. 'I . . . I really wouldn't know, Inspector. Étienne was someone she and I never discussed.'

'Even though she was so worried about him and had done everything she could to secure his release?'

The girl didn't answer. Cramming her mittened hands deeper into the pockets of her overcoat, she waited in silence. And what was it Hermann had said Frau Schlacht had told him about the half-sister and half-brother? That the beekeeper had complained to her that Danielle's one mistake was to blindly trust Étienne and to encourage his every endeavour.

'You posed for your brother, mademoiselle. You were the best of comrades. He made sketches of you and at least one superb bronze we know of.'

'Did I pose naked for him – is this what she told you?'

'She?'

'Mother, of course. She hated my being close to her son. Étienne and I used to tease each other about it. Jealous . . . she was so jealous, I'm not surprised she told you I was naked when I posed.'

'And were you?'

'What do you think, Inspector? Do I look the type?'

Wryly she tossed her head at his silence and said, 'When I was three or four I did when bribed with the whole of a peach flan, but not since then.'

Yet that father of yours believed you had done so right up to when the boy went off to war, thought St-Cyr and heard himself ask harshly, 'Was Étienne de Bonnevies' release arranged and paid for by Herr Oskar Schlacht?'

'Did Étienne poison my father – is this what you're wondering? If so, then the answer is no, Inspector. Étienne couldn't kill anything. Not in this war we lost and not before it either. "All who are born have a right to life," he'd always say and leave the job, if absolutely necessary, to me. To *me*, Inspector. Me, the fumigator *par excellence* of my father's hives. You'll not have forgotten that, I think!'

'When questioned in your father's study, mademoiselle, you tried to keep me from the microscope he'd been using and denied having been told why he felt a disaster was so certain.'

'Acarine mites in Caucasians from Russia. All right, I knew that Herr Schlacht was causing diseased hives to be brought into France. Does that satisfy you now?'

'How long has it been going on?'

'How long did *papa* and I know of it? Since early last summer. We knew it had to be stopped. Things like that can be so easily spread – in one season half the hives can be wiped out in any apiary, sometimes all of them.'

'So when Frau Schlacht wanted honey for facial masks and bee stings for her arthritis, your father was only too willing to supply them?'

'She'd been a client right from September of 1940.'

'And the candle-making has been going on since when?'

'The . . . the fall of last year, I think. Earlier perhaps.'

'The fall of 1941?'

'Yes . . . yes, perhaps.'

'And where is the factory located?'

'The factory . . . ? I . . . We . . . *Papa* and I tried to find out, but then I . . . I told him that it was best if we . . . we left the matter alone.'

'Why? Because you knew that fifty thousand francs had been paid?'

'And Étienne had come home yet mother didn't know of it? I'd have told her if I'd known such a thing, Inspector. Believe me, I'd have gladly ended the little hell I've had to endure with her. Going out in search of food – peddling my merchandise and constantly running the controls, so much so my nerves are all but shot? *Shot*, do you understand? Only to come home to nothing but silence and disapproval from her? You saw the way she slapped me when I asked if she'd put the oil of mirbane into that . . . that bottle of Amaretto. You and your partner questioned her thoroughly, didn't you? Well, didn't you? You saw how she feels about me, the "accident", the "tragedy" her womb committed, its betrayal – God, why couldn't she have drowned me at birth? I . . . Ah *nom de Dieu*, forgive me. You see the state I'm in.'

But had the outburst been deliberate? wondered St-Cyr, forcing himself to question, as Hermann did, if the girl might well be guilty.

Thinking it best to give pause to his questions, or perhaps wanting to better plan his little campaign, the Inspector indicated that they should walk towards the promenade that would lead them to the terraces and his partner. He wouldn't leave her alone now, but would keep on asking things, felt Danielle, and she would have to answer with sufficient truth to counter disbelief.

'That bottle, mademoiselle. You stated that when you left the house at five a.m. on Thursday it wasn't in the study.'

'I'd never seen it before.'

'But you stated first that your mother had poisoned your father and then . . . then felt one of the Society might have done it?'

'Mother couldn't have, and I told you this, that I'd spoken out of despair. As for a member of the Society, come and meet them. Hear what they have to say to me, then decide for yourself!'

It was nearly two o'clock and still there was no sign of Louis. Had he left the Jardin du Luxembourg? wondered Kohler anxiously. Had he realized Schlacht would have to offer a deal that couldn't be refused because Oberg and the SS had first been consulted?

Louis would feel a need to sort things out and redefine his side of the partnership. He'd want to be by himself. *Mein Gott*, the *Bonze* made gold wafers for the SS of the avenue Foch, and sure as hell Oberg wouldn't want Old Shatter Hand finding out about it! That was why Oona was a hostage. No other reason. Oona . . .

With difficulty, he hobbled back up the steps to the highest of the terraces, to stand again, leaning on his crutches, forcing himself to let his gaze sift calmly over the Jardin. A Wehrmacht concert band, oblivious to peace and quiet, struck up *Deutschland über Alles* as if to thumb their noses at the loss of the Sixth Army – 24 generals, 150,000 dead, 100,000 taken prisoner, tanks, guns, everything – and to let the French know the Occupier was here to stay. Few turned to pause and listen, most just kept on as they were and tried to ignore the racket.

A Bach fugue followed to crash sorrowfully around the ears, but then the oompah-tubas and other brasses hit their stride with that old beerhall favourite *In München steht ein Hofbräuhaus!*

'I feel like an idiot standing out here like this,' he swore softly. The French would hate him when this Occupation ended, as surely it must, and never mind Rudi's talk of flying bombs, or the *Milice*, or the *Cagoule*. The *Résistance* would grab Oona and Giselle if he didn't do something soon and fast. They wouldn't understand that he wasn't one of the Occupier, not really, and that neither Oona nor Giselle had given themselves to the enemy. They'd blame Louis for collaborating. They'd hang that patriot or slam him up against the post without even a blindfold! They *wouldn't* listen to a word his partner screamed.

It was at times like this that a priest, if one believed in such, might be helpful, and as sure as that God of Louis's had called them, one hurried past. Was it a sign? wondered Kohler bleakly. Knitted dark black, bushy brows formed thatches over dark brown, harried eyes that were behind heavy black horn-rimmed bifocals. The black overcoat had been carefully brushed, the black beret cleaned and ironed . . .

'Father, just a minute!'

Swiftly the priest took him in at a glance. 'Not now. Can't you see I haven't time?'

'Kohler, Father. Gestapo Paris-Central and that little murder in Charonne, eh?'

'My son, forgive me, but . . . but if I don't hurry, a young life may be lost. The métro was stopped by your people, and now . . .'

'Now you're late and worried about Danielle de Bonnevies.'

'Now I greatly fear she is about to make a terrible mistake.'

Brusquely Father Michel indicated the greenhouses that were behind hedges and a high stone wall next to the School of Mines, in the southeastern corner of the Jardin.

'Then I'd better come with you,' sighed Kohler. 'Here, let me rest a hand on your shoulder. These crutches of mine are a curse.'

'Is she suspected of poisoning that father of hers?'

'Did she?'

'No. No, of course she didn't. What makes you think so?'

'Aren't I the one who's supposed to ask the questions?'

'Then stop her from speaking out. Let me defend her.'

'Against whom?'

'Herself and them. Juliette also, for I'm certain she has tried to prevent Danielle from doing this and has failed.'

Forbidden territory, open only to a select few and then but rarely, the greenhouses of the Jardin were the domain of its gardeners who understandably resented any and all intrusion. But oh *mon Dieu*, thought St-Cyr, forgetting their troubles for the moment. It was like stepping into spring.

Tulips, crocuses, daffodils and cyclamens, begonias and baby's-breath – the tiny-flowered variety so affectionately called Paris Market – were here en masse. There were freesia and alyssum and forget-me-nots, and over the weathered lattice of an arbour that divided the long length of the greenhouse in half, soon a vibrant display of orange-flowering nasturtiums.

Shrubs were in terracotta pots and tubs on the crowded banks of trestle tables along whose aisles the members had filed: acacia, soon with its delight of tiny clusters of yellow; star jasmine in its late blooming, the perfume mingling with that of calla lilies and around them, masses of anemones, primroses and sky-blue scilla.

'Monsieur . . .'

The gardener sternly indicated the crowd of forty or so who had finally made their way to the far end where chairs had been set up in the aisles. 'It's not the Orangery,' muttered St-Cyr, 'but is every bit as pleasant. I envy you.'

'Few would.'

A pessimist? he wondered. Every fall the oleanders, date palms, orange and pomegranate trees, grown in large wooden planters about the garden, were taken indoors to the Orangery, but it, too, must be reserved for the Occupier and out of bounds even to such a long-standing and respected group as the Society.

Instead of it, they had to be content with row upon row of magic, a veritable jungle of colour where hot-water heating pipes banged because it was their nature, and moisture constantly dampened the flagstone floor.

Bees unobtrusively went about their business. 'They're working overtime,' he quipped, for the man was trying to hurry him into joining the others. 'Like detectives, they're not allowed vacations.'

A coat sleeve was urgently plucked at.

'Was he really murdered?' asked the gardener, his expression now one of deep concern.

They were still some distance from the assembled. Danielle de Bonnevies had hurried on well ahead of them. 'St-Cyr, Sûreté, Monsieur . . . ?'

'Lalonde. Paul-André, *sous-jardinier.*'

Assistant gardener. 'What do you think?'

Short, wiry and dressed in unbelievably faded coveralls, and wearing an old grey fedora, Lalonde was over seventy, the face thin and with a high forehead and bony hands that had been wrinkled and blotched by a life spent largely outdoors.

No glasses, though, and an enviable clearness to deep blue eyes that now gave the frankest of gazes.

'What you mean to ask, Inspector . . .'

'It's Chief Inspector, but yes, I want to know which ones.'

'Any of several.'

'Please save me time I can't spare.'

'Then any of the most vocal three. Monsieur le président de Bonnevies was not an easy man. Oh *bien sûr*, one could always ask his advice but he was far too unyielding a scientist for them, too much the perfectionist. It was his idea to release a few bees here, so as to bring more meaning to the winter's lectures he will now no longer be able to give. Monsieur Baucour, my superior, tried many times to get him to remove the bees, but Alexandre refused to hear of it. Once his mind was made up, it stayed that way, but . . .'

Lalonde gave a sheepish grin and sucked in on his grizzled cheeks. 'But I, myself, have become quite accustomed to them and find them most restful.'

A man after my own heart! thought St-Cyr.

Lettuces, radishes, shallots and green onions were being grown in among the flowers and as they walked along the aisle, the assistant gardener kept an eye on everything.

'Alexandre was a very worried man, Chief Inspector. He and the three you will hear most, fought constantly. They didn't want him to . . .'

Danielle had stepped up on to the rostrum. Suddenly her voice sang out with, '*Mesdames, Mesdemoiselles et Messieurs, attendez-vous. My father is gone and I must take his place.*'

'STOP HER, PLEASE!'

Father Michel and Hermann had just entered the greenhouse and were at the other end, the priest with an arm raised.

'NO, FATHER, THEY MUSTN'T!' shouted Danielle.

'INSPECTOR, I BEG YOU!' cried the priest as he hurried along an aisle, with Hermann trying desperately to catch up.

'Mademoiselle de Bonnevies, you are out of order!' shouted one of the men at the front.

'ORDER!' shouted another.

'Please let her speak,' said an older woman tartly. 'She has every right and more than enough experience.'

'Madame Roulleau, you mind your tongue!' seethed the one who had cried for order.

'My father . . .' began Danielle again. 'Many of you know he planned to give an important address today but . . . but was prevented from doing so – *was poisoned, do you understand?*' she shrilled, her voice echoing under the glass.

No one moved in their seats or said a thing. Were they too afraid of or embarrassed by what was to come? wondered St-Cyr. The speech de Bonnevies had been working on was still tucked in his jacket pocket – *merde*, there'd been so little time and he'd put off reading it! But now the girl, having denied any knowledge of its substance, was freely admitting she had lied.

As Father Michel, and finally Hermann, caught up with him, he indicated the offending document. The three of them stood side by side in the centre aisle at the back of the gathering, the girl up front on a makeshift dais that gave her the advantage of but a half-metre of height over those who were seated. There were several of the Occupier – two SS from the SIPO, the Sicherheitspolizei, their security police who specialized in investigating enemies of the State – *Jésus, merde alors*, why had they come?

The German overseer was here, too. Every segment of French agriculture and industry, even apiculture, had one, usually a specialist in his field.

'Frau Käthe Hillebrand,' breathed Hermann, nodding towards a smartly dressed blonde in a light beige, camelhair overcoat, soft lemon-coloured cashmere scarf, brown leather gloves and a wide-brimmed tan fedora that all but hid the right half of her brow and was, yes, very provocative.

'That is our *Bonze*'s secretary, Louis, but what the hell is she doing here?'

'Listening, perhaps.'

Madame Roulleau was knitting a pullover from scavenged unravelled wool, but held the needles poised for more dialogue, the fingers pudgy, the face lined with worry and with deep pouches under soft brown eyes.

De Bonnevies was to have paid her a visit on Friday. Beside her sat an elderly gentleman who wore the yellow and green ribbon of the *Médaille Militaire*. 'Captain Henri-Alphonse Vallée, of 2 place des Vosges, Hermann,' said St-Cyr quietly. '*Confident* in all difficult matters.'

'*Mesdames et Messieurs* . . .'

'SIT DOWN! YOU'VE NO RIGHT!'

This had come from one of the three men at the front: a grey business suit, and with immaculately groomed grey hair.

'I have every right, Monsieur le vice-président Jourdan, but let us put it to a vote,' countered Danielle, clearly flustered and upset, yet determined to carry through. 'All those in favour of allowing me a few moments of their time; and then, those not in favour. Monsieur l'Inspecteur Kohler of the Gestapo has just arrived with Père Michel, our parish priest and an old friend of my father's. Perhaps these two could count the votes.'

'THIS IS INSANE! SIT DOWN!'

'TAKE YOUR PLACE, MADEMOISELLE!'

'AT THE BACK, WHERE I WILL NEVER BE HEARD, MONSIEUR DE SAUSSINE? You who have fought so hard to stop my father from speaking out, should at least have the courage to allow his daughter to do so, if for no other reason than to honour the man who taught you virtually everything you know!'

'Let us listen to her,' grumbled Mme Roulleau, stuffing her knitting away in its bag. 'Oh come now, *mes vieux amis*, what can a mere girl say that offends so much?'

You wise old owl, thought St-Cyr. You know exactly what that girl plans to tell them.

'Those for letting her continue,' sang out Kohler.

Hands were raised, some hesitantly and only after others had been lifted.

'And now the nays!' he cried.

The SS played no part in the voting, and neither did any of the others of the Occupier, including two Obergrenadiers on leave, a Hauptmann, a Major and another *Blitzmädel*.

'Praise be to God,' sighed Father Michel. 'The nays have it in abundance!'

'Oh no they don't, Father,' swore Kohler softly and then, much louder, 'Thirty-five to eight say she speaks!'

'*Merci*,' managed Danielle and tried to smile.

Father Michel crossed his chest and said softly but acidly, 'May God forgive you, my son.'

'Mesdames, Mesdemoiselles et Messieurs, will no one speak for the bees of Russia? Reliable estimates tell us that over one-half of all Russian honeybees have already perished – one-half! This tragic loss is not just due to the fierce shelling of tiny villages and hamlets, you understand, nor to other acts of war which leave the farms in ruins and the hives untended. It is also due to disease and its rapid spread. Since few are left to trap the swarms when each colony divides, these establish themselves in the wild and there, too, the diseases spread to decimate those few colonies that are still being carefully tended.

'But . . . but it's not simply of these matters that my father wished to speak. There is theft on a massive scale. In most rural areas of the Ukraine and in Poland and elsewhere in the east, the peasants are still using the woven wicker or straw skeps, and now . . . now especially in winter, these hives are being gathered by German soldiers. Skeps are piled one on top of another without regard to their brood clusters or to disease, and these . . . these are being shipped by rail to Paris.'

Again she paused, but this time opened her left hand to release a bee which lingered until gently blown away.

'Normally in the late fall the peasants would examine each hive, and would drown the oldest and heaviest, but also the lightest and weakest colonies, both to destroy any disease and to harvest the honey. But now these diseased colonies, and the healthy ones, too, arrive here. *Papa* knew that among them some carried acarine mites and European foul brood, also chalk brood which, as many of you know, makes the dead larvae appear as if Egyptian mummies wrapped in white cotton. He tried to stop what was happening, and for this . . . for this was poisoned.'

'*VOYOU!*' sang out one of the men at the front, leaping to his feet to shake a fist at her. Delinquent . . .

'*SALOPE!*'

'*C'EST SCANDELEUX!*' cried another, joining him.

'God forbid our guests should have to listen to such rubbish!'

'À TOUT PRIX, MONSIEUR DE SAUSSINE!' shrieked Danielle. At any price!

She caught a breath and hastily wiped away her tears, calmed herself a little and at a sudden thought, even tried to smile. 'After all, hasn't the Maréchal Pétain told us that no neutrality is possible between truth and falsehood? Why, then, should we lie about this matter?'

'Silence, girl. You've already said too much!'

'MURDERER!' she shrilled. 'ASSASSIN! I WILL FINISH AS IS MY RIGHT!'

One of the SS nodded at her to continue and in spite of their presence, she found her voice. 'Those hives are joined by crushed and mangled honeycomb and broodcomb from the Vaucluse, from Normandy, Brittany, Anjou, Touraine and other regions, and this . . . this is not for the honey they contain but for the wax which is made into candles. The wax!'

She let that sink in.

'And we all know which of our most revered of institutions must burn only beeswax candles, don't we, Père Michel? The Église de Saint-Germain-de-Charonne, your very own church, n'est-ce pas? The Notre Dame, aussi, and Sacré-Coeur, and all others, since all have found ways to purchase them on the black market at highly inflated prices. Even in wartime such candles are necessary. Especially so, I think, since no others are available. But some of you here have used the honey from these diseased hives to augment your winter stores – admit it, messieurs. My father knew very well one of these three was selling it to you and lying about it.'

Either Jourdan, de Saussine, or the man who sat between them, thought St-Cyr.

'She's a dead girl, Louis. She's just committed suicide but we had to let her speak out.'

'Agreed. Brave yet foolish, Hermann, but did she have another reason for doing so and is that not why this priest didn't want her to?'

'You fools,' swore Father Michel. 'You call yourselves detectives but are so blind. There is my reason, and hasn't that woman suffered enough?'

Not two metres behind them, Juliette de Bonnevies had stood silently watching the daughter whose existence she had hardly acknowledged. Now she gazed steadily at each of them in turn, and the black veil she wore only served to emphasize the hardness of her betrayal and their suspicions of her.

The uproar had subsided but now the charges were being laid and a deathly calm had settled over the members of the Society, all of whom had been confined to their chairs and placed under an armed SS guard.

Wary of putting his foot too deeply in the shit, Louis had wisely stayed in the background.

'The girl is accused of buying and selling on the black market, Kohler.'

'And that represents two counts against her, eh?' he panicked, taking in the blue-eyed, hawk-eyed, greying son of a bitch in the snappy field-grey uniform who was the same SS major as had had him arrested at the Club Mirage! The Golden Party Badge put the bastard among the first 100,000 members of the Nazi Party. The silver *Blutorden*, with its red and white ribbon, narrowed things down to the Blood Purge – all 1,500 of them had received one in 1933, on its tenth anniversary.

The SS *Dienstauszeichnungen*, the Long Service Award, only had a silver swastika with SS runes on the ribbon – twelve years, but this one would be anxiously awaiting the twenty-five-year gilt swastika, since he'd damned well been around since 1923.

'Lots of people buy and sell these days. She's only a kid.'

'Discipline, Kohler. *Discipline*! She has also fomented discord by accusing the Army of a criminal act.'

'*Mein Gott*, since when did the SS ever take up the cause of protecting the Wehrmacht's enviable reputation? And here I thought they were well able to do that themselves.'

Kohler would never learn. As a prisoner of war in 1916, he had come to love the French so much he had even learned to speak their inferior language. 'The girl is under arrest, and will be considered *Sühneperson*. She'll be shot as soon as her name is selected.'

'But . . . but, Sturmbannführer, she's a suspect in a murder investigation. Both Gestapo Boemelburg, my superior officer, and the Kommandant von Gross-Paris have ordered us to look into the matter.'

'And that takes precedence over acts of terrorism?'

'Look, be reasonable. We need to question her.'

'Then do so. You have exactly one hour.'

Schiesse! 'Then begin by hauling before us the pigeons who fingered her on the black-market charges. My partner and I had best question them first.'

'As you wish.'

Oberg must really be in a rage. 'Would it help if we found it wasn't murder at all, but simply an accident?'

'Perhaps.'

'That way, our reports would contain nothing other than statements from the wife, the daughter and the priest. I'd vet everything. You have my word on it.'

'And that of your partner?'

'Louis will be made to see we have no reason to declare anything else. A clean slate all round and a happy funeral.'

'But . . . but this would surely not eradicate the criminal charges, Kohler? I, too, must file reports. The Brigadeführer und Generalmajor der Polizei, the Höherer SS und Polizeiführer of France is most thorough and accepts only total loyalty, absolute thoroughness, and the truth above all else.'

Ach du lieber Gott, what the hell did this one really want?

'Giselle le Roy, Kohler. The Dutch alien, Oona Van der Lynn, to be sent into exile to one of the camps.'

And never mind the deal Schlacht had offered, even though this one would have known all about it. Never mind even admitting that such an offer had been made.

'Then take me to see your boss. I've things I have to say to him.'

'And your partner?'

'Leave him here to do what he does best.'

Without a word or even a nod, Hermann was gone from the greenhouse and that could only mean trouble, thought St-Cyr. Some of the members simply stared emptily at the backs of the chairs ahead of them; a few smoked cigarettes. All were afraid – this was abundantly clear. Several were embarrassed by, and ashamed of what had been done to Danielle, but all prayed they'd not be arrested themselves.

That is only human, he cautioned himself. Madame Roulleau and Captain Henri-Alphonse Vallée, from widely differing worlds, held each other by the hand. War did things like that, the Occupation especially. It broke down social barriers and cast aside the customs of centuries.

Both were much shaken by the girl's arrest and, though they would earnestly want to speak out on her behalf, knew well what that would almost certainly bring.

Under guard, Danielle sat in a chair on the dais, her head bowed, the not quite shoulder-length, pale auburn hair falling forward. That she was silently praying seemed evident, and he couldn't help but feel sympathy for her. The worry of always having to run the controls had finally caught up with her, but as with so many these days, she'd been accused by people who had known her for much of her life, and they'd done so, not out of any sense of public duty, but simply to save their own asses or to get back at her, and never mind the hundred thousand francs reward that might or might not be paid.

Jourdan, de Saussine, and the third member of their front-row coterie, Bertrand Richaux, stonily kept their counsel. They'd wait to be questioned, and perhaps it would be best to let them, since they'd expect to be among the first and every moment of delay would serve to further put them on edge.

Alone among the Occupier, apart from the guards, Frau Käthe Hillebrand had stayed behind, and when his gaze met hers, she smiled as if to say, What now, Inspector? She was calmly smoking a cigarette and had taken out a notebook and pen to record things for her boss. A woman, then, who would know more than she'd let on and would now be very careful about what she said.

Father Michel had tried to comfort Juliette de Bonnevies but without success. Both still stood near him, the woman with her back to the priest, her gloved fingers delicately caressing the petals of a crimson cyclamen as if trying desperately to find a moment's peace.

'Your son, madame. Has he been released?' he asked, closing the gap between them as though on impulse. 'You begged Herr Schlacht to intercede on his behalf, didn't you?'

'Inspector . . .'

'Father, later. It's with this one that I must begin. Please leave us immediately. *Well*?' demanded St-Cyr of her.

Startled, she stiffened and, lifting her hand from the cyclamen, briefly touched her veil as she turned to look at him, the dark brown eyes now rapidly moistening.

'I begged him to, and he agreed that if I would do as he asked, the fifty thousand francs the waiter had demanded would be paid.'

Her lips had quivered as she'd said this, but quickly she overcame her nervousness.

'Madame, you knew of Herr Schlacht through your husband's contacts with his wife.'

'Yes. All right. I . . . I did go through that little book of Alexandre's not once but several times. It wasn't hard to contact Frau Schlacht's husband. The Hôtel Drouot . . . We met six months ago and he decided what he wanted from me in exchange, while I, poor fool, believed him. I did! damn you. I was desperate.'

'But he didn't pay up.'

'No, he did not. Two or three times a week I'd go to that filthy place of his and . . .'

'The Hôtel Titania.'

'Room 4–18. From its little balcony there is a rather pleasant view of the Sacré-Coeur, even in winter.'

'Then in so far as you know, Étienne is still in Oflag 17A?'

'Yes, and I would willingly give myself to anyone, male or female, who would see that he was allowed to come home.'

'But your husband didn't want him to, did he?'

'What do you think?'

The dark, almost black hair and sharply defined features with their pale complexion suited the veil most admirably and she knew it and used it to good advantage, so much so, he was reminded she'd been very much of the Sorbonne and the rue du Faubourg Saint-Honoré, but never of the quartier Charonne.

'He wanted his sister to return and you couldn't have that, could you?' asked St-Cyr.

'As I've already told you, Inspector, I didn't poison him. Oh *bien sûr*, if I'd known how to, I most certainly would have tried to, but . . .' Her slender shoulders lifted in a nonchalant shrug as she looked away.

'But would Danielle?' he asked.

'Have told me how to – Is this what you're after? Well, is it?'

'No, madame. Would Danielle have told your son?'

'Who despised his father for the way he treated me and would want to stop it?'

'Before Angèle-Marie was allowed to compound your suffering.'

'Étienne isn't in France, Inspector. Oskar always promised to pay for his release. He'd always say, "Next week, or tomorrow, or in a few days," and I'd let him do whatever he wanted to me. I'd even beg him to do it and willingly I'd allow others into the room to watch or participate, if that was what he wished. What did it matter, really, so long as Étienne came home?'

'Then could anyone else have paid for that boy's release?'

'His real father – Is this what you're wondering, because if it is, then I must tell you that he died in 1938.'

'His name, Madame de Bonnevies? I'm sorry, but it's necessary.'

'But . . . but it has no bearing on my husband's death. How could it have?'

'All things have bearing, even the rape of a fifteen-year-old girl in the Père Lachaise on 20 August 1912.'

How cruel of him. 'Henri-Christophe de Trouvelot. His widow has since remarried, and now the mother who refused her son the joy of his one true love, lives alone.'

'Where?'

'Forty-two boulevard Maillot.'

In Neuilly, overlooking the Bois de Boulogne, and money . . . lots of money. 'Ah *bon*! that's all I want from you at present. Next . . . who's next?' he called out and then, in *deutsch* to a guard, 'You may release this one.'

But no one was to be released until the major had returned.

The conservatory was warm, huge and humid, and stepping into it like entering a verdant jungle where one expected monkeys to chatter and pythons to lurk.

Or scorpions, thought Kohler uncomfortably as he leaned on his crutches. The major and his adjutant had ushered him through the entrance of this dripping glass house and now stood guard outside it!

Merde, what the hell was up? This wasn't the Luxembourg but the Jardin des Plantes where, not so long ago and in its zoo, a bomb had been left for him to defuse. Sweat and all the rest of it. Suspicions of *Résistance* people – Gabrielle no less – and a safe-cracker named the Gypsy.

Scheisse! Oberg couldn't have liked the outcome of that affair, nor what had happened in Avignon, and had deliberately chosen to meet him here as a reminder. But that could only mean the meeting had been decided on well before he'd even asked for it. And why, please, the secrecy?

There were flowers – things called Flame of the Woods and Bleeding Glory Bower. Orchids, too, and hadn't Oberg liked them? They grew on the ribbed trunks of the palms, and in among the creepers. One was high above him, another over there . . . Pretty things that seemed to wait in silent judgement.

Bananas, too. Their thick stalks and long, broad leaves all but hiding pale green bunches.

Spiders, most probably. Black widows maybe.

In 1926 Karl Albrecht Oberg had landed a job with a wholesale tropical fruit importer in his home town of Hamburg. Perhaps he had dreamt of jungles like this while tallying the books, perhaps of naked Polynesian maidens, but he'd have thought of them with disgust, no doubt, for he had been, and still was, contentedly married and was as strait-laced, severe and no-nonsense a son of a bitch as one could find. A plodder with women. A man of little joy.

Within three years he'd left to join a competitor, only to have the Great Depression shove him out the door and into the tiny tobacco kiosk he'd managed to buy in the Schanenburgerstrasse, near the town hall.

In June of 1931, he had joined the Party – number 575205 – and months later the SS, where Reinhard Heydrich had put him in the Sicherheitsdienst and had shot him up the ranks.

September 1941 saw him as S.D. und Polizeiführer at Radom, where he earned the epithet 'The Butcher of Poland' for his ruthless suppression of resistance and passionate extermination of Jews and other so-called undesirables, most especially the Gypsies, ah yes.

At forty-five years of age, and with the power of life or death over every living soul in France, he had landed in Paris. Hardly a word of French to him – he'd leave all that to others.

One had to pause and gape, for there he was at last, coming out from the jungle. The field-grey greatcoat, with its wide parade lapels and shining cap, with its silver skull and crossbones, went with the highly polished jackboots and the black leather gloves which were impatiently being slapped into the left hand. Behind him, water from a tiered and sculpted fountain shot up into the air before showering into streams beneath the glass dome of the conservatory, and flanking Australian tree ferns towered above him.

A man of little more than medium height, round and fleshly of face, and with a slight paunch and double chin, and a small, closely clipped, Führer-style moustache, tight sardonic smile, and pale, blue-grey, bulging eyes behind thick and steel-rimmed spectacles.

When approached, the look he gave was simply one of mild impatience as if to say to himself, I can squash this bug any time I like.

It was impossible to clash the heels together, and one crutch would fall away to clatter on the floor as the salute was given!

'Heil Hitler, Herr Höherer SS und Polizeiführer. Kohler, Kripo, Paris-Central. You wanted to see me?'

'Kohler . . . Ah yes. You've been wounded.'

The crutch was snatched up. 'It's nothing, mein Brigadeführer und Generalmajor von der Polizei. A small accident. I was careless.'

'Then you mustn't let it happen again. These days, good men are becoming harder and harder to find.'

Oberg let that sink in. 'This entanglement with the Procurement Office, Kohler. *Das Amt* is a Wehrmacht organization but most useful to the SS.'

The office . . . the bureau . . . 'That is understood, Herr Höherer.'

'*Gut.* Then in your reports to the General von Schaumburg you should emphasize two things. First, that we have no interest whatsoever in it, and secondly, that this compound is really quite remarkable.'

The tin was about ten centimetres in diameter and the same in height, the label showing an industrious *Panzergruppe* polishing their boots in a Russian flax field while bees floated happily around them.

'The Soldier's little Friend?' he bleated.

'Beeswax and lanolin. Herr Schlacht manufactures the compound for the Wehrmacht, Kohler, and has just been awarded a two-year contract. I, myself, find it excellent, and have enthusiastically recommended it to the General von Stülpnagel.'

Oberg had been in the same regiment on the Western Front in 1916 and, as a lieutenant then, had been awarded both the Iron Cross First Class and Second. They were still on speaking terms, von Stülpnagel leaving all 'political' matters to Oberg.

'One first warms the boots a little, with a candle flame perhaps, then works the compound well into the leather, Kohler. It has a pleasant smell and is also good for the skin, particularly if the hands are chapped. You'd best keep that tin, I think.'

'Herr Generalmajor, are you sending me to Russia?'

'And now you're shitting your pants, is that it?'

Ach du lieber Gott, how shrill can the bastard get? 'I . . . I only ask because our investigation is not yet complete.'

Reports – whispers – stated clearly that this one engaged in pornographic debauchery with the women he kept, and with both of them at the same time! 'This murder, Kohler . . .'

Louis wasn't going to like what was said but might understand if told. *If.* 'It was an accident, Herr Generalmajor. I'm positive of this, but that fool of a French partner of mine can be very pigheaded. All I need is a little time.'

'A few formalities, then?'

'Absolutely nothing more.'

No plea to save his women, none whatsoever for the beekeeper's daughter who had spoken out like that, and nothing for his partner. Was Kohler at last learning to be loyal? 'Then that's settled and I'll not detain you further. Oh, there was one other matter. Now what was it? Ah yes, candles for the Reich, Kohler.

Herr Schlacht buys what he can on the black market but the quantities fall far short of the quotas set by Berlin.'

A constant problem, no doubt. 'So he buys the wax and manufactures them,' sighed Kohler.

'And supplies both the home market and the Wehrmacht. Candles for our boys in the trenches, Kohler. Please don't forget this in your reports to the General von Schaumburg. Candles and boot grease.'

And a saint, a loyal member of the Party, and one of the *Förderndes Mitglied*.

'There are no slackers in *Das Amt*, Kohler. It is far too useful an organization for me to let an idiot like you help to close down. Now get out of here and let me enjoy a few moments to myself.'

Close it down . . . Slackers? *Ach, mein Gott*! thought Kohler. No wonder they were worried. The Führer must be shrieking his head off over Stalingrad and must have ordered a witch-hunt. Namely for all those hiding in cushy jobs well behind the lines, and in Paris especially.

'Be careful, Kohler. You may yet have friends in Gestapo Boemelburg and the General von Schaumburg, since they both still find a need for you. But don't mess up this time. Praise *Das Amt* to the hilt while saying nothing of our interest. Let Herr Schlacht buy what he needs and sell what he makes, and leave that wife of his out of things. Agree to go along with the offer he has extended and keep everyone happy.'

They were desperate. Schlacht had been told to pay up or else!

'*Jawohl, mein* Generalmajor und Höherer SS. Heil Hitler.'

8

The observation hive was walled with glass and one standard frame in width and thickness, by perhaps two in height, and everything the bees did in there could be seen. Maraldi, the Italian astronomer, had, in 1687, recalled St-Cyr, seen observation hives in the Paris gardens of Louis XIV's Royal Observatory. De Bonnevies had kept up the tradition and had used this one to help train his students.

It was not difficult to locate the queen, and to find brood cells that held eggs or larvae, nor to differentiate the larger drone cells from those of the workers and to watch as the larvae were fed by the 'nurse' bees – fed royal jelly perhaps – while others capped cells and still others foraged afar for nectar, pollen and the resin with which to make propolis, and still others guarded the entrance against robbers and other predators.

'A maze of cells,' he said as the girl was brought to him by one of her guards, 'but the mites can't be seen, can they, without a microscope?'

Ashen, she didn't say a thing, only suffered his scrutiny. 'Your mother tried to keep me from finding a name in that directory of your father's, mademoiselle; you tried to keep me from looking through his microscope.'

'I was afraid. You were the police. I needed time.'

'Yet you first accused your mother of poisoning him, and then one of the Society, and now . . . why now have publicly stated that Monsieur de Saussine is the murderer, the . . .'

The Inspector flipped open his little black book, startling her.

'The "assassin", mademoiselle. How is it that you are so certain now that Monsieur de Saussine poisoned your father?'

It would do no good to lie. To hide what had to be hidden, one must give as much of the truth as possible. 'I meant, merely, that he was responsible for the deaths of so many of our bees, and for what was happening, the crisis my father tried to stop.'

'Mademoiselle, you knew very well what your father intended to say in that address, yet when interviewed in his study you denied this.'

'I did, and I am sorry for it. Will that satisfy you?'

Not even a perturbed sigh was given, the Chief Inspector simply took out his pipe and tobacco pouch as if preparing to stay for ever, should the interview be extended and the police van be delayed. '*Acarapis woodi*, Inspector. Until this Occupation of ours, the acarine mite had not been a big problem in France, or Belgium, or Holland and the Reich, for that matter. Indeed, we did not even suspect it had shown up in numbers in Russia, not until Herr Schlacht began to bring in so many hives. With some, the bees were still alive and these escaped and would most certainly have tried to join other hives, if not in Paris, then en route, or formed their own colonies.'

She paused, and as he lit his pipe, the Inspector looked steadily at her, a hard man when it came to the answers he wanted. 'It's . . . it's always difficult to positively identify acarine infestation, Inspector. During the honey flow so many bees are being born, it's sometimes impossible to detect those that are unwell, especially if carrying the mite, but in winter when brood laying ceases, there are only the older bees. Several die off, and one wonders. More die off and you know you have a problem, but what is its origin, you ask. Only by using the microscope, by dissection and staining, too, sometimes, can you determine it is the mite. Mme Roulleau and others began to have problems last year in the early fall but by then *papa* had already identified the cause, so what they showed him simply reinforced his belief that the disease was rapidly spreading.

'The mite can only be transferred by contact from bee to bee, Inspector. It lodges on the body hairs of the young bees and from there makes its way into the tracheae, where the female lays her eggs and the mites multiply until perhaps there are as many as a hundred and the bee, now a full adult, is first weakened and then dies.'

As she spoke, the girl would often catch sight of a forager

returning to the observation hive, and when one landed on his coat sleeve, she reached out to let it crawl into her hand before blowing it towards the hive.

'The disease is terrible, Inspector. It was first identified in 1919 by J. Rennie, in England, but had begun on the Isle of Wight in 1904 and has caused severe losses ever since. But as I've said, we did not have a major problem here, though a watch was always kept and my father insisted this be done, even to training me, as a child, in how to deal with it.'

The sound of the bees came to them, so subdued were the other members of the Society who sat some distance from them, the mother standing behind them, the priest near her but still being shunned by her.

'The very young bees drift, Inspector. During their play flights, their orientation flights when they get to know their hive and its immediate surroundings, they often enter other hives, the drones especially since they, alone, are always welcome because the virgins need them. Bees also love to rob one another's hives.'

'So the mites are spread from hive to hive in any one apiary and the queens are also infected.'

'Once started, it's insidious. At times the bees become so weakened they can't fly and will crawl around the entrance in desperation.'

'And the treatment with nitrobenzene is the only way to get rid of them?'

'The most effective way so far. One could kill all of the bees and destroy the hives, I suppose. The mites can't live long without a live host.'

'And the honey that is taken from those hives?'

'Will be fine unless the bees have been infected with foul brood, chalk brood or other diseases which do get into the honey. In spite of the danger to his own hives, Monsieur de Saussine was selling it to other beekeepers. *Papa* tried to stop him. They often argued vehemently, and Monsieur Jourdan, the vice president, and Monsieur Richaux were against him also.'

'Yet all three must have known the honey was contaminated?'

The girl glanced at her guard and shuddered, but was determined to reply.

'Of course but . . . but when your winter stores have been depleted by the ever-increasing demands of others and you cannot buy sugar with which to make syrup so that the bees can feed on it, you do what you have to and buy what you can. We didn't. We refused the excessive quota demands and made certain our little friends would always have what was needed to best tide them over the winter. Good, clean, disease-free pollen also, for that, too, is necessary at times.'

'How many hives does de Saussine keep?'

'Forty in out-apiaries about the city; thirty in each of two home apiaries – he fights the disease and fumigates also, but believes my father was overreacting. Monsieur Jourdan has only fifteen hives; Monsieur Richaux, about twenty.'

'And de Saussine works for Herr Schlacht?'

'Very much so, both as an adviser and in selling some of the honey, so you see, Inspector, my accuser deals on the black market himself!'

'How much of the honey?'

'A considerable amount. After all, he's a beekeeper, isn't he, and what could be more natural than for him to sell it to those he first provides with extra ration tickets?'

'Which Herr Schlacht gives him?'

'As a way of legitimatizing everything so that Monsieur de Saussine will not have to face arrest, should the authorities question his dealings.'

Had the girl finally agreed to tell them everything? wondered St-Cyr, or was she merely giving what she could in order to hide something else? 'My partner and I are almost certain, mademoiselle, that the bottle of Amaretto sat unattended on your father's desk for at least a few hours.'

'From when he had returned from the Salpêtrière, until after the brothel, yes.'

'Did you know the two he went with?'

'No, of course not.'

'A moment, then.'

The notebook was again consulted. Danielle felt her heart sink as the Inspector found what he was after and said tersely, 'Georgette purchased a cigarette lighter from you.'

'All right, I do know of them. I'm not proud of myself, Inspector, but . . . but I had to see who they were.'

'Did Georgette and Josiane let you visit his cemetery room?'

'Angèle-Marie was my aunt. I had a right to . . . to know what had happened to her.'

'And what your father had been up to for all those years since he had returned from the war. Did you know of Héloïse Debré? Well, did you?'

'And of Monsieur Leroux, the custodian? Yes! I . . . I visited the catacombs once. Only once to . . . to see what kind of a man would . . . would do such a thing when but a boy.'

'On last Thursday afternoon, mademoiselle, were the gates to the apiary and garden left unlocked?'

'They shouldn't have been, but . . .'

The girl looked desperately across the aisle to where her mother gazed steadily back at her from behind the veil of mourning.

'But *maman* could have unlocked them, yes.'

'Using whose keys?'

'Mine. I left them in my room.'

'Unlocked for whom, then?'

'For that one, perhaps.'

'Father Michel?'

'*Oui.*'

'Mademoiselle, please explain yourself.'

'Many times over the past few months Father Michel has watched us fumigating infected hives. He *knew* where my father kept the nitrobenzene, knew exactly how poisonous it was. He . . . he was receiving candles for his church, was benefiting from what was happening.'

'The candles, yes.'

'The mother church,' she said harshly. 'Any of them could have . . . have done it.'

'Any priest, bishop, or cardinal?'

She bowed her head and, choking back a sob, said, 'Please, I . . . I can't give you more. I'm so afraid.'

'Mademoiselle, did you return to the house on Thursday?'

'In time to poison that bottle?' she yelped.

'Please just answer the question.'

'Then no, I did not!'

'The names, please, of those who can corroborate this?'

'The guards on the controls. Ask them! I . . . I stayed overnight at . . . at the country house, as I told you earlier.'

'Near Soisy-sur-Seine.'

'Yes. I . . . I arrived late, and well after dark, as is my custom always, and I left in darkness before dawn.'

'Then your half-brother, mademoiselle. Is it that you're afraid he really has been released and that, to free the mother you both share and put a stop to Angèle-Marie's return, he killed your father?'

'My brother would have had to have known what was happening, n'est-ce pas? But, you're right, of course. War hardens us all, doesn't it, Inspector? It makes monsters out of house painters, butchers out of banana merchants, so why not killers out of sculptors?'

'It also makes liars out of decent, law-abiding citizens, mademoiselle. For now that is all I want from you.

'Herr Unterscharführer,' he said in *deutsch* to the guard who had understood little, if anything, of what had been said, 'you may escort this one back to her chair. Next . . . ? Who's next?'

The small glass jar of honey was twisted open by work-worn fingers that might, at one time, thought St-Cyr, have cared about manicures and lotions, but had long since set all such concerns aside.

'Lifelong apiculturists, especially those such as myself, are nothing compared to Alexandre, Inspector,' said Mme Roulleau. 'To comprehend what has happened regarding his sister, it is necessary for you to understand this.'

A forefinger was dipped into the honey and held up. 'Immediately *les abeilles* are attracted to the aroma and greedily rush to gorge themselves – it's easier, since the honey is ripe and the whole process of making it cut short. They show no fear, neither do I, and this, too, they intuitively know, but . . .'

The rheumy, large and soft brown eyes, with their sagging pouches and scars, looked up at him. 'But unlike others, Alexandre loved bees as a man sometimes loves a woman.

Intensely, you understand. Fiercely, passionately, protectively and possessively.'

'Angèle-Marie was the cross he had to bear for his love of all things about bees,' coughed Captain Henri-Alphonse Vallée, clearing a chest that had obviously been gassed several times during the Great War. Quickly he brushed a fingertip over his moustache to tidy it. 'Often he would have tears in his eyes when we discussed that sister of his, Inspector. At Verdun, on 21 February of '16, he broke down completely when *la tempête de feu* seemed like all the world had come crashing down upon us and death swept too close. He was badly wounded and begged me to look after her and to see that the wrong was righted. She was his little queen.'

The tempest of fire . . . The shelling . . . *Das Trommelfeuer*, Hermann had called it from his side of that terrible war. The drumfire.

'He was her worker, Inspector. Never her drone,' interjected Mme Roulleau with a curt nod to dismiss all such Sûreté suspicions.

'But he was always conscious of who she should marry?' he asked.

'Ah *oui*. He wanted Angèle-Marie to have a good match. Position, enough money and all the rest. A foolish thought, of course, for life is seldom so kind.'

'Others shamefully mated with her, Inspector, and because of this, Alexandre knew no peace and vowed he would punish them for the rest of his life. Many times I implored him to go to the police. He said too much time had elapsed and that, you will forgive me, the police seldom cared about young girls being deflowered against their will and would only accuse her of seducing her attackers.'

'His queen had flown, and several drones had mated with her, Inspector. It's what would have happened quite naturally among the bees, only the queen would have ripped out the *parties sensibles* of each of them on completion of their coupling.'

'They'd have died,' said Vallée, clearly uncomfortable at discussing such things.

'And Danielle?' asked St-Cyr. 'Did he feel the same about her?'

Bees now covered Mme Roulleau's finger, the woman watching them with keen interest. 'Danielle,' she softly said. 'Danielle and Étienne.'

'Alexandre feared those two were far too close,' muttered Vallée fidgeting uncomfortably. 'He always regretted that he'd had to give Étienne the family name. "That boy is useless," he would often say, "yet Danielle, who should know better, will have nothing said against him."'

'An artist, a sculptor . . . She posed for him, I gather.'

'Posed?' snorted Mme Roulleau. 'As mannequins will before the artists who hire them. *Toute nue* and without even a feather!'

'But as a child of three or four, and surely not since then?'

'Not since this war and the Defeat took him away,' huffed the woman. 'But who am I to say what went on in that country house where the boy lived alone and she went regularly and often stayed for nights on end until Alexandre was forced to fetch her home?'

'Étienne and he fought, of course,' said Vallée. 'The boy hated his stepfather. Ah! it was not good, Inspector. A girl of fifteen in 1939 . . .'

'Alexandre was certain the boy had designs on her,' swore Mme Roulleau. 'Certain, too, that he did not want Danielle taking after her mother!'

'Did he know of his wife's attempts to have her son released?' hazarded St-Cyr.

'Know of them?' seethed the woman. 'He refused absolutely to let her do so.'

'He despised that wife of his, Inspector. He knew she had begged this German, this Schlacht to intercede on her son's behalf.'

'And if the boy had returned?'

'Alexandre would not have let him enter his house and . . .'

'Captain, please continue. It's important,' urged St-Cyr.

Vallée looked to Madame Roulleau for guidance and saw her nod. 'Inspector, Alexandre vowed he would go to the authorities and accuse the boy of being among the terrorists. He even swore he could find evidence enough to have him shot.'

'What evidence, please?'

Afraid of speaking about such things, Vallée nervously glanced at the guards who were standing some distance from them. 'My service revolver. Though I had asked him to do so for me, Alexandre never turned it in when we were demobilized. "I might need it some day," he always claimed. "Leroux or one of the others might try to do something." '

The custodian . . .

The Inspector did not ask where the revolver was hidden, but rather, thought Mme Roulleau, if Danielle would have access to it.

'For this you must ask her,' she said, and placing the opened jar among some primroses, patiently removed the bees from her finger, tut-tutting when they insisted on returning to it. 'Or perhaps Madame de Bonnevies might know. A wife always has the keys to the house, Inspector, even if she claims not to, and Alexandre was often away on his rounds.'

'He kept that study of his locked.'

'Of course, but perhaps it was only locked to some and not to others?' offered the woman. 'Juliette de Goncourt was, and still is, *très belle, très adorable, n'est-ce pas*? One of the Saint-Honoré crowd, that also of the Sorbonne and things I know little of. But when it comes to a pregnancy out of wedlock, one shopkeeper's daughter is the same as another, no matter the class of shop. The boy responsible refused to marry her and daily poor Monsieur de Goncourt would look at her growing belly and wince!'

'It's not the past that I want at the moment, *mes amis*, but the present. Could the mother of that boy have paid to have her illegitimate grandson freed?'

'*Mon Dieu*, what is this, Inspector?' exclaimed Mme Roulleau.

'It's just a thought.'

'Then who, please, was the father of that bastard of hers?'

'That sculptor, madame,' chided Vallée uncomfortably. 'The boy is talented. Even though Alexandre would never acknowledge this, I myself happened to see some of his work in a gallery before the Defeat and was much taken with it and surprised.'

'*Who*, Inspector? Was it Henri-Christophe de Trouvelot? I've long considered this matter, though of course such circles were not mine to question.'

'It's confidential.'

'And when you catch the killer?' she hazarded.

'Perhaps then Mme de Bonnevies will no longer care.'

'But it is only to you that she gives a secret she has guarded all these years?' muttered Madame Roulleau, concluding that she'd been right all along. Yes, right! 'What reason, please, did she have for suddenly breaking a vow she had kept even from the Père Michel, her confessor?'

'Has the boy been released, Inspector?' asked Vallée. 'If so, then God forgive me for saying it, but there is your poisoner.'

'And Madame de Bonnevies must, if she doesn't already know what the boy did, be thinking it,' said Madame Roulleau.

'And Danielle?' asked St-Cyr.

'Danielle?' leapt the woman. 'Oh for sure the girl would worry about such a thing, should the half-brother have come home, but she loved her father dearly and worked constantly with him. She would never have . . .'

'Well, what is it?' asked St-Cyr.

It made her sad to have to say it. 'Alexandre would most certainly have told her what he intended to do if . . . if the boy was released. She'd have been terribly hurt – he was never one to let the feelings of others intrude once his mind was made up. But as for Danielle trying to stop him in such a way, ah no. No, I can't believe it.'

But she would consider the matter, thought St-Cyr and said, 'Then let us move on to Monsieur de Saussine and his associates.'

'Who had every reason to kill him,' hissed the woman, 'and who knew exactly how to do it!'

'Alexandre always considered M. de Saussine to be beneath him, Inspector,' confided Vallée. 'A student to whom he had devoted considerable energy, and had helped to become established, but a great disappointment. Not dedicated enough, he'd say. Too greedy.'

'Too cavalier. Monsieur de Saussine had little interest in selective breeding to produce disease-resistant stocks, Inspector, and was more interested in selling his queens which he shipped to beekeepers in competition with Alexandre.'

'Disease-free queens?'

'Ah!' clucked the woman. 'How could they have been in times

like these? Alexandre would never do such a thing, no matter the circumstance, and had sent notices out to warn others, even though Monsieur de Saussine threatened legal action.'

'And Messieurs Jourdan and Richeaux?'

'Are like most politicians, simply front men for others. The one has been placed in a position of power by his friends so as to be used by them. But always, as in a hive, there are parasites to guard against and battle.'

'Alexandre knew M. de Saussine was a threat, Inspector, and feared he would convince Herr Schlacht to take serious measures against him.'

'To clip his wings. To not let him speak out,' said Mme Roulleau, 'and to silence him for ever, perhaps.'

'Inspector, is it true that Mme de Bonnevies was having an affair with this German?' asked Vallée. 'Alexandre was convinced that she was. I tried to urge caution. One of the Occupier, but he wouldn't listen and swore he had followed her to a hotel near the omnibus yards and the freight yards of the Gare du Nord. "Many German servicemen go into that hotel," he said, "and so does that wife of mine, though she always looks first to see if there are those who are waiting for her."'

'And Herr Schlacht?'

It was Mme Roulleau who touched his arm to softly confide, 'Monsieur Durand, over there, kept bees on his roof for Alexandre, who found his daughter Mariette a job as housemaid to the wife of this businessman. But that was before our troubles started.'

'The girl followed Madame de Bonnevies to that hotel,' said St-Cyr.

'And then confided to her *papa* what she knew was happening,' went on Mme Roulleau. 'Mariette was very worried, Inspector, and insisted that Frau Schlacht was insanely jealous and very angry.'

'This German woman wanted him to poison her husband, Inspector. He was to lace a bottle of Amaretto with the nitrobenzene but had adamantly refused in spite of her many threats.'

'To have done so would have brought the Gestapo down on

238

him, Danielle also, *n'est-ce pas?*' said Madame Roulleau. '*Mon Dieu*, to poison one of the Occupier, at least the firing squad. That also for Juliette and her son, of course, though he didn't care about them, only Danielle.'

She caught a breath. 'That bottle of Amaretto was in his study, on his desk, wasn't it?' she sighed. 'The doors would have been locked, the gates also, but were they really locked?'

'Could M. de Saussine, or one of the other two, have had access to it?'

'For this they would have to have known of it,' muttered the woman, again lost in thought. 'But then . . . why then, someone must have told one of them of it and, of course, Monsieur de Saussine could well have brought along his own nitrobenzene.'

'Why not ask him and the other two, Inspector?' advised Vallée. 'Why not demand the statement, the *procès-verbal* they must sign and swear to?'

The furnace and boilerworks in the cellars of the School of Mines were gargantuan and warm . . . *mein Gott*, so cosy, thought Kohler. Coals glowed when the firebox door was opened – coals like he hadn't seen since before the Great War.

Leaning the crutches against the bin where sacks of anthracite, no less, were piled, he pulled off his greatcoat and draped it over some of the hot-water pipes.

Neither Jurgen nor Hans had ever experienced a fire like this – at least, he didn't think the boys would have. He warmed his hands and, when female steps hesitantly picked their way in from the Jardin du Luxembourg's greenhouses, gingerly lighted a twig and brought its flame up to the cigarette he offered to Frau Käthe Hillebrand.

'Inspector, what's the meaning of this?' she shrilled in *deutsch*, not liking things, for the SS major's adjutant had brought her to the cellars in silence and then had departed.

'A quiet word, that's all. Why not sit down? The caretakers use that broken chair, but I've given it a wipe just for you.'

The Höherer SS Oberg must have been convinced of the usefulness of the meeting, Käthe warned herself, but why had Kohler left the door to the firebox open? Why had he switched off the electric light? 'I'll stand,' she heard herself saying emptily. Flames licked upwards from around each glowing coal and clinker, but every now and then gases would erupt and the flames would rush to unite and race about the firebox. The smell of sulphur was in the air . . .

Unbidden, the woman's fingers began to nervously pluck at the top button of the beige overcoat she wore. Light from the firebox flickered over her, making her lipstick glisten and burnishing the fair cheeks. Uncertain still, her blue eyes tentatively sought him out, and finally she took a hurried drag at the cigarette.

'What the hell do you want with me that couldn't have been asked in the greenhouse?' she demanded. The boyish grin he gave only upset her more.

'Look, if I'm to help that boss of yours, I'm going to have to know everything you can tell me.'

Oberg must have agreed. 'All right, a private conversation. Just the two of us.'

'I've been the blindest of fools, haven't I? Herr Schlacht is up to his ears in mischief and wallowing in the shit.'

'I . . . I'm only a part-time secretary for him. I've others I must look after.'

'Others you've had sex with?'

'*Verdammt*! What if I have? It's got nothing to do with this business!'

'But one that must have kept on for a good long time, otherwise, why would he have blamed you for losing his little pin?'

'That was a mistake.'

'Then why did the affair end, if it did?'

'I was new. I was inexperienced. It . . . it just happened, that's all.'

'Maybe yes, maybe no, but how many of those gold wafers does he agree to let you send to Switzerland with that wife of his?'

'Switzerland . . . ? *Bitte*, I . . . I don't know what you mean.'

A button came undone, and then another, and when he'd undone them all, Kohler took her coat, hat and gloves and, indicating the chair, said in best Gestapo form, 'Get comfortable. It'll be easier for you.'

The dress she wore was off-white, of cashmere like the scarf he had let her keep. Fine goods, thought Kohler appreciatively, but not suitable for a furnace room, and she knew it and was worried about this, if not about other things. Silk stockings, too, and high heels. Bracelets of gold, and a citrine brooch to match the superb stone on the middle finger of her left hand. No wedding ring, of course, he reminded himself and heard her tartly ask of his scrutiny, '*Well*, what is it?'

'Lovely,' he said and grinned as he turned to hang her coat on a nail, 'but I told you to sit down, and I really do want an answer to that question I asked.'

'From time to time Oskar lets me send the few wafers I can manage to buy from him. A small favour, in return for the one that I rendered,' she said acidly.

'And what, exactly, is that favour worth?'

There was no feeling in the look he gave, only an emptiness that made her tremble. 'Five each quarter. Sometimes a few more; sometimes a few less.'

'Then that wife of his is important to you and you wouldn't want anything to happen to either of them.'

'No . . . No, I wouldn't.'

'It's big, what he's doing, isn't it, and I really have been blind?'

'Candles aren't the only thing he deals in.'

'I didn't think they were, but what he does for one, he does for all, right? He claims to buy the beeswax on the black market, even though his relatives steal much of it for him.'

'There are prices and prices.'

'And no accounting beyond what he writes himself and you type up for him – that's another little service you offer, by the way, but never mind. The wax is "bought" many times over, even though he's already acquired most of it. The candles are made and sold to that same black market and then . . . then, and this is where I've been so blind, they're bought back at even higher prices.'

'And are shipped to the Reich. Well, most of them. What he . . . he doesn't sell to the churches here and . . . and to the catacombs and other places.'

'But the ones that go to the Reich are at vastly inflated prices, so the profit is pretty good.'

She would sit down now, Käthe told herself. She would cross

her legs and finish her cigarette while gazing openly up at this Hermann Kohler who had such a reputation with the ladies but was far from the brutal Gestapo he had tried to indicate.

'As I've said, Inspector, Oskar isn't just into candles. He makes a water-proofing compound as well.'

'For the Wehrmacht – *ja*, I've heard all about it.'

'Propolis is bought and made into varnish, and this is shipped at a modest profit which is donated to the SS, as a loyal member of the *Förderndes Mitglied* should.'

'And the honey?'

'Some of it is donated to the *Secours National* – the National Help – for the soup kitchens, where it is doled out to young children and nursing mothers.'

'But not much of it, I'll bet. And the rest?'

'Is sold to beekeepers, to the black market, and also "bought" back from it and shipped to the Reich.'

'Again at a very healthy profit.'

'He's a businessman and everything he does for the Palais d'Eiffel is done under that mandate, so what, please, is wrong with that?'

'Nothing but the ten or twenty or fifty times profit the "creative" book-keeping allows.'

'Nobody cares so long as the needs are met.'

'And they'll only become greater now, won't they, with the defeat at Stalingrad?'

She shrugged and did so beautifully, thought Kohler. He'd take the cigarette from her now and would stub it out. 'For my little tin,' he said. 'With us, nothing is wasted.'

'Us?' she asked.

'My partner and me, and the two women I live with but seldom see.'

'Look, I really must get going. Herr Schlacht—'

'Wanted you to keep track of things here for him. De Bonnevies was a distinct threat – bitching about what was happening; going to the Kommandant von Gross-Paris with tales of robbed and butchered hives and diseased bees. Old Shatter Hand's no fool, Frau Hillebrand. He's not some dumb *Detektiv Aufsichtsbeamter* like me.'

'Oskar didn't kill this beekeeper.'

'I didn't say he had but we both know he's in deep trouble, and not just with von Schaumburg.'

'Trouble . . . ? What trouble, please?'

'Rumours – whispers – that there are slackers behind the lines. People in cushy jobs who are helping themselves and getting too greedy while others do the fighting for them.'

Sickened by the thought that the good times were about to end, Käthe tried to stop her eyes from smarting. Herr Kohler found another cigarette and lit it for her, and though she took it from him and said softly, '*Danke*,' her fingers trembled and she knew he had noticed this. 'Are there really rumours the Führer might shut us down?' Oberg would be furious; Oskar in a panic . . .

'They're not just rumours. They're serious. Oberg's just asked for my help.'

Ah Jesus, sweet Jesus! 'Oskar was very worried, yes. He . . . he didn't want de Bonnevies to give that address his daughter gave this afternoon. It would ruin everything, would make things very difficult for him, as it will. Always word of such things is passed so quickly. He . . . he wanted him stopped, that's all I know. I swear it is, but . . . but felt he couldn't have him arrested.'

'Too obvious, eh? Too blatant for the Kommandant von Gross-Paris to swallow. Besides, there was this other little matter of Frau Schlacht's having one of his mistresses followed to a certain hotel. The beekeeper's wife, to be precise.'

'Frau Schlacht had purchased a bottle of Amaretto. Oskar, he . . . he watches constantly, or has others do the watching for him, so he knew Uma was up to something with that bottle, but . . . but didn't know exactly what.'

'Does he like the stuff?'

'Yes!'

'Then let me elaborate. Fearing the worst, he had me taken to that smelter of his and had his friends in the *Milice* try to pry the answer he wanted from me, but since the beekeeper had refused to help Frau Schlacht poison your boss, who added the nitrobenzene to that bottle?'

The cigarette was teased from her lips to be shared. Nervously she touched the base of her throat, then fiddled with her scarf.

'Oskar learned of the poison from one of the other beekeepers – de Saussine, I think – but . . . but said it had to be done so as to make it appear as if Juliette had done it. She despised her husband and was very unhappy in her marriage. She knew where the poison was kept and had told Oskar of this. A tin on a shelf in the study, above the workbench. A skull and crossbones on its label . . . Oil of mirbane in bright lemon-yellow letters, mono . . . mono-nitrobenzene beneath this in brackets. Juliette was to suspect nothing. The daughter would be away . . .'

'Did you do it for him, since you knew where it was kept?'

'NO! I . . . Look, I didn't, I swear it.'

'But he asked you to?'

'And I refused.'

'Then what about the stepson?' demanded Kohler.

He was so anxious now she would have to smile weakly at him, she told herself, and softly say, 'Oflag 17A, you know of it, of how desperate Juliette was to get her son home? She would do anything Oskar wanted her to and went with many men in that place of his. Two . . . three at a time, if he wanted her to – prostitutes as well – what did it matter, so long as Oskar would buy the boy's freedom?'

'Did you watch them?'

'Once. Oskar . . . Oskar thought it was funny. He throws dinner parties and then we . . . we all go back to that hotel of his to . . . to observe things.'

But that was more than once. 'And did he buy the son's freedom?'

'To put her out of her misery – one of the French? What do you think?'

'That he'd prefer to spend the money on a bit of sculpture for *der* Führer.'

'Leda and the Swan, ah yes.'

'No freedom, then?'

'Not from Oskar. This I know.'

'Good. Now let's stop pissing about. Tell me where he's keeping Oona.'

'Oona? Who is this, please?'

Abruptly Kohler moved away from her to deeply thrust into

244

the coals the long iron hoe that was used to pull clinkers from the firebox. 'The candle factory, where is it?' he demanded.

'On the rue Championnet, across from the Omnibus Yards.'

'How many employees?'

Would he threaten to burn her with that rod? 'Thirty, I think.'

'How many shifts?'

'Two. Each of twelve hours, when . . . when there is sufficient wax.'

'Any guards?'

'Why should there be?'

'Lorries?'

'Two.'

'*Gazogènes*?'

'Their roof tanks are filled at the Omnibus Yards. Oskar has a . . . a deal with the manager.'

'Deals and deals, eh? So where do the *Milice* who keep an eye on that smelter of his hang out?'

'Did they hurt you badly?' she winced and heard him answer, 'Not badly enough.'

'The gymnasium on the rue Bonne Nouvelle. They . . . they have a room at the back and . . . and use the gym for parades and . . . and other things.'

'Like beating people up and raping girls they've hauled in for questioning?'

'When it's necessary, yes.'

'Since when were either necessary?'

'You . . . you know what I meant.'

'So, where is Oona?'

'At the Hotel Titania. There's a room Oskar uses for . . . for the girls he's preparing.'

'Guards?'

'One or two.'

'French?'

'Of course.'

'Gangsters?'

'Yes.'

'Anything else I need to know?'

'Nothing! Will the Führer really shut us down?'

It took all types to make up the Occupier, but he'd best say something to calm her, thought Kohler, setting the rod aside to help her on with her coat. 'Not if I can prevent it. That's what the Höherer SS wants and we aim to deliver.'

'We?'

'My partner and I, though he doesn't know about it yet, but don't go telling your boss that we've had this little chat, not when Oberg agreed to let me question you.'

'Did he really?'

'If I were you, I wouldn't even ask. Oh by the way, I'll want to interview you again about your use of the name "Juliette" for Mme de Bonnevies, and your knowing all about that tin of . . . What did you call it?'

Verdammt! 'Oil of mirbane.'

Honoré de Saussine was in his mid-forties, the picture of health in these days when the sick got sicker and most others became ill through worrying. He did not back away from anything, thought St-Cyr, but met each question with a confidence that was troubling. A civil servant, and no doubt once a lover of *la petitesse*, the virtue of living small, he had come up in the world. No longer was his tie worn loose so as not to wear it out, nor did he bother to save his cigarette butts.

'Inspector, as assistant director of building codes in the Ninth arrondissement, I was at my desk on Thursday from eight a.m. until noon, and from two until six. I could not possibly have gone to Charonne, nor had I any intention of, or wish to harm Alexandre. Oh *bien sûr*, we disagreed. Among scientists is disagreement not a fact of life? But to poison him . . . Ah no. No. It's impossible.'

'And you've those who will swear to your being at that desk?'

'My secretary and my assistants, the director also. Let me tell you nothing escapes that one's eye. Nothing.'

'Then that's settled. A moment. I'll just jot it down in my little book. "De Saussine at work." '

The Sûreté took his time and wrote far more, so as to be unsettling, but one could only smile at such a ruse, thought de Saussine. St-Cyr would find no paste-pot pinching civil servant here, no shifty-eyed accumulator of the rubber bands and erasers of fellow employees.

From time to time Juliette de Bonnevies would glance their way and he had to ask himself, What has she told the Inspector? That I hated Alexandre even more than she did? That I knew very well where the nitrobenzene was kept – had I not been in his study many times? Had I not my own to use, in any case?

At the flash of a lewd and knowing grin from him, the woman quickly averted her veiled eyes and turned her back on them, a back that, when naked, had been seen by many.

The Hôtel Titania, eh, madame, he silently taunted. Was Alexandre aware of the things you did in that place, things Herr Schlacht bragged about to me?

'Your lunch, monsieur,' said the Sûreté, suddenly looking up from his notebook. 'Where, please, did you have it on Thursday?'

'My lunch . . . ? In the café at . . . at the corner of the rue Rossini and the rue Drouot, near the office. We always go there. Myself and two others.'

'The soup, the *pot-au-feu* . . . a glass of wine?'

'No wine, Inspector. It was a no-alcohol day, remember?'

'Bread?'

'Two of the twenty-five gram slices.'

'The National?'

That grey stuff that was made of sweepings and a lot of other things. 'Yes.'

'*Bread*,' he muttered and wrote it down. '*No wine.*'

'Inspector, is this necessary?'

'As necessary as is the truth, monsieur. You see my partner has spoken at length with . . .'

'All right. I . . . I dined with Herr Schlacht at *l'Auberge de Savoie.*'

'Thirty-six rue Rodier, but still in the Ninth and not far from that office of yours in the town hall, not far from the auction house either. Before the war, the porters at the Hôtel Drouot were its regulars. They all came from Savoy, a prescriptive right Napoleon insisted on, but now . . . Now I do not know how things are.'

'Occasionally a few of them still eat there, but . . . but it's a busy place and the clientele has changed.'

'Black market?'

'The *gratin de pommes de terre de Savoie* was superb.'

Baked, thinly sliced potatoes, cheese, eggs, milk and garlic, with pepper, salt and butter, optional nutmeg and sometimes sliced onions or shallots . . . in a city where most hadn't seen a potato since the winter of 1940 to '41, to say nothing of the butter and cheese!

'The *soufflé de truite à la sauce d'écrevisses* was magnificent.'

Mon Dieu, trout with a crayfish sauce! 'The Reblochon and the Boudane?'

Cheeses from Savoy, the latter matured in grape brandy. 'Those also, and coffee. Herr Schlacht likes to dine well.'

The Inspector painstakingly wrote all of this down, then took a break to pack his pipe and light it. The match was blown out, not waved out, and then, as an added precaution, spittle wetted a thumb and forefinger and the thing was decisively extinguished.

'One never knows, does one?' he said. 'The threat of fire in winter seems even more imminent than in summer.'

Fire in a greenhouse! 'Inspector . . .'

'Monsieur, I am certain Herr Schlacht expressed to you his thoughts regarding your president.'

'He was concerned, yes.'

'Not simply concerned, monsieur. The two of you . . .'

'What, exactly, did Madame Roulleau tell you, Inspector? That I was *deutschfreundlich* and assisting one of the Occupier? Since when is that a crime?'

'Madame Roulleau and I did not even discuss you, monsieur.' This was a lie, of course. 'But it is interesting that you should think she has accused you of murder.'

'I didn't say that! I . . .'

'But the possibility arose between you and Herr Schlacht, didn't it, and you were asked advice on how best to do it?'

'I refused absolutely to even speak of such a thing.'

'At what time did you finish your lunch? Please remember that the *patron* will be consulted.'

'At three forty. We . . . we talked of other matters.'

'The honey you were selling for him. Honey you knew carried diseases and yet . . . and yet you sold it to your colleagues to augment the winter stores of their hives.'

'Inspector, to not have done so was for them to have lost their colonies. If Madame Roulleau were at all honest and reliable, she would have acknowledged this.'

'You deal on the black market, monsieur; you sell diseased queens.'

'What else did that interfering old woman tell you?'

'That you threatened your president with legal action; that the two of you argued vehemently and that Monsieur de Bonnevies sent out notices to warn others of the diseases you were so thoughtlessly spreading.'

'He had no proof! It was all a figment of his "scientific" imagination. Acarine mites . . . A crisis in the making? A tragedy? It's absurd. Idiotic. Their numbers were far too small. Only a few hives showed any signs of it. All were fumigated most thoroughly. All!'

'And Herr Schlacht, monsieur? Didn't he offer you a substantial reward if you took care of things for him?' This was another lie, of course, but when needed, could lies not be forgiven in these difficult times?

'I refused. Ask him.'

'Two hundred thousand francs?' It was a shot in the dark.

'A million. It . . . it was insane, Inspector. I . . . I couldn't agree to such a thing – how could I? Alexandre and I go back too far. When I was but a boy of thirteen, he took me under his wing and shared his love of bees. I . . .'

'Inspector . . .'

It was Lalonde, the assistant gardener. 'Well, what is it?'

'A moment, please. I . . . I have found something you must see.'

'Can it not keep?'

'Forgive me, Inspector, but it can't. Your partner also wishes to speak with you in private.'

Hermann . . . *Merde*, what the hell had happened? 'He's always in a hurry. Monsieur de Saussine, please remain ready to continue. A million you said? Ah! I must jot that down and get you to . . . Sign here, please.'

'It . . . it's in code. I can't re—'

'Just sign it, monsieur, and date it. Thirty-first January, 1943 at . . . four ten in the afternoon. No wonder I'm hungry. I've totally missed my lunch!'

Hermann was waiting in another of the greenhouses and didn't look up when approached. Humus was scattered. Two of the potted flowers, set well behind a screen of others on the trestle table, had been uprooted and hastily replanted. Broken, blackish-brown rootlets formed a tangled spaghetti on the leaves of adjacent plants.

'*Merci*, Monsieur Lalonde,' sighed St-Cyr. 'You may leave us now, but were absolutely correct to fetch me.'

'Mademoiselle Danielle could so easily have come in here before the meeting, Inspector. The girl is considered almost as one of us and knows well where each type of flower is grown.'

The gardener was clearly much distressed and with good reason, but had best be told. 'Say nothing. Let us deal with it. Now go. We will return to the others in a moment.'

'*Helleborus niger*, Louis. The Christmas rose . . .'

'Yes, yes. A cure for madness in the days of Pliny the Elder, Hermann, but as to how many patients survived, the historical records are understandably vague.'

The flowers, of a very uncomplicated but proud look, were large and white or purplish and stood tall and straight, with golden, pollen-covered anthers to which the bees, excluded from this greenhouse, could not come.

The leaves were serrated and leathery; the stems, a purplish-brown.

'Did she wear gloves?' asked Kohler.

'If it was Danielle – if, Hermann. We don't know this yet, but if gloves weren't worn, then the skin of the fingers – especially that around the nails – will definitely show signs of inflammation.'

'There'll also be earth under her fingernails, idiot!'

'Unless whoever did this washed their hands afterwards, or wore gloves.'

'The roots, Louis.'

'When dried and ground, they have the look of powdered liquorice and can, at times, unfortunately be mistaken for it. A dram of the tisane has been known to kill, but with the powdered root, the exact dosage is unknown and probably varies, though it has to be much less than a gram.'

'She either killed her father or thinks that half-brother of hers did it and now plans to kill herself.'

'And if not Danielle and not Étienne?'

'Then Frau Käthe Hillebrand, or Madame de Bonnevies.'

'Or Honoré de Saussine, or Father Michel?'

'You tell me. Look, we have to talk. The Palais d'Eiffel is about to be shut down. Oberg insists we do everything we can to prevent this. We can find our murderer, but had better leave Schlacht and his wife well out of it, or else.'

Hermann was clearly agitated and didn't look well. 'And Oona?'

'To Spain. It's what has to be, Louis. I'm sorry, but I've no other choice. I'm one of them, remember?'

One of the Occupier. 'We'll discuss it later.'

'*Verdammt*! An order is an order.'

'And Oona? Oona loves you, Hermann. You and Giselle are her link with sanity in a world gone mad. Take the two of you away from her and what remains?'

'Ashes.'

'Then let's pay the morgue a visit. Let's both calm down and do what we have to.'

'I knew you'd help. I was just worried about asking you.'

'Then don't be. We're in this together. How are the toes?'

'Terrible.'

The Citroën was packed. Hoarfrost had quickly formed inside the windscreen and windows, and Hermann, his hands not free, what with the crutches and Danielle sitting on his lap, could do nothing to improve visibility.

Frau Hillebrand sat squeezed between them, with Father Michel, Juliette de Bonnevies, and Honoré de Saussine in the back. The SS followed in two cars; the city was, of course, in darkness. When one lamp, its bluing streaked, signalled that they had finally reached the place Mazas, the forty-watt light bulb that was above the door to the morgue had gone out.

A bad sign? wondered St-Cyr. Hermann would think so. Hermann hated visits to the morgue, but this one was necessary. Even so, he sighed and said, 'Louis, there are things you need to know; things I can't tell you in present company, or in any other, for that matter.'

'This won't take long, *mon vieux*, and will, I think, save much time.'

'And if we refuse to go in there?' shrilled Frau Hillebrand.

'Then my partner will have the SS drag you in, *meine gute Frau*,' said St-Cyr in *deutsch*. 'If you've nothing to hide, you've nothing to fear.'

Father Michel said in French that it wasn't right and that the deceased deserved to be left in peace. 'He never did that to me, Father!' countered Juliette. 'Why not tell the Inspectors everything? Why not confess?'

'My child, you're overwrought.'

'You came to the house on Thursday afternoon, Father. You had just been to see Angèle-Marie.'

'Inspectors, is this really necessary?' asked de Saussine.

'I guess it is, eh, Louis?' snorted Kohler.

Danielle de Bonnevies said nothing but was so tense, he could feel her pulse racing and, finding an ear, whispered, 'Don't even think of it. Those boys behind us have two dogs and Schmeissers. We'd only be laying you out on a slab.'

'I heard no dogs,' she replied.

'Well, maybe not, but you do understand, eh? Now you first, and easy, then me. Here, hang on a minute, I need to lean my crutches against the door.'

'Forgive me,' she muttered as the door was opened.

'Forgive . . .' echoed Hermann, only to shriek in agony as the girl stamped on his wounded foot and tumbled out of the car. She fell. She dragged herself up and began to run as the guards cried, '*Halt!*' and Juliette shrilled, '*Danielle* . . .'

'Don't shoot! Please don't!' yelled St-Cyr in German, and then, 'Ah *merde*. Mademoiselle, *arrêtez-vous!* You cannot escape.'

Cursing, the SS bundled back into their cars, one racing up the avenue Ledru-Rollin with high beams fully uncovered and the fronts of the buildings staring out into the passing light as if suddenly awakened; the other tearing up the boulevard de la Bastille. Simultaneously they must have reached the rue de Lyon, for two sets of tyres screeched, both horns blared. A bicycle taxi had perhaps got in the way.

'Louis, shouldn't we go after her? Those roots . . .'

'What roots?' demanded Frau Hillebrand in perfect French.

'Hermann, we had best leave her for now. Inside, I think.'

They heard the cars taking the short little side streets that lay between the rue de Lyon and rue de Bercy.

'*Verdammt!*' swore Kohler still gritting his teeth in pain, and gathering up scattered crutches. 'Why the hell couldn't she have listened to me, Louis?'

'The half-brother, I think. Now come on, let me help you.'

'No. I'm all right. I should have listened to myself. I knew she was going to make a bolt for it.'

They crowded into the entrance, blinking as the electric light hit them. Frau Hillebrand was nervous and withdrawn; Father Michel tense and watchful; Juliette de Bonnevies sickened by what Danielle had just done and by the nearness of what they must now go through.

And de Saussine, wondered St-Cyr, and answered, is no longer sure of himself.

'This way, *mes amis*. Monsieur,' he said to the attendant on the desk, 'St-Cyr of the Sûreté and Kohler of the Kripo to see the autopsy reports on Alexandre de Bonnevies and to view the corpse.'

'Louis, must I?' muttered Kohler.

'Why me, why you, why us, eh?' It was a plea Hermann often made.

'My son . . .'

Stung, Kohler swung round. 'Father, get that butt of yours in there and speak only when spoken to!'

They went into a room so big and cold and white, her shivering would be noticed, thought Juliette and swallowed hard. There were several corpses on table-like slabs, with draining boards and sinks and blood . . . blood seeping from a cut-open chest and abdomen. Blood pooled around someone's heart and lungs and splashed on a limp penis and marble-white thighs.

Alexandre was hideous. His iron-grey hair was parted in the middle and slicked down hard with pomade – he'd never worn it that way. Not like a gangster or pimp! The nostrils were blackberry blue, the eyelids and lips, the fingernails . . .

Turning swiftly away, she choked and threw up.

'And you, Frau Hillebrand?' asked the Chief Inspector St-Cyr, watching her closely, too closely, thought Käthe. 'You're not sickened, but are fascinated.'

'In shock!' she said harshly in *deutsch*, and dragging a handkerchief from her purse, clapped it over her nose. Rage moistened her lovely eyes – guilt also? wondered St-Cyr.

Father Michel had kissed the rosary he had dragged from a pocket and was muttering an *Ave*.

De Saussine was pale and shaken. Slowly, gradually, his gaze moved from the blue-black lips and gold-filled teeth to the scars of war that had lacerated and punctured the chest and arms, to the varicose veins and putrid, greenish-yellow blotches that were spreading under the pale, blackberry-hued and hairy skin.

'Ah *bon!*' sighed St-Cyr. 'He's been opened twice and . . .'

The Inspector consulted a sheaf of typed pages, pausing when he found what he was after, thought Juliette. 'A good sixty cubic centimetres were downed in one gulp from that bottle. The "Amaretto" was between thirty and forty per cent mononitrobenzene, but its excess, beyond that which had dissolved in the alcohol, would have risen to the top so he did not even look at the drink he took.'

'Oil of mirbane,' whispered Kohler to Frau Hillebrand who darted a startled and hurtful glance at him.

'Apparently our victim had eaten little since the early morning, Madame de Bonnevies,' went on Louis. 'A "coffee" taken without milk, a small piece of the National bread and a teaspoon of pollen.'

'He always swore it gave him energy,' she said emptily.

'A little wine during the day. A dried apple, a few chestnuts and one or two of your daughter's vitaminic biscuits.'

The woman shrugged and said, 'I really wouldn't know what, if anything, he ate during the rest of that day. I took him his breakfast at seven. We didn't even speak. We . . . we seldom did.'

'And that afternoon?'

'Father Michel came to see me after he'd been to the Salpêtrière. He said . . . I'm sorry, Father, but I have to tell them. He said that it had all been taken care of and I need not worry any longer about Alexandre's bringing Angèle-Marie home.'

'I gave that poor unfortunate a taste of honey, Inspectors, and freely admit it.'

'Later, *mon Père*. We'll deal with you later,' grunted St-Cyr. 'Madame, at what time, please, did your husband return from the hospital?'

'At . . . at about ten past four.'

'And where were you at that time?'

'In the kitchen. Father Michel hadn't wanted Alexandre to find him there but my husband came through as usual, saying only that he was going out again.'

'And your answer, madame?'

'My answer . . . ? Why, the silence of a wife who knows, Inspector, exactly where her husband is going.'

'To *Le Chat qui crie*.'

'Yes.'

'And early that evening?' asked Louis, glancing again at the autopsy reports as if there was information he had deliberately withheld, thought Kohler, and saw the priest warily watching Juliette.

'At eight thirty Alexandre went out to unlock the gates.'

'And where were you when you heard this?'

'In . . . in Étienne's room.'

'And you *heard* your husband from behind closed windows, black-out drapes and closed doors – remember, please, that the study is quite separate from the rest of the house?'

Ah damn him! 'I had opened my son's bedroom window a little. I . . . I felt Alexandre must be meeting someone because he . . . he had been so agitated. Nothing had been right. It never was, but . . .' She shrugged. 'I just had to find out who could be coming at such an hour.'

255

'Yet you had hardly spoken during the whole of that day?'

Merde alors, would he not leave things alone? 'It . . . it was a feeling I had. Nothing else.'

'Then we'll let the matter rest, shall we? Death occurred between eight twenty and nine twenty, give or take a half-hour on either side.'

'Alexandre hurried back through the garden. I heard him quickly close the outer door to the study. There were a few minutes of silence and then . . . then . . .' She gripped her forehead and, covering her eyes in despair, said, 'I heard him cry out suddenly, heard him shrieking my name and . . . and gagging. I thought he was just angry. Really I did. Oh *mon Dieu, mon Dieu*, why could I not have gone to help him? I didn't, Inspectors. I waited, and may God forgive me.'

A reasonable performance, thought Kohler, but not quite believable. 'And then?' asked Louis with that same unruffled patience he always had when a corpse was between himself and a suspect.

'I heard him vomiting and wondered at this, but . . . but someone was opening the gate at the back of the garden. It needs to be oiled, you understand, but there is no oil to be had. This person came on and opened the outer door to the study. Light fell briefly on her and I . . . I saw who it was.'

'The time, please – as close as you can estimate?'

'Nine, I think, or . . . or eight forty-five.'

'And the name, madame?'

'Frau Schlacht. She . . . she didn't stay more than a minute or two and, making certain the lock was on, closed the door and hurriedly left by the way she had come. I ran downstairs and went out the front door to the street and nearly collided with her, but . . . but she simply hurried away and got into a *vélo-taxi* that was waiting for her. Only then did I hear her voice, in German. She was swearing at her driver and telling him to hurry.'

'And then?' asked Louis.

'I went back inside and tried to get my husband to open the door to the study, but . . . but there was no sound.'

'No sound . . . Ah! a moment, madame. I have it here.'

Kohler knew the look Louis gave the woman, that of a Sûreté who hadn't believed for a minute what she'd said.

'By itself, and simply drinking the nitrobenzene, madame, any reaction would have been delayed for at least an hour, but your husband, as you know, realized what had happened and immediately tried to check the contents of the container, and during this, spilled the oil of mirbane and got it on his hands and clothes. As a result, the reaction was much more rapid and death took place within an hour. An hour, Madame de Bonnevies.'

'Between eight twenty and nine twenty,' muttered Käthe Hillebrand, 'or between seven fifty and eight fifty . . .'

'Or between eight fifty and nine fifty,' said St-Cyr, 'which would be suitable, of course, but we want that hour prior to death, don't we, and Madame de Bonnevies has just told us her husband had gone out to open the gates at . . . ?'

'At eight thirty. My watch, it's . . . it's not so good any more.'

'Off by an hour?' asked the Sûreté. 'Still on the old time perhaps?'

She swallowed hard and admitted that this was possible.

'Then let's get it straight once and for all, madame. Your husband lay on the floor in agony – vomiting, passing out only to awaken moments later with a ragged gasp. Twitching, getting up – falling – knocking things over and . . . ?'

'And crying out my name, but . . . but I did not kill him. I swear it. I . . . I thought he was drunk.'

Her tears were very real, but still it would have to be asked. 'Had he ever been drunk before in his study?'

'No! Father . . . Father, tell him I didn't do it. Tell him I sat in the kitchen, listening to Alexandre – knowing something must be wrong and that I should go to him, but that the years of bitterness had been too many.'

'Inspector . . .'

'Later, Father. Later. And Frau Schlacht, madame?' asked St-Cyr.

'She came to the front entrance and I let her into the house. Together we broke a pane of glass in the back door and found my husband on the floor.'

'Dead?'

'Of course.'

'At what time, please?'

'Time? I . . . I don't know! How could I? My watch . . .'

'Was it at the Hôtel Titania on a night table, madame? Were you nowhere near your house at the time of your husband's death?'

'Louis, when first interviewed she claimed she couldn't possibly have known he was expecting a visitor.'

'Absolutely a conflict, Hermann.'

'All right. I . . . I didn't find him until about three in the morning when Herr Schlacht dropped me off at the corner of the street. Alexandre's bedroom door was open and he wasn't in his bed. That's . . . that's when I broke the window and found him on the floor.'

'And Frau Schlacht?' asked Louis.

'Must have put the lock on the outer door he had left open for her. I . . . I really don't know but didn't want you to find her name in his little book because . . . because Oskar had said she was up to something with my husband.'

He would give her the curt little nod of dismissal he usually gave on such occasions, thought St-Cyr, and then would distract her by going after the priest. 'And now you, Father. Let's get this over with quickly.'

'I didn't kill him. I would never have done that.'

'Perhaps, but as his priest and confessor you knew all about what he'd been doing to Héloïse Debré and to Jean-Claude Leroux, the custodian of the catacombs, and you knew he wanted his sister to come home.'

'Angèle-Marie was a madness of his. I couldn't allow him to destroy Juliette's life any more than he already had.'

'So you gave the sister a taste of honey.'

'Things had gone too far. Alexandre could be and was a monster and yet . . . and yet, he had much good in him.'

'And after you'd been to see the sister?'

'I went straight to the house to counsel Juliette, as she has stated.'

'You knew where the nitrobenzene was kept, Father,' said Kohler, 'and unless I'm very mistaken, madame confided to you that she had been questioned by Herr Schlacht as to its whereabouts.'

'The bottle of Amaretto was on the desk,' continued Louis. 'Monsieur de Bonnevies would pay the brothel his customary visit.'

'He'd been very vocal, hadn't he?' said Kohler.

'And had told you, Father, exactly what he'd do if madame's son should return.'

These two would not stop until they had the truth, sighed Father Michel and said sadly, 'Alexandre was beside himself with rage to which I, poor humble servant that I am, tried only to plead for reason. Étienne had done him no real harm. How could he continue to blame the boy for a love affair the child in its mother's womb could have known nothing of.'

'Your husband, madame,' said St-Cyr. 'I believe you knew very well what he intended to do should your efforts to free your son succeed.'

'And these two were *both* in the house when that bottle sat alone on the desk,' interjected Käthe Hillebrand.

'No poison in it, eh, Louis, and then more than sufficient, even if he hadn't cooperated by spilling it on himself.'

'And a million francs,' swore Honoré de Saussine. 'Herr Schlacht must have offered it to you as well, Madame de Bonnevies.'

'A million . . . ,' countered Juliette lividly. 'Neither Father Michel nor I went into that study, Inspectors. The door was locked and I *don't* have a key. I've *never* had one. Not even when Alexandre first brought me to the house of his mother and introduced me to the hatred and resentment he bore me.'

'But you do have keys to the gates?' asked St-Cyr and heard her saying, 'Danielle has those for when looking after the hives. Not me, Inspector. Never me.'

'But she has told us she left them in her room when out of the city?'

'This . . . this I wouldn't have been aware of.'

'Of course you were.'

'All right, I was, but I didn't touch them.'

'And could Danielle, knowing only too well what her father would do if Étienne was freed, not have left the city on Thursday as she claimed, but returned to the house late that afternoon?'

'Danielle . . . It's . . . it's possible, but . . . but Étienne has not been freed. I would have known of this. My son would not have denied his mother the news I've been praying so hard for.'

'Louis . . .' Kohler indicated the SS major and two others who had come into the autopsy room. 'They haven't found her.'

'Then let us hope the half-brother has come home.'

In total darkness 42 boulevard Maillot faced on to the Bois de Boulogne. Her heart sinking at what she must now go through, Juliette recalled that before the Defeat there had been tall iron gates, such handsome gates, bearing the de Trouvelot coat of arms, but these had been taken by the Occupier and shipped to the Reich as scrap metals. 'To the Krupp factories at Essen!' Madame de Trouvelot had charged, as if she had caused the loss and was still to blame for . . . What? she asked herself. For bearing her son's only child and keeping silent the family name.

She remembered begging the woman to free Étienne before he died in the camps. 'On 5 November of last year I went down on my knees to her, Inspectors,' she confessed, her voice breaking. 'Tears that should never have fallen in front of one such as her, wet my cheeks and I could not stop them just as now. I told her the name of the waiter at Maxim's that Oskar had said could help me. Fifty thousand francs . . . a hundred thousand – they were nothing to her. Oh *bien sûr*, the Occupier has requisitioned her beautiful house but pays her a healthy rent, and yes, she now lives in one room – the library. Henri-Christophe loved that room and, when forced to move, she chose it above all others, but the Generalmajor who lives here and commands the Luftwaffe in Paris and the Île de France is an understanding man. Her meals deny her nothing. She has the use of the garden and is free to come and go as she pleases. Sometimes even the car is available, but you'll get nothing from her. She hated me and hated the thought of her son marrying me. To her I was a tramp and nothing Henri-Christophe could do or say could ever change her opinion. My father was a shopkeeper. I had lured her son into illicit sexual encounters to elevate my own status, disregarding entirely that I would bring down that of his family.'

'Louis, let me stay here with madame and the others,' sighed

Kohler. 'Don't bugger about looking for answers we might or might not need. Just ask the woman if she paid up and if the boy was freed.'

'She didn't!' wept Juliette. 'She laughed at my attempts to beg and told me that now I must really pay for my sins. *My sins*, when Henri-Christophe and I were so in love our hearts ached to be with one another and we could hardly wait to go to a hotel. A hotel . . . Ah! I'm sorry. Please forgive me. Ours was a secret, an *amour fou*, and I can still feel the first time he kissed me, the first brush of his hands on my breasts, the tenderness of his caresses, the first time he entered me, the rush of it, the joy, the eagerness of us both.'

'My child . . .'

'Father, don't you dare patronize me! You knew the agony I was living. You, who married me to that bastard!'

'It was for the best.'

'*Sacré nom de nom*, how can you say such a thing? You who knew him far better than anyone else!'

Pocketing the keys, Louis got out and came round to the other side of the car. Kohler saw him look up to that God of his to ask for help. Danielle de Bonnevies was terrified and on the run and probably trying to reach her brother before it was too late for him, but if no brother, then what? he asked himself and answered, A quiet place where the roots of *Helleborus niger* can be ground or simply eaten as is.

A sentry challenged Louis as he stepped between the stone gates, and the beam of a blue-blinkered torch swept over him before alighting on the proffered Sûreté badge and identity papers. Madame de Bonnevies gave a ragged sob to which Father Michel impatiently said, 'If Étienne de Bonnevies has come home, Inspector, then I greatly fear you have no need to look further for your murderer.'

Frau Hillebrand simply smoked a cigarette in silence and stared out her side window while Honoré de Saussine muttered things to himself.

The sofa and armchairs had been in the library since well before the Franco-Prussian War of 1870 to '71, felt St-Cyr. Their wine-red morocco was crackled and faded but also wore that dark patina of solid comfort and many cigars. Books climbed to the ceiling.

'Inspector, I'll be frank. I'm a woman who never had any patience for waiters, street beggars, or the police and other civil servants. Please state your reason for this invasion of my privacy.'

Madame de Trouvelot was in her early eighties, a tall, slim, dignified woman in a soft grey prewar suit of immaculate cut. The single strand of pearls was worth a fortune, the rings and brooch, too, but exactly the right amount of jewellery was worn, no more, no less. The face was narrow, the nose bringing together a sharpness whose deep blue eyes perceptively assessed this Sûreté and plumbed for the depths of his little visit. No matter what Hermann had advised, one did not go quickly with a woman such as this because she simply would not allow it. The *bourgeoisie aisée*, the really well off, could often be so difficult.

'The aristocracy,' she said, having read his thoughts. 'Oh do sit by the fire. You find me in much reduced circumstances, Inspector, but living in one room saves on my having to employ a lot of ungrateful servants. My cook is considerably happier, since he can now steal far more and his new employer is apparently oblivious to it. The maids smile because they are fed a daily diet of compliments and little presents by the Generalmajor's staff who want, no doubt, to get under their skirts. The chauffeur, however, still considers himself above such plebeianisms, since I've always turned a blind eye to his philandering, even to his disgusting habit, when I am not present, of using the back seat of my automobile for his *liaisons sexuelles*.'

'Madame, a small matter. A few questions. Nothing difficult, I assure you.'

'Must you be so tiresome?'

'The library is pleasant.'

'Am I to understand that you are interested in real estate?'

'Madame, the watercolours that hang among the Old Masters, the exquisite array of small bronzes on your mantelpiece, that portrait photograph . . . May I?'

'Since you have already picked it up, who am I to deny the police their pleasure in these days of trial?'

She would take a cigarette now, thought Marie-Élisabeth. This presumptuous Sûreté would try to offer a light she would coldly refuse.

'I have sufficient,' she said, flicking the lighter the Generalmajor Krüger had given her. She'd let this Sûreté see that it bore the SS runes and swastika, a piece of cheapness the Generalmajor had not wanted on his person perhaps, but an item also that necessity had forced upon her.

'Madame, this portrait photograph is of Juliette de Bonnevies née de Goncourt.'

'Beautiful, wasn't she, at the age of nineteen? Pregnancy always makes a girl radiant in its first month or two. Flushed, warm, soft, tender. A seductress, Inspector. The earrings dangling like that. Cheap seed pearls and rhinestones that fooled no one.'

'Diamonds, madame. Two strands of magnificent pearls which match in lustre the seeds but are larger and far more expensive. Your son . . . Did he, perhaps, give them to her?'

'How dare you?'

The dress, of a white silk crêpe de Chine, was worn well off the shoulder and with double straps. On the right wrist there was the slim, black leather band of a Hermès watch, on the left, some bracelets, no doubt from Cartier's and again of diamonds. The straight jet-black hair was parted in the middle and pulled back tightly, the dark eyes magnificent and full of warmth and happiness, nothing else. A young girl who was sitting sideways, so as to look over her right shoulder at the camera. Not shy, not bold, just herself and totally in love.

'A girl of few morals and loose ways, Inspector. Oh *bien sûr*, she seduced my son and the boy wanted desperately to marry her, but passion and love are the least of reasons for one to marry and we could not allow it. A position was found in the *Service Diplomatique* for Henri-Christophe and we sent him to Indochina. The girl married and had her child, a son, I believe, and then a daughter.'

'And you've not seen her since?' He indicated the photo.

'Not since.'

'Then why, please, have you the photo out? Why the bronzes, the watercolours, all of which were done by Étienne de Bonnevies?'

The Inspector leaped from his chair to touch the bronzes. 'Sandpipers,' he said. 'Swans. A girl of fifteen, Madame de Trouvelot, a mermaid rising from the Seine near . . .'

'Do you really think I would let that woman know I had bought them, Inspector? Ah! you police, you're all the same. Of course I had them removed before she came to see me. I had to have my revenge, but one mustn't go too far with such things.'

'You bought some of the boy's work.'

'As a way of encouraging him and because Henri-Christophe had genuinely admired his talent. They never met, of course. To have done so would have been for my son to have broken his solemn promise to me.'

'Then how did he know the boy had talent?'

'Because that mother of his once stopped my son in the street and gave him some of the boy's sketches.'

The Sûreté put the mermaid back. 'The boy's sister,' she said, 'but he does not, I am forced to say, and glad of it too, think of her in the way a man usually thinks of a naked girl.'

She would give this one a moment to digest such a morsel, thought Marie-Élisabeth, and then would leave him to consider it. 'Inspector, Juliette should have come to me long before she did. To think that the boy has languished in prisoner-of-war camps all these years since the Defeat. I went the very next day, the sixth of November, to Maxim's and made enquiries. Fifty thousand francs was, of course, outrageous, but waiters have never known their proper place and times like these only make them far more arrogant. The boy is never to return to the house of that mother of his, you understand, but has sent me a note that he is safely back in France and staying at the country house where he had, before the war, a studio. He will pay me a visit only when I ask it of him. He has, I gather, started to paint again.'

'At the country house . . .'

'That is just what I said. Really, Inspector, you can't have expected me to have told Juliette? Surely not.'

'And have you paid this waiter the final fifty thousand francs?'

'As agreed. I did so as soon as I received the boy's letter. It was written on the fourth of this month and arrived on the sixth – the mail these days is simply not what it used to be. I went to the restaurant on the seventh.'

'Might I see the letter?'

'It's there beside the rose my son gave me when he was called away to Berlin.'

'As a diplomat?'

'Thirteenth September 1938. A road accident. There was heavy rain and fog. The other car was totally demolished. Three people . . . The police claimed they were driving too fast and that my son was in the right, but . . .' She shrugged. 'These things are never clear when they happen in such places and at such times, are they?'

A nod would be best, since the son could well have been on sensitive business and murdered by the Nazis. The letter seemed genuine enough but, still, he'd best ask, 'Have you ever had any other letters from Étienne de Bonnevies?'

'The signature matches that on his sketches, Inspector, and I am satisfied as best I can be.'

'Good. Madame, you stated that the boy would pay you a—'

'Inspector, I thought I had made myself clear. He's very talented and most of what you have seen of this house, and whatever else I possess, will soon be his. I have no other heir to whom I would wish to leave my estate.'

'But he doesn't look at naked girls in the way your son looked at Juliette de Goncourt?'

A slight tremor caused her to put her cigarette down, though she said nothing, which was to her credit, since she was trying to protect the boy and still uncertain of this Sûreté.

'Madame, my partner and I are of the law, but believe it should be tempered with reason and compassion wherever possible. Homosexuality is deemed illegal these days, and both our Government in Vichy and the Occupier wish vehemently to stamp it out. As a result, such men, and women, are imprisoned and sent into hard labour in the Reich, or shot.'

'Or beaten to death, but you and your partner are open to reason. Is it not dangerous for you to admit such a thing?'

'Yes.'

'Then understand that this is why I have insisted the boy stay out of Paris and away from that stepfather of his who will, I greatly fear if aware of his true nature, do everything in his power to have him arrested. Please prevent it from happening.'

'Do you know Alexandre de Bonnevies?'

'I know of him, Inspector. I've always known. A woman in my position has to, though these days I am not so able to find things out as quickly as I would wish.'

'And the daughter, Danielle?'

'When I decided to purchase my grandson's freedom, I had the girl brought here and told her. I wanted to be absolutely certain no harm came to him, and was fully satisfied by her responses and manner. She struck me as being a very intelligent, very capable young woman who loved my grandson dearly. She explained his need to use her as a model, since he had so little money and could not hire another, and while I did not agree, I understood perfectly the sincerity of her reasoning. He is extremely talented, and she wanted only to help him.'

A match was struck, hands were cupped, and out of the night, the left side of Kohler's face appeared briefly as he lit a cigarette. Then the match went out and there was only that tiny glow as he leaned on his crutches and secretly shared the cigarette with the sentry. Their voices were muffled. Maybe they'd be talking of home, thought Käthe. Maybe Kohler would joke about a little, but as sure as she was sitting here watching him, she knew he had deliberately left the four of them alone in the car.

Again the image of that scar came to her. Kohler had defied the SS in his and St-Cyr's holier-than-thou pursuit of the guilty and they had savagely struck him with a rawhide whip some months ago. Ever since then, both men had been distrusted and reviled by many in the SS and Gestapo, and the Höherer SS und Polizeiführer Oberg would be fully cognizant of this and wouldn't want the Palais d'Eiffel to be closed and a scandal to erupt.

Oskar was worth too much to him, and to others in high places, but also knew too much and would be a decided embarrassment should things go wrong. Oberg had been very clear on this. Settle things or else. Get de Bonnevies out of the way. Never had she seen Oskar in such a state. 'Juliette will open the door of the house and ask you in when you tell her I've sent a message. She won't suspect a thing.'

Oil of mirbane. It would be on a shelf in the study. The bottle of Amaretto had been on the desk . . .

Glancing up into the rearview mirror, she tried to meet the gaze Juliette must give, but there was only darkness. I know she's watching me, said Käthe silently. Oskar had been so tired of Uma and had wanted his little bit of fun, and it had been exciting – lots and lots of laughs and sex; sex like she'd never experienced before, but now . . . Would Kohler and his partner really try to smooth things over and hide the truth?

Juliette had pulled off a glove. Her fingertips were cold when Käthe felt them touch the nape of her neck. 'A cigarette?' asked the woman. 'Could I have one, please?'

I know you speak and understand French. How else could Oskar have managed when he first came to the city?

'Of course. Here . . . here, let me light it for you.'

The lighter was flicked twice, the flame lit up the front seat of the car, but then . . . then the light went out so quickly, thought Juliette, and said diffidently, '*Merci*,' as she took the proffered cigarette and put it between her lips. Lips that have kissed yours, Frau Hillebrand? she silently asked. I was blindfolded, wasn't I, each time you came into Room 4–18 at the Hôtel Titania to find me naked and with my hands tied behind my back? Was it you who insisted on the blindfold? You would always say a few words in French to calm me, but I sensed you were afraid if you said more I might be able to recognize you. You trembled, you were so anxious sometimes. Later the smell of the Javel would always be on my fingertips, and you, Frau Hillebrand, are a part of the reason for this. Of course I wanted that husband of mine dead. Of course I lied when questioned by St-Cyr. When one has so much to hide, what are a few more things?

Oskar knew where the oil of mirbane was kept, Käthe, because I had told him when asked. And getting the keys to the study and to the gates presented little difficulty. There was beeswax on my front-door key one time. Was it wax from when an impression had been made? With that key, it was then possible for someone to enter the house, but will the detectives believe this if I tell them?

Alexandre usually left his keys on the bureau in his bedroom when he hung up his suit, Käthe. He slept soundly for a man of such cruelty and was so arrogant he never believed for a moment anyone would dare to enter his room at night.

Danielle, when away, would leave her keys behind and when at home would set them on her night-table before bed. Danielle whose breath came uneasily in a sleep that was often troubled. She fears the worst, poor thing, and has run for her life, but can't run to Étienne who would surely have come home if he could have to instantly free me from my agony.

Étienne who is so sensitive a creature, an *original* in his own right, but never one like Alexandre.

Étienne who is locked up with hundreds and hundreds of lonely men, Käthe, most of whom will only abuse him terribly.

'Father, I did what I had to do,' she said and offered to share the cigarette, an offer that wasn't refused, for he answered softly, 'My child, God hears and understands.'

'But will He forgive me?'

'Yes. Yes, of course, as He forgives all who truly repent and accept His love.'

'Then will He forgive my son for being the way he is?'

'And what way is that?'

'You know, so please don't ask me to say it.'

'Then yes. Yes, He will. My child, did you manage the boy's release? Danielle would not have run like that unless she believed Étienne had come home and had killed Alexandre.'

'Father, Madame de Trouvelot adamantly refused to help me. Étienne will not have come home.'

'That boy poisoned Alexandre, didn't he?' snapped Honoré de Saussine. 'While we're all being held for something we didn't do, he runs free and that sister of his runs after him!'

'You were offered money,' countered Juliette swiftly. 'Oskar must have had a set of keys made to the house and study, *mon ami*. Please don't forget that when the opportunity arises I will definitely inform the detectives of this!'

'*Salope!*' swore de Saussine. '*Putain!*'

Kohler yanked open the rear door and leaned into the car to confront him. 'Our beekeeper was one hell of a problem, wasn't he, *mon fin*? He'd have let you have your day in court and willingly would have seen you thrown out of that Society and shut down hard.'

'*I didn't do it!*' shrilled de Saussine. 'I didn't need to because Herr Schlacht had arranged for . . .' Ah *merde*, had he walked himself to the widow-maker? he wondered, sickened by the thought. 'I . . . I shouldn't have said that. I . . . I spoke in haste.'

'Had arranged for whom, exactly, to do the job, eh? Frau Hillebrand?'

'*I didn't!*' cried Käthe. '*I couldn't!* I . . . I went there, yes, to the house in the afternoon but . . . but didn't even ring the front bell!'

'We'll see then, won't we, but it's good of you to have let us know you were there on the day he died. Now which of you knows anything about *Helleborus niger*, the Christmas rose?'

'The leaves, the stems and roots are poisonous,' said Father Michel. 'But why, please, do you wish me to say this?'

They listened, Juliette swallowing hard but saying nothing. 'Violent inflammation of the skin where the plant has touched it. Vomiting and purging that can't be stopped – the bowels ache to pass waste and constrict but can't void a thing because you're totally empty. Severe abdominal cramps and numbness – one of its ingredients, helleborin, is a narcotic; another, helleborein, is a cardiac poison. There is copious sweating – you constantly drool, but can't figure out what the hell is happening to you. Your heartbeat is very rapid but so faint you can hardly feel it. Consciousness remains until about ten minutes before death, but you drift into and out of it until, at last, the nerve centres that control the heart finally become paralysed. Your daughter, madame, intends to kill herself.'

The driver's side door was yanked open. Breathlessly Louis crammed himself behind the steering wheel and jammed the key into the ignition. The tyres screeched. He made a sharp U-turn on the boulevard Maillot and they shot eastwards towards Charonne. There were a few bicycles and bicycle-taxis, a *gazogène* lorry . . .

Tiny blue-blinkered red brake lights, a pedestrian crossing, a traffic cop . . .

The horn was leaned on and they were through.

'The grandmother paid up, Hermann. Étienne de Bonnevies has come home and Danielle will try to reach him before we do or the SS take her. There's also a gun, the service revolver belonging to Captain Henri-Alphonse Vallée, madame. A Lebel *Modèle d'ordonnance*.'

A gun . . . Ah *Scheisse*! 'The black-powder cartridges, Louis?'

They might be damp because of their age. 'Perhaps, since Vallése is definitely of the old school, but if not the 1873, Hermann, then the 1892 and the 8mm smokeless. Madame, where is it hidden?'

'I . . . I don't know. How could I? Alexandre . . .'

'Come, come, madame, we've no time to lose. Please understand that if the SS or anyone else should arrest your daughter and find that on her, there will be nothing my partner and I can do to save her.'

9

At 8:10 they gathered in the kitchen of the beekeeper's house. The gun was gone; the girl was gone. Louis held the oilcloth the Lebel had been wrapped in while hidden under the floorboards of the honey-house.

A broken-open packet of 11mm cartridges revealed that a handful had been hastily pocketed. The suit, stockings, sweater, blouse and shoes the girl had worn to the meeting had lain in a crumpled heap on the floor of her bedroom. She had dressed warmly in her khaki trousers, and no doubt a flannel shirt, two sweaters, woollen knee-socks and hiking boots, and had taken her rucksack, with what food, matches, blankets and money she could grab.

The Terrot bicycle was also absent.

'An hour's start, at most, Hermann, but it's a good fifty kilometres to Soisy-sur-Seine. The road follows the river for some distance to Villeneuve-Saint Georges, then moves inland and doesn't return to it until south of Draveil. There are short cuts she will know of and use. The Forêt de Sénart also presents a problem, since it will offer easy retreat should she and her half-brother feel it necessary.'

An hour in this weather . . . Ten kilometres, fifteen at the most since she was used to winter cycling, thought Kohler. 'But the snow . . . Louis, she might have to ditch the bike. If so, we'll never find her.'

'Inspectors, sometimes I would find the two of them at a hunters' hide near the Carrefour du Chêne-Prieur. My husband always thought the worst; I knew the truth but could not bring myself to tell him for fear of his hurting the boy.'

The Crossroads of the Prior's Oak . . . 'Your son must have

271

come into the city, and finding that bottle, added the poison, madame,' said Kohler. 'Look, I'm sorry, but that's how it appears.'

'And Danielle, who loves him dearly and understands him totally, has finally realized this and is trying to save him – is this what you mean?'

'You know it is.'

'*Sacré nom de nom*, why couldn't Madame de Trouvelot have told me she had secured his release? I could have spoken to him, calmed him. He'd have listened to me.'

'Madame, would your daughter have written to your son about how terrible things were for you at home?' asked St-Cyr.

'Yes, and often, I think.'

'And did you tell Herr Schlacht of the country house?'

'I did, yes.'

'Louis, that SS major will have let our *Bonze* know the kid's on the loose.'

'And that waiter at Maxim's, Hermann, would have contacted him as soon as Madame de Trouvelot had paid the first fifty thousand.'

'Schlacht knows the boy has come home, then,' sighed Kohler, 'and exactly where the girl will run.'

'But do the SS?' asked St-Cyr. 'Has he told them of the house?'

'Drive, damn it! Drive! We've still got to get Oona.'

'Calm down. Have courage, Hermann. *Courage!*'

'Louis . . . Louis, why the hell would Schlacht have to get to Danielle before we do?'

It was a good question to which Frau Hillebrand offered no answer, and neither did Honoré de Saussine. Only Father Michel had anything to say as they raced out of the city. 'I was afraid of this tragedy. When we first spoke, Chief Inspector, I feared the boy had come home and that Juliette had not yet learned of it, but that Danielle not only knew her half-brother had returned but that her father would have him arrested. I knew I couldn't let it happen and begged God to intervene.'

'And did God listen, Father, or merely guide your hand?' demanded Louis, negotiating a difficult bend in the road.

'God doesn't choose to notify the messengers of His will,

Inspector. Men like myself are simply here to pick up the pieces and salvage what we can.'

'As you did with Héloïse Debré and with the rapists of Angèle-Marie?' asked Louis sharply.

'Héloïse was being punished and so were the others. My position has always been not to interfere but to counsel patience, hear confessions, and beg all to make their peace with God and those they have wronged.'

'That custodian wants you dead.'

'He's a weak man, and I have known for years of his disregard for me.'

'Then don't go into the catacombs, Father, or he'll do what he tried to do to me!'

Just south of Saint-Mandé, they cut through the Bois de Vincennes and then crossed the Marne before returning to the Seine. There was so little traffic, the road was like a blind, dark tunnel across which the falling snow tried only to obscure everything. Left to themselves, the three in the back seat had clammed up. Frau Hillebrand went to offer Hermann a cigarette from her case only to find it empty. 'My purse, Herr Kohler,' she said, trying to reach for it. 'It's on the floor at your feet.'

'Let me,' interjected St-Cyr. 'I have to get out anyway to remove the black-out tape from the headlamps. A moment, please.'

The purse was heavy, and as he handed it to the woman, she held her breath, and he had to wonder if she'd a gun of her own.

To the south of Choisy-le-Roi there were railway freight yards. Here they were stopped at a control and their papers demanded, and it was all Herr Kohler could do to keep them from having to get out of the car, thought Käthe. But then they were on their way again. Forty . . . fifty kilometres an hour, often less. St-Cyr knew the roads and was an excellent driver. They were so different, these two, and yet . . . and yet that same intuitiveness existed between them. When Kohler, impatient at their progress, drummed his fingers on the dashboard, St-Cyr was ready and calmly said, 'Oona will be all right, *mon vieux*. Schlacht won't touch her, not after Oberg has said she's to go to Spain.'

'And since when could the SS ever be trusted?' scoffed Kohler, and took to irritably scraping the frost from his side window. 'Our *Bonze* wants Giselle in exchange, Louis, and the SS have agreed.'

'Then we must settle things for the good of all.'

But how? wondered Käthe, as the two of them dropped into silence and only the throb of the engine was heard. Danielle de Bonnevies knew too much as did her mother. If taken before the Kommandant von Gross-Paris and questioned, either one or the other, or both, could so easily destroy everything. The Höherer SS Oberg had been adamant about this when he'd given her the pistol.

And what of the priest? she asked and told herself, it would be best if he, too, were silenced. But would Oskar really go back to Uma? Oberg would insist on it until this whole business had blown over and he had made up his mind what to do about the woman. Uma knew things the Führer must never hear; Oberg would want all the account and safety deposit box numbers and keys, especially those Uma had used for Oskar. He had said, 'Don't fail me, Frau Hillebrand. Do it for the Fatherland and as a loyal SS should.'

'We are entering Draveil,' said St-Cyr companionably to her. 'Once beyond it, you will find one of the finest stretches of the river. A gentle peace before the storm of the city, a reprieve for those wanting to get away for the weekend. On the Left Bank there are the smokestacks, cranes and loading docks of increasingly crowded industrial complexes; on the Right Bank, as if by pure magic, the villas with their expansive lawns and tennis courts, the sailing clubs and quaint little hotels of the bourgeoisie.'

'My father loved our country house, Inspector,' said Juliette from behind them, 'but it was far from being a villa!'

'There are riding trails throughout the forest and along the river bank, Frau Hillebrand,' he went on, ignoring Madame de Bonnevies as if he was a tour guide for some low-priced agency, thought Kohler. 'Peaceful walks, picnics and diligent hunts for morels, but always the river which here flows quietly. No barges these days, of course, but do you know, Hermann, I have yet to investigate a murder along this stretch of the river. Such contentment has to mean something.'

'He's overtired. Ignore him. If you don't, he'll soon be going on about the little farm he wants to retire to!'

'Messieurs, *please*! It is not a joking matter. The turn-off to the house is but a few kilometres now. Once past a little wood on your right, Inspector, you take the first turn towards the river, but . . . but we will have to walk in, I think.'

And Étienne? wondered Juliette. Should she cry out a warning? Would he then attempt to escape or use the gun to defend himself?

The road was even lonelier than the one they'd come along and it was covered with about fifteen centimetres of snow. As light from the headlamps passed quickly over the house and then returned to settle on it, the two detectives searched the ground ahead for footprints and tyre marks but could see none.

'Wait here,' breathed St-Cyr softly. 'Make a sound and you will answer for it. Hermann, let me go in alone, but follow at a distance.'

'Then take my gun.'

The head was shaken; the Lebel Louis carried was preferred. Danielle de Bonnevies had stated that she had stayed overnight here on Thursday and Friday, arriving well after dark and leaving well before dawn.

Finding her footprints under the fresh snow would take time, the tyre marks of her bike also.

But had she really stayed here on Thursday night? wondered Kohler. Had the kid not lied about that, too?

It was not good walking in here alone, thought St-Cyr. Though a dark shape on a moonless night, he would still show up against the snow-covered ground. Fruit trees, old, many-branched and left to nature, marked the remains of a small orchard and offered cover. Four beehives had been set out in a tidy, well-spaced row among the trees and as his gaze passed quickly over them, he realized Danielle and her father had kept one of their out-apiaries here. A logical place, a perfect location, but there were no recent tracks under the snow when he crouched to brush it away, and perhaps it was true what she had said, that she tried not to use the house often, so as to keep attention from it. 'I arrived well after dark, Inspector, and left well before dawn.'

From the hives, it was but a short walk to the house whose dark silhouette gave a sloping-roofed shed, a ground-floor wing, with attic dormer, and then, at a right angle, the main two-storeyed part of a stone building that probably dated from about 1850. Peering through a window revealed only a lack of black-out curtains. Trying the doors as stealthily as he could yielded only a decided need for their keys. But there were recent tracks, though not since this snowfall or the one before it. The prints were those of the girl's hiking boots.

'Thursday and Friday nights, then,' he whispered to himself. '*Merde*, I wish Hermann was with me. Hermann is far better at this and can see things I don't.'

The door to the shed wasn't locked. Danielle had pushed her bike in here on those two nights but there was no bike. There were garden tools as old as the centuries, fishnets, two pairs of oars, and he couldn't help but admire Juliette de Goncourt's father for both having kept the house as a family retreat and making sure Étienne de Bonnevies had the use of it and perhaps even its ownership.

Soisy-sur-Seine had been lovely. Marianne had adored the little holiday they had managed when Philippe had been six months old. They had left him nearby with a farm woman and had danced to an accordion on the grand porch of one of the fabled *guinguettes*, the rustic riverside restaurants and dancehalls. They had gone out on the river in a skiff, he with his shirtsleeves rolled up and wearing an old straw hat, Marianne in a brand-new flowered print dress that had been so light and gay, he could remember it still. The *fritures*, the deep-fried little fish from the river, had been superb. They had shared a chocolate mousse and she had spilled some on the dress and been so worried about it he had bought her another the very next day.

'But such holidays were always too rare and brief, and now she's gone and so is Philippe,' he reminded himself and, passing the torch beam over the remainder of the shed, felt his heart sink.

On the other side of a wheelbarrow, hidden as if set out of sight in haste, there was a tattered khaki rucksack. Atop this, tightly rolled and tied with linked bits of old boot laces, was a darkly stained French Army trench coat that still bore a frayed and faded Red Cross armband. A metre-long, stiff, leather-covered map tube from the Great War lay on the stone floor and beside it there was an artist's paintbox. Étienne de Bonnevies had indeed come home.

Kohler leaned on his crutches and listened hard to the night. Louis had been gone too long. There wasn't a sound, save that of the wind in frozen reeds now dry and old along the bank. 'I knew I shouldn't have let him go in there alone,' he softly swore. '*Verdammt*! What the hell am I going to do if something's happened to him and I haven't his help?'

Try to get Oona to Spain, no matter what? Try to outrun the SS with this foot? And what about Giselle, eh? Giselle . . .

Sickened by what would surely happen to both of them if he tried and failed to get them to freedom behind Oberg's back, he started out again. Louis had often paused, and that was good. He had done the wise thing and had approached the house obliquely.

When he came to the shed, Kohler leaned the crutches against the wall and hobbled inside. Only then did he switch on his torch and curse Gestapo stores for the lousy batteries they supplied. Striking two matches which flew apart in a rush of sparks, he again cursed, this time the State-run monopoly Vichy now managed but no better than the Government of the Third Republic. The French had been putting up with the same lousy matches ever since the damned things had been invented!

Finally one of them lighted and his frost-numbed fingers added two more. As though it were yesterday and he still deep in that other war, he saw the map tube and rucksack. He remembered the battery of field guns he had commanded, the fierceness of the shelling, the constant stench of cordite, wet, mouldy earth and death, of opened French bunkers and upheaved trenches, the scatterings of last letters from home. 'Ah *Scheisse*,' he said. 'Louis . . .'

Hobbling as quickly as he could, he raced to find the main door of the house and bang on it. 'Open up!' he yelled. 'Police!'

'Louis . . .' he bleated. 'Louis, I heard no shot. Has the kid killed herself?'

Only silence answered, and as he nudged the door, it swung open.

It was freezing in the car, the endless waiting an agony, and when Honoré de Saussine got out, Juliette did so too.

Then Father Michel decided to stretch his legs. 'It is not good, this silence,' he said. 'I think we'd best go to the house and find out what has happened. I might be needed.'

'Suit yourselves,' said de Saussine. 'For me, I will walk back to the main road. There must be a small hotel or restaurant nearby – is there one, madame?'

'All will be closed. It's nearly curfew,' she answered emptily. Had Danielle done something terrible; had Étienne?

'You've no *laissez-passer* or *sauf-conduit*, monsieur,' cautioned Father Michel. 'If I were you, I would stay with the rest of us.'

'What makes you so certain the German woman wants to remain here?' asked de Saussine.

'We'll ask her, shall we?' countered Father Michel swiftly.

'A moment, *mon Père*,' cautioned de Saussine. 'She knows far more than she's letting on. Herr Schlacht had keys to Alexandre's gates and study. Since I did not take them when offered, who, obviously, do you think he gave them to?'

'Madame de Bonnevies and myself were in the kitchen, monsieur. We would have heard Frau Hillebrand. And please do not forget that from the window there is a clear view of the honey-house and garden. I myself sat facing that window; Madame de Bonnevies with her back to it.'

'And you didn't look away, didn't go into any other room, Father?' scoffed de Saussine.

'We spoke in earnest.'

'And couldn't have done much looking up and out of that window, eh?' taunted de Saussine.

'But . . . but, Father, you do remember that I went upstairs to Étienne's room to bring you his last letter,' said Juliette in distress. 'I couldn't find it on his writing table. I searched the drawers, searched Alexandre's bedroom and only when I went

278

into Danielle's room, found it beside her bed. It was so censored I . . . I wanted your opinion as to how it must originally have read. You do recall this, don't you?'

Merde, why had she had to mention it? cursed Father Michel silently, only to hear de Saussine sigh and say with evident delight, 'Then madame was away sufficiently, *mon Père*, and I will be certain to inform the detectives of this.'

'You're forgetting, my son, that for me, and not the German lady, or yourself to have poisoned one of my oldest and dearest friends I would have needed a key to his study.'

'Madame de Bonnevies left one on the table for you! Her absence had been agreed upon and was deliberate. Admit it, this "oldest and dearest of friends" was a distinct liability. He would accuse his son and have the boy arrested. He'd have that sister of his brought home from the madhouse, and . . . and, Father, he'd continue to make madame suffer.'

'You took the million francs Oskar had offered, didn't you, Monsieur de Saussine?' swore Käthe, having quietly got out of the other side of the car.

There was something in the woman's hands, thought de Saussine, and she was resting them on the roof of the car and pointing it at them. 'I was terrified,' he said, his voice climbing, 'but refused, so that leaves only yourself.'

'Or the Father, or madame, or the son or his half-sister,' she answered calmly.

'Or Oskar himself,' said Juliette anxiously wondering if the woman was about to shoot them. 'Oskar wanted you, Monsieur de Saussine, to do it, and you, too, Frau Hillebrand, but if neither of you were willing, then what was he to have done?'

'You knew where the poison was kept, didn't you?' said Käthe. 'You had a set of keys!'

Was she going to shoot her first? wondered Juliette and tried to keep calm . . . calm. 'Oskar knew my husband would go with those two whores after visiting his sister because Alexandre had always done so and I had told Oskar of this often enough.'

'You knew about the bottle of Amaretto, didn't you?' said Käthe.

'A liqueur which smells of bitter almonds, as does the oil of mirbane,' interjected de Saussine nervously. He'd run. He'd have to, he told himself.

'Which is why it was chosen,' sighed Father Michel, 'though Alexandre would not have cared for it in the least.'

'But Oskar *does* like liqueurs,' countered Käthe. 'And Uma *knew* he would sample it and not just casually, isn't that right, Juliette? Well, isn't it? Oskar would have had you pour him a tumblerful and would have downed it all at once and you . . . you knew he would because when naked you had served and serviced him often enough!'

'What's in your hands?' quavered de Saussine.

'A Beretta 9mm, but Herr Kohler seems to have removed its clip, although I did not hear or feel him do so.'

The studio, some distance beyond the house and closer to the river, must once have been a carpenter's shop, thought St-Cyr. Skylights and French windows had been added, and a nineteenth-century Belgian cookstove with inlaid ceramic tiles. But it was the almost unbelievable clutter that drew the beam of the torch and caused it to flit from place to place. Tubes of oil paint, canvases and easels were everywhere. Fruit jars held upended fistfuls of cleaned brushes, others, a dried stew of paint and brush. There were plaster and clay maquettes and figurines and these threw shadows, small bronzes, too. Experiments with pottery and the firing of sculpted heads and figures were mingled with dried leaves and wild flowers, hanging bits of coloured glass, ropes of it and spirals . . .

Imprints of dead fish, in slabs of sunbaked river mud that must have been carefully excavated years ago, were near prints of the half-sister's bare feet and those of the boy, as if the two of them had walked out from the dawn of history. The bleached skeleton of a seagull flew towards that of a rook some farmer must have shot and the boy or girl had carted home one day. Among the many portraits were sketches of Danielle that had been done in charcoal, in a soft, reddish ochre, in watercolours, too, and in oils. Yet everywhere the torch shone, it seemed the dust had settled.

'Except on the chaise longue,' said Kohler, having found him at last. 'The kid must have slept here on Thursday and Friday nights, Louis.'

She had been going through a number of sketches of herself. Whatever pose the half-brother had wanted, she had adopted. Naked at the age of four, and often up until that of fifteen, she had let him draw and paint her, had been completely at ease. Just as often, though, she was fully dressed; often, too, in a bathing suit or an old pair of coveralls and weeding the vegetable garden or cradling, with evident delight, an errant hen she had just captured.

They had gone rowing on the Seine, had swum naked and not, had fished and explored and done so many things together.

There were photographs, pinned to a cupboard door, of the blind near the Carrefour du Chêne Prieur, snapshots of the boy in uniform, September 1940.

'Two notes,' said St-Cyr, shining the light more fully on them. A pencil dangled from a string into which a drawing pin had been recently stabbed.

Friday 29 January, 1943

Mon cher Étienne,

It has been some time since I've stayed overnight here, so I don't know when you arrived. A week, two weeks . . . Perhaps as long ago as the three and a half weeks since my last visit ended on the third of the month. When I got here late last night, I found your things in the shed. I cried, Étienne. I laughed. I ran to the house calling your name but could not find you even here in the studio and pray you haven't gone into the city to see *maman. Papa* will not allow it. He will swear things about you to the police that are untrue and will try to have you arrested and taken away. He wants Angèle-Marie to come home and insists *maman* must look after her, myself also.

Today I will visit some of our old haunts and friends in the hope of finding you, but I must also go to Brie-Comte-Robert, as I have a farmer there who has promised me a good breeding pair of rabbits, some sausage and cheese. It's a deal I mustn't pass up, so please forgive me and wait for me if you return.

Étienne,

It is now very late and I am so tired. Still there has been no sign or word from you and I have worried all day. Please don't let it be that you've gone to see *maman*. I couldn't bear having *papa* do that to you. I would kill myself, but I know you've always had a set of keys to the gates, the house and his study. I had them made for you years ago so that you wouldn't feel hurt, but these keys, Étienne, they are missing from the tin box where you always kept them. Missing, *mon cher*!

If you should read this, please stay put as you will be far safer here. There is some food, not much, that I've stored in the stove's oven, so don't light a fire before removing it and then only late at night, as there are those in the district one can no longer trust.

I will try to return on Monday but must be careful, as the controls are becoming increasingly difficult and we now have the *Milice* who watch the métro, the railways and bus stations and the streets as well. *Maman*, though she cares nothing for me, will be beside herself with joy, Étienne, but I must be very careful how I tell her. We can't have her running here without thinking of the consequences, but I will try to find a way to bring her to you in secret.

For now, may the love I have for you keep you safe and warm.

Your dearest friend and companion, as always, Danielle.

Like the footprints in dried river mud, the notes stepped out from the past.

'Admit it, Louis. She couldn't have poisoned that father of hers. She was definitely here.'

'The girl accuses her mother, then one of the Society, then publicly de Saussine, but lies so badly she gets confused . . .'

'She *knew* her brother was coming home and felt he must have done it. All along she's been trying her damnedest to hide this from us.'

'And Father Michel opens a parish wound to keep us from finding out what he believes has happened: that the boy has returned and is responsible.'

'When she left us, the kid was heading here to save him. They'll die together, Louis. That's what she intends.'

'But he isn't here, Hermann, and yet . . . and yet, Madame de Trouvelot received a letter from him written on the fourth of the month from here.'

'A letter?'

'On its receipt she paid the final instalment.'

'That kit in the shed . . . It reminded me of the war, Louis, of the things we had to send home for so many.'

'And there's a fruit jar of fine white sand by the sink in the kitchen.'

'Sand?'

'Don't worry so much. It may mean nothing.'

'Frau Hillebrand had a loaded pistol in that purse of hers, Louis.'

'Could she have written the letter Madame de Trouvelot received?'

'We'll have to ask her, eh, since I've got what she may well have been ordered by Oberg to use.'

In the shed, torchlight fell on the rucksack which yielded only pieces of worn clothing that could have been the boy's. The map case held the few rolled sketches of life in the POW camps that the censors hadn't removed, but each one of them bore, dead centre, the heavy black imprint of the official rubber stamp.

The paintbox had a few dried-up tubes of oil paint, one brush and some bits of charcoal.

Hermann turned the map case upside down and like last leaves, the boy's identity papers fell out. All had been officially stamped as '*Cancelled. Died 28 December 1942. Pneumonia.*'

'Schlacht must have known, Louis, yet he let Madame de Bonnevies continue to beg for her son's release.'

'And the girl, Hermann? What if she, too, has known of this all along?'

'She can't have.'

'But if she had?'

'Then she wasn't heading here at all, but has gone after our *Bonze*. Oberg will kill us, if she succeeds. He'll make it slow and painful and will insist Oona and Giselle watch before he also hangs the two of them with the same piano wire.'

Like the rest of the city's streets at 4:20 in the morning, the boulevard Ornano was dark in the grip of winter and empty. Breath billowed, and as they went up the street, Louis shone his torch over the entrances until at last he had picked out the soot-streaked placard on a flaking wall beside the rat-hole entrance to the *maison de passe* Schlacht had bought.

HOTEL
Chambres et Cabinets
TITANIA
au jour et nuit ou à la semaine

The blackened, doorless cavern that was the entrance led immediately to a narrow flight of wooden stairs. There was no light except that of the torch. At midnight the *patron* would have doused the faint, blue-washed beacon that would have drawn in the passing moths, with or without their yellow work cards, but with the boys they would love 'for ever'.

Now, of course, and since midnight, they'd all have been locked in until the curfew ended. Snores and farts and spills of *vin ordinaire* or brandy, or the 'champagne' that was flogged even in places like this, the beds covered not with sheets and blankets, but with a single, greasy, stained and worn length of oilcloth. Cold as Christ; wet as Christ. Drunken legs sprawled, naked bodies dead to the world beneath scatterings of greatcoats, dresses, trousers and underpants, as if these could ever keep out the cold while snoring it off in the sweaty, unbathed clutches of a lover who was lying, like as not, in a puddle of piss.

Kohler knew he had seen it all; Louis had, too. They had left the Citroën opposite the rue du Roi-d'Alger and its *passage*, had parked Juliette de Bonnevies and the others in the cells of Charonne's Commissariat de Police on the rue des Orteaux, and had refused to listen to their objections so as to come here alone.

Just the two of us, as always, he said silently to himself but would Oona have been raped by several? Would they find her half out of her mind with Danielle naked in the same room, the kid stone-eyed and beaten into submission?

'Louis, let me go first. You know I'm better at this.'

'That foot of yours will only complain of the shoe you've forced it into.'

'Me first. That's an order. We'll take our time.'

'We haven't much of it and already are late, and at five we both know this can of worms will empty and we will be trampled in the rush.'

There were no hidden tripwires, no 'alarms' to warn *résistants* who might be hiding in such a place and were fond of using them.

But not this hole, thought Kohler, checking the stairwell out anyway.

Hermann *was* good at this sort of thing, conceded St-Cyr. His night vision was so clear he could see things in a darkened room or stairwell that no one else could. And hear things, too, and yet not be heard or seen. But Hermann was afraid of what they'd find and now felt great sympathy for Danielle, having forgotten entirely that it was he who had first thought she might have poisoned her father.

There had, as yet, been no sign of the bicycle, though they had watched the sides of the country roads and had tried to find it.

'Louis, this door's not locked,' came the whisper. Hermann's fingers trembled as he emphasized the point. Pistol in hand, he nudged the door open. The carpet was frayed, and as he felt for the tripwire that might be here, hole after torn hole was found.

The 'desk' was vacant. The *patron* had been told to bugger off. There were no snores, only Louis's breathing and that of his own. 'Switch on the torch,' he sighed. 'Come on *mein lieber Oberdetektiv*, this place has been emptied in expectation of our little visit.'

'So have my batteries.' But had Herr Schlacht prepared a welcome for them?

Time was lost, all sense of its passing gone. On his hands and knees St-Cyr crept forward to another door which, he knew by now, must open at a touch but one could never touch without searching first.

Dust . . . a feather in a place where there were so few . . . a coin, a pfennig dropped as *Reichskassenscheine* or francs were hauled from a pocket and one mark or twenty francs given for a little moment, or cigarettes, for these had fast become the preferred currency. A packet of twenty for the night, maybe with an extra ten if there were two girls and the soldier boy was living the dream he'd had while lying up in a barracks, waiting to go on leave.

There was no wire, no taut bit of string but still . . . the door could have been booby-trapped from within. They'd had that happen before. A safe cracker, the Gypsy, the Ritz and not so very long ago. Was it a week or ten days? One lost track of time. Before Avignon . . . yes, yes. Before its *Cagoule* had taken such an exception to them.

Sacré nom de nom, were friends of friends simply out to silence Hermann and himself, and never mind Oona and Giselle, never mind the murder of some beekeeper who had, one must agree, done everything to ensure sufficient would want him dead.

Not just his wife.

The room held no one but himself. The *vase de nuit* had been used but accidentally overturned in the rush to get out. A raid, then, he said. A raid . . .

A door banged; it banged again and the sound of this carried through the pitch darkness of the attic where garrets, close under the roof, held filthy mattresses, rags and scatterings of female clothing. A torn dress . . . a brassiere, a shoe . . . Was it Oona's? wondered Kohler, moving silently and swiftly from room to room for that door hadn't been banging until now.

Stepping out on to the roof, he hooked the door open to silence it. 'Oona . . . ?' he called softly. 'Oona, it's me.'

There was no answer. A flat stretch of tarred roofing had been swept clear by the wind which had piled the snow up against the base of a brick wall that rose a storey and a half.

Crossing the roof, Kohler looked up through the darkness at the iron ladder that was bolted to the wall and would lead whoever it was to the chimneypots of the adjacent building. 'Don't do this to me,' he sighed. Louis . . . should he get Louis?

Someone had put through an alarm and the Paris *flics*, the Sûreté's vice squad *and* Gestapo's bully boys with guns had come running.

Résistants? he wondered. Had the person told them that? No doubt Schlacht had clearance and had paid off the local sous-préfet and all others, but who among the rank and file was going to worry about such little details at two or three in the morning when the alarm must have come in?

His foot hurt like hell and he really didn't want to climb the rungs. His hands were freezing, but he had to tell himself Oona would have gone up this in her bare feet if necessary. Oona could be up there.

Had she been missed in the raid? Had she heard something or sensed there was someone else in the attic and not known it was him? She must have. But it hadn't been Oona. Jammed between the chimneypots at the top of the ladder was a thick Manila folder that had been put there while clambering on to the roof, and then left in haste.

The folder held sketches and snapshots of Danielle de Bonnevies at the age of fourteen and fifteen, and in most of these the girl wore nothing but her birthday suit. But there were others in Room 4–18, some tucked in around the mirrored doors of an armoire, some pinned to the walls, or, if a large sketch, framed and hung, and all must have come from the studio. While most recently there, she had realized that several were missing and must have wondered where they were and who had taken them.

'Frau Hillebrand and Schlacht,' said Kohler, nursing his right foot and trying to rebandage his wounded toes. 'Our *Bonze* didn't just want to raid the hive for the mother, Louis. He was intent on the kid.'

'And the mother must have known of it, Hermann.'

'And done something about it, eh? Like lacing a bottle that was intended for him.'

'Perhaps, but then . . . Ah *mon Dieu*, this murder, Hermann. Positively no time to sort things out except while on the run. The run, *mon vieux*. Turning in an alarm is not so easy after the curfew has begun. Mademoiselle Danielle would have needed to either tell the *flics* in person and risk certain arrest, or have had access to a telephone.'

An instrument the Hôtel Titania lacked as did most of the quartier Clignancourt.

'But what the hell had she really in mind?' asked Kohler. Room 4–18 was a cut above the others. Plush wine-red drapes covered French windows that must lead to the little balcony Juliette de Bonnevies had said had a view of the Sacré-Coeur. There were carpets on the floor, pillows on the iron-framed double bed, silk sheets, too, soft woollen blankets and an antique, white lace spread. Two straight-backed chaises, an armchair, a footstool . . . Champagne flutes placed in readiness – there was even some ice left in the bucket, no bottle of Krüg, though, for those who had raided the hotel would have helped themselves with pleasure.

The ashtrays were clean. Sash cord for tying up the willing and unwilling had been neatly coiled, a gag laid out, a blindfold . . .

In a drawer, beneath heaps of lingerie, were boxes of Wehrmacht regulation-issue condoms, jars of petroleum jelly, rolls of surgical tape any hospital in the city would have been glad of, since they had none or very little. 'Even *godemichés*, Louis!' Dildos. 'Look, I know our *Bonze* wasn't having it off tonight, or watching through some peephole as others went at it, but what I want to know is why the hell did that kid see fit to lay on a raid?'

Hermann was really worried and had best be calmed. 'To get at the truth of the missing sketches. To see for herself the room where her mother had been forced to prostitute herself and perhaps even offer up her daughter in hope of freeing her son.'

'Whom Danielle believed had returned, but then discovered after writing the last of her notes, that he couldn't have.'

'She didn't want us knowing this, Hermann, until she had done what she felt she had to.'

'Which was to give that lecture and then poison herself. Louis, Oona may be in the cells at the rue des Saussaies with the rest of those who were carted away from here.'

'Or Herr Schlacht has now had time to free her and has taken her with him.'

'Where to?'

'The candles.'

'What about them? Danielle . . .'

'Though she has denied knowing the whereabouts of the factory, she has patiently discovered everything else.'

'And will now try to put an end to our *Bonze* and everything he's been doing.'

Goods trains shunted in the freight yards, which Kohler knew were just to the east and along the rue des Poissonniers. In the maintenance sheds and yards of the Omnibus Depot across from him and off the north side of the rue Championnet, the racket of misfiring *autobuses aux gazogène* mingled with that of the others to break the cold, hard darkness, as *vélos* and their earnest riders hurried to work through the ink of what had, before the Defeat of 1940, been 4:45 a.m. A light snow fell to dampen the rank air from the distillation units which used charcoal to produce the mixture of methane, carbon monoxide and hydrogen that, when burned in the cylinders, powered the buses. A lorry parted the stream of bicycle riders; a bus followed, honking furiously.

Louis was to enter the candle factory by another route. He would negotiate the inevitable *passages* and, on the way, try to find where the girl had hidden her bike. Just precisely what she planned, they didn't know yet, but would have to stop her. They couldn't have her trying to kill Schlacht, couldn't have her causing trouble here and alerting von Schaumburg and the rest of the OKW to the iniquities of the Palais d'Eiffel any more than she already had, couldn't have her infuriating Oberg.

When a lorry turned in at a courtyard whose entrance had been meant for horse-drawn carriages and wagons, its driver violently cursed and finally, at a lumbering crawl, managed to squeeze it through.

One cylinder wasn't firing, another missed a beat, so the banging and clattering was intermittent, but it wasn't wise to switch these things off when the engine was warming up and would soon fire on all cylinders, albeit at three-quarters the power, or less, of a gasoline-fired engine.

Words erupted with the *argot* – the slang of the quartier. Wax was to be unloaded; candles taken to the Gare de l'Est for shipment to the Reich. Another lorry soon negotiated the entrance, and now the racket of the two of them filled the courtyard and rose up the slot of it to escape into the night sky some four or five storeys above him.

Vacated most probably in the early days of the Great Depression, the building had, no doubt, been cheap and available, and with all the room for expansion Schlacht could possibly have wanted. But it had one big drawback, thought Kohler grimly. There would be far too many places for that kid to hide.

The day shift of fifteen souls began to filter in, their female voices muffled under the constant drone. Kohler thought to join them, but knew he'd stand out as they lined up to punch in at the time clock.

Hacking coughs, sneezes, constant bitching, two teenaged girls discussing a film, a car . . .

Schlacht's Renault drew slowly into the courtyard behind the lorries. Out tumbled Frau Hillebrand and the others, along with Oona and Giselle. A full house. Not only had he been up all night, he'd been to the lock-up in the cellars of the rue des Saussaies, and also that of Charonne's Commissariat de Police.

Soft on the violent air came the sweet scent of beeswax to indicate that after Sunday's lay-off, the foreman and his assistants had come in at midnight probably to get the wax melted and everything ready for the day's production.

Soon the clanking of ancient machinery was added to the sound of the *gazogènes*.

The *passage* was as dark as pitch and no more than two metres in width, felt St-Cyr, not liking what he'd come upon. It ran the length of the rear of the building and separated it from one of the tenements the Société Anonyme des Logements à Bon Marché had put up years ago out of concrete blocks to house, at low rents, the then increasing waves of immigrants from North Africa. But now this latter building would be all but empty. Blacks, Arabs and other non-whites had been forbidden re-entry to the Occupied Zone after the Defeat and had had to stay in the south, to where they had fled along with so many others. Those who had remained in Paris would be exceedingly careful about where and when they went out, for anyone of colour was suspect and likely to be stopped in the street and, if not vouched for by an employer, then taken for forced labour.

Makeshift doorways had consequently been cut into this wall, and inside one of them, he found the girl's bike. The rucksack was open, the gun gone. When barred windows and locked doors prevented entrance to the factory, he found the fire escape and went up it just as Danielle must have done. A broken window gave access to an even deeper darkness through which the distant sounds of slowly moving machinery came.

Pausing to feel the gap where the lift doors should have been, he found, instead, an emptiness that sickened. When someone stepped on broken glass, he hissed urgently, 'Mademoiselle, it is Jean-Louis St-Cyr of the Sûreté. Please give yourself up.'

She made no further sound, and after a while he told himself that she had left him. Her half-brother was dead, her father dead, her life in ruins. With nowhere else to run to, she had come here to do what she felt had to be done. But had she caused her father's death? he asked himself as he blindly searched for the staircase. Had she returned to the house on Thursday to find that bottle on his desk?

The beekeeper would have turned Étienne in and had been very vocal about it. Had he written a letter of condemnation to the Kommandant of Oflag 17A and told her of it? She'd given no hint of this but must have known Frau Schlacht would come to the study on that evening to collect the bottle. Yet much of what Danielle had done and said since they had first met in the garden seemed to indicate she had been terribly afraid the half-brother *had* committed the killing. Father Michel had sensed this and had believed firmly for some time that the boy had indeed returned.

A set of keys. Those from the studio? he wondered, dreading the possibility, for Frau Hillebrand and Honoré de Saussine had each known the whereabouts of the poison, as had Herr Schlacht who had had, by far, the most to lose.

Pneumonia . . . At least it wasn't the 'cardiac arrest' the Gestapo were so fond of using, but had the boy been shot? Had the beekeeper, knowing that Juliette would stop at nothing, finally written to the Kommandant of Oflag 17A, denouncing his stepson?

They would probably never know, and certainly the mother, not having been informed of the boy's death, had had reasons of her own for adding the poison.

When he found the staircase, it descended to a landing where there was light, and as he looked up, St-Cyr saw that the building was in two parts, with a forward hoist bay that extended to the roof above, and rearward offices and storerooms. Down below him, where once electrical generators had been assembled, horizontally mounted, cast-iron wheels, a good two metres in diameter and positioned some three metres above the floor, had candle hoops hanging from them at regular intervals. Each hoop had been vertically strung with an outer and inner cage of wicks, and as each wheel advanced, and each cage came round, an operator pulled down on a lever to lower it into a vat of liquid wax. Dripping, the hoop's cage was then lifted to cool and set, while successive others were dipped, a candle and cage taking some forty or fifty passes before being completed. Each outer cage held perhaps thirty candles, each inner one, perhaps twenty, and there were sixteen of the hoops suspended from each of five separate wheels.

More rectangular cages and vats held the larger church candles, the *cierges* without which the Mass would not seem the same. But short, squat, votive candles were also being made – cast in water-jacketed tables that held perhaps thirty dozen at a time and whose piston arrangement pushed the finished candles out and automatically cut off the wicks which were fed from below and through the pistons. For this operation the wax was being melted in galvanized iron drums that stood atop gantries at one end of the tables. There were lighted gas rings under them, and each drum was equipped with a spigot which, when opened, would let the molten wax run down a trough before spreading out to flood and fill the moulds.

Elsewhere, machines braided cotton threads into wicks of various sizes, while others inserted wicks into candles that had been cast without them. Of the fifteen or so females who operated the machines, sorted, polished and packed candles, only two were white and not of North African descent. The foreman, his assistants and two others, all of whom were busy unloading lard pails of wax and honey, were Caucasian.

Behind the windows of an office on the far side of the working floor, Schlacht was clearly in a rage. Frau Hillebrand stood next to him, irritably smoking a cigarette, while Juliette de Bonnevies sat beside Father Michel and Honoré de Saussine was with Oona and Giselle.

There was no sign of Hermann.

The Senegalese was tall and thin, and when he came upon her suddenly in the room where the wax was being separated from the honey in a press, Kohler touched a finger to his lips.

Startled, confused, she didn't know what to do. Should she cry out a warning; should she remain silent? she wondered.

He threw an anxious glance over his shoulder towards the door through which he'd come, this giant who was even taller than herself. Everything about him smelled of fear and yet . . . and yet . . .

Her dark eyes settled on him. 'You're from the police, but are afraid,' she said.

An observant woman. The jet-black hair was all but hidden under a tightly knotted kerchief. 'Visitors,' breathed Kohler. '*Miliciens* from the quartier du Mail et de Bonne-Nouvelle. Old friends your boss has called in for a little more help.' And *nom de Jésus Christ*, why had it to be this way?

They had arrived in a hurry in two cars and had parked these across the entrance to the courtyard, thus sealing it. 'They'll soon be after a girl,' he said sadly, only to hear the woman anxiously ask, 'Which one?'

'Not one of yours.'

'What's she done?'

'It's not what she's done but what she intends to do.'

Once separated from the honey, the wax was cleaned by placing it in flour sacks which were submerged in boiling water – the woman used a stout stick to prod these. 'As the wax melts,' she said, 'it passes through the sacks and leaves behind the . . .'

'*Ach*, I know all about it. The unwanted bits of bee carapaces, et cetera. The wax rises to the surface of the water and you skim it off. No problem, madame, except that there are lots of extra sacks on that washing line of yours and some of them are missing from the end next to that door I came through.'

'Missing . . . ?'

'Four, I think.' Soaked through with residual wax, and then dried, as they now must be, any of them would make an ideal wick, but all the kid really had to do to set fire to the place was to turn up the gas rings under the drums that fed the votive candles. Wax should never be boiled or allowed to get too hot, because if it reached its flash point, it would rapidly expand to vapour and ignite with a deafening bang.

'Pass the word, will you? Tell the others you'd best go on strike and leave the building while you can.'

Louis . . . he'd better find Louis. 'Go on, damn it. Hurry!'

Seen from above, there were seven *miliciens* and as they poured from the office, St-Cyr watched Juliette de Bonnevies press herself against the windows to cry out, 'Danielle . . . ,' though he could not hear her. Each of the *miliciens* carried a lead-weighted, black-leather truncheon which they now used to herd the shrieking workers into a corner, refusing to let them leave. They knocked things over in their haste. The iron wheels continued to turn; the pistons to spit out the votive candles. The two white girls were joined by another who called out, 'The burners, messieurs. I must shut them off!'

They let her go and, from high above the working floor, he watched as she went to the gantried drums. She wore a kerchief, a block-printed smock, and wax-covered, charred asbestos gauntlets, showed no fear or uncertainty, knew exactly what she would have to do.

Some of the *miliciens*, still not realizing who it was, began to search for her and went up the stairs. She gave them time, called out firmly, '*Un moment*,' when yelled at to join the others, then, having turned up the burners and flung off the gauntlets, pulled the Lebel from under her waistband.

Firing only once, Danielle put a hole in one of the drums and let a stream of molten wax pour out over the floor.

'Mademoiselle!' called out St-Cyr. 'Mademoiselle, you mustn't do this! We know your brother couldn't have come home.'

Against the thud and clank of meshing gears, the sound of his voice echoed.

'I must!' she cried. 'Herr Schlacht had my brother killed!'
Killed . . . Killed . . .
'No he didn't! If anyone, it was your father.'
'*Papa* . . . ? But . . . but how could this be, please?'
'By writing to the Kommandant of Oflag 17A.'
'Ah no. *Maman*, is this true?'
Someone must have switched off the machines, for the wheels and gears soon ground to silence.
Allowed to leave the office, the mother walked out on to the floor, was pale and badly shaken. 'Is Étienne dead, *chérie*?' she quavered.
'*Maman*, I thought he was alive and had come home to us. I thought he was staying at the studio but . . .'
'But couldn't have?' asked Juliette.
'He wasn't there, *maman*, and only later did I find what had happened to him. I . . . STAY WHERE YOU ARE! DON'T MOVE!' she shrieked at *miliciens* who had been tempted to close in on her. 'THIS PLACE IS FINISHED, MESSIEURS. I DO IT FOR THE BEES OF RUSSIA AND FRANCE!'
'Danielle, you mustn't! You're not a murderer. Some may be killed, others badly burned.'
'*Maman*, did *papa* write such a letter?'
Letter . . . Letter . . .
'He . . . he threatened to, yes. He . . . he even showed it to me. To me!'
'And did you know Herr Schlacht had been to the studio?'
The studio . . . The studio . . .
'*Chérie*, listen, please. I could not have stopped him. He . . .'
'You knew he wanted to rape me, *maman*! *Me*!'
Some of the wax from the hole was flooding down the side of the drum. It was only moments away from curling under to the burner. The burner . . .
'The other drum, Louis. The kid was going to come up here and, after torching these, throw them down, but must have felt they wouldn't work.'
There were flour sacks in Hermann's hands. 'Do I shoot the daughter?' asked St-Cyr.
'You're the diplomat. Try that first and buy me a little time. Oona and Giselle are still in that office with our *Bonze*.'

'Madame de Bonnevies,' called out St-Cyr. 'If my partner and I can negotiate a reprieve for your daughter, would that not be best? The two of you to Spain, perhaps, with sufficient funds to make a new start.'

Juliette looked questioningly at Schlacht as he came out of the office with Frau Hillebrand; she looked at Danielle. 'Spain, *chérie*, and a chance to leave it all behind. Is it possible?'

'THE INSPECTOR IS LYING!' shrilled Danielle. The fountain of wax was still pouring on the floor; she still had the revolver and would use it if necessary . . .

'We'll die together, is this what you want?' asked Juliette. 'I felt certain Étienne wasn't coming home, Danielle. I had only to look at those sketches that Herr Schlacht had taken from the studio to remind and taunt me, and I knew that something terrible must have happened and would also happen to you. I did not know what to do. Should I add the poison and hope Frau Schlacht's husband would drink it, should I not do so? And all the while I was so worried about Étienne.'

'Pneumonia.'

'Don't cry. Turn off the burners. You've done what you really had to do. You've made me see how much my silence has hurt you.'

'HERR SCHLACHT,' called out Louis. 'WILL YOU AGREE TO GET THEM *AUSWEISE* AND LET THEM ACCOMPANY MADAME VAN DER LYNN TO SPAIN?'

TO SPAIN . . . TO SPAIN . . .

Kohler had reached the working floor and would now, thought Schlacht, begin to make his way up behind the two of them. He hadn't yet drawn his gun, so must be planning to grab the revolver and switch off the burners. But the drums were separated by a good three metres, and while the one began to boil and clouds of heavy white vapour poured from it, the other continued to piss its stream.

'Oskar, agree! You have to,' hissed Käthe. 'If you don't, and this place goes up, it really will be the end of the Palais d'Eiffel.'

'Those two to Spain. The Van der Lynn woman stays in Paris,' called out Schlacht. Father Michel crossed himself; Honoré de Saussine began to slip away, but was held back by Frau Hillebrand.

'*Dieu merci*,' said Louis as the girl handed the revolver to her mother and crouched to switch off the gas ring under the leaking drum, then turned off the other one.

'The office, I think,' said Kohler, 'so that we can clean this mess off our shoes, eh? You've nothing else planned, have you?' he asked Danielle and saw her shake her head.

The morning grew, the rays of feeble sunlight at last finding the streaked and grimy outer windows of the office. Juliette de Bonnevies tried to clean the windowpane in front of her, to stare better at freedom, but it was no use. Behind her, she knew the others sat or stood waiting, too, to hear what the detectives had to say.

Father Michel would be looking inwardly, his gnarled fingers moving the beads of his rosary as he silently recited the decades. Frau Hillebrand was sitting next to Herr Schlacht who, though impatient, would have to let the detectives proceed.

Honoré de Saussine would be pale and silent, nor would his gaze meet hers or anyone else's, except but briefly.

'*Mesdames, Mesdemoiselles et Messieurs*,' said St-Cyr, and there was a watchfulness to him she sensed right away. 'A bottle sits alone on a desk for but a few hours. We now know how it got there and what happened those few hours later. We also know that the gates to the apiary and the garden, and the door to the study were locked that afternoon and would have had to have been opened had someone other than the immediate family or Father Michel poisoned that bottle. Frau Schlacht wanted our beekeeper to add the oil of mirbane so that she could give the Amaretto to you, Herr Schlacht, but by then you knew what your wife had planned. Using *miliciens* to question and torture my partner on Saturday only confirmed your worst fears.'

'Get on with it. *Verdammt*, I haven't all day!'

'Louis, he had the set of keys he and Frau Hillebrand had removed from the studio.'

'Yes, certainly, *mon vieux*, but were they used that afternoon by himself, his secretary, or M. de Saussine?'

'*I didn't do it!*' shrieked de Saussine. '*I couldn't*! I . . . I was too afraid Alexandre wouldn't drink it. *Mon Dieu*, how the hell did

297

anyone know he would? He didn't *like* that stuff. His was always the . . .'

'Yes, yes, monsieur, but you had been offered a million francs and I have your signature to this statement as proof!'

'I signed it under duress. You forced me!'

Schlacht had taken a bottle of cognac from his desk and had set out several glasses which he now filled, laughing as he did and downing one after another. '*So, bitte, meine lieber Detektivs,* will you join me?' he asked, enjoying his little joke and causing Juliette to shudder as she turned at last to face them.

'Of course,' said St-Cyr, and taking two of the glasses, crossed the room to where the ones called Giselle and Oona sat tightly holding each other by the hand. 'Relax,' they heard him say gently. 'I think we can settle this.'

Impulsively the one called Giselle leapt to her feet to kiss and hug him and let her tears spill down his cheek while the one called Oona smiled faintly and said, 'Spain. It's not possible for me, Jean-Louis. You know it and so do I.'

'This murder,' said St-Cyr, when the two had downed their cognac. 'Always there has been the problem of its being intended and yet also accidental. Had de Bonnevies not panicked and thought you had done it, madame, he might well have recovered, had he taken only a sip and spat it out. But he downed a good sixty cubic centimetres, and the rest of what he did only speeded up his demise.

'Mademoiselle Danielle, you were always a suspect. First with my partner, and then myself. You had continually left candles for Father Michel and yet had denied any knowledge of the whereabouts of this factory. You had, I think – and this is crucial – firmly believed for some time that your brother would return.'

'Back in November of last year, Madame de Trouvelot asked to see me and revealed that she had paid for Étienne's release but that it would, of necessity, take much time.'

'*Chérie* . . .'

'*Maman,* I couldn't tell you. Madame de Trouvelot made me promise.'

'You believed,' said St-Cyr, 'and Father Michel sensed this and also came to believe that the boy had, or would, return but that, for very good reasons, you hadn't told your mother.'

'*Papa* would have had him arrested. Everyone knew this. He made certain of it and I . . . I shuddered every time he yelled it at me.'

Oh-oh, thought Kohler, now it's coming.

'On Thursday, mademoiselle, you stated that you left at just after curfew, that your father was already at work, and that the bottle was not present.'

'That is correct.'

'What was he wearing?'

'Pardon?'

'Mademoiselle, you know exactly what I have asked and why.'

The sand, thought Kohler. The kid had realized it, too, or that something she'd done and forgotten about had come to light.

'A flannel shirt. A waistcoat, jacket, scarf, beret and fingerless gloves. Old tweed trousers, two pairs of socks, the gumboots he used when working with the hives. A laboratory coat also.'

'And what did he demand of you?'

'He . . . he asked for a clean shirt. He . . . he said, "You know I have to do my rounds and that that woman is coming to see me this evening."'

'And your mother, mademoiselle, could she not have done this for him?'

'She was asleep but would have silently refused as you well know, so why, please, do you ask?'

'Just tell us, mademoiselle. Leave nothing out.'

Why could he not simply accuse her? wondered Danielle. Why must he insist on making her say it? 'Though he knew I had to leave very early to get past the controls, my father was too filled with his own concerns and wouldn't listen. I washed a dress shirt for him and hung it up but he said it wouldn't dry and that I would have to light a fire in the stove and could use some of our old frames for this. Afterwards, as it was then about six, I . . . I hesitated to leave the city. One has always to be so very careful. I . . .'

'You knew Frau Schlacht was coming that evening to collect the bottle she had yet to give him.'

'Yes, I knew, and may God forgive me.'

'You also knew or felt that Father Michel, thinking it best, would go to the Salpêtrière to give Angèle-Marie the taste of honey that would bring on one of her attacks and convince the doctors she wasn't fit to return home.'

'I . . . I did not specifically know this, Inspector, but yes, I did believe he might do something like that. *Mon Dieu,* the house was in a constant state of crisis. No peace. Never a kind word or any love, just a hatred I could no longer stand. I had to leave before the day grew light. Many times I told myself something terrible would happen and that I should not leave, but . . . but Étienne might finally arrive at Soisy-sur-Seine and I . . . I knew I had to warn him.'

'Mademoiselle, the notes you left at the studio clearly stated that you hadn't been anywhere near the place in three and a half weeks and yet . . . and yet you have just said, "might finally arrive?"'

'It . . . it was not safe for me to visit the country house too often. I . . . I had to force myself to wait.'

'For three and a half weeks?'

'Yes! There are those who watch for me. I . . . I was afraid of them and for him also.'

'And before you finally left the house in Charonne at . . . What time was it, please?'

'Six a.m. I listened to my father's harangue, Inspector, listened as he cursed Frau Schlacht and Étienne and everyone else, including *maman* whom he said was fucking – that is the word he used – fucking every man she could at the Hôtel Titania and enjoying it. *Enjoying it!*'

The girl was desperate and so very afraid of the truth, but it would still be best to force it from her. 'You arrived at the first control at about what time, please? It can and will be checked.'

'Inspector, what more do you want from me? That I stayed in the city but kept out of sight? That I went to the Salpêtrière and while hiding among the milling crowd saw Frau Schlacht hand that bottle to my aunt? That I saw *papa* take it from her and then . . . then, later, set it on his desk? That . . . that it was then that I listened to his hateful harangue and how he cursed me for loving my brother? I . . . I knew *papa* would have Étienne arrested and shot. I knew that bottle had to have the poison added to it – yes, yes, a thousand times yes, damn you! But . . . but . . .'

Tears filled her eyes as she hung her head in despair. 'But if you had added the poison,' said St-Cyr, 'and your father hadn't drunk from the bottle – indeed, why should he have – Herr Schlacht, who did like liqueurs, would have done so and died.'

'And every member of your family, including yourself and your half-brother,' sighed Kohler, 'would have been taken in reprisal. That's the law.'

Louis poured a glass of cognac and gave it to the girl, and as the kid took it, she looked up at him and tried to smile. '*Merci*,' she said. 'Oh *mon Dieu*, I've been so afraid and ashamed. I left that bottle untouched, Inspector. I could have taken it with me that afternoon when I rode all the way to Soisy-sur-Seine, but I didn't. I found Étienne's things in the shed. I was so excited. He'd understand how I felt and wouldn't blame me, but . . . but he wasn't there. He wasn't.'

Louis poured her another cognac and then handed one to the mother who quickly passed it to Father Michel and said brittlely, 'Drink it, *mon Père*. I greatly fear you are going to need it.'

'God is my comfort, my child, and as God is my witness, I could not do it. I, too, knew that if Herr Schlacht had been poisoned, Inspector, Alexandre would surely be blamed and that would mean Étienne and he would go to the firing squad, Danielle and Juliette into deportation. Oh *bien sûr*, I wanted Alexandre dead. He had become a monster even I could no longer tolerate. The bottle was there in the study and I knew this because I'd seen him bring it home from the Salpêtrière and take it into the study to leave it there before going to the brothel. And yes, I could so easily have done it had I fiddled with the lock and opened that door, but . . .'

'But someone came in through the garden,' sighed Kohler. 'A very attractive German lady. Not Frau Schlacht but another.'

One who would later go to the Society's meeting with a loaded Beretta in her purse.

'Oskar, stop them. I did it for us.'

'Don't worry. These two have been told to leave me and my affairs out of things. Oberg won't allow it.'

'Your wife, *mein* Herr,' said Louis, 'was to have been accused of buying the Amaretto and attempting to kill you. That would, I think, have been sufficient for your courts to have given her a lengthy sentence and you the divorce you so dearly wanted.'

'She'd have had an "accident", Louis. Don't be so kind,' snorted Kohler. 'Frau Hillebrand would then have become the courier to Switzerland, and the happy couple could have continued to salt away as much as possible for everyone.'

'And now?' cautioned Schlacht.

'We'll have to arrest her, *mein lieber Bonze*,' said Kohler firmly. 'Our reports will go in – we'll cite extenuating circumstances. That speech de Bonnevies was to have given. Very much against the interests of the Reich, et cetera. If she's lucky, they'll pin a medal on her. Right, Louis?'

Hermann always liked to have the last word, but was not the law – the law; truth sacred – and yet . . . and yet the Occupier a formidable presence? 'Right, of course,' he sighed. What else was he to have done, especially when they still had two arrests to make? That of the custodian of the catacombs, and of Madame Héloïse Debré, both of whom the French courts would be only too happy to deal with.

Two glasses were filled with the *Bonze*'s twenty-year-old cognac. 'One for you, *mon vieux*,' said St-Cyr, 'and the other for . . . Why, for your chauffeur, I think. Yes, the title suits and the Citroën is, of course, mine to drive, at least until the toes heal. How are they, by the way?'

'Perfect.'

'Good.'

When he held the second-class tickets out to Juliette and Danielle, Kohler felt his fingers trembling at the loss and knew that for Oona and himself, and Giselle and Louis, there could only be more of the Occupation.

'Take care,' he said, and felt the kid's lips as she kissed him warmly on both cheeks.

'Madame,' said Louis, 'you will travel only as far as Orange where, leaving your suitcases behind, you will get off the train during its brief stopover. Buy a copy of *Le Provençal* if possible, but if one is not available, then simply wait beside the news kiosk with your daughter always on your left. When someone asks if you're from the north, don't answer or look around. Simply follow this person at a distance towards the toilets. There's an office near them, and then an outer door to freedom. It's all been arranged. A farm in one of the remotest parts of the Cévennes, a few hives, a new start.'

Gabrielle had contacted friends in the *Résistance*. 'We can't trust Herr Schlacht, madame, nor can we trust Oberg and the SS,' said Kohler. 'You're carrying five million francs and are just too easy a target.'

'We know too much,' said Danielle sadly.

'All but fifty thousand will be taken by your *passeur* to be used by others,' said St-Cyr.

'And Father Michel?' asked Juliette.

'Has been sent to a monastery in the Haute-Savoie and has already left the city.'

'Then it's goodbye,' she said. 'You two . . . ah *mon Dieu*, how can I ever thank you?'

'By being the friend this one needs,' he said, and helped them on to the train.

They watched, they waited, these two detectives, as the train began to pull out of the Gare de Lyon. They would not leave, thought Juliette, until certain they had done everything possible to get them safely away.

'Louis, when you were up in the gods of that factory and calling down to them and to our *Bonze*, you knew Schlacht would compromise and save face by saying Oona had to stay in Paris. You knew he'd let those two go, at least for the time being.'

'By keeping Oona here, Herr Schlacht still believes he has a hold over us, Hermann, should he ever think to let the Kommandant von Gross-Paris know what's really been going on. I admit, however, that I also had self-interest at heart, for with Oona here, I can depend on you to be the person you are. Giselle as well, of course, for she'd give you up in an instant if she felt you had become at all loyal to the Occupier.'

'Then read these!'

Je Suis Partout's and *Le Matin*'s thin and heavily controlled newspapers shrilled outrage in bold black letters: TERRORISTS DYNAMITE HEADQUARTERS OF QUARTIER DU MAIL ET DE BONNE-NOUVELLE MILICE. FOUR DEAD, FIVE TERRIBLY INJURED.

'It's those *gazogène* lorries, Louis. Their lousy gas tanks invariably leak. Smoke a careless cigarette or cigar near one of them and you damn well know what's likely to happen.'

'Candles . . . They say the lorries were loaded with them and that the fire volatilized – that's a big word for the Occupation's *Le Matin*, but no matter – volatilized the beeswax causing it to explode as well as . . .'

'As the dynamite their fertile imaginations felt must have been necessary. *Mein Gott*, don't those idiots in the press know anything about wax? Now read this little item my boss so thoughtfully ripped out of yesterday's rags.'

'I didn't know Walter had the time.'

'It's Gestapo Boemelburg to you, *mon fin*, and don't ever forget it even if you *did* work with him on international police business before the Defeat!'

Paris welcomes the General Unruh, the Hero's Friend, who has set up offices in the Hôtel Majestic.

Unruh meant, literally, trouble!

'He's already begun a thorough review of the Palais d'Eiffel, Louis. Apparently the Führer has had his eye out for slackers for some time.'*

'And Schlacht?'

'Is still looking for his little badge and now trying to explain to the authorities how honey and wax could have been stolen by him from under the noses of armed Wehrmacht guards and air-raid sirens that shouldn't have sounded. He'll just have to go along with the rest of the staff. After all, there's a war on.'

And the Führer is always right.

'Now read this.'

It was a telex from Pierre Laval, no less. The Premier, in Vichy,

---

* Early in 1943 General Unruh arrived in Paris and within a few weeks had disbanded the staff of the Procurement Office and closed it.

the internationally famous spa and home of the Government of France in these terrible times and since June of 1940.

Flykiller slays mistress of high-ranking Government employee in Hall des Sources. Imperative you immediately send experienced detectives who are not from this district. Repeat, not from this district.

'Not from his jurisdiction?'

'Outsiders. Of course it smells just like one of those lousy waters they insist are so good for you, Louis, but who the hell can be killing flies in winter? There aren't any!'

But apparently there were.